WE ARE THE FIRE

WE ARE THE FIRE

SAM TAYLOR

New York

A Swoon Reads Book
An imprint of Feiwel and Friends and Macmillan Publishing Group, LLC
120 Broadway, New York, NY 10271
swoonreads.com

Our books may be purchased in bulk for promotional, educational, or business use. Please contact your local bookseller or the Macmillan Corporate and Premium Sales Department at (800) 221-7945 ext. 5442 or by email at MacmillanSpecialMarkets@macmillan.com.

Library of Congress Cataloging-in-Publication Data
Names: Taylor, Sam, 1986-author.
Title: We are the fire / Sam Taylor.
Description: First edition. | New York : Swoon Reads, 2021. | Audience: Ages 13-18. | Audience: Grades 10-12. | Summary: Teens Oksana and Pran, stolen from their families and forced into the army, dream of a life together after tearing down the tyrannical empire but their radically different methods strain their relationship.
Identifiers: LCCN 2020017589 | ISBN 9781250241429 (hardcover)
Subjects: CYAC: Fantasy.
Classification: LCC PZ7.1.T3967 We 2021 | DDC [Fic]—dc23
LC record available at https://lccn.loc.gov/2020017589

First edition, 2021
Book design by Mike Burroughs
Printed in the United States of America

ISBN 978-1-250-24142-9 (hardcover)
10 9 8 7 6 5 4 3 2 1

To Steve, North, and Oak,
the brightest sparks in my world

THE TULIIKOBRETS

Fire Warriors

Soldiers of the Vesimaan Empire

RANKS AND COLORS

Commanders, *white*

Nightmares, *blue*

Hellions, *orange*

Goblins, *bright red*

Imps, *dull red*

Novices, *no color*

SCAMALL

LINN

MENNICK

KIVI

VESIMAA

Veriki

VAINO

NYÍTA

HÄRMA

NOVOSEL

HORÁDIM

PAKASTRA

UTSAH

PART ONE

THE FIRES WERE BORN

CHAPTER ONE

PRAN

He hadn't taken off his heavy gauntlets and greaves, didn't even have a chance to sit, when the Commanders gave their next order: night patrol.

Pran cursed and rubbed his already aching leg. He'd been awake since fifth bell that morning, Commanders ordering him to training, then morning patrol, on to battle practice, then still more training, with no rest in between. But the Commanders did not tolerate complaints or dawdling, and Pran had no say in how he spent his days. None of the young soldiers in this fort did, not since they'd all been ripped from their families, dragged hundreds of miles to this copper fort, and told they belonged to the emperor.

And a soldier late to patrol—or sleeping during it—fared almost as badly as any rebels they caught scheming against His Imperial Majesty.

At least tonight Pran had splendid company. Down in City Center, where chemical lamps glowed and breezes drifted around stonework arches and imposing imperial offices, Pran leaned against a wall, shifting his weight off his bad leg, and elbowed Oksana beside him. "See any disturbances?"

"Yes, there's a ridiculous boy who thinks the Commanders ordered naps instead of night patrol."

She winked, and the look was heart-stopping when paired with her uniform: sleek leather with a stark red fire-demon patch across the tunic, clawed gauntlets, scaled greaves, brass antlers bound into the vibrant red braid pinned around her head. Her eyes were stained black—the Demon's Mark, their Commanders called it. One glance at eyes without pupil or iris—without *light*—made even the fiercest enemies tremble. If Pran were some cornered miscreant, he'd be on his knees begging for mercy.

Instead, he pulled Oksana in for another kiss.

"Pran!" she protested, even while leaning so close her breath brushed the hollow of his throat. "If the Commanders catch us . . ."

"Nothing's happening," Pran whispered against her mouth. "No one's around to see."

That was all the coaxing Oksana needed to return the kiss: first quick, then longer, deeper, her lips parting beneath his touch. Their antlers—twisted and terrible, like deer straight from hell—tangled and locked. But with Oksana pressed against him, Pran didn't care. She rose on her toes, wound her arms across his neck, and he lifted her off her feet.

Or would have, but his leg chose that moment to seize. A spasm ripped through his right thigh like someone had wound a crank inside, and he doubled over with a yelp.

Oksana yanked their antlers apart with an almighty

wrench that left his head aching. "Didn't you get your medicine today?"

He slouched back against the stone wall behind them and hissed through his clenched teeth. "The Commanders will grant me a stronger dose if I wait until after patrol."

Her jaw stiffened. "Because you work so much better in pain?"

Pain keeps Tuliikobrets alert. For once, the Commanders were right—gods, those were awful words! But with his leg in this state, he could stay awake until tomorrow's fifth bell. Another wave of pain surged through him and bile rose with it, searing his tongue.

Instead of swallowing that bile as the Commanders would have demanded, Pran spat it onto the pristine cobblestone streets. He wished a Commander were around to see what he thought of their rules, even if all that would earn him was a few lashes across his back. Let them see they didn't control him completely.

"Hey." Oksana cupped a hand around his cheek, her woodsmoke-and-clove scent fragrant and familiar, instantly soothing Pran's nerves. "Do you need to sit?"

With her so near, Pran could see stars reflected in her night-dark eyes. Saw himself in her brass antlers, all the color also blacked out of his eyes, while his own antlers—ebony to blend with his midnight hair and brown skin—had gone crooked after their kiss and subsequent tangle. He'd have to adjust the straps before they toppled off and crashed onto the street. Moonlight shimmered against Oksana's white skin, and though she was tiny, her head tucking neatly beneath his chin, when they stood side by side he felt positively unstoppable.

His hand strayed to the ring hidden in his pocket. She deserved this, something pretty from her homeland. Yet the words engraved inside, *I promise,* made it into so much more than a delightful surprise. *What* did he promise?

She deserved freedom. But he didn't know how to give her that.

"I could find a way to get medicine whenever I want," Pran grumbled, ignoring her question. "The Commanders are starved for flattery. With the right words at the right moment, I could—"

"Don't do anything reckless." Oksana thumped his shoulder. "Come on, let's walk it off."

Her hand on his elbow, she steered him through Mennick's streets. The autumn breeze was ripe with frost, and on the horizon the emperor's palace loomed, thorny spires of white marble. Following Oksana, Pran limped past empty markets, silent government halls, and the station where a steam-powered train roared in with wares from all over the Vesimaan nation. He hobbled around Imperial Square with its fire fountains and statues of the emperor and his grandfather the Great King. Both bronze sculptures clutched massive torches, symbols of the fire-summoning soldiers, Tuliikobrets, who'd protected Vesimaa from oppressive invaders, the Scamall nation—then, enabled Vesimaans to conquer their own neighboring countries and kidnap children to feed the ranks of their flame-wielding army.

Last week, a vandal had crowned these statues with velveteen donkey ears.

Pran fiddled with the flint starter tucked in his belt, toying with its metal striker that launched a shard of steel against a scrap of flint embedded in the long ivory handle. "That boy had the right idea with those ears. If I'd seen him, I'd have let him carry on."

Oksana wrapped her hand around Pran's, stopping him from hitting the striker hard enough to raise sparks. "If you had, your ashes would be cooling alongside his."

Her voice wobbled over the words, and she turned toward a road that led out of the city. If they followed it long enough, that road would take them to Horádim, her home country. In a better world, they might make it all the way there, but even the most fleet-footed soldiers couldn't outpace the Nightmares who chased after deserters.

Another pain stabbed through Pran's leg, so fierce a whimper wormed from his throat.

Oksana whirled to Pran, holding him upright until his pain ebbed to a dull ache. "One more hour on patrol," she whispered. "Then I'll take you back and get your medicine."

But her gaze flitted once more to that road through the woods, and her shoulders drooped.

Pran was sick with himself, how he couldn't give her that escape. "Oksana . . ."

"Enough." She squeezed his hand, then led him deeper into the city.

They slunk past rows of darkened restaurants smelling of blood sausage and pickled pumpkin. Down a street where the elite and comfortable lived in houses boasting elaborate stone facades and shallow balconies with gilt railings. Occasionally, a curtain twitched in a window as they passed, but no one crossed their path. When the emperor's monstrous Tuliikobrets prowled, good Vesimaans stayed out of their way.

"Should we turn back?" Pran asked as the streets narrowed. The homes here were crooked and crowded together like too many unwashed Vesimaans packed onto a donkey cart.

"Not yet. If we time our walk perfectly, we'll pass the fort the moment our shift ends." Oksana glanced to Pran's right leg, how he rested hardly any weight on it. They'd have to be efficient in their steps, if he'd get back on his own feet at all. Pain might keep him awake, but it certainly didn't keep him functional.

Pran cursed, hobbling after Oksana through City Center. Sometimes he didn't know what the Commanders were playing at. Did it make them feel big, watching young soldiers scramble like rodents after bait? Nights when the pain kept him awake, he'd lie on his bunk and imagine all the terrible things he'd do to the Commanders if he ever mastered fire.

But for now, he clutched Oksana's arm so tightly his

fingers ached while he limped through every step—until a fragment of sound stopped him short. "Do you hear that?"

"What, my stomach grumbling? I swear, if Meal Hall serves cabbage-and-mince stew one more time this week—"

"No." Pran held his breath, then spun to his left, back toward City Center. Toward the fort. "There. A scream."

"Probably drunks brawling." Oksana shrugged, though a shadow passed over her face. "I'll look. You wait here." She tried to lean him against the stone wall of another shop gone cold and empty for the night, but Pran grabbed hold of her shoulder when she turned to step away.

"You can't go alone," he argued, even as another spasm twisted through his thigh. "Please."

"If it's trouble, we have to find out. We have to report it." Her face crumpled as she spoke the hated words. "And no more of this 'letting vandals carry on' talk. I mean it."

If he were alone tonight, it'd be tempting to join in any revelry, smash down pompous fire fountains, heave burning coals against the palace's disgustingly pristine walls. But of course he wouldn't put Oksana in danger, no matter how he admired those who dared defy the emperor.

When they turned the street corner, however, it wasn't protesters or even drunks brawling in the streets.

A troop of fellow Tuliikobrets, around a dozen of them, swarmed forward. Most of these weren't in full gear—some were missing their antlers or horns, others the scaled greaves. None had stained their eyes black, either, as all

Tuliis were required to do when stepping outside the fort. But their expressions were no less terrifying, faces contorted in boundless fury. Some frothed at the mouth like rabid dogs. The fire-demon emblem adorning their dark uniforms was a dying ember red, in contrast to the violent scarlet of Pran's and Oksana's. These were one of the Imp troops, the lowest-ranking soldiers in the fort. None were more than fifteen years old.

Pran and Oksana barely scrambled out of the way before the Imps stampeded down the road. With echoing shrieks they stormed toward the edge of town, sparking jets of flame through the air. Their cries still split the night when the fort alarm tore through the sky, and Pran staggered as the bells' horrible clanging reverberated through his skull.

Oksana sucked in a breath. "Saints alive. What's going on?"

Pran's whole mouth went dry. No more than three or four Imps ever left the fort at a time, and never without a Hellion or Nightmare rank to supervise them. Add to that their screaming frenzy . . . even in their worst training sessions, Tuliikobrets didn't behave this way.

"Follow them," Pran choked out. "The Commanders will expect us to stop them." They'd be looking for someone to *blame*, never mind whether the accusations were fair. He and Oksana had to show they'd at least tried to end . . . whatever this was.

But they couldn't keep up. He and Oksana were barely back on the street when the Imps had already disappeared up the road into the night's thick shadows. The way they ran would put to shame even the Nightmares, the highest-ranking of the fort's troops. And with Pran lurching through every step, running was out of the question for him.

"Go on without me," he wheezed, though the words stung straight to his bones. Whatever chaos was stirring, he didn't want to leave Oksana to face it alone. Nor was it a good look if Pran skipped out on patrol, no matter the reason. The Commanders wouldn't hesitate to punish him. He'd proudly endure their fury arising from his own defiance. Not so much, if he'd failed because they'd left him in too much pain to work.

To his immense relief—not that he'd admit it out loud—Oksana tightened her hold on him. "If another group is behind them, you'll be trampled. You're staying with me."

When his leg buckled, she leaned him against her side, steering back through the roads with crowded, crumbling houses. Doors burst open, rusty hinges screeching as people stomped into the street.

"What's happening?" someone called.

"They're crossing the bridge!" another person shouted.

"They're headed for the village! They're headed for Linn!"

How could the Imps have gotten so far already? Pran didn't want to believe it, but the truth made itself known as he and Oksana passed the last row of houses on the city's edge. Across the Terhi River, Imps charged into the village, gibbering and hurling fireballs toward the stars.

A cottage door slammed open and two villagers darted out, waving farming rakes. "Get away from us!" The shout echoed across the river as the villagers swiped at the Imps with their rakes.

The Imps' shrieks and howls shifted into snarls. They rounded on those people and the homes behind them, raising fire and casting flames until every thatched-roof cottage blazed.

Pran's legs buckled. Tuliikobrets never burned whole towns here in Vesimaa—or at least, the Commanders had never ordered them to do so.

"We have to stop them," Pran said, more urgently this time. If they didn't bring these Imps to order, there'd be worse problems than delayed medicine or a few lashes for so-called laziness during patrol.

Oksana's face went slack with shock. "Why would they do this?"

The bigger question was, what would the Commanders do to these Imps after they were caught?

By the time Pran and Oksana crossed the bridge and reached Linn, there was nothing left to save. The entire village was a blaze that climbed toward the thumbnail moon—every house, stable, cart, and watering trough swallowed by fire. A couple of chickens, their feathers smoking, fled the area with indignant squawks, but no one else would escape that wall of flame. Yet the Imps still sparked their flint starters, raising fireballs that they hurled into the inferno with screeches and grating howls.

Oksana lunged forward, snatching the nearest Imp. "Stop! Whatever you're doing, it's not worth this."

Pran hobbled to another Imp, who'd dropped her flint starter and was scrabbling in the dirt after it. He caught her by the shoulder, turning the girl until she met him face to face. "What are you doing?" he demanded, then lowered his voice. "Who organized this?"

Her eyes were feral and unfocused, yet there was something still human about them, free as they were of the midnight-black stain. For a moment, it seemed Pran had gotten through to her, connected with some last reasonable scrap of her mind. She licked her sooty lips, opened her mouth . . . and screamed. Not words in any language Pran knew, just a screech that knifed against his ears.

None of it kept him from hearing the small cry through the billowing smoke. The Imp Oksana had grabbed was lobbing fireballs at her so fast she had to lunge away, slipping farther and farther from the Imp as she dodged every flame. Oksana yanked her flint starter from her belt and raised a fireball of her own, but her throw went wild when she had to duck another plume jetting toward her head.

"No, you don't!" Pran barked at that Imp. He whipped the flint starter from his belt and pressed the striker with his thumb. Steel grazed across flint, and hissing sparks sprang to life. As they flared molten-bright against the dark, Pran summoned the heat forever lurking deep inside his lungs, and with one gasping breath it burst out, searing his throat and scalding his tongue. With another huff and hiss, Pran breathed those sparks into billowing flames, then snatched the roaring fireball with his gloved hands, arms tensed to throw.

His leg seized, muscles wrenching as though a demon dwelled inside him, gnawing on his flesh. Pran dropped the fireball and collapsed to his knees, his cry piercing the night.

The Imp who'd attacked Oksana rounded on Pran, an animal hunger sweeping across his face. His lips pulled back in a snarl, and he lifted his flint starter to spark and flame once more.

Bonfires erupted through the air, ravenous and unrestrained. Oksana was flame incarnate, the blazes rising from her outstretched hands and roaring furiously behind her back.

"Enough!" Oksana cast flame after flame until the Imp fled. Then, wielding three fire plumes at once, she chased a handful of Imps out of the village, back toward the bridge. "Get away from here! Go to the fort. Or . . ." *Run away*. Her lips shaped the words, but the sounds never left her tongue. The fire in her hands withered, dwindling to tiny tips of flame.

It was too late.

A line of Tuliikobrets charged across the bridge toward the Imps and the inferno. The demons fronting their uniforms gleamed eye-stabbing blue, while their antlers twisted skyward like unholy stags. These soldiers wore masks as well—ones that covered all but their mouths, painted like skin peeling away to reveal bodies made not of muscle and bone, but flame.

The Nightmares had arrived.

Pran's mouth went as dry as the ashes drifting through the air, and he scrambled to his feet. It was not good to be caught among these Imps while they destroyed a village, and one right outside the emperor's capital city, no less.

"Sir!" he called to the Nightmare leading the troop.

"Halt!" the man yelled back. "Nobody move."

The rioting Imps didn't listen, of course, still screeching, hurling their fireballs, securing their deaths with every spark. In a few steps the Nightmares were on them, knocking the younger Tuliis to the ground with pillars of flame made blue-hot with the tanks of liquid fire—Demon's Tongue—strapped across their backs.

The lead Nightmare rounded on Pran and Oksana, eyeing the bright red demon on both their uniforms. "Goblin ranks? Report."

"Pran Nayar and Oksana Artemivna, of the Crimson Sparks troop, sir," Pran said. Oksana bit her lip as she watched the Imps struggling on the ground. "We were put on night patrol and came to see what the trouble was. To *stop* it."

"Well, we've ended it," the Nightmare said, then yelled over his shoulder, "Everyone back to the fort."

CHAPTER TWO

OKSANA

On the city's far edge, opposite the burnt village, the fort loomed. It was a ghastly sight: glaringly bright walls covered in enormous strips of woven copper, the red-roofed Commander Tower standing sentinel behind them. The Nightmares charged toward it, dragging the Imps, bound together with thick, scratchy rope meant for docking boats, not restraining children.

And these *were* children. Whatever had possessed them to ignite a village had vanished. Now, bloodied and scorched, they shambled through the streets, looking as confused as Oksana felt.

Why? she yearned to ask them. *Why did you do it? Why did you* dare?

At her side, Pran lurched and groaned. His leg gave out, nearly knocking them both down. Oksana tugged his arm across her shoulders and scooped her other around his waist, cursing that she was too tiny to haul him on her back. At least the Nightmares hadn't bound them, too, but they weren't about to help, either. *True Tuliikobrets are strong enough to stand on their own,* as the Commanders loved to say.

Revolting. It was just their excuse to be cruel.

She tipped her head against Pran's, slumped onto her shoulder. "Almost there. You can do this!"

But they were falling desperately behind, Pran lagging with every step. One Nightmare glared toward them. "Goblins, keep up!"

"Nayar needs help," she pleaded, but the Nightmare stomped back to the sobbing Imps. Oksana swallowed her curses and turned to her saint. *Yeva. My ally, my defender, my guardian. Help me get Pran inside.* She yearned to touch the icon hidden beneath her tunic, clutch it for strength. But she needed both arms to keep Pran standing.

"You can do this." She didn't know if she spoke to Pran or herself.

When they finally passed through the copper fort gates, a trio of Nightmares stood ready to receive them, along with Commander Tamm. The pale woman had even paler hair cropped short, while the white fire demon fronting her uniform glared stark as exposed bone.

The Nightmares guarding the gates allowed those leading the Imps to storm into the fort and disappear with the young Tuliis into the shadows. But when Oksana moved forward, steering Pran, the gate guards stopped her.

"Halt!" One of the Nightmares barked, grabbing Oksana by the arm as the gates slammed shut.

Another lifted his chemical lamp high, its green-gray light blinding. "Surrender your flint starters, Goblins."

Wretched protocol. Oksana tossed her starter to the Nightmares' feet. Pran collapsed across the cobblestones, barely stirring. She tossed his starter to the Nightmares as well, then shook Pran's shoulder. "Let's get you to the hospital wing. Let's—"

"These were at the riot, too." A Nightmare, one of those who'd captured the Imps, strolled back toward the gates, jabbing his thumb toward Oksana and Pran.

Tamm glowered at Oksana. "You and Nayar were assigned to City Center!"

How very like a Commander, to find fault no matter which way a Tulii stepped. Oksana bit back every retort brimming on her tongue. Being right wasn't important; helping Pran mattered most. "When we saw the Imps running through City Center, we followed to *stop* them."

"And they reached those rebels first," the Imp-catcher cut in. "Even chased a few from the village. They did as expected of loyal Tuliikobrets."

Oksana swallowed hard, gut-sick at those words. Doubly so when Tamm eyed her with renewed interest and remarked, "So noted."

Pran stirred on the ground, letting out a guttural groan, and Oksana stomped down her queasiness. She had a real job to do.

"Commander," Oksana called, as the woman turned away. "Please, Nayar, he needs—"

As though they'd arranged it, Pran vomited in great heaves across the cobblestones.

"Good gods. Get him out of here." Tamm retreated, tossing a medicine token as she went.

Oksana caught the token, then crouched beside Pran. "I can get your medicine. Can you stand?"

He muttered sounds that weren't words, eyes rolling back in his head.

"Pran!" He wasn't big, but she couldn't carry him alone. She glanced to the Nightmares, but of course none of them moved to help. Especially as Pran retched again.

"Oksana!" Another voice echoed toward the gates, pealing like a bell. Anu jogged forward, weaving between the guards, the dull red demon on her Imp's tunic as cheerless as her grimace. Her pale face had gone blotchy, and strands of white-blond hair spilled untidily from her braids, yet the girl's dark blue eyes were as calm as still water.

At the sight of her friend, Oksana breathed again. "Please, help me move him."

"This is no place to sleep, Pran," Anu chided. "Come along, there's a slightly better bed for you in the hospital." Anu took one of his arms, Oksana the other, and together they heaved him to his feet, then staggered toward the red-turreted Healing Hall. As they waddled, Pran's leg spasmed and he let out a keening cry.

"Stay strong." Oksana squeezed his hand. When he squeezed back, the knot in her chest loosened the smallest bit. But that knot tightened right back up when they entered the hospital wing on the first floor. Not one physician stood in sight among the linen-covered cots.

"We could use some help," Anu called toward the adjoining chamber, where physicians sometimes gathered for meetings. But that room was silent; no one answered her shout.

"Should I look around?" Anu stumbled as Pran slumped against her shoulder. "They can't be far."

Oksana shook her head. "I don't need them. Get him on a cot."

While Anu got Pran settled, Oksana snatched a suture needle off a table and used it to pick the lock on one of the many steel cabinets lining the walls. The shelves within were crammed with bottles and jars—none labeled, all different sizes and shapes. She grabbed three and poured two spoonfuls from each into a bowl. Pran would need a strong dose tonight.

"Stir that well." She shoved the bowl toward Anu and turned to fetch a syringe.

Someone stood in her way. Oksana smelled him before she saw him and choked: Rotten eggs. Scorched metal.

Rootare, the imperial alchemist. His round glasses caught the light until he looked like an insect with enormous, gleaming eyes, and his high-collared white lab coat was stained with smears of red, black, and silver. The man's skin was ashen, even his blond hair peppered through with gray, though his face wasn't wrinkled with age.

He peered at the bottles on the table. "Where did you get those?"

Acid bubbled in Oksana's throat. She stepped between Rootare and the bowl, drawing herself up as tall as she could. Still, she didn't reach his shoulder. "None of the physicians were here to help. I have a medicine token."

She tossed it over. He snatched it in midair, though his hand trembled so badly it was a miracle he caught it at all. His brow furrowed as he stared at her. "None of those bottles are labeled. How did you figure out which to pick?"

"I know some things about chemicals." Even as a young child, Oksana had already been exploring, experimenting, before being kidnapped for this army.

Peering over Oksana's head, Rootare studied the bottles she'd selected, then snatched the bowl from Anu's hands and examined the mixture inside. A slow smile carved across his face. "Indeed you do."

When Oksana didn't grin back, Rootare turned to Pran, looking him over as he might a rotted cabbage in the market. "Injured in that fight with the Imps? There's a mess that will have heads rolling. At least my Demon's Tongue saved the day. With proper help, I could really change this country." He peered out the window, frowning toward the palace glowing in the distance.

Oksana clenched her jaw, fighting to keep her temper in check. Rootare's wretched work was the reason Pran was sick. "Nayar needs his medicine."

The man unlocked another cabinet and selected a syringe. Oksana reached to take it, but Rootare clucked his tongue. "Now, now, you've already crossed a line, poking through the cabinets. Don't make me report you to the Commanders. *I* will administer the dose."

Oksana didn't trust him with needles. She didn't trust him near Pran. But another spasm tore through Pran and he thrashed on the cot, crying out.

Rootare wagged the syringe like a scolding finger. "Don't you trust your own work?"

Biting her tongue, Oksana watched Rootare fill the syringe from the bowl, then stick it into a vein in Pran's arm. As the medicine poured into him, Pran sighed, his breath evening into the steady rhythm of sleep.

"It . . . worked." Rootare tossed the used syringe into a vat of pure ethanol.

"Disappointed?" Oksana asked. But the rising light in the man's face spoke the truth. Not dismayed. *Delighted.*

The alchemist rounded on her, peering with an intensity that sent chills down her spine. "What else do you know about chemicals?"

A warning knell echoed through Oksana's heart. "Nothing of interest."

Rootare's grin widened to a smirk. "Care to change that? I could teach you a thing or two. I've even gotten Demon's Tongue to burn underwater. Tell me that's not more interesting than medicine for crippled Tuliis."

Bastard. Oksana yearned to toss a beaker of scalding serum into his face. "I have to get back outside," she said. "Commanders' orders."

Beyond the window, shouts erupted like firecrackers. Commanders' voices, calling for attention and order.

With a scowl, Rootare stalked from the room. Oksana didn't follow, sinking instead onto the cot beside Pran. She yearned to hold him but didn't dare. Affection between Tuliis wasn't forbidden, but anyone who displayed dedication to something—especially some*one*—other than the army invited trouble. So she settled for the smaller comforts of a mere comrade, pulling off his gauntlets and unbuckling his antlers and greaves.

While Pran slept, Oksana untucked the pendant hidden beneath her tunic. It was painted with an image of Yeva, her favorite of the Twelve Sainted Siblings from her country. Yeva, defender of life, smiled demurely in the portrait, dark eyes shining and black hair flowing wild.

Thank you. Oksana touched a finger to the icon. *Thank you for speeding my steps.*

Anu tucked a blanket around Pran as Oksana hummed a song from his homeland, Pakastra, about monsoons watering the rich green jungles. She hummed a second song, from her country, Horádim, about the wind sweeping over the meadows and sifting through sheaves of wheat. These were the songs she always turned to when Pran suffered.

And there'd been no shortage of suffering in the seven years since they'd been dragged to this fort. Their first four years here had been consumed by transformation and training. Rootare had injected them with serum after serum until with a single gasp, they could breathe sparks into a raging inferno. Many of his prisoners died along the way, the harsh serums corroding their bodies instead of remaking them.

Oksana had weathered the serums well enough, but each new dose left Pran violently ill and in agony. And Rootare and the Commanders did nothing to help, saying that true Tuliikobrets survived on their own. So Oksana had tended to Pran: bringing food, cleaning up when he'd been sick, cradling him through the worst of the pain.

She'd kept him alive, but his leg was ruined by the injections. And the Commanders and Rootare gave little help, insisting Pran earn his treatments. As if he *owed* them something.

Oksana breathed slowly to hold back her tears, then yanked off her gear, especially the gauntlets that kept her from touching Pran's skin.

Anu settled onto the next cot over. The girl hummed the ballad of the first Tuliikobrets: legendary, ancient fire demons said to have once guarded Vesimaa. A Vesimaan herself, Anu would have grown up with that tune as an anthem.

Some days Oksana could almost find beauty in its haunting melody. But tonight, with Pran in a drugged stupor while shouts echoed through the windows, she bristled at every measure. "Anu, could you please—"

The girl halted her tune and brushed a hand across her face. She'd penned new words on herself again, a band of long-tailed script stretching down her arm: *Out in the mountains the fires were born.*

"Is it true? Linn . . . it's gone?" Anu asked, then added in a whisper, "So close to home. That could have been my village."

The memory of acrid smoke scorched Oksana's lungs. "It all burned before we got there. There was no chance to save anything. *Anyone*. What set off those Imps?"

Rebellion would be the easy—*easy?*—answer. But no Imps should have been able to escape the Nightmares patrolling the gates. Or charge through the city at such unnatural speed, then burn an entire village as completely as if every cottage was drenched in kerosene.

No Imps should have outrun Nightmares, or needed Demon's Tongue to stop their havoc.

Anu scrubbed a hand across her brow. "It was the Scarlet Embers troop. One moment they were in their barracks, bedding down for the night. The next, they fled the fort, shrieking like ghouls. It was like they'd just . . . Snapped."

"Tuliikobrets!" a voice barked from the door. Oksana jumped so hard, she jolted Pran.

A messenger leaned into the room, the fire-demon tattoo on his neck slick with sweat. "All Tuliikobrets are to report to the south courtyard to learn from the Scarlet Embers' mistake."

Oksana's stomach plummeted. From the moment those Imps had stepped outside the fort, there'd been no other end for them. If only they'd kept going, past that village and into the woods, maybe they could have escaped. Now . . .

As she heaved to her feet, Pran opened his eyes. The

black stain had faded and his irises were back to deep brown, though his gaze was still unfocused.

"Take me with you." Still affected by the medicine, Pran's words slurred into one long, tangled sound that Oksana understood only because she'd spent so many years helping him.

"You can barely stand," she protested as he clambered off the cot. His limp was almost gone and his bad leg didn't buckle. But he was still unsteady, bumping into the table and knocking the empty medicine bowl to the ground with a clang.

"Is Rootare still around?" With tremendous effort, Pran lifted his head, squinting across the room. "I'm not staying here alone."

For that, she couldn't blame him. "All right. Hold on to me."

Outside Healing Hall, shouts thundered through the air. Gold-uniformed messengers streamed between the gates and red-roofed Commander Tower. Atop the fort walls, Nightmares prowled every walkway, peering into the city.

Oksana and Anu led Pran away from them all, toward the south courtyard. They tugged him around tousle-haired Tuliis stumbling from barracks, bleary-eyed with sleep, confusion, and fear. Kept him away from Commanders screaming at those Tuliis to step faster. When Pran stumbled, Oksana pulled him upright. When he mumbled, Oksana pushed his head down so the Commanders didn't think he was complaining. With Anu's help, she steered him past Meal Hall, the dirty pub, and training yards, heading straight to the south courtyard's cast-iron gates.

The yard inside blazed with green-gray light from chemical lamps mounted across the walls. Tuliis huddled in order of rank: Imps nearest the stone platform, Goblins behind, then Hellions. More Nightmares prowled about, chasing stragglers into line with bursts of flame.

Anu took her place among the Imps as Oksana steered Pran toward the Goblins. Across the courtyard, a Nightmare shot flames at another Goblin who teetered half-asleep on his feet.

Pran staggered like the worst drunk. Oksana uttered a prayer of relief when she spotted Pran's friend Yalku, his sleek black hair a beacon among so many paler heads. She beckoned, and the boy elbowed forward. He was only a little taller than Oksana but was built like a rock. In one movement he shifted Pran's weight against his side.

"Pran looks like hell," Yalku said.

"He's had better nights." She flicked hay off Yalku's uniform. "Come from the stables?"

"Couldn't sleep. And those horses need looking after."

"You smell like animals, Yalku." Pran recoiled, wrinkling his nose.

"And I help you stand. I'm an excellent friend."

"I *can* stand. Lemme go!"

"Of course you can." Yalku patted Pran's shoulder. "Now hold still before you land on your face."

"Can you believe him?" Pran scowled toward Oksana, his cheeks so apple-red with annoyance it was all she could do to keep from kissing them in front of everyone.

She bumped his arm. "Stop wobbling like you're wasted and I'll believe *you.*"

Fighting the smile at war with his scowl, Pran bumped her shoulder back when a frigid wind gusted through the courtyard. He shuddered, Oksana shivered, but Yalku didn't so much as blink. An autumn chill didn't bother him, one of the few Tuliis kidnapped from the frigid Nyítan tundra and its clans of nomadic reindeer herders.

Oksana burrowed deeper into her jacket. "Did you see the Scarlet Embers when they Snapped?" she whispered to Yalku. "Did—"

Hands yanked her from behind, spinning her around. Commander Lepik glared down. "Questions for you, Artemivna."

She'd thought she was cold before. She was wrong.

One hand on her neck, Lepik hauled her from the courtyard and shoved her against the wall. Throat tight, Oksana craned her head back as far as it would go to meet the man's ice-blue stare. The Commanders, all of them Vesimaans, stood pale as ghosts and tall as young trees, like most from their nation. But their bodies were inhumanly, *grotesquely* bulked from the fiercest serums of all. Whether with fire or their fists, Commanders could destroy anyone they chose.

"What did you see tonight?" Lepik's spiky, graying hair

caught the chemical light like a crown of thorns. But his hand squeezing her jaw trembled.

Oksana frowned. What *would* Emperor Juhan do to the Commanders for letting the Scarlet Embers rampage, killing who knew how many Vesimaan citizens?

Whatever happened, she'd shoulder none of the blame for them. Not her, and never Pran. "It's as I told Commander Tamm. Nayar and I were patrolling City Center. When the Scarlet Embers stampeded past, we pursued."

"But you didn't stop them from destroying Linn?"

"The *Nightmares* didn't stop them."

At that, Lepik fell silent.

"Everyone gather round!" a voice shouted through the gloom.

Not ten paces away, all the Commanders, nearly two dozen of them, clustered together. Lepik joined them, leaving Oksana beside the wall, rubbing her aching jaw. The man hadn't dismissed her, and none of the other Commanders seemed aware of her presence.

Oksana sank into the shadows and went still.

"What news?" Lepik asked as he joined the group.

"There are riots in every street surrounding the palace." Commander Tamm lifted a square of parchment stamped with a gold seal. "Emperor Juhan demands an explanation."

"We'll be lucky if that's all he demands," another said.

Faces paled. Tamm licked her lips. "Emperor Juhan must understand that we need time to train fighters. His council presses for too many troops too quickly."

"His Majesty is desperate to conquer Scamall," Lepik replied.

"His Majesty is desperate to conquer *anything*," someone muttered.

In front of the troops, the Commanders pretended absolute confidence in their emperor. But Oksana knew Juhan was a disappointing excuse for a leader, even by Vesimaan standards. Great King Heino, Juhan's grandfather, had put an end to years of invasions by Scamall, the mighty northern nation fierce with its iron mills and craggy mountain peaks. And Juhan's father created the empire when he'd led Tuliikobrets to conquer Horádim, Pakastra, and the tundra lands of Nyíta. But for the nearly twenty-five years Juhan had ruled—half his lifetime—he hadn't added a pig's field to the empire. And that was with conscripting Vesimaan children like Anu into the army, something his father and grandfather had refused to do.

"We can't supply troops strong enough to defeat the Scamalls in their own lands," Tamm argued, "when the new soldiers are advanced before they're fully trained."

"The emperor doesn't want excuses," Lepik said. "He wants action. And proof that our troops are competent and disciplined."

"Troops can't be prepared on demand like bread for a banquet!"

Lepik pursed his lips. "Emperor Juhan would not approve of your criticism."

"Enough!" shouted the tallest Commander—Kraanvelt,

a man with soulless gray eyes. "We must prove that we can and will stamp out rebellion. If we don't exact a sufficient price against the Scarlet Embers, Emperor Juhan will do so against *us*."

Oksana's breath tangled in her throat. She wished she weren't standing by this wall. She wished she weren't alone with these people.

"Collect the Embers' trainers." Kraanvelt beckoned to the Commanders, turning toward the courtyard. He spotted Oksana. "Why are you here, Goblin?"

Oksana swore silently, then faced Lepik. "Am I dismissed, sir?"

"Get with the others already!"

She didn't push her luck further. Oksana ran into the courtyard and burrowed within the crowd. The Tuliis pressed together too tightly for her to reach Pran. Just as well. She didn't want him to sense the tension rising off her like steam from boiling water.

Commanders stalked through the crowd, pulling aside the Hellions who'd trained the Scarlet Embers. Behind them all, the courtyard gates clanged shut. Heavy footsteps pounded as more Commanders marched the Scarlet Embers forward, bound together by clinking chains. The rest of the Commanders hauled metal stakes, kindling, and wood toward the stone platform.

A sob threatened to burst from Oksana's throat. She clamped her jaw shut and stared toward the sky, at the stars flecked across like tears, until the cry withered behind her teeth.

"Eyes on me!" Kraanvelt ascended the platform. He was ungodly tall and so corded with muscle, he looked like a creature out of a tale written to terrify children. On his uniform tunic, the white demon shone as bright as the chemical lamps mounted throughout the courtyard. Its color was absurdly vivid, absurdly *pure,* next to the demons on the Imps' tunics, dull red like drying blood.

Oksana faced Kraanvelt. For one moment, she didn't temper the hatred coursing across her face. She wished it were poison that she could spit and he'd shrivel at its touch.

Then she took another breath and made her face absolutely blank.

"Perhaps you think yourselves mighty," Kraanvelt called across the courtyard, "because of the powers you've been given, by the grace of our emperor, to defend this land."

He made the transformation sound so pretty. She'd been ten years old when the Nightmares came to her village, Novosel. They'd dragged her into the street by her red hair. When her father came after them with his hammer, they beat him to the ground. When her older brother Borys launched forward, swinging his fists, they'd kicked him in the head. They'd set the house on fire, then turned to Oksana's sobbing mother and tiny sister Iryna.

"No, stop!" Oksana had pushed to her feet. "I'll go with you."

Every Tulii had such a story. This was how Juhan bestowed his gifts.

"You do not betray the man who granted you such powers," Kraanvelt shouted. "Anyone who does . . ." He gestured to the Commanders chaining the Scarlet Embers to metal stakes.

Kraanvelt strode toward the Embers. "So, you *do* like to burn things? Too bad you never showed such initiative during training."

They sobbed, tears cutting across their soot-smudged faces. One shrieked, a cry more animal than human.

Oksana's stomach clenched.

Kraanvelt raised his hand. "We challenge you. One final opportunity to raise flame."

The Commanders shoved flint starters into the Embers' hands. The Imps gawked at the instruments, their pink tongues and white teeth stark against their ash-stained faces.

"Flame," Kraanvelt said. "Now."

A few stopped quaking. Others brightened with hope.

Oksana bit the inside of her cheek. These Imps were too new; they didn't understand. This wasn't a chance to redeem themselves.

"Flame," Kraanvelt demanded.

The Embers lifted the flint starters. Clicked the strikers. Blew sparks into fire. One hurled his blaze toward Kraanvelt, howling in triumph.

Reckless, foolish boy.

A single moment before the fire would have hit him, Kraanvelt flicked his wrist. The flame roared up until it was a pillar as tall as the Ember who'd cast it. Taller.

It reversed course, surging back toward him.

The boy flapped his hands. Swung his arms. But the fire had become Kraanvelt's, and no Imp could overpower such ruthless flame. The blaze was on him before he could shout, swelling taller than the stake, taller than Kraanvelt, taller than the courtyard walls.

The Embers screamed. Some tried to snuff out their flames. But the Commanders caught their fires, too, and twisted them back until every Imp burned.

Somewhere in the courtyard, a voice cried out. "No!"

Don't! Oksana wanted to shout. *Keep the hurt inside or you'll die, too.*

But the boy screeched again, "You can't do this! It isn't right." Others sobbed openly.

Nightmares dragged the protesters forward. More Imps. The youngest soldiers fought and flailed, but they were no match for Nightmares. After a nod from the Commanders, the Nightmares threw these Imps onto the pyres as well.

When Oksana clenched her teeth, ash gritted between them. She flicked her wrist as Kraanvelt had done, but taking control of another's flames was a Commander's feat.

Kraanvelt glared across the yard. "Does anyone else object to punishing rebellion?"

The only sounds inside these walls were roaring flames and the howls of dying Tuliis. Oksana wasn't sure if anyone else dared breathe. She didn't. Couldn't. Her throat knotted at the thick smoke and the reek of scorching hair and burnt flesh.

Another group of Nightmares marched the Hellion trainers forward.

"These Imps were your responsibility," Kraanvelt declared. "They failed, therefore *you've* failed. So you will share their fate. Throw yourselves into the fire and die with dignity. Or"—he gestured to the flint starter on his belt—"we will ignite you."

The Hellions hesitated only a moment before leaping into the flames.

When the last dying Tuliis had stopped moving, Kraanvelt paced the platform's edge. The sky behind him glowered red, as if the Commanders, in their fury, burned even the heavens.

"Rebel with flame," Kraanvelt said, "and you die by flame. We are watching."

Oksana couldn't look away from the pyres. Ash crumbled, flames shriveled, and smoke ascended like ghosts clawing free. *Yeva,* she prayed. *Those Imps weren't of our land and didn't know you. But will you still give them peace? Will you accept their souls?*

She didn't move when the other Tuliis shuffled from the courtyard, dismissed. Didn't stir until Anu clasped her arm. It would be so easy to Snap like the Embers. So easy, one day, to break and lose all sense. So easy for her to end up on a pyre.

Or Pran. Or Anu.

A sob rose in Oksana's throat. Hidden beneath the noise of hundreds of shuffling feet, she finally let it speak.

CHAPTER THREE

PRAN

"Get to your barracks!" Kraanvelt shouted. "Report to training at the fifth bell."

Imps and Goblins skittered toward the gates, while Hellions and Nightmares loomed alongside. As long as those younger Tuliis hustled, they wouldn't feel the sting of the Nightmares' flames . . . for now.

"Come on, Pran." Yalku gripped his arm. "I'll help you."

Stumbling, Pran cursed that he needed any help, especially from the medicine that numbed his wits and senses along with his pain. He batted away Yalku's outstretched hands and staggered forward, searching the crowd for Oksana. "Did they send her back into the yard? Is she all right?"

"If the Commanders had any grief against her, they'd have thrown her onto those pyres as well."

That might still happen before this night was over. Pran's head spun, and it had nothing to do with the medicine pulsing through his veins. "The Commanders will cut down anyone to save themselves, especially tonight."

Yalku shook his head. "They have limits. Every Tulii they tear down weakens the army."

His words trailed off as a Hellion—a Vesimaan, her silver-blond hair twisted high on her head in double buns—approached a Commander, gesturing to different Tuliis. The Commander clapped her on the shoulder and stalked after one of the Imps.

"Self-important sycophants, those Hellions," Yalku muttered. "Think their rank makes them special?"

"If it saves them from being trampled," Pran said, "why not take the advancement?"

Yalku shot him a frigid look. "Didn't think you'd stoop to their games."

"Is it stooping if we use them as stairs?"

"Nayar!" a messenger barked through the crowd, shoving past Tuliis until she stood at Pran's side. "Commander Tamm wants you in her office. Now."

Pran blinked at the girl. Tamm had just spoken to them, collecting their report the moment Oksana had dragged him back. With everything going on tonight, why would she spare them another thought? He'd heard, barely, the Nightmare's defense at the gate: *They did as expected of loyal Tuliikobrets*. She couldn't believe, then, that they'd been part of the Scarlet Embers' rebellion.

Rebellion. Pran turned that word over as though coating his tongue with its flavor. What had made them so bold, these Imps advanced from Novices only a few weeks before?

Shame burned through him, that he hadn't thrown the first flames of dissent.

"*Now*, Nayar," the messenger pressed. "It's urgent."

Even when he had no idea what was happening—whether the Commanders would try to blame them, somehow, for what had gone down in Linn—Pran knew his place in this fort. So he kept his expression steady, his tone light. "Of course. Take me to her."

"See you at breakfast." Yalku lifted his eyebrows high, the words more promise than farewell.

Pran had taken one step alongside the messenger when a blur of red sprinted toward him: Oksana, unharmed and unbound, free of a Commander's clutches. He sighed so long and deep the breath could have put thick clouds in the frozen air, then reached for Oksana. His arms ached for the feel of her—even if it was a ridiculous risk in this yard with so many eyes watching.

But the messenger slipped between them, blocking Oksana from his grasp. "What timing, Artemivna. Commander Tamm wishes to meet with you as well."

Those words were as sobering to Pran as a bucket of ice water to the face. With Tamm summoning him, there'd been a chance, albeit small, that she'd simply wanted his own version of the night's events. But wanting to see Oksana *again* . . .

The Commanders would tear down anyone to save themselves.

Pran choked, throat as dry as the ashes settling across

the platform. When the messenger marched them past walled training yards toward Commander Tower, Pran's gaze locked with Oksana's. He reached his hand out, brushed the tips of his fingers against hers, so quick that to any onlookers it would appear only an accidental touch, a bump in passing.

But Pran's hand lingered just long enough that Oksana tapped his fingers in return. For less than a moment, their littlest fingers intertwined.

It wasn't nearly enough comfort, but it would have to do.

At the tower, the messenger led them through the metal doors with iron bars twisted in the shape of a leaping fire demon, the same demon fronting the Tuliis' uniforms and tattooed onto the messengers' necks. They climbed three flights of spiraling stairs and stepped into an office where Tamm, seated behind a wide steel desk, pointed to a pair of wrought-iron chairs across from her. "Have a seat. Would you care for coffee? We've all had a long night."

Pran had lost count of how many times he'd seen this game from Tamm, opening meetings with pleasantries whether she intended to praise or punish. It kept Tuliis on edge, and even he couldn't help the way his heart tightened over what might follow. He perched on the offered seat, stretching out his leg, which throbbed after all those stairs—would it kill the Commanders to meet with him on the first floor?—and accepting the cup of coffee Tamm offered. But he didn't drink it, and neither did Oksana as she settled into the next chair, watching Tamm as if the woman were a viper coiling to strike.

"I confess, Nayar," the Commander said, dumping sugar and cream into her own cup, "I was astonished to see you in the courtyard. Foul shape you were in when you returned."

"All Tuliikobrets were summoned to the courtyard, and I follow every order."

"I trust you'll extend that same diligence to your next role." Tamm took a long swallow of coffee. "We need more trainers. *Better* trainers."

"T-trainers?" Before they could rattle in his hand, Pran set his cup and saucer on the desk, because *trainers* meant—

"Congratulations are in order." Tamm beckoned behind them, and another messenger swooped into the room carrying two tunics, the leather demons on them a harsh orange. The messenger gave these to Pran and Oksana, along with long-handled flint starters.

"Welcome to Hellion rank," Tamm said. "Effective immediately, you are reassigned to the Bronze Bonfire troop. After your commendable attempts tonight to stop the Scarlet Embers . . . Well, we need Tuliikobrets of your caliber in leadership roles. We must instill in young fighters the importance of following commands. Even when it's painful." She glanced blatantly at his bad leg.

What the Commanders needed, really, was to replace the Hellions they'd just cooked alongside the Embers. Hellions were young Tuliis' first instructors, training them to become emotionless puppets who burned on command.

They did as expected of loyal Tuliikobrets. And if he and

Oksana wanted to walk out of this tower alive, they'd embrace this new role.

Beside him, Oksana said nothing, her face a blank mask. But the tips of her ears had gone as red as her hair, as they did whenever she was barely holding herself together.

But maybe, Pran considered, this new rank didn't have to be a snare that entangled them further in the Commanders' power. Maybe they could craft it into something *else*.

He hefted the flint starter—his own to keep, not surrender at the gates—and his blood buzzed at its sturdy weight against his palm. "We are honored to accept this duty, Commander. To whom do we report?"

Tamm grimaced. "Commander Lepik insisted his troop was the best place for you. He wants you to begin by training Novices. You'll help Commander Sibul with her group tomorrow. In the future, you may be assigned failing Imps as well. A few should have progressed to Goblin rank long ago. Like that Anu Tarvas. They must improve, or there will be consequences."

The little color left in Oksana's face flushed away, and this time, Pran couldn't blame her. "We'll report to the Novice training yard at fifth bell," he said while she caught her breath.

"Perform well, help us reaffirm our value to this empire," Tamm said, "and within a year you may be promoted to Nightmare rank."

Nightmare. Now that was a portal to hell—forcing Tuliis

to stand at attention while their fellows burned, murdering for the emperor, kidnapping children to be tortured into new fighters.

Sometimes, when the Nightmares stormed past him in the fort, eyes utterly empty beneath their painted masks, Pran's senses spiraled until he was back on his doorstep the day Nightmares had come for him: brutal hands, hot through their leather gloves, hauling him out by the wrists. His mother sobbing, *No! Leave my son alone*. Pran turning back to tell her not to cry, only to find his older brother, Nanda, in the doorway, pleading with the Nightmares. *Not my brother! He's frail, he's sickly, he's so young. Take me instead!*

Right then, Pran had stopped resisting the Nightmares. *Stay here,* he'd said to Nanda. *Don't give up your life for me.* When his brother protested, Pran had glared so hard tears sprang into his eyes as he hissed, *I don't need anyone to save me.*

Nanda had crumpled as if Pran had reached between his ribs and torn out his heart. But those words became Pran's vow behind these copper walls, even when it seemed the world was bent on proving him wrong—starting with the transformations that would have killed him if Oksana hadn't come to his aid.

Every day, Nanda's words echoed through his skull like a challenge: *frail, sickly, so young*. Pran was, in fact, older than many of the children transformed alongside him, and frail? Not now, not ever. He'd prove exactly what he was capable of, overcoming everything this fort threw in his path.

"I trust," Tamm added, "that you will perform better than the Hellions we lost today."

The rank memory of smoke and charring meat made it hard for Pran to breathe, but he cleared his throat and forced words to come. "We won't disappoint, Commander."

Outside the tower, Pran and Oksana trudged toward the barracks, the fort silent except for their footsteps and the distant call of one messenger to another. Behind them, Commander Tower glowed with gray-green light in almost every window, but before them, the grounds were dark and empty as Tuliis attempted to get a few hours of sleep before fifth bell.

Oksana still held her Hellion tunic at arm's length. "How can we become *this?*"

Pran glanced around, but there was no sign of anyone else, so he led Oksana into the shadows between two training yards. Leaning against a wall, shifting all his weight to his good leg, he drew her close until their breaths blended and their hearts beat as one.

"It's a role," he said. "A part to assume, and these uniforms, a costume. We can play the Commanders' games, and in the meantime transform this rank into whatever suits us."

"What are you talking about?"

He wasn't sure exactly, but an answer lurked in that bright orange demon burning up from the uniform, if he could only scrape together the pieces. "This rank gives us power here, and there must be some way we can use it to do more. The Scarlet Embers made a statement tonight. Maybe we could make a bigger one, finish what they started."

"We don't know *what* they were doing! We never will, because they're *dead*. They destroyed an entire village—people, *families*, murdered in their homes. That's not a statement. That's horrific."

A chill pulsed through Pran's veins. He had little love for any Vesimaans, but still . . . no one knew better than a Tuliikobret what it was to have a home shattered. "The Embers were too new and inexperienced. They didn't have the skills or authority—in fire, planning, control—to do better. As Hellions, we do. We *must*. We can't go on living this way."

And his wrecked leg, always so helpful, so outstanding with its timing, flared with a pain that sucked away his breath, killing the strength in his last words and leaving him slumped across Oksana's shoulder.

"How, Pran?" She pressed her head against his. "How will we do better?"

He wished he had an answer, a plan for how they could break from this fort. Leave it all behind and stay free, not be dragged back in chains and burned at stakes with a fire of their own creation. It hurt as much as his thigh, admitting he didn't know, that all he had was hope.

But after seven years in this fort, hope was nothing to scoff at. Seven years surviving meant they were capable of so much more.

"We'll find a way. You and I, we've always found a way. When we were Novices, you didn't want to cast fire, but you learned it to teach me, so I'd stay alive. We'll do that again but stronger, learn everything they demand from us as Hellions, and use all of it to turn this fort on its head. We'll make our lives our own, and we'll do it at each other's side."

Before he could talk himself out of it again, he plucked the ring from his pocket. It was silver, a thin band engraved with roses, poppies, yarrow, and peonies, exactly like the wreaths she'd talked of wearing at dance festivals with her mother and sister.

Oksana's jaw dropped as he passed the ring to her. "Where did you get this?"

He'd stolen this ring during a mission last spring. He'd been sent out before nightfall, when the markets were still open, and while slinking through the shadows behind stalls, a silver gleam caught his eye. The moment he saw this ring, he wanted it for Oksana, something so clearly from her homeland.

Then he'd seen the words inside—in Horádimian, no less: *Ya abetschayu. I promise.*

A flush bloomed across Oksana's cheeks as she caught sight of those words. "You promise . . . what?"

That was what he hadn't known for so long. How could he promise anything when he had no control over his life? But after tonight, this change in rank . . . he would not spend such power bending to the Commanders' whims.

He lifted the ring from Oksana's trembling hand, though his own shook so badly he could hardly slide the ring onto her finger. "I don't know what our future holds." He cupped her face in his hands, and only then did they go still. "But I want to give us freedom. And I'd like to share it with you."

She was silent for so long he feared he'd said the wrong thing. Perhaps these claims, this ring, were too absurd, too much this impossible night.

But then she leaned close until her breath fluttered like a moth against his jaw. "That is a future worth fighting for."

And before he could laugh, before he could say a word of his own, she tangled her hands in his hair and kissed him until Pran could have summoned a fire with the heat surging through him. He pressed her against the wall, her soft lip caught between his teeth, and kissed her until they both gasped, their ragged breaths tangling together. They kissed until his heart pounded so fiercely he thought it might burst from his chest. They kissed until he could barely stand, until he didn't *want* to stand, and his shirt was in the way, too. But when he scooted from her to tug it off, Oksana leaped on him, closing the distance.

They kissed until the first bell clanged, reminding Pran where they stood, and that no place in this fort was safe.

"I'm sorry," he said, as he broke away. Oksana's shoulders slumped when she glanced to the training yards and Commander Tower always looming above them.

He caught one of her hunched shoulders and squeezed. "In the morning, when we walk into that yard, we'll be together. We'll figure this out together."

The east training yard was primarily used for Novice lessons, so the space was plain and bare, offering few obstacles for clumsy soldiers-to-be. A few stone benches stood along the walls, and a well hunkered in the center with tin buckets to douse errant flames.

The Novices huddled in one corner. The oldest among them couldn't have been more than thirteen years old, and the youngest, perhaps ten. Drab uniforms hung like sacks on their twiggy bodies. Their skin was ashen from serum treatments, and their hair lank and dull. The flint starters they hefted, the thick ivory handles longer than their forearms, would have looked comically absurd if there were anything humorous about children forced to become soldiers. They flinched as Commander Sibul strode near, her colorless hair bound in a tight knot high on her head, making her appear even taller and meaner.

Pran stepped between her and the Novices. "Where are they in their training?"

Commander Sibul pursed her lips. "Halfway through serum treatments. They're skittish, careless with flame. You must be strict with them. Today, I want you to observe my methods. Next session, you'll teach."

She stalked toward the Novices and clicked her own flint starter, raising a pillar of fire. The Novices cowered, casting their arms over their faces and whimpering. One wept openly.

"Silence!" Sibul barked. "Back in line." After another burst of flame, the Novices scrambled into a ragged row.

Pran banished the fury from his face but couldn't dismiss the memories. How long since he'd been here, a half-transformed Novice still struggling to walk—five years?

"No more lazing about, Nayar," one Commander had said after a session where Pran spent more time clutching his leg than throwing flame. "If you don't complete the training by the week's end, we'll remove you from service."

They did not mean they'd send him home.

That whole night, Oksana had stayed up with him, stretching and exercising his throbbing leg until he'd had enough strength to both stand and raise sparks at once.

Oksana's stare went murderous as she nodded toward the opposite wall, where Rootare perched on a bench, notebook and nib pen in his hands. As the Novices copied Sibul's movements, swooping their arms through the air while clicking their flint starters, Rootare jotted notes, shaking his head and frowning whenever they stumbled or raised flames that were sputtering and weak.

"What is *he* doing here?" Oksana hissed.

As though feeling their attention, the man turned toward them. No, not them. *Oksana.* Rootare stared as though she were a secret he couldn't figure out, and he'd never know peace until he'd cracked her down the middle.

Bile surged in Pran's gut. He hefted his flint starter, thumb pressed to the metal striker, but Oksana shook her head. "Don't give him reason to hurt you."

The alchemist ought to be scared of Pran, if he kept looking at Oksana as if she were some substance—a *specimen*—

to claim. He was about to say as much, when Sibul's shouts echoed across the yard. "No, no, no! Hold your ground."

A young Pakastran girl wailed as a fireball swooped too near her face. She threw her arms over her head, ducking down.

"Emperor Juhan didn't grant these powers so you'd cower like mice!" Sibul yelled.

The girl rubbed a burn on her forehead. "I want to go home."

Sibul struck the child with her flint starter so hard, the girl tumbled to the ground. "The homes and families you knew—forget them. Your life now is only this fort and the tasks we assign. If any of you mewl again for home—"

Beside him, Oksana stiffened, her whole expression strained. "I can't watch this," she whispered.

"Might we step in?" Pran called to the Commander.

The woman whirled toward them. "I told you to observe."

"My first Commander said we learned best by *doing*. It was good advice; that's why I advanced to Goblin rank so quickly. And it seems you have your hands full." He gestured toward two Novices who'd managed to set their own hair on fire.

Sibul glowered. "Put them out," she snapped. While Pran dumped a bucket of water over their heads, she announced to the rest of the group, "Nayar and Artemivna are your new trainers. Heed them as you'd heed me."

As Sibul stalked to the far side of the yard with a group of the Novices, Oksana helped the fallen girl to her feet.

"Bend your elbow as you hold the starter." She wrapped the girl's fingers around the handle. "You have power over these flames. You decide where they go, what shape they take. Not everything that comes from fire is terrible and ugly."

Pran wasn't sure if the girl registered Oksana's words. She stared only at the orange demons on their tunics, hunching her shoulders and shuffling back. He splayed a hand over the demon. "This doesn't define us. We aren't here to hurt you."

"If we don't do as the Commanders say, they beat us. If we keep failing, they kill us. Last week Bijan tried to run away, and Nightmares caught him and they—" Her voice broke.

"I'm sorry." Pran barely got the words past the knot in his own throat.

"They took you from Pakastra, too." Her voice was steeped in longing—and accusation.

He was no stranger to such anguish; the Nightmares who'd dragged him from home had also been Pakastran. It was one thing to be trapped by the Commanders—all Vesimaans, strangers, none of them knowing his home and people. But the Hellions and Nightmares who'd also come from Pakastra, who looked like him and had once been like him . . . those were hardest to forgive and impossible to trust.

Pran would not be like them. He'd help this girl and other young Tuliis, and he'd start by proving he was different. He leaned down until their eyes were level. "Shall I tell you how I learned to make fire? How she taught me?" He nodded toward Oksana.

The girl's chin wobbled.

"In your lungs, their deepest depths," Pran said, "there's a heat forever burning. Close your eyes, try to find it."

Though she scowled, the girl did as he asked, her brow furrowing so tightly she went as wrinkled as an old woman. "It's there. I feel it," she said, and winced.

"When you raise a spark"—he clicked his flint starter, flecks of fierce orange raining down from stone and steel—"at the same time, call to that heat inside you, nudge it forward with your mind. Summon it from your lungs and direct it out your throat. Breathe hard, like you're trying to put a fire out. But instead, your heat, *your power*, will turn that spark into a bigger fire. With practice, you can throw that fire wherever you want." He hurled a flame high above Sibul's head and into a water bucket across the yard.

"You are mightier than the flame," he said as the girl gaped, "and with practice, you can be stronger still."

Her eyes welling with tears, the girl took up her flint starter again and pressed the striker. Sparks scattered in every direction and the girl whimpered, until Oksana rested a hand on her shoulder. "You can do this. Try again."

The girl did, and on the second attempt, one of those sparks blossomed into a flame, flaring white as a star.

"Like that," Pran said. "Now, try again. Just watch, I'll teach every one of you to fight."

CHAPTER FOUR

OKSANA

"Wake up, Artemivna!" Someone seized Oksana's shoulders, jolting her upright.

She pushed her tangled hair from her face and squinted at the barrack window. Amber sunlight slanted through hazy glass. Oksana groaned as a headache throbbed in the depths of her skull. After a day of training, she'd found her new barrack, where the girls of Bronze Bonfire lived. She'd sunk onto her bunk, tugged off her boots, and must have fallen asleep the moment her head hit the pillow.

A Vesimaan a year or so older than Oksana, her silver-blond hair twisted up in double buns, hurled those boots toward her. "Get to the courtyard."

Oksana barely stopped the boots from hitting her face. "Another assignment *already*?"

"Emperor Juhan has summoned everyone."

Oksana froze, foot halfway in a boot. "He's here? In the fort?"

"You have two minutes before the Commanders close the courtyard gates. Don't be left on the wrong side." The girl slammed the barrack door behind her.

Oksana shook so badly she could hardly get her boots on. She ran with the straps half undone, Kraanvelt's words thundering through her mind: *If we don't exact a sufficient price against the Scarlet Embers, Emperor Juhan will do so against* us.

When she barreled into the courtyard, brow damp and boot buckles drooping, Anu slipped to her side. "You join us at last! I waited to walk to supper with you when suddenly the messengers darted about and—and—" She gaped at Oksana's tunic. "Holy Maiden of the Grave!"

Oksana pressed a hand over the orange demon. "Tamm did it after the burning. Pran, too. They want us to train—it's still me!" she blurted, as Anu's brow furrowed. "I won't become one of *them*."

Anu glanced at the Nightmares prowling around the courtyard and the Hellions tailing them like eager dogs. "That will take some real mettle. Not that you don't have it, but—"

"In line!" Commanders stalked through the courtyard. "Order, for His Imperial Majesty."

Anu scurried toward the rows of Imps. Oksana remained with the Hellions. She spotted Pran the moment a Nightmare shoved him toward a cluster of fidgeting Novices huddled in front of the platform.

Yeva, keep him safe. She clutched her pendant hidden beneath her tunic, Pran's ring strung onto the chain alongside her saint's icon. *Don't let those Novices make trouble.*

All twenty-two Commanders gathered on one side of

the platform, faces grim. Rootare lurked among them, stark against all the dark uniforms in his stained lab coat—did he never take it off? Meanwhile, on the opposite side of the platform, messengers stood at ease in neat rows.

Not transformed by serums, the messengers held almost as lofty a position as the Commanders. Only Vesimaans could assume either role. Wealthy Vesimaan families were sometimes permitted to gift one of their children into Juhan's service in exchange for political favors. Of these, the strongest were transformed into Commanders. The rest carried the empire's news in their pockets.

It was a disgusting gamble that Juhan forced onto his own people: Give up a child for power and prestige. Or keep their children, and pray that the Nightmares didn't come and steal them anyway to be tortured into Tuliikobrets.

A hush fell over the courtyard as Kraanvelt approached the platform. "All hail His Imperial Majesty, Emperor Juhan Edvin Visnapuu."

Juhan ascended from behind the platform, flanked by two Nightmares from his personal guard. In the day's dying light, streaks of silver gleamed through his dark blond hair, while his copper-red jacket was as lurid as spurting blood.

The man clenched a gloved fist, his square jaw stiffening. "Whichever one of you directed the Scarlet Embers, I want you on this platform. Now."

The Commanders froze. Even Kraanvelt went rigid. Then one who'd hunkered in the back of the group staggered forward, his feet hardly lifting from the ground. Tamm touched his arm as he climbed the platform steps.

"Commander Mälk?" Juhan's mouth thinned to a line so sharp it could cut. "How disappointing."

Juhan extended his hand, staring until Mälk took it as though to shake. "Y-your Majesty," the Commander choked.

"Do you understand what your failure has wrought?" Juhan tightened his hold as though to break Mälk's fingers, tugging the Commander closer. "My palace is beset by protesters. Early this morning, renegades from Kivi mauled two members of my council and left them for dead. These malcontents promise more violence unless I disband the Tuliikobrets."

From across the courtyard, Oksana saw Anu's head whip upright, her jaw dropping. Kivi was Anu's hometown; her family still lived there. But . . . surely they wouldn't—*couldn't*—risk Juhan's fury by attacking council members . . . ?

It didn't matter. If Juhan decided to strike back, the whole village would come under fire. Oksana's heart clenched as Anu's shoulders shook.

Mälk gaped at the other Commanders, but none moved to help him. "Your Majesty," he gasped, "we are most aggrieved—"

"I told these protesters"—Juhan tugged Mälk even closer until his shadow eclipsed the Commander—"that disbanding the Tuliikobrets is akin to the Horádimians surrendering their bows. Pakastrans giving up their sabers. Nyítans handing over their reindeer-bone knives. But they've already done that, haven't they? Because of the Tuliikobrets."

Juhan leaned down, leveling his gaze at Mälk. "I told them destroying the Tuliikobrets would invite Scamall to descend again from the highlands and invade our nation, once more plundering our fertile lands and commandeering the verikivi mines. I reminded them that my grandfather had freed Vesimaa from Scamall's relentless attacks, and by what means? The Tuliikobrets. One day, these Tuliikobrets will conquer Scamall, bringing their forges, shipyards, and mills into our power and forever ending their threat against us."

"L-long live the Visnapuu line." With his free hand, Mälk dabbed at his brow. "All hail their Tuliikobrets."

"And yet"—Juhan tilted his head as he considered Mälk—"Vesimaans were murdered by those sworn to keep them safe. The people deserve retribution. Don't you agree?"

Mälk opened his mouth, but no sound followed. He scrubbed his face with an open palm, shuddering visibly.

"Blood for blood. It is our way." Juhan finally released Mälk's hand.

The Commander collapsed. He writhed on top of the platform, fingers scrabbling at his chest as spit foamed on his lips. He uttered a gurgling wail, his whole body spasming.

Then he went still, eyes glazing over, rattling breaths ended.

Everyone in the courtyard was silent. Not even the Novices squirmed, as if by remaining still Juhan might forget their presence. Might let them live.

"He killed a Commander by looking at him!" a Tulii whispered.

But that wasn't it at all. Oksana stared at the thick leather gloves Juhan stripped from his hands. Rootare, meanwhile, oozed smugness, while the Commanders nearest him gave the alchemist a wide berth. What had he put on Juhan's gloves? Aconitine? Arsenic mixed with cantharides? Most likely some sick brew of his own, to kill Mälk this quickly.

"So it goes for any who fail their duties to Vesimaa." Juhan peered at the Tuliis nearest the platform, then jabbed a finger. "Pakastran Hellion. Up here."

And Pran—oh saints, *Pran*—limped up the platform steps.

He stood a whole head taller than Oksana, yet next to the emperor he looked like a child's doll. With one slap of Juhan's meaty hand, Pran could be on the ground, broken.

Yet he faced that man with a steady jaw and steadier stare. "What do you wish, Your Majesty?"

A sob tangled in Oksana's throat. *Yeva, do not let this happen.*

"It seems some have forgotten the reason for their existence," Juhan said. "Refresh your comrades on the Tuliikobrets' history. Remind them why they are here."

Pran faced the courtyard, shifting his weight to his good leg so he could stand without having anyone or anything to lean against. He glanced toward Oksana, tapping his ring finger and mouthing, *Ya abetschayu.*

I promise.

She bit her lip to keep from crying.

"Speak, Hellion," Juhan commanded.

"We defend Vesimaa's borders." Pran raised his voice until, like Juhan's, it echoed across the courtyard. "We defend the nation's interests, throughout all of Vesimaa, and in the . . . the lands beyond. We fight so the nation—"

"Stop," Juhan interrupted. "Tell it right. Start from the beginning."

Tell it, he meant, as they'd learned when carted to this fort, their first months immersed in learning the Vesimaans' language, history, and excuses for the Tuliikobrets.

Pran drew a long breath. "Great King Heino knew that to defeat Scamall, send them running back to their mountains, he must confront them with a force they'd never encountered and could not match. He worked in secret with his alchemists, and, using the incendiary verikivi stones that the Scamalls coveted, they made fire serums. The first Tuliikobrets were volunteers from Vesimaa's original army, and they struck fear into the Scamalls' hearts. But fear alone doesn't end a war, and King Heino's alchemists discovered that when the fire serums were administered to . . . those not fully grown . . . the recipients developed powers over fire that were otherworldly. Mythological."

Demonic. Monstrous. Oksana's breath hissed through her teeth.

"King Heino's son, Niilo, conquered the surrounding nations and claimed child soldiers from these lands," Pran continued. "The young fighters were doubly effective because, with their non-Vesimaan features, the Scamalls didn't suspect them. These Tuliikobrets could wreak havoc within Scamall camps before those soldiers realized what had struck them. It didn't take long for Scamall to abandon its attacks on Vesimaa and retreat home."

"But we aren't finished," Juhan called across the courtyard. "Not with Scamall, nor with asserting Vesimaa's might." He peered at the Commanders. "Some of you feel the demands of training troops aren't adequately considered."

Tamm blanched corpse-pale. Oksana wasn't sure if her heart should sing or quake at the sight of Commanders squirming beneath Juhan.

The man grinned, showing all his teeth. "I understand organizing troops fit for battle is no small task. And my councilors could benefit from your insights and experience. So, a proposition: I will add Commanders to the Imperial Council. Those who do the most to get this army back on track will be granted seats. These appointments will be announced in five weeks, on Jubilee Night—my Silver Jubilee, this year." Juhan lifted his eyebrows, as though everyone in this courtyard should applaud his long reign.

"In addition to the new council members," he continued, "I will invite to my jubilee celebration any Commanders who make impressive contributions to this army and Vesimaa's safety."

Whispers broke out among the Commanders. Atop the platform, Pran gaped at Juhan.

"But do not forget," Juhan called above the hubbub. "Never forget."

The whispers died with a hiss like water poured over embers.

"The Tuliikobret army is essential to the empire. But individually, you are not."

He snapped his fingers, and one of his Nightmares hurled fire toward Pran.

Oksana reached for her flint starter but came up empty. She must have forgotten it in the barrack, in her rush to get to this courtyard. And between her and Pran stood the whole army of Tuliis. She'd never reach him.

A gasp escaped her lips as the flames surged forward.

But a finger's breadth from Pran's face, they halted, the fire licking toward his skin but not quite touching. The Nightmare crouched on the platform, fingers clenched to hold the blaze in place.

Juhan circled them both, the glow from those flames brass-bright across his brow. "The serums are instilled into your flesh. I can't take away these abilities. But if you don't perform as expected, I will have you replaced."

He nodded to the Nightmare. The Tulii twitched her thumb and a tendril of flame lashed Pran's face. He doubled over, clutching his cheek.

Oksana bit her tongue to keep from crying out, even as her blood smoldered.

Once again, Juhan snapped his fingers and the Nightmare smothered her flame.

Pran straightened, dropping his hand from the red burn seared across his cheek. He stared at Juhan as though dazed. Then his shoulders stiffened, and he lifted his chin. When he spoke next, his voice was anything but small. "What would you have us do now, Your Majesty?"

"The Hellions will attack Kivi. I won't have more councilors maimed, nor my authority mocked. Make those reprobates pay dearly for their rebellion."

No. Across the courtyard, Oksana spotted Anu shaking her head, bright spots flaring on her cheeks. Anu met her stare, then glared toward the orange demon fronting Oksana's tunic.

With a curse, Oksana spread her hand over the insignia. There was no escaping an order from the emperor himself. But she couldn't attack her friend's family, no matter who decreed it.

Atop the platform, Pran bowed. "As you wish, Your Majesty."

Oksana's stomach turned over and her palms went slick and cold . . . doubly so when Pran rose, his eyes vivid with a frightening gleam.

She knew that look. Whatever he was scheming, she wished he'd stop, at least until he was far from that man.

"Send the message strong and clear," Juhan said to Pran, to the Commanders, to every Tulii in the yard. "Do the job right. Do not make me come back here."

He shoved Pran aside and descended the dais steps. Juhan strode past the Commanders without a glance, marching with his Nightmare entourage out the gates.

The moment he'd departed, Tuliis fled the courtyard, elbowing to be the first beyond the cast-iron gates. Oksana, however, shoved toward the platform. Toward Pran.

At his side, she cupped a hand around his jaw, her fingers hovering above the burn angry-bright across his cheek. "I really thought Juhan would kill you," she whispered. "And that I'd be stuck in the crowd watching you die."

He shuddered. "Me too."

But then that strange light flashed back into his eyes. "He's done it, Oksana. He's given us their end. Him, and all the Commanders."

"What are you saying?" Stepping back from Pran, she glanced to the Tuliis and Commanders still pressing toward the gates. "No, don't answer that here."

Pran rubbed his temples. "I need a drink. Meet you at the pub?"

CHAPTER FIVE

PRAN

The fort's pub was particularly crowded that night, Tuliis packed onto every crudely cut bench. It seemed many came to forget the emperor's visit. Some busied themselves with cards made from scraps of paper, gambling their ale tokens. Others cavorted on a table while bellowing folk songs, replacing lyrics with lewd suggestions.

But the rest of the crowd discussed the courtyard events, leaning close and recounting the scene as though it were some legendary battle. While Pran waited at the bar, trading his weekly ale token for a mug, more than a few Tuliis gawped at him. "The Hellion who faced the emperor," they murmured, and speculated how he'd survived when Emperor Juhan had killed a Commander with his eyes.

Pran tried to drown the churning in his stomach with a swallow of ale, but his gut clenched worse when a group of Tuliis raised their mugs to him and cheered. Devak, a Pakastran Imp, joined their shouts while fiddling with the braided band around his wrist. Faithful Pakastran Tuliis plaited those from seven strands of twine, knotting each string in a different place, a unique and complex knot for each of the Seven Gods they insisted still watched over them. *Ridiculous,* Pran thought. If the Seven Gods were so benevolent and powerful, why had they let any Pakastrans be taken into the Vesimaans' army?

But Devak cheered again, staring as if Pran were one of those gods incarnate. Pran grimaced, but still lifted his mug in acknowledgment, then slipped away the moment Devak turned to his own drink.

A trio of Nightmares huddled at a table in Pran's usual shadowy corner, the blue demons on their tunics uncannily vibrant in the dim pub. They threw back shots of liquor, still wearing their towering antlers and rotting-skin masks—they were never without them—then stalked outside. Pran seized their abandoned table as the door opened again and Oksana and Anu strode in, whispering furiously.

"I don't care," Anu said as they approached the table. "I *will* warn my family."

"You're in trouble with the Commanders already. Tamm told me that you aren't making enough progress. She said there'd be consequences. They're watching you."

"And here I thought I was improving. Only a special kind of awful draws their attention."

"How can you joke about this?"

Anu sat and pulled squares of wrinkled paper toward her, what passed for playing cards in this pub. She took a piece of charcoal from her pocket and sketched across the back of those cards, singing a line from "The Demon's Ballad"—an old Vesimaan folk song—as she worked. "*Out in the moun-*

tains the monsters arose, all embers and fire, to fight the land's foes."

Its usual melody was peppered with restless measures, demanding fear, yet these notes Anu crooned were sweet as a lullaby.

"That's the reason Tuliikobrets exist," she said over sketches of willowy Mother Forest and stern Master Thunder. "I won't stop helping people I love no matter the danger to me. *You* wouldn't."

"I advanced to Goblin rank a year ago precisely *so* I could help people I love!"

Oksana glanced to Pran, her earth-dark eyes lingering on his burned cheek. She frowned and brushed her fingers below the wound. "You should have bound this up."

Her touch soothed him like a balm, better than anything the physicians could offer. Pran leaned into it, clinging to his chair to keep from tugging Oksana close and begging for more of that medicine here in front of everyone.

"What were you saying in the courtyard?" she asked, yanking him back to reality.

He peeked over his shoulder, checking whether anyone might overhear. The door swung open and Pran instinctively leaned away from Oksana until he saw the newcomer was Yalku. Grinning, he beckoned the boy to their table.

He nodded to the hay on Yalku's tunic. "Still tending the Commanders' horses?"

"Some of them can hardly tell the hooves from the head. It's disgusting."

"Benevolent of you, to consider the animals."

"Horses are as close to reindeer as I can get here."

"I'm sure the extra drink tokens have nothing to do with it."

Yalku twitched an eyebrow and held up his hand, displaying a fistful of ale tokens. He disappeared toward the bar and returned moments later with three mugs of beer and a glass of kali—a drink brewed from fermented bread—for Anu. It was much too sour for Pran, and never strong enough when there was real beer to be had, but Anu loved the stuff.

"Such a gentleman." She winked at Yalku.

He dropped into a chair, his gaze lingering on Pran's burned cheek. "Are you—?"

"I'm still here, aren't I? The emperor wanted to teach a lesson, nothing more."

Shoving away his mug, Pran peered around the pub. Though many Tuliis jeered over games, their eyes remained joyless. Others huddled near the windows, their expressions vacant, silently nursing drinks. Meanwhile, the dancing soldiers tipped over their table, sending themselves and crockery crashing to the ground. With a shout, the pubmaster threw down his rag and stalked around the bar, his face going vibrant shades of red and purple.

"What if we could take this army into our hands?" Pran said quietly.

Anu's charcoal snapped, Yalku paused mid-sip of his ale, and Oksana blanched. She peeked around the room, though no one could hear anything over the pubmaster screaming about ruined crockery. "What do you mean?"

Yalku shook his head. "Don't speak of this. At all. Do you want to die?"

"This"—Pran swept his hand across the room—"isn't living. Surely you see that."

"Neither was battling the Scamalls," Anu countered. "Vesimaans almost lost everything. And Scamall wouldn't have stopped at conquering our nation, you know."

"It was Vesimaa's verikivi mines they were after," Pran said. "I don't want more Pakastran children dragged here to protect *your* country's riches."

"Do you think because you're a Hellion now you're invincible?" Yalku cut in. "Or what, because you survived the emperor? He *let* you go."

"None of us are helpless if we unite our powers and minds."

While the pubmaster shoved the dancing Tuliis out the door, Oksana nudged Pran with her elbow. "What did you mean before, about Juhan handing us his end?"

He scooted his chair closer to the worn table, meeting each of them in the eye. "By inviting Commanders to the Imperial Council, and more specifically, his jubilee."

The others stared. "That will make the Commanders meaner," Oksana said. "They'll be watching us more than ever, because a slipup of ours will cost them dearly."

"The offer divides the Commanders," Pran pressed. "They'll try to outdo one another to secure a seat, become rivals. And then their ranks will be weakened further when some leave the fort on Jubilee Night. That is when we take action, while they're distracted and not all present to fight back."

Yalku scowled. "That's only five weeks away. In five weeks, you believe we can make ourselves strong enough to challenge them? The Commanders can rip fire from our hands just by thinking about it. One of them could take down dozens of Imps and Goblins. Dozens of Hellions."

"Open battle isn't the only way to challenge Commanders. They have their weak points, they let things slip. Like the Scarlet Embers."

"Pran." Oksana gripped his elbow. "You saw what they did to the Embers. If we rise against them, they'll slaughter us and make everyone watch."

He did watch—as the Tuliis resumed mindless card games or drowned themselves in cheap ale, their shouts raucous even as their eyes glazed over, numb to their cores. "There's a story my father loved to tell, about how the small and weak took down the strong."

At home, Pran had grown up on stories, his mother filling his days with tales of the Seven Gods, legends she taught at the Grand Temple where she ministered. But his father, chief justice of the High Court, put Pran and Nanda to bed each night with stories of the cases he worked through. Those had been Pran's favorites, and the ones that still inspired him even trapped behind these fort walls.

"There was an apothecary in the city," he began. "He

was small of stature and poor. Most of the herbs he sold, he grew himself or gathered from the jungle, but he made enough money to get by until a crime lord, the Saw-Scaled Viper, targeted this man and others. The Viper forced them to pay for protection from his gang until he ruined many of the smaller merchants, bringing them utterly into his power. This apothecary was in danger of losing all to the Viper, too, when he discovered that the crime lord had a lung condition, and he knew the poisons that would aggravate it. He rubbed tinctures onto his money and the coins his neighbors paid, too. Week after week he did this until the Saw-Scaled Viper was no more."

Yalku cocked an eyebrow. "You want to us to poison the Commanders and emperor?"

"I want us to focus on what actions lie in our power, and unite with other Tuliis who dare rise against the Commanders. That apothecary's coins alone would not have taken down the Viper, but when the man brought his neighbors into the plan, the city's weakest ended that monster. We can succeed, too, if we recruit the right allies and work shrewdly."

"How far are you willing to go?" Yalku asked. "These people aren't neighborhood bullies to be defeated with trick coins. This won't be a clean victory, if we can win at all."

"You think I don't know that? Yes, there will be hard choices. I can make them."

Oksana sucked in a sharp breath. "Pran! This is too much."

The words were worse than a slap. Her doubting him, when she'd always been first at his side, left him feeling like his whole world had been knocked off-center. "What wouldn't you do to be rid of the Commanders and emperor?"

"Never sacrifice you! If this goes wrong, the Commanders will kill you like the Scarlet Embers."

"Or with the right allies, we can all know freedom. Please." He swept his gaze over each of them in turn. "Do I have you?"

Anu brushed a hand over her intricate sketches: a wrinkled man strumming a kannel, a curly-haired woman gathering cornflowers, a grinning boy and girl dashing through a field. "My country can be better than this. We *need* to be better. There must be another way to defend our lands. But I don't know how to do that yet. And my family is too near. The Commanders might retaliate against them if I'm caught in open rebellion. I can't."

Pran had expected more from her, and disappointment sat bitter on his tongue. After all, Anu had been forced from her home and family, same as them. Still, she was a Vesimaan. This was her land; this army defended her people's interests.

Downing a gulp of ale, Pran turned from her and faced Yalku. "What about you?"

The boy snorted. "Seems like I'd be signing up to die."

"If we do nothing, we *will* die, in this fort or in some worthless battle for the emperor. Is that how you'd spend your life?"

"I'm not afraid of death. My father was almost killed trying to keep me from the Nightmares. I'd suffer the same for my family—all of them, every last Nyítan. But I need to see there's a real chance we can win. I won't risk everything for nothing, like the Scarlet Embers."

"The Embers weren't organized," Pran said. "They didn't have the strength or skills to win. But we don't have to fail like them. There are plenty of Tuliis among us capable of this fight, if they'll only commit to the cause."

"I know what you're trying to say—" Yalku began.

"Do you? Because an effort like this needs fighters like you. That's what will make the difference between freedom and the half life in this fort."

Yalku crumpled a card in his fist. "All we'll have is a half life, no matter where we stand. We're half human, half monster, pulling fire from a crackle of light. No one can change that."

"No, we can't." Pran didn't know if the strange weight settling in his chest was resignation or relief. "But if we're stuck with these powers . . . wouldn't you rather use them to protect your own people? We can lead these troops to fight for our own homes, rather than die for an emperor who only sees us as tools. You'd do anything for your people. Won't you help me free them from Vesimaa's rule? You can help me make a difference for all."

With a grumbled curse, Yalku pushed back his chair so roughly it screeched against the floor, then stalked toward the bar and plunked down a token for another ale.

Pran's head throbbed, but at least his words had hit

their mark. For now, he would wait for his friend to make the right choice.

While Yalku stayed at the bar, slurping down more ale, Pran turned to Oksana. She didn't shrink from his stare, but her brow was damp, her whole expression strained.

"I mean it," she warned. "You have to think this through."

"Why do you believe I haven't?" He took a breath until all bite faded from his tone. Venom wasn't what Oksana deserved. She was not the source of his troubles, and she was right to be worried.

"Under the cover of our new rank," he said, "we can strike deeper. I'm telling you, with the Commanders distracted by the jubilee, we'll have our best chance to claim control of this fort and the troops. From there, we can challenge the emperor himself."

Instead of looking assured, Oksana went rigid. "I don't want control of the fort. I don't want to keep fighting and burning. I just want to go home."

She buried her face in her hands, as though the confession cut deep.

"Fight for that," he whispered. "Because for now, we *will* fight. If not for ourselves, then for the emperor, until he's spent us through."

He wished he had a better answer, but they were fire soldiers—monsters in everyone's eyes. The chance at a life without fighting had been stolen from them long ago. Still, his heart ached as Oksana's shoulders slumped.

He clutched her hand. "After we've defeated the

Commanders, I won't force anyone to stay. My army is by choice. If you want to return to Horádim, I'll get you there. You want a field with a hundred woolly lambs? Fresh loaves of braided bread each morning? Forests for mushroom hunting? Want me to learn to play the bandura so you have music to dance to every summer? A cottage near your parents' home, with a better chemistry lab than anything your Professor Melnyk can boast? I'll do it all. I'll fight for lives worth living. Ya abetschayu."

She squeezed his hand so hard his knuckles popped, but Pran held on.

He would never be the one to let go.

CHAPTER SIX

OKSANA

Half the night she lay awake in her barrack, staring into the darkness surrounding her. Oksana slipped Pran's ring off her necklace chain. Clutched it tight against her palm. Ran her thumb over the engraved flowers. Sank onto her mattress and remembered the taste of his kiss: oranges and toasted sugar. Her lips were hot, as if a flame crackled beneath the skin.

When he'd given her his promise, she'd thought her heart might take wing. But knowing what must happen first clipped those wings to the bone. The Commanders weren't to be trifled with. They could end every Tulii, at any time, in flame and agony. There was no end to what the Commanders, or Juhan, would do to preserve their power.

Sometimes, Oksana still felt the Scarlet Embers' ashes between her teeth. *Rebel with flame, and you die by flame.*

When she finally slept, she dreamed she was with Pran, kissing him until her lips were swollen. She dreamed of returning together to Horádim, sitting with him in a wheat field while orioles sang and snow-capped mountains stood sentinel. They visited her older brother Borys in Professor

Melnyk's chemistry lab. Visited her mother and younger sister, Iryna, teaching the village dances to children. Admired the swirling patterns her carpenter father carved into a table.

It was everything she remembered of home but better, because Pran was with her.

She woke with tears on her face, heart sore beneath her ribs. Oksana wasn't sure what hurt worse: the memories of what had been stolen, or the fear that they could only ever be memories.

The sun had just barely thought of rising. Meal Hall wasn't opened yet for breakfast. Not that Oksana was sorry to miss another bowl of mushy kama—barley, rye, pea, and oat flours, whatever the kitchen had left over, mixed with tepid milk—especially with her stomach already clenching over what was coming.

The meeting to plan the attack against Kivi.

Inside the tower, the meeting room's wooden benches were packed with all the Hellions stationed in Mennick, nearly four dozen. Every hair on the back of Oksana's neck prickled until she spotted Pran sitting against the far wall. He scooted down the bench, making space beside him, and nodded her way. Oksana settled next to him, and he pressed his fingers to the back of her hand. The gentle touch eased the tightness in her throat. When she gave a tiny smile, Pran bumped his elbow against hers. *Together,* he mouthed.

Then he went back to studying every face in the room as

though he could pierce through their bones straight to the secrets within.

"This planning," Pran whispered, "it's a glimpse into how their minds work, where their loyalties lie. Whether they might help us."

But Oksana's skin crawled as Lepik and Tamm strode into the room, along with Commander Haamer, who led another troop of Hellions. For a Vesimaan, the man's hair was shockingly dark, like freshly plowed earth after rain. His face held a trace of softness, too, around the edges. Once he might have been a kind soul, though that had been long beaten out of him.

"You heard Emperor Juhan last night," Haamer told the Hellions, his voice raspy like a Nightmare's. "The people of Kivi have made trouble for His Majesty. We must send a clear message that rebellion is not tolerated."

Oksana twisted her fingers until her knuckles popped. She couldn't let them attack Anu's family because they'd spoken out for their massacred neighbors. Even if all Vesimaans were complicit in the Tuliis' pain, going along with this terrible army for so long . . . it wasn't right to murder families. And the people of Kivi weren't wrong to speak against it.

"We should sneak to Kivi in the evening," one Hellion declared in overconfident tones. Marten, an arrogant boy several years older than Oksana. "As they settle down in their homes. We'll fall on the villagers before they can organize themselves or summon help."

That girl from Oksana's barrack, silver-blond hair wound

high on her head in two knots, leaped to her feet. "No, it's better to arrive in the dead of night and wake them with fire. Any lives spared will be at our discretion. There will be no question where true power lies."

Both these Hellions were Vesimaans. So strange, seeing them plot against their own people. Oksana shuddered. This fort truly made monsters in ways that had nothing to do with serums.

Tamm's mouth thinned. "We must be strategic about any damage inflicted. The goal is to instill obedience, not give more cause for rebellion."

"But there must be punishment!" Lepik clenched a fist. "Rebellion cannot stand."

The Hellions erupted in noisy debate, some calling for one grand spectacle, others for stealthy, repeated attacks that would wear down Kivi's drive to fight. Each word seized Oksana's lungs until she could barely breathe.

Beside her, Pran brushed Oksana's shoulder as though sweeping away ash. She leaned into him, and the familiar warmth, the way her shoulder fit against his, dulled some of her heartache. Pran reached around her back, squeezed her other shoulder, until she felt steady enough to sit upright.

Beneath the noise, Pran murmured, "Is Anu really going to warn her family?"

Oksana bit her lip and nodded. "When she was taken, she swore she'd use this role to keep them safe. That's what's gotten her through all these years."

It was a sentiment Oksana understood. If it had been her family and home slated for attack, of course she'd warn them. She'd do whatever it took to protect them.

"If these villagers are protesting," Pran muttered, "do you think they might help us?"

"We should help them because it's the right thing to do." Oksana shot him a sharp look, stomach clenching at the strange hunger in his eyes. What good was any freedom they might claim, if along the way they stood back and let other people suffer?

That wasn't freedom. It was nothing they should aspire to. Nothing she'd take part in.

All the same, she couldn't keep this attack from happening. Juhan had decreed it; changing it would be like bending a stone with her hands.

But maybe she could alter its nature. An idea took root in her mind, just outlandish enough that it might work.

Oksana thrust her hand into the air. "Light their water fountain on fire!"

Every voice fell silent.

Pran gaped, terror burning in his eyes. "What are you doing?" he hissed.

He should know to trust her. Oksana fought back a frown and kept her gaze on the Commanders, all three of them scowling.

"Is this a joke?" Haamer demanded.

"Demon's Tongue." Her voice rang with confidence. Chemicals, properly mixed, never disappointed or failed.

"The alchemist has gotten it to burn underwater." She recalled Rootare's boasting in the hospital wing, as though he'd expected her to fall over herself, begging to learn the secrets of his twisted work.

Lepik uttered a throaty sound of disbelief, but Tamm nodded. "That's true."

"Light it, and launch it into the fountain," Oksana continued. "Do it at sundown, the night of their weekly market. When everyone will be present to see."

All the fear in Pran's eyes was replaced by glowing admiration. "That's quite the plan," he whispered, and bumped her fingers with his fist. Oksana barely held back a smile at his approval.

Around the room Hellions lifted their eyebrows. Even Tamm was stunned, her face steeped in awe.

Haamer glowered. "There's no lingering damage. Where's the lesson?"

"If we can set fire to water, what *can't* we burn? It demonstrates power without creating martyrs. It will terrify them." Oksana prayed that would be enough.

There was a beat of silence as the Commanders considered her plan.

"An excellent approach." Tamm nodded, and Oksana could suddenly breathe again. "Sends the message without handing the villagers more excuses to fight."

Haamer opened his mouth as if to object, but the Hellions broke into another babble, already scheming the best ways to march upon Kivi and its fountain.

"All right," Haamer declared. "In four days, we show Kivi how water burns."

Supper was more cabbage-and-mince stew. Of course.

Oksana got in line, groaning, but Anu pulled her aside. A shining burn stretched from the girl's jaw down to her collarbone.

Oksana sucked in a breath. "What happened to you?"

"This? Just Commander Igarik. I ran through my drill too slowly. She said next time I'd get five across my back." Anu scowled. "You're distracting me. Kivi. My family. What will—"

"I'm training you. Now." Oksana tugged Anu toward Meal Hall's doors.

Anu waved a dismissive hand. "Igarik was just in a mood. Afraid with her sad-sack Imps she'll never win a council seat."

"Igarik reports to Tamm, and all she has to say is—"

"I'm not here to talk about me. I want to know what the Hellions will do to Kivi."

"I'll tell you when Commanders aren't threatening you with fire whips!"

Anu yanked from Oksana's touch. "Sometimes you're a real hypocrite, you know that? There's not a thing you won't do for someone you love, and I adore it. But you're not the only one who can take risks for people they care about."

The words stung. "I can help you. If I don't do anything, and you get hurt, I'd—"

"You're not responsible for my choices or what follows them."

Her heart went as raw as the welt across Anu's cheek. "Looking out for you and Pran is the only good thing I have here. Don't take it away."

"Honoring my family is *my* good thing." Anu shook her head. "I thought you'd understand. I thought I could count on you."

"You can. Listen." She steered Anu from Meal Hall and through the rows of barracks until they reached the storage sheds on the far side of the fort. Those wind-weathered, graying wooden frames slouched to one side or another. Oksana checked the area three times, then tugged Anu behind a shed so dilapidated it seemed it would fall apart with one wild gust of wind.

"The other Hellions wanted to burn the village," Oksana said. "I said to light up their water fountain with Rootare's liquid fire. Played it off as sending a message about our power." With a small smile, she added the words she'd given the little Novice in the training yard. "But not everything that comes from fire is terrible and ugly."

Anu wrung her hands. She'd penned new words across them: *All embers and fire*. "It's a clever plan. But when my family and neighbors see Hellions marching, they won't wait for the blow to fall. They'll strike first, protect themselves. Then the

Commanders will retaliate. But if they know what you have in store . . . maybe they'll hold back. I have to warn them."

"You're already in trouble! And after the Embers . . . if the Commanders catch you sneaking out of the fort, they'll kill you."

"Messengers regularly trade news with villages. I'll disguise myself as one."

"You might pass as a messenger, but *I* won't."

"I never said you had to—"

"If you're doing this, I won't stop you. But let me help." Whatever happened to Anu outside the fort, Oksana wouldn't leave her to face it alone. She could do that much.

Anu waved a hand. "A little chalk powder and mudroot will do wonders on you."

"What about the Commanders' seal? The Nightmare guards check for it on every letter."

"You're the Hellion. Arrange a meeting with a Commander. Tell Sibul you have concerns about Novice training, and when you're in her office, snatch her seal."

Might be safer to steal the emperor's own seal than toy with Sibul's. Another idea shivered to life in Oksana's mind, one that chilled her to her bones. But once it awoke, it dug its claws in, refusing to leave.

"Rootare also sends messages."

The next day during training, when a Novice lost control of his fire, Oksana pretended to trip and thrust her shoulder in front of the errant flames. The blaze bit through her leather tunic and into her skin. A disgusted Sibul sent her to the hospital wing. ("You'll be useless the rest of the day!") There, while physicians tended to her burns, a group of Novices slumped into the room—right on schedule, their training finished for the morning—fighting back tears from their own injuries.

"Is it eleventh bell already?" one physician groaned.

"Here we go again. Wait a moment, Artemivna." The physicians crowded around the sniffling Novices, taking stock of their injuries and sorting the children into groups.

They were quick. Oksana was quicker. It was but a moment's work to pick the lock on one of the medicine cabinets and slip a vial of saltpeter into her pocket.

That night, in the chaos before supper, she stole sugar from the food stores for Commanders and messengers. While Tuliis crowded into Meal Hall, Oksana hid in her barrack and mixed the sugar with saltpeter and water. She picked threads from the seams of her scorched tunic and dipped them in the mixture to make fuses. With the rest of the paste she made lumpy balls, one fuse in each, then set them beneath a loose floorboard under her bunk to dry. This was the first trick her brother Borys had taught her, back at home when they'd tinkered in old Professor Melnyk's lab.

Let them work for us, Yeva, Oksana prayed, as she slid the floorboard back in place.

The following day, after her salves and bandages were refreshed in the hospital wing, instead of walking out of Healing Hall, she crept upstairs to the second floor. To the lab.

Rootare's voice barked from his office at the end of the hallway. "Let the brew simmer twelve hours, I said. What was unclear about that?"

"We needed more hands in the hospital. When the Novices came in—"

"Now those serums must be brewed again and I'm twice as behind schedule."

Oksana clicked her flint starter, breathed sparks into flame, and lit the fuses. One by one, she tossed her little bombs inside the lab.

Small pops rang out and smoke vomited into the air. Leaving the double doors open so smoke could billow into the corridor, Oksana ducked into a nearby doorway and clung to the shadows.

The arguing in Rootare's office fell silent. "Is that smoke?" said the second voice.

A chair screeched back. Rootare and a physician sprinted from the office toward the lab, where smoke belched past the open doors in heaving gusts.

"Get down!" the physician shouted. "The verikivi will explode!" He threw himself to the floor, but Rootare leaped over him and charged inside, his lab coat flapping behind him.

Oksana darted into Rootare's office. She checked his desk drawers, pawing through loose sheets of paper, fountain pens, and canisters of tea leaves, but found no seal. Her blood ran cold as more voices shouted. "The lab's on fire! Bring sand!"

Smoke drifted into the office, making Oksana's eyes water. She swallowed hard to keep from coughing. Footsteps thumped too near. Biting back a cry, Oksana dropped to the floor. As she went, her motion knocked a wooden canister off the desk. Before it smacked against the ground, she caught it, but the lid still tumbled off.

Out rolled the letter seal and red wax.

Thank you, Yeva, for guiding my hands. Fighting a wry smile, Oksana snatched paper, scribbled some nonsense about a serum, then lit the wax's wick and dribbled a few globs onto the folded page. The seal left an impression of a Tuliikobret fire demon surrounded by a dotted circle: the symbol for alchemy.

More shouts echoed. "What do you mean, there's no fire? Then what made this smoke?"

Heart in her throat, Oksana slipped from the office, fleeing down the back stairs and out of Healing Hall.

With the forged letter tucked inside her tunic and the path ahead clear, Oksana allowed herself a grin. She had their ticket out of the fort. Whatever happened tomorrow night, at least she'd be there to see Anu through it.

Oksana found herself wanting to show Pran, too. Wanting to see the look in his eyes when she told him how she'd snuck around Commanders and Rootare. Scheming was empowering; her blood buzzed with the energy of all she'd done. If she could do this, what more might she do for his plan to set them free?

Maybe his plot *could* work.

Maybe *she* could help make it happen.

But as she rounded a bend in the path, her barrack in sight, a hand clapped down on her shoulder. A smell hit her like a punch to the gut: rotten eggs and scorched metal.

"Hello, Oksana." Rootare stepped in front of her. "I believe you paid a visit to my lab and left this." He held out a charred white lump. "Smoke bomb, was it?"

She stared at the lump, her lungs knotting. Those had always dissolved quickly. They weren't supposed to leave any trace.

Still, he couldn't prove *she'd* made it. "You think that was me?"

"Who else in this fort knows 'some things' about chemicals? Certainly not the second-rate physicians serving as my so-called assistants."

Oksana bit her lip so hard she tasted iron.

The alchemist smirked. "Oh, I'm not angry. If anything, I find it fascinating. How do you know 'some things' about chemicals? Are you sneaking into my lab?"

"I had a good teacher. At home," Oksana blurted. She couldn't bear him thinking she wanted anything to do with his lab, where children were tortured into monsters.

"Clearly. If you can do this much—identify medicines

in unlabeled bottles, make a smoke bomb with stolen ingredients—what might you accomplish with real access to chemicals?" Rootare bounced the bomb on his palm, his lips curling in a grin. "Would you like to find out? You're wasted on Novice training, my dear."

Oksana bristled at the scorn in his words . . . and the queasy feeling that he was right. She *should* be doing more. "It's my job. Commanders' orders."

"Ah, but the Commanders aren't the only ones who issue orders. I could give you different work. I need a proper assistant, one who knows chemicals. I'm developing another serum. Always stronger Tuliis for Vesimaa."

"I won't help you poison Novices!"

Rootare stepped so close his breath rustled her hair. "This work isn't optional. There's much that must be done, and it can come only through my lab. I need good help to make it happen. Besides . . . I want your inquisitive little hands where I can watch them."

"Or what, you'll report me?"

"Now, that wouldn't serve either of us, would it? Consider this, instead: I don't have time anymore to develop new serums *and* brew medicine for those still struggling from transformation. Which do you think I'll set aside?"

Oksana's mouth went sour. Pran could seldom go more than a couple of days without his medicine. During an excellent span, he could do three, maybe four. Most often, he needed a daily dose or his leg pained him so much he could barely walk.

The truth was ugly, loud, and clear: Rootare didn't have to report the smoke bomb. There were worse ways to torment her.

But she couldn't become Rootare's puppet. "You're not my Commander. I don't have to obey you. I won't help."

Rootare scowled. "Remember what I said about those medicines. When you do change your mind, send word. I can have you reassigned within a day."

When he walked away, she spat where he'd stood.

CHAPTER SEVEN

PRAN

Two days after the Hellions had planned their attack against Kivi, Pran woke to a tap on his barrack window. He rolled from his bunk, snatched up his boots and jacket, and slipped through the door. Once outside, he whistled, watching the sky—barely lightening on the horizon—for a telltale blur of black and orange. His heart kicked against his ribs like it was trying to break through. He never knew what to call this feeling buzzing through him while waiting for the bird to appear. It wasn't excitement, dread, or irritation.

Somehow, it was all three at once.

When Pran whistled again, a series of cheerful notes responded. The copper crown—sleek with shining feathers, all black except for the cap of bright orange atop its head—landed on his outstretched hand, its tiny talons digging into his finger. Pran plucked out the letter rolled into the slim canister bound to the bird's back.

After sending the creature on its way with a whispered farewell, he crept through the rows of barracks, clutching that letter against his chest, until he was hidden within the shadows between storage sheds. There he held the paper at arm's length, turning the letter over in his hands without opening it.

He knew he should be grateful. There were Tuliis in this fort who would do many terrible things for the Commanders—bully Novices, spy on fellow soldiers, set fire to literally anything—if it meant receiving word from home. And here his brother had found a way for them to exchange letters in secret, thanks to a hardy copper crown with commendable speed and a knack for getting in and out of the fort unseen. Too often, the exchange was one-sided—Tuliis had little access to paper and ink, much less private time and space to write forbidden correspondence—but Nanda kept his letters coming. Never too often; they both knew they couldn't risk the copper crown drawing attention. Yet he steadily supplied Pran with news from home, along with sketches of familiar people and places.

Except this letter, when Pran opened it, held little of Pakastra at all:

Bha'ee,
We've heard what happened in the village Linn. We aren't supposed to know, of course. That might, gods forbid, encourage sedition here in our untamed land. Well, too late. Jiyn and I tapped the Vesimaans' new telegraph here in our city. We know about those Imps rebelling. We know what happened to them after.

You've never possessed a quiet soul, bha'ee. If Tuliis are speaking out, rising up, I know you're among them. I won't bother telling you to stop. I know you won't listen. All I ask is that you be mindful of the enemies and battles you take on. When smoking out an enemy, don't build a fire stronger than you can control.

You know flames better than I ever will. You've seen how quickly sparks can become a bonfire. And bonfires show little discretion in what, or whom, they devour—even the hands that made them. As you're burning your way out, I don't want you overtaken by the blaze.

Tumha Bha'uu

Pran sat between the sheds with the letter in his hands, staring at the sky until it went from gray to rose. If Oksana were at his side, she'd say his brother meant well. He'd feel monstrous complaining to her about this letter at all when she, like most every Tulii, had no way to communicate with her family.

But these words sent Nanda's last declaration to the Nightmares clanging again through Pran's mind: *He's frail, he's sickly, he's so young*. None of those things had been true! Pran had been eleven and strong, climbing walls and towers all around the city from sunup until whenever his father came looking for him in the evening. Nanda, who at thirteen had been too old to be transformed anyway, was waifish and gangling, spending his days hunched behind mountains of books and blathering with their tutors. The fact that he'd tried to protect Pran, that he'd *lied* to do so, that he'd thought he *needed* to, made Pran so angry he wanted to punch his fist straight through the fort's copper-clad walls.

That his brother still thought he needed to step in, save Pran from his enemies and even himself after he'd survived this fort for *seven years,* advancing in rank when no one had expected he'd even complete Novice training . . . and all while Nanda and his partner Jiyn tapped Vesimaan telegraph lines and wrote about it in letters?

Pran pulled the flint starter from his belt and clicked until sparks crackled. Sometimes he held on to Nanda's letters for a day, pulling them from his pocket during safe moments alone, looking over the words until he had them memorized. But this one he burned straightaway. These doubting words deserved nothing else.

Nanda would know the truth soon enough. When Pran set the Tuliis free, when he sent divisions marching back to Pakastra, Horádim, and Nyíta, when Nanda and everyone in his hometown saw Tuliikobrets coming to defend them and Pran leading the way . . . then they would see just how frail, sickly, and young he was *not.*

It was time to find sparks of his own—fellow Tuliis he could trust to rise with him on Jubilee Night. Fellow Tuliis who would recognize everything he could do, and believe in him.

That night after another terrible supper—had the fort cooks forgotten how to make anything besides cabbage-and-mince stew?—Pran joined Yalku in the pub to vet recruits.

"How about him?" Pran inclined his head toward a Goblin from his old troop.

Amid the noise of so many drunken Tuliis, this was the best place to talk, hiding in the open. Pran had wanted to invite Oksana as well, but she hadn't been at supper for the third day in a row. They seldom shared a meal—outside of training, it was prudent to limit their time seen together—but at least she'd be there to share a smirk or disgusted scowl from across the room, over the latest atrocity masquerading as food.

She was up to something, skipping meals and getting herself burned on purpose during Novice training. No doubt it was to do with Anu and Kivi. But if he spent too much time searching for her, he'd draw the wrong attention to them both. Best he could do was get themselves free of this mess, once and for all.

"That one will get you killed." Yalku flipped through a deck of hand-drawn playing cards. "He's too volatile, already watched for trouble. Don't let him near your recruits."

Pran stretched his aching leg across a chair, stifling a groan; earlier that day the physicians had claimed they had no medicine for him. *Nobody gets more until the alchemist provides us with a new batch. What's left is for emergencies only.* Gritting his teeth against the pain, he steered his mind back to the task at hand. "There are a few Hellions in my new troop who might be good candidates."

"You'd trust Hellions with this cause?"

Pran pointed to the orange demon on his tunic.

"You've only been Hellion a few days," Yalku said.

"And when I remain one?"

Yalku shuffled a new deck of cards. "Hellions have more to gain serving the Commanders than rebelling. Imps and Goblins would fight back. It hasn't been stamped out of them yet."

"How about him, then?" Pran nodded to a boy slouching alone at the next table. Devak, the young Pakastran Imp. Bruises mottled the boy's face, and he winced whenever he sipped his ale. He sat watching another table packed with Imps, all of them shouting over a game involving dice, ale tokens, a withered apple, and a bootlace.

"He's not strong enough," Yalku said. "We need Tuliis with backbone."

But Pran's throat tightened as he considered the boy: Devak by himself, none of his fellow Imps inviting him to join their game, his spine drooping while he guzzled ale, all but drowning himself with those endless swallows. That might have been Pran, once, if Oksana hadn't reached out. Did Devak have no one to care about him?

All I ask is that you're mindful of the enemies and battles you take on.

This wasn't a battle Pran had envisioned, but as he considered the lonely boy . . . why not? Or rather, how *could* he not? He could fight for the whole fort, and that was an incredible feat, but he could also fight for the one. The forgotten, the dismissed, the underestimated. He could fight for that one, uplift him, show all he was capable of doing, small and great.

He could claim a brother for himself, a little brother, who might recognize and value everything he could do.

Pran leaned across the aisle and tapped the boy's shoulder. "Sit with me."

"What? No!" Yalku hissed, but Pran ignored him.

"I mean it," he said, while Devak gaped like a beached fish, his gaze fastened on the burn scar across Pran's cheek. Pran gestured to the empty seat at their table. "Come."

Devak perched on the edge of the seat as though expecting some cruel trick, like Pran yanking that chair out beneath him. Instead, Pran motioned to the bruises on Devak's face. "You've had a rough day."

The boy downed another too-large gulp of ale. "My Commander said I throw flames dismally. Nothing I do is enough."

"Nothing you do will ever be enough for the Commanders," Yalku said. "Stop trying to get on their good side. There's no such thing."

Any other time, Pran might have shot Yalku a warning look, but his friend's acerbic tongue set the perfect contrast for this conversation.

"I could help you," he told Devak. "We'll claim a training yard when the Commanders aren't around to get in our way, and I'll teach you a few tricks that should get you through training. Maybe even onto Goblin rank."

"You'd do that? For me?" The look in Devak's eyes was so astounded that Pran's heart hurt. It wasn't right that this boy had no one to care for him.

That would make it all the more memorable when Pran did.

Devak blinked at the bright red demon on Yalku's tunic and the orange on Pran's. "Does it get easier? After advancing?"

Pran didn't want to break this boy's heart with the truth. That wasn't why he'd brought him over. He leaned across the scuffed table, meeting Devak with a firm stare. "Are you brave?"

"Huh?"

"I think you can be." He tugged the ale mug out of Devak's hands. "I think you *are*, to have made it this far. You're a survivor. You're strong."

"I—" Devak glanced at the other Imps. Most still ignored him, though a few cast curious glances when they spotted him at Pran's table.

Pran returned all his attention to the boy, as though he was the most important person in this whole pub. In this moment, he was. "You fight every battle the Commanders throw at you, and so far you've overcome them. Wouldn't you like to choose your next battles? You could lead in this fort. You could lead those other Imps"—he inclined his head—"into something better. Isn't that right, Yalku?"

His friend scowled as though he'd guzzled vinegar and

eyed Devak with distaste. "You have to be bolder. Stronger. You can't crumble under every setback."

"I know how to be strong!" Devak bristled, then peered toward Pran. "And I know who holds the power in this fort. It isn't any of us Tuliis."

"The Commanders are powerful, but they're not infallible. You've seen how a few sparks can bring down a building."

Devak studied, again, the burn on Pran's face, then straightened in his chair. "Tell me how to be fierce. Like you."

CHAPTER EIGHT

OKSANA

The next evening, on her way to Anu's barrack, she saw him walking out of the pub. "Pran!" she called, before her brain could catch up with her heart.

He whirled, and then was at her side so fast, she barely saw him move. "Where have you been?" His hands closed around her shoulders. "I've hardly seen you since the meeting."

Now that they were finally side by side, Oksana didn't know what to tell him. Bragging about her forged letter suddenly seemed absurd. There was no sign Rootare knew what she'd really been up to. But he had figured out she'd been in his lab . . . while she'd been congratulating herself on a job supposedly well done.

It would be even harder than she'd imagined, striking out against this fort, keeping their actions secret from prying eyes. And if they failed, the price would be so much higher than Rootare threatening to withhold medicine.

Oh saints, Pran's medicine! "How are you? Are you feeling all right?"

"Of course." Though he leaned heavily on his good leg,

his face was serene, breath calm and even. So she believed him. At his touch, she melted, dropping her head onto his shoulder while he cradled her against his side. It was a relief to have someone to lean on. To hold tight, to be still with. Oksana never wanted to part from him or this moment.

Until Pran whispered, "Our meeting, it's tonight."

She went rigid. "Meeting?"

"Yalku and I have been vetting recruits the past few days. We spent today inviting some Tuliis to come discuss ways to take down the Commanders on Jubilee Night. Just spoke with our last candidates." He tipped his head toward the pub behind him. "We're meeting at eighth bell, in the old armory. You'll come?"

She broke from his warmth, blood throbbing through her veins. "You trust them with your plan? What if one gives you away?"

"On our own, we'll never overthrow the Commanders. We need allies. I've thought about each one, personally invited them. Yes, I trust them. Will you be joining us?"

He reached for her hand, but she scooted back. "I can't," she said, cursing the timing. She wanted to watch these Tuliis Pran trusted enough to stake his life on. But Anu was waiting, and she couldn't abandon her friend. "Anu and I, we're going—"

"To warn the village?" Pran's eyes lit with anger. "How does that help us? It only endangers *you*. We have to focus on what's most important—escaping the Commanders and emperor, defending our own homes."

"There's no guarantee we'll escape, or ever go home." *Home.* The word filled her with a gnawing despair. It had never felt farther away.

The hurt seeping across Pran's face stung her heart. "I thought you wanted this," he pressed.

"I do!" Saints alive, her body ached with longing to be back among Horádim's wheat fields and wooded hills. Yet she wouldn't throw away her whole soul after what might be only a mirage. "But along the way, if there's good we might do, we need to try for it. That might be all we achieve. Tomorrow, the Commanders will march on Kivi. *Anu's family.* We know it."

"And you've made a plan to keep them safe."

"With the Commanders, no one is ever safe. Tonight Anu *will* warn her family, and if there's trouble along the way . . . I'm doing this to help my friend. If you don't like it, I'm sorry. But if there's help I can give, I'll give it. That's why I still have anything good in my life."

It was why she had him. All her fury spent, Oksana slumped forward. She pressed her head against his chest, wound her arms across his waist. He hugged her back, and for a moment they stood still, warm together despite the icy wind wailing around them.

"Look," Oksana said, voice softening, "you had a point: if we're going to reclaim freedom, we need support outside these walls. If Kivi sees we'll help them, maybe they'll help us. No matter which way we look at it, this is the right move."

Pran scowled as though he intended to keep arguing,

but huffed a breath. "Be careful," he said, and kissed her brow. "When you come back, I'll have good Tuliis on our side. We'll be a step closer to freedom. Someday, this will all be behind us. Ya abetschayu."

She couldn't breathe—could barely feel anything around her—with how much she wished that could be true.

At Anu's barrack, she knocked a staccato beat. Immediately, Anu swung open the door, a messenger tattoo already inked onto her neck. "You have our letter?"

Oksana gaped at the deftly forged tattoo, but that wasn't their only hurdle. "How will you make me into a Vesimaan?"

"Sit!" Anu jabbed a finger toward her bunk and scooped up a bowl of pungent slop. "Mudroot paste," she said while unraveling Oksana's braid. "My cousins and I used it every summer when performing *The Dark Maidens of Härma*."

Oksana winced as Anu dropped a glob of the reeking mess onto her head, though she knew she should be delighted to disguise her hair's color. After all, the Nightmares had taken her *because* of this hair. It was red, like most Scamalls'. *She* was part Scamall.

But her red hair was also a connection to home. As a child, the story had been her favorite, more than any folktale or fable: Decades earlier, a lost Scamall soldier wandered through the Horádimian meadows, his sole possessions a broken dagger and patched set of warpipes. He found her grandmother dancing there, red boots twirling, flowers and ribbons wound up her braids. Instantly, they'd fallen in love, and they'd married and had a son.

Then the man's officer found him and dragged him back to Scamall. That son, however, shared his father's deep red hair, in Horádim the color of joy and life. When Oksana was also born with bright red locks, her village said she was blessed.

But when the Nightmares came to her village, they'd seen in her an enemy to subdue. One they *must* subdue.

Oksana had never given them the satisfaction.

Now she watched in the washstand's rippled mirror as Anu worked the mudroot through her hair until the strands were as dark as her eyes.

"This makes me Vesimaan?" If anything, she appeared more Horádimian with the dark hair. She looked like her mother.

A sliver of homesickness shot through Oksana's heart.

"Stop fussing." Anu bent her over the basin and rinsed her hair with a jug of cold water. "They'll think you're from the eastern border. Hence *The Dark Maidens of Härma*."

And there was Commander Haamer, of course, with his strange dark hair. Still, Oksana's heart didn't ease. "But tomorrow, will I still—"

"Hush, hush. It washes right out." Anu dried Oksana's hair and twisted it into a knot at the nape of her neck, the way female messengers wore their hair. She brushed cream-colored paste over the burn on her own cheek and layered more paste and powder across Oksana's face. The blend paled her skin and made her cheekbones appear rounder and eyes wider. In the end, Oksana wasn't sure she passed as a Vesimaan, but she looked nothing like herself, either.

"Lift your chin." Anu snatched a nib pen off the wash-stand and dipped the tip into the rest of the mudroot. Oksana watched in the mirror as Anu etched the messenger's tattoo onto her skin, duplicating every swirling line, every arc of flame, until a fire demon stretched from her ear to her collar-bone. The job would have taken Oksana half the night and wouldn't have tricked a Novice. But before Oksana's neck could cramp, Anu leaned back and smiled.

Oksana brushed her fingers across the tattoo. "You're amazing."

"I know that. Now get dressed! And bind your chest." Anu threw a rag her way. "You're so short, we'll have to pretend you're a child."

As Oksana and Anu approached the gates, the Nightmare guards stiffened. "Odd time for messengers to depart," one said.

Anu held up their letter. "This can't wait until morning."

The other scowled at Oksana. "You're young to be a messenger. What are you, twelve?"

She met the woman's gaze, suppressing a shudder as she faced the burning soul mask and heartless black eyes. "My family serves our emperor early," Oksana said, mimicking the clipped vowels of a Vesimaan accent.

"It's our first mission." Anu squared her shoulders as though she deserved a medal.

The Nightmare kept frowning. "Let's see this message."

"It's from that man with the glasses," Oksana said as Anu handed it over. "The alchemist? I can't remember his name . . ."

"Rootare." The Nightmare tossed the letter back as if it were poison. "Get on your way."

Anu grabbed Oksana's elbow and dragged her through the gates. "Remember, when we hand off a message, ask for confirmation that it's the right person. Like a family crest, or . . ."

When they'd left the Nightmares behind, Anu barked a laugh. "All those years spent quaking whenever they swooped near, yet *I* tricked *them*."

"Clearly the Commanders have missed your chief talents."

They followed the path through Mennick's center, down streets wide enough for three carriages to roll abreast. Stone archways stretched overhead, connecting offices and imperial courts, where Vesimaans paid taxes or argued before judges, though all the offices were of course dark and silent this time of night. The steam train screamed into the station as the girls darted past, its wide cars hauling cargo from the farthest reaches of the empire.

A few aristocrats, their tailored jackets decorated with copper embroidery and ruby beads, stood conversing at the nearby square. As Oksana and Anu approached, the group fell silent but nodded at the gold messenger uniforms and let the girls pass with reverent salutes. Still, Oksana didn't stop clutching her flint starter beneath her coat until they were well outside the city's borders.

"Kivi is beyond those trees." Anu gestured to a patch of forest crouching on the horizon. "When we get there, let me do the talking."

The sliver moon did little to light the world, but the path ahead was clear, the road so worn that the dirt shone like polished stone. Oksana ran with Anu past empty fields, the last crops already harvested. They skirted pastures where sheep nodded in sleep. Fallen leaves crunched beneath their boots, some still scarlet and gold, others faded dirt-brown. As they dipped into the woods, a frosty breeze numbed Oksana's hands and face, and the sharp tang of pine was strong in the air.

Anu hummed the demon ballad, but Oksana ran in silence. Her gaze flitted toward the horizon peeking through the trees, where the world stretched on farther than she'd ever seen. She was outside the fort, and the Commanders didn't know she was loose. She could run for that horizon, and maybe, *maybe*, if she fled fast enough the Nightmares would never catch up . . .

But Pran wasn't with her. Even if he had been, he couldn't run for long. Probably he wouldn't, anyway, bent as he was on fighting the Commanders.

Oksana sighed to the bottom of her lungs and didn't feel lighter for it. Pran had never stopped hungering for life beyond the fort. Probably his strange grievance with his brother—his obsession with proving Nanda wrong and making clear all he could do—fueled that longing. Whatever the reason, Pran was one of the few who dared try for more.

One of the few who'd ever stood up for her.

During their transformations, tending him had given her a reason to rise each morning. It gave her a path she chose for herself. It kept her from caving into the Commanders' lies that her only purpose was to serve Juhan. Kept her from descending into the monster they wanted her to become.

Yet she'd never forgotten the night when Pran had gone from being a cause to an ally.

It had been halfway through their Novice training. Pran was thirteen and she was twelve. Each day he'd still battled pain, but he could rise from his cot and spent more time awake than asleep. One night she'd tried to sneak extra food to him, but the Nightmare guards caught her.

"Stealing food?" They tore the bread from her hands and threw her to the floor. The other Novices cowered in the room's corners as the Nightmares closed in, fists swinging.

Oksana had learned not to expect anyone's help, nor to fight back. The Nightmares were too big, too fast, and wouldn't stop until they were bored. So she curled into a ball as their fists pummeled, biting back her cries . . .

An earth-shattering crash had thundered from the far side of the barrack.

The blows stopped. Oksana was left alone as the Nightmares stalked toward the noise.

Pran knelt beside an overturned table, surrounded by the shattered remains of a clay water pitcher. "I tripped! Bumped the table . . ." His wide eyes pretended innocence, but a sly smile teased across his lips.

"Watch what you're doing!" One Nightmare walloped him across the face, then shoved Pran away as the barrack's door flew open.

Two Commanders stormed in. "What's going on here?"

The Nightmares hustled toward them, stammering excuses. Aching in her corner, Oksana gritted her teeth and pushed to her hands and knees. Pran would need help.

But he reached her first, holding out a hand to help her up. "Are you all right?"

She gaped from him to the Nightmares ushered away by the shouting Commanders. "Thank you," she whispered.

And he'd grinned, blood dribbling from his nose and lips.

For five years since that night, she'd stood by him with renewed vigor, as a *partner*. With him on her side, the darkness of the fort still weighed on her heart but never overcame her. Every deed of hers, for good and ill, aimed to keep him safe. That became the creed she lived by.

Anu snatched Oksana's arm. "Look!" She gestured toward a light beyond the trees, like the moon shining on a lake. But as she steered Oksana forward, that light split apart. Not moonbeams, but kitchen fires and lanterns glowing from windows. The trees thinned into sloping fields dotted with unpainted barns and thatch-roofed cottages.

Anu nodded to the second home along the path. "When

we step through that door, stay behind me. And *let me talk first.*"

As they trod forward, a voice inside the cottage lifted in song, and a group joined in. Anu cracked open the door, and Oksana stood on her toes to peer over her friend's shoulder.

The cottage was packed with rosy-cheeked people. Many crowded elbow to elbow at the wooden table in the room's center. The rest perched on trunks, on windowsills, atop overturned buckets, or up and down the ladder leading to the loft. An iron pot squatted on the table, filled with yellow pea stew. One woman carried steaming loaves of black bread from a brick oven. Another set down a honey cake. All sang while an old man in the corner strummed a kannel.

"'The Flame with Three Faces,'" Anu whispered.

Oksana recognized the song, a majestic tune about a fire that could grant wishes, a fire that could predict the future, and a fire that offered good fortune . . . as long as the wisher leaped all three in one bound. The family sang with great gusto, if not entirely on-key, voices swelling as they returned to the chorus:

Jump the flames with me, my love
Jump the flames so high
Jump the flames with me, my dear
Together we will fly.

Anu clapped her hands, cheeks flushing pink, and stepped into the room. Oksana followed close, heart slithering into her throat as Anu joined the chorus. The moment her flute voice pitched in, the music died and every head whipped in her direction.

"Is that . . . *you?*" A woman with Anu's round cheeks and pointed chin leaned closer.

"Tadte." Anu threw herself forward, wrapping her arms around her aunt.

The woman squirmed from Anu's hold, her already pale face going bone white as her gaze raked over the messenger uniform. "But . . . we thought—"

Screams erupted throughout the cottage as the whole family scrambled back like a wolf had stalked in. One woman fled outside with several small children in tow. A thickset man steered the aunt away while another pinned Anu at his side, twisting her arms behind her back.

Oksana gaped in horror. This was the greeting from Anu's beloved family? Saints alive, if this was how family treated a Tuliikobret who found their way back . . .

"*Let her go!*" Oksana dove for Anu, but an iron-strong hand snared her mid-jump. She lunged backward to slam her skull against the man's, but he was as big as a bear and her head thumped harmlessly against his shoulder.

"We've come to warn you!" Anu shouted. She blinked at the man pinning her, all the pink in her cheeks gone blotchy. "*I* came to warn you. Please."

Oksana tried to slip through her jacket, but her captor hooked his arm around her neck. "What's this you've brought into our house?" the man barked at Anu. "A spy?"

"Please," a woman called. "Let them go. It's a crime to assault a Tuliikobret."

Instead, the man tightened his hold over Oksana's throat, cutting off her air. "I'd rather show Juhan that we'll protect our families, if he won't."

"There must be a reason for what happened in Linn," another man spoke up. "Perhaps they harbored traitors. There were rumors of Scamall sympathizers among them."

"That's a lie," said the man holding Anu. "They criticized the emperor for stealing their children and still failing to conquer Scamall. So he sent soldiers to silence them."

"Take the short one outside," drawled a young man near the window. He stroked the knife hanging from his belt. "Leave her body where it won't be found."

"NO!" Anu kneed her captor in the stomach. When he doubled over, Oksana's captor yelled in alarm. In his distraction, Oksana kicked free and clicked her flint starter, raising sparks.

So much for winning support. She and Anu would be lucky if they made it out alive.

Oksana didn't know what was worse: the hatred woven into every face, despising her even though she'd been stolen from *her* family and *her* country to serve *theirs* . . . or the despair eclipsing Anu, as she was slapped with rejection from the one group who should have been on her side.

Oksana had feared this night wouldn't end well. She'd never dreamed it would be because Anu's family had closed their hearts to her.

With a wail, Anu vaulted onto the table. "We came to warn you! Tomorrow the Tuliikobrets will march on Kivi!"

More shouts rang out, but Oksana silenced them with a burst of flame. "The plan is to burn your central fountain. *Only* that fountain."

The air grew heavy. "Tuliikobrets never strike so gently," said the old kannel player.

"Nor do Tuliikobrets give warnings." The young man with the knife pushed toward Anu. "What are you really after, cousin?"

Anu crouched on the table's edge, bringing herself eye to eye with him. "When I was taken, I swore I'd serve our family. I swore to *you*, Peeter. My allegiance was never to Juhan."

Her aunt approached Anu as she might a rabid wolf: each step laced with terror, caution, her whole body tensed to run at any sudden move. "You've been inside that fort for seven years. I don't know what they've done to you there, but these past years we've watched the soldiers become more and more brutal. We *miss* you, Anu. But after what happened in Linn . . . we can't trust you anymore."

"My loyalty is to you, Tadte. I want to give you better lives, in any way I can!"

"Go." The aunt turned away. "Leave us in peace and we'll believe you care."

Anu sank to her knees atop the table, all the light in her eyes snuffed out.

"Listen!" Oksana snapped at the family. "Anu risked her life because she couldn't bear the thought of you hurt.

Tomorrow, during your weekly market, Hellions will attack in retribution for those councilors your village attacked. But no one here needs to suffer. It's as I said: we'll burn the central fountain. And that will be the only fire, as long as *no one fights back*. Don't give the Commanders a reason to strike."

"They don't need reasons," cried the old man with the kannel. "Look at Linn."

"We will not be silenced!" the knife-man snarled. "We won't cower before Juhan."

Oksana faced the man. He could have been Anu's twin, except his deep blue eyes were lit only by hate. "When we light the fountain tomorrow, act terrified. Subdued. The Commanders will believe they've made their point and leave. I swear it."

"Oh, really? Did you make this plan?"

"I did," Oksana said, and the whole cottage fell so quiet, the only sound was the ale dripping out of someone's overturned mug.

"Some Hellions wanted to burn your village. Instead, I talked them into setting your fountain on fire," Oksana said, even though the last thing she wanted was to help these cold-blooded cowards. It was still the right thing to do, even if they didn't deserve it. They were Anu's family. They were *people*, and ones who'd spoken up for neighbors murdered in their homes.

"Tomorrow, be smart," she continued. "The day after, you can do whatever you want. Wage battle against Juhan. Defend your *own* country for once. But tomorrow, don't provoke the Commanders while they can torch you where you stand."

The family exchanged grim stares. No one turned to Anu as she reached toward them, a tear sliding down her cheek.

"We did what we came to do," Oksana said. "Come on, Anu."

She helped her friend off the table and steered Anu toward the cottage door. The family moved aside while they passed, as though the girls carried some contagious disease. But as the two stepped by the aunt, Anu tugged a paper from her sleeve. "You don't trust me, but I swear by the heavens, earth, and flame that I haven't forgotten you, Tadte."

She pressed the paper into her aunt's hand: a drawing of Anu beside that same woman, and two men, one older like the aunt, another closer to Anu's age. The knife-man. Peeter, Anu had called him. Her cousin.

The woman's hand shook so badly she dropped the sketch. She opened her mouth but no words came out, though her lips silently formed Anu's name.

Oksana swept the room with her gaze, no mercy, pity, or energy left for people who treated family this way. "Pass this news on. Help your neighbors understand. You will not be hurt tomorrow if you don't push back."

With her arm around Anu, she pulled her friend into the dark, cold streets, slamming the door behind them.

CHAPTER NINE

PRAN

One by one Imps and Goblins, around a dozen of each, slipped into the old armory. At their steps, dust shivered into the air, stirred from the wooden floor as they clustered in small groups. Pran studied them from atop his makeshift platform of stacked crates. Imps tapped their cheeks where his own was burned and whispered, "The Hellion who survived the emperor!" And Goblins, who only days before had rubbed shoulders with him during training, now gazed with curiosity and even something approaching respect.

A bolt of nerves iced through Pran, overwhelming him with the impulse to leap from these crates and disappear somewhere secluded, a place where maybe his lungs would remember how to breathe. Somewhere he could sit, because his leg had chosen this moment to flare up, and every time a spasm bit through, it was all he could do to keep standing, much less keep his thoughts together.

But these Tuliis hadn't come to see a Hellion cringing because of something Commanders had done to him years ago. They'd come to hear promises so grand no one had dared speak them before. Pran knew that what he reached for was enormous—impossible, many would argue—and that was never clearer than when these Tuliis gathered around, their lives in his hands.

All I ask is that you be mindful of the enemies and battles you take on. The words echoed unwelcomely through Pran's head. Worst was that if his brother stood before him this moment, Pran wouldn't be able to argue, as a spasm roared through his leg and stole his breath, and all his words along with it.

In moments like this, he'd lean on Oksana. She was always at his side when he needed her, without him even having to ask. But she wasn't here tonight. She was out risking herself for others because that was what she did, what she'd keep doing until there wasn't a reason to anymore—until this army was in his hands.

Think of that, Pran urged himself. *Remember.* He swallowed a groan and lifted his head, facing these Tuliis he'd chosen.

Devak had joined the group, shoulders back and chin high. Pride burst through Pran, to see the change a little attention and confidence had made for this boy. He nodded, the boy beamed, and a handful of Imps scooted closer and copied Devak's stance.

When the eighth bell clanged, Pran gestured to Yalku, keeping watch by the door, for him to shut it. But as Yalku pressed his hand to the knob, a Hellion from Pran's new troop darted in—the Vesimaan with her pale hair in double buns.

Every whisper in the armory fell silent. Pran leaped off the platform, gritting his teeth as he jarred his bad leg, and stalked toward her. As he drew near, the Hellion spoke, her words tripping over themselves. "Hear me out, Nayar. I know what you're doing, and I want to help."

The demand in her tone rankled, as if she were in charge here. It didn't help that he had to crane his head back to meet her gaze. Good gods, what band of giants had the Vesimaans once mated with for them to be so obscenely tall?

He slipped between the girl and his Tuliis. "Why should I listen? You're the Commanders' lapdog."

"Do any of us have a choice? That's why I'm here. To make more options."

"I don't trust her," Yalku muttered.

Of course he didn't; he'd made his opinion of Hellions clear. But Pran didn't trust her, either, showing up without invitation or a chance for him to vet her real interests. He opened his mouth to tell her . . . what? He could hardly send her away when she knew they were meeting here, and why.

"Nayar, listen to me, please." The girl clenched her hands into fists. "Do you think because I'm Vesimaan I *like* serving in this fort? I didn't choose to be here any more than you. If I'd wanted to make trouble, I would have gone straight to Lepik and he'd be here now instead of me."

A bright flush bloomed on her cheeks and her breath came in hard gasps, like she was terrified. Of him? That he'd reject her? She might be an excellent actor; in this fort that was an essential survival skill. But even Pran had to admit there was no faking the desperation on her face and the quaking of her hands.

"What's your name?" Pran demanded.

"Sepp," she said, voice breaking. "I've been trapped in this fort for nine years, half my life. Don't leave me to endure any more. I can help you, if you'll just trust me."

He didn't know if he could, but she was here now and it would be best to keep her under watch. "Give me a reason to doubt, any at all, and I will make you pay."

She swallowed, but pressed a fist to her heart and joined the crowd.

Yalku seethed. "How can you—"

"Resume your post. We'll talk after." Pran clambered onto his platform.

Every Goblin and Imp stared, jaws slack.

Pran gripped his flint starter to hide the jittering in his hands. He could not let the others believe he was less than confident in anyone's presence here, else they'd never risk themselves for his plan.

Resting his elbow on a stack of smaller crates Yalku had arranged on their improvised platform, Pran leaned into a stance that he hoped looked collected and confident. Really, it took all the weight off his bad leg so he could stand before this group long enough to say everything he'd brought them to hear. With a gaze both stern and proud, he peered at the Tuliis and nodded. "Each of you are capable of more than this fort has dealt you."

He spoke only loud enough to be heard, not so loud that

his voice would leak outside the shed. The Tuliis in the back of the crowd leaned in to listen as Pran continued. "I believe you are capable of leading yourselves to freedom, empowerment, and happiness. What we are about to discuss, you must guard as though your lives depended upon it. Because they do."

All attention remained on him, the group's breathing hushed and stares rapt. Yalku's indignant glower softened, and Pran couldn't deny that eased some of the tightness in his own chest.

"In Pakastra, we have a certain bird in abundance: the glorious copper crown." Pran snapped his fingers, and the orange-capped bird dove from the rafters and landed on his raised hand. "As you can see, it looks like a delicate creature, nothing more than a fragile songbird. But these birds are hardier than one might expect. They can fly great distances at incredible speeds, and they're one of the few creatures that can challenge the dagger-beaked shrike. We Tuliis have much in common with this copper crown. We, too, are in the best position to challenge our oppressors. The emperor, yes, but first and foremost our Commanders."

"How? We can't possibly battle them," a Horádimian Goblin said.

Pran gestured to the bird on his arm, who studied the gathered Tuliis with its shiny black eyes. "Many copper crowns could argue the same about the dagger-beaked shrike. Shrikes are brutes to the core, snapping the necks of their prey with a vicious shake, then impaling the bodies on thorns. And a dagger-beaked shrike's favorite meal? Newly hatched copper crowns, left alone while their parents search for food. No single copper crown is a match for any shrike. But when whole flocks of copper crowns join together and mob the shrike, they can fight off that fearsome bird and protect themselves. For all their cruelty, dagger-beaked shrikes aren't invincible, and the same is true of our Commanders."

Pran's copper crown flapped its wings and ascended back to the rafters with a screech.

Around the room, a few Tuliis' shoulders lifted and their eyes shone bright. But others shook their heads, scowling. "This is real life, not some sappy story about birds," a Nyítan Imp protested. "If we challenge the Commanders, we'll die. Just like the Scarlet Embers."

"All of you will have to sacrifice, perhaps dearly, for this cause." Pran's quick admission shocked the Tuliis into silence. "Fighting against the likes of the Commanders—and, ultimately, our emperor—will not be comfortable or clean. I can't promise anyone's safety. But are you content to continue attacking and burning for the people who've torn you from home? Will you sit by while your neighbors and family are dragged behind these walls and forced to join the troops as well? Or will you use your fire to protect your *own* people, your *own* countries?"

"If I must burn, I'll burn for home!" a voice called, and others murmured in assent.

"Our opportunity comes soon," Pran said, silencing the

scattered whispers. "In just over four weeks, the emperor will host Jubilee Night—his Silver Jubilee, this year. That night, both he and the Commanders will believe us subdued. They won't expect us to act, and they'll be distracted by his grand celebration. That night, we can overpower and trap the few Commanders left in the fort, those not invited to the council or jubilee celebrations. We can then use them as bargaining chips against the whole army."

"Let them see what it's like to be used as an object!" a Pakastran Goblin called.

"But to do this," Pran continued, "we need more numbers than what's gathered here. Think on your fellow troop members: Who among them would aid our cause? Recruit the ones you trust. Be discreet. It takes only one mistake to send this plan to dust, and all of us with it. But by rallying the most courageous, fierce, and determined Tuliis within the fort, this plan *can* become more than talk."

"F-freedom to the flames," Devak whispered, his voice quavering as though he couldn't believe he was speaking aloud. But when Pran smiled, the boy stood tall. "Freedom to the flames!"

The others joined his pledge. "Freedom to the flames! Freedom to Tuliikobrets!"

Brightness rose through Pran, to see such hope and loyalty. This plan started with him, but freedom was not the work of one. Without their help he'd never achieve it.

"I will not fail you," he said. "Never forget: in the grand scheme of the world we may be only copper crowns, but together we can challenge the shrikes. Leave now, quietly. When it's time for the next meeting, I'll send word."

Imps and Goblins slipped into the darkness outside, their steps light. Sepp caught Pran's eye, nodding as she left. He returned the nod only, not her smile.

A hand came down hard on his shoulder, almost knocking him off the platform. "You still trust them to bring others," Yalku growled, "after that Hellion showed up?"

Pran sighed, suddenly tired to his bones, and of course his leg chose that moment to spasm so hard he nearly choked. "Think, Yalku. How many Imps and Goblins are friendly with Hellions? We won't come back to find this room overrun with high ranks. Even if we did . . . we'll need all the help we can get. I won't turn away anyone who will fight."

"I stand by what I said: it serves Hellions and Nightmares to aid Commanders, not fight against them. If nothing else, they're used to pushing around Goblins and Imps, not working alongside them."

"There's only one Tulii raising hell right now, and he's standing in front of me. Are you on my side or not?"

Yalku cracked his knuckles. "So much depends on Jubilee Night. Don't let us down."

In his mind, Pran saw the Tuliis with their fists pressed against their chests, and this time, that pledge settled like a weight on his shoulders instead of wings at his back. "I'd die first."

"Don't do that, either." Yalku clapped Pran's shoulder and strode from the room.

❦

After he'd returned the old armory to its former neglected disarray, Pran slipped back outside, shutting the door firmly and sliding the bar in place. He was checking the dirt for stray boot prints when a voice split the silence. "Nayar?"

Resisting the impulse to whirl around, Pran kept his breathing steady even though his heart punched against his ribs. He peered over his shoulder as though he expected this intrusion, *welcomed* it. The man approached, and through the shadows Pran recognized him by the thorny silhouette of his hair—his new Commander, Lepik.

Pran cursed softly, but as Lepik drew near, he clicked his heels together. "Sir?"

The man's scowl was sharp enough to slice leather. "I could have sworn a pack of Tuliikobrets came up from this way. Now I find you here. What's going on?"

A ghostly hand reached inside Pran's chest and squeezed his lungs. If Lepik uncovered the truth, this cause was lost before it began.

But Lepik would have no reason to doubt if he firmly believed that in Pran, he had an ally.

"I saw the same, sir," Pran announced, keeping his voice calm. "I came to investigate."

"Is that so?" The Commander's expression did not lighten.

"You requested me for your troop. I consider myself your eyes and ears throughout this fort, keeping peace when you aren't around. *Especially* then. When Tuliikobrets believe themselves free of a Commander's eyes, there are things they'll say and do that betray their true intentions. After the Scarlet Embers, isn't it more critical than ever that we pick out troublemakers and stop them before they cause more chaos? I'd like to help you there, Commander, if you'll accept my assistance."

Every word felt so strange on his tongue. He didn't know what he was committing to, exactly, but he knew if he didn't, he'd fail his Tuliis, whose own eyes had just begun to shine with hope.

Though the man's brow remained furrowed, he pursed his lips thoughtfully. "Come talk with me after this mess with Kivi is over, first thing the next morning."

CHAPTER TEN

OKSANA

As they ran back to the fort, Anu trailed slightly behind, silent. Every time Oksana glanced back, her friend's face was blank as an unmarked page. When Anu spotted Oksana watching, she picked up her pace. "I'm fine. Fine."

Oksana didn't believe it. She wouldn't be fine, to sneak from the fort only to have her family reject her so cruelly. Getting home had always seemed the impossible part. If she made it all the way to Horádim only to have her family say they didn't trust her, didn't want her, threaten to drag her behind the house and . . .

Oksana stumbled, nearly landing on her face, because she couldn't see the ground for all the tears blurring her sight.

They were on the outskirts of Mennick when she heard Anu stagger to a halt, sniffling. As Oksana stopped running and turned around, Anu scrubbed at her face. "I told you, I'm *fine*!"

But Oksana still saw the tears glistening on her friend's cheeks. When she pulled Anu close, the girl drooped against her shoulder.

"Isn't my family charming?" Anu said. "You should

see them on Midsummer's Day, when they race in potato sacks. They'd stab their brother to win—and stab you for looking cross-eyed at that same brother." She laughed, but her voice had gone thick. "I thought they'd remember my promise!"

"I'm sorry." Oksana held tight, even after Anu stopped shivering. "You risked so much tonight, and for that to be their response . . ."

Anu leaned back and swiped at her eyes. "I'd do it again. Every time, I'll choose them. They're my family, and Kivi is my home. Even if nobody remembers."

"But the way they looked at you . . . those things they said . . ." Oksana felt hollow inside, scraped out like a husk. If they ever did get free of the Commanders, what would Anu have to go back to?

"I'll be all right." Anu caught Oksana's hand. "A person can have more than one home. There's the one we're born with, and it will always matter. But home is also what we make of the people we're with. And there, I'm beyond blessed. It's just like you told me: not everything that comes from fire is terrible and ugly."

She touched her forehead to Oksana's, then threw back her shoulders and led the way, singing as she ran: "*Out from the mountains the demons came forth, avenging all wrongs wrought from east to north. Tuliikobrets, come, come along! Guardians to keep Vesimaa strong.*"

Oksana followed at a distance, her steps plodding where Anu's bounced. They'd done what they'd set out to do. That was what mattered, and the only part in their control. She tried to take comfort in it.

But the night still felt far from a victory.

The next morning, she looked for Pran in Meal Hall to ask how his meeting had gone. Though nothing would replace her having been there for him, studying these Tuliis he trusted with his life. She wasn't sorry to have gone with Anu, she only wished there were a way to be in two places at once.

An apology quivered on her tongue, but it faded like smoke when she spotted him slumped at a table, head in hands, teeth gritted. A bowl of kama and milk sat before him, but he wasn't eating, not with his face shifting through ghastly shades of green.

"Pran?" She rested a hand against his back. "Haven't you been getting medicine?"

"Supplies are low," he gasped. "The physicians are saving them for emergencies until Rootare brews more."

A whimper slipped from his throat, and Oksana was nearly sick as Rootare's voice stung like poison through her mind: *I don't have time anymore to develop new serums* and *brew medicine for those still struggling from transformation. Which do you think I'll set aside?*

It was never a question, really, of whether he'd make good on the threat. But Oksana had hoped she'd have more time. "How long since your last dose?"

"Nayar!" A Pakastran Imp elbowed between her and the table. "Tonight?" He lowered his voice in a truly poor attempt at subtlety. "Can you help me? You said—"

"Not now, Devak," Pran groaned, still slumped forward, head in his hands. The boy slunk away, but Oksana couldn't spare him more than a sympathetic frown. She rubbed Pran's shoulders, aching for something real she could do to help. If she snuck into the hospital wing again, broke into another cabinet, could she steal away what medicine was left?

That might help Pran today, but what about tomorrow, and every day after?

When you do change your mind, send word.

Damn Rootare to the pits of hell.

"Oksana!" Now Anu pushed toward her, pale as though she'd seen her own ghost.

Just when Oksana thought she couldn't feel worse. "What's happened?"

"Last night . . . if anyone asks, you can't say you were with me, or they'll take you, too—"

"Tarvas!" Commander Igarik shoved between the tables and snatched the girl by her elbow. "You missed last night's training. Where were you, having a lie-around?"

Training? The floor tilted. Oksana caught the edge of Pran's table to keep standing.

Anu straightened, turning her back to Oksana without another glance. "I'm sorry, Commander. I was sick."

"You weren't in the hospital wing. You weren't in your barrack. Where were you?"

"I didn't get the announcement. I wouldn't have skipped—"

"Last night you missed an advancement test. I warned what would happen if you failed again." Igarik dragged her out through Meal Hall's doors.

All the Tuliis seated nearby fell silent, wincing as those doors banged shut. Even Pran lifted his head, face slack with shock.

"I didn't know!" Oksana spluttered. She wasn't sure if she was trying to convince Pran, herself, or her saints.

Next time I'll get five on my back. For missing an advancement test, Anu would be lucky if that was all she got.

Oksana dropped onto the bench beside Pran, slouching against his shoulder even though she ought to be the one supporting him. And yet he stayed there, propping her up, until the last Tulii left the hall.

Anu didn't come to the midday meal. Didn't march yard to yard between trainings. At least she wasn't burned on the platform in the south courtyard, all the Tuliis made to watch. But with no other sign of Anu or her fate . . . all day, Oksana clutched her icon of Yeva. Prayed that her saint would look out for Anu.

Hated that there wasn't more she could do.

A few hours before sunset, Oksana stood before the narrow mirror in her barrack. She put on her gauntlets and greaves, bound on her antlers, squeezed in the dark eye drops. When they finished stinging and her vision cleared, a monster with night-black eyes stared back.

Out in the mountains the monsters arose, all embers and fire, to fight the land's foes.

Perhaps this monster could be what saved Kivi from its enemies. If she couldn't spare Anu from the Commanders, then Oksana had to at least protect her friend's family.

It didn't make her feel better, of course. After last night, Oksana would give up every person in that cottage to keep Anu safe. But it was what her friend would want, and right now that was all Oksana could give her.

Dressed for a battle she wasn't ready to fight, Oksana followed her troop from their barrack to where the rest of the Hellions clustered around the fort's gates. Some stood in elaborate armor: gloves with shining claws, twisted antlers or barbed horns, and wings of leather and animal bones. Three of the largest Hellions carried on their backs brass tanks filled with Demon's Tongue, nozzles molded into the shape of fire demons peeking over their shoulders.

Oksana uttered a silent prayer. *It's for the fountain. Nothing else.*

A muffled groan rose on her right. Pran hunched against the stable wall, his breath gone ragged.

"They still haven't given you medicine?" Oksana whispered.

"Emergencies only," he grunted.

"You're about to become an emergency!"

"Then the physicians can't deny me again."

Oksana scooped his arm across her shoulders and leaned him against her side. Most Tuliis sickened by the serums had died years ago, but a few other Hellions slumped near the gate, clutching shoulders or arms, their jaws clenched. Bile stung Oksana's throat. No matter how strong they pretended to be, they were all at Rootare's mercy.

A bitter tear slipped from her eye and trickled down her face.

The fort gates groaned open. Commanders Lepik and Haamer, in their own battle gear complete with horned helmets, ushered the Hellions out those gates. When the last ones passed through, another Commander approached, also dressed for battle. Not Tamm, as Oksana had expected from the meeting, but Kraanvelt.

His words in the courtyard, as the Scarlet Embers had cooked on their pyres, echoed through her mind: *Rebel with flame, and you die by flame. We are watching.*

Oksana's heart withered and she stumbled, nearly knocking Pran to the ground.

"Whassamatter?" he moaned, gloved fingers digging into her shoulder.

"Keep walking." She steered him beyond the gates.

The Commanders led them on foot; horse carts would make too much noise and draw attention. Silently, they wove through the pines surrounding Kivi. Oksana lingered at the back, steering Pran, pausing every time he needed to retch. The girl with the pale double buns from Oksana's new barrack frowned at them, but no one else paid attention, much less offered help.

True Tuliikobrets are strong enough to stand on their own.

May they remember that when it was their turn to suffer.

When the troops could see Kivi's first cottages through the trees, Haamer called for a halt. "At my signal," he told the Hellions carrying the tanks of Demon's Tongue, "pump and flame. Any other suggestions, Artemivna? This is your plan."

She mirrored Haamer's stance, flint starter in one raised hand. "We move like the demons we're named for. Swiftly in, swiftly out. These people won't know what hit them."

Please, Yeva, she pleaded as they slipped into the village. *Let it be so.*

Kivi's streets were empty as the Hellions marched through, but market sounds gurgled from the village square: voices bargaining, arguing, or trilling songs.

But those sounds died as Hellions poured into the square. Nor were there signs of any market: no booths of baked goods, no stalls with the harvest's last vegetables, no tables of winter boots or woven shawls. The villagers were not decked in fire-colored festival clothes, but quilted jackets and boiled-leather armor. They stood elbow to elbow, so many they filled the square and spilled back into the surrounding streets.

There were far too many people gathered, for all of them to dwell here in Kivi. Not only had Anu's family ignored her warning, they'd *recruited*. Oksana peered at their iron-stiff faces, and sour dismay curdled through her.

"You've wronged our emperor," Haamer declared to the crowd. "He has a message for you."

"We have one for him," a villager countered. He signaled, and half-dozen more dumped armfuls of charred rubble onto the ground: Wooden beams. Roof shingles. A cart wheel. A soot-stained hand broken off a statue.

"We lost cousins and friends in Linn," a woman cried. "Yet Juhan still defends your existence. Whom, then, does he protect? It's not good Vesimaans."

"You assaulted two of his council," Kraanvelt said. "This deed cannot go unpunished."

"Unpunished?" The first man strode forward. "Your troops destroyed a village, and the next day Juhan offers you council seats. We ask again, whom does he protect?"

"Stand back," Lepik said, "if you value the safety of your village."

"We seek more than the safety of *this* village," the woman said. "We want security for all Vesimaans. We want our children to stop being taken and turned into monsters that slaughter their own people. We want our whole country to know peace. For that, we'd sacrifice anything."

"Remember whom you challenge." Haamer lifted his flint starter.

The Hellions with tanks of Demon's Tongue aimed

the nozzles and worked the pumps until a deep red liquid spurted into the fountain. Three more Hellions lunged forward, flinging sparks from their flint starters.

A pillar of fire erupted in that bubbling fountain, flames clawing toward the crimson sky. The fountain's stonework blackened and the frosty autumn air boiled.

Oksana sucked in a breath, staggering back. *It worked.* This was her outlandish idea, a desperate shot cobbled together in the space of a moment. And there, before them all, water burned.

Villagers shrieked and scrambled away, trampling each other in their panic. Except for one—a child no more than ten years old, who flung a handful of mud into a Hellion's face.

"Vesimaa!" the boy shouted, until others joined in. "For Vesimaa!"

But their cheers died as the muddied Hellion went rigid, uttering a snarl that wasn't human. With a piercing scream that lanced through Oksana's bones, the Tulii lunged forward, torching the nearest villagers in a screeching burst of flame.

"Enough!" Lepik shouted. But the Hellion raced deeper into Kivi, incinerating everything in his path with sweeping pillars of fire taller than the cottages.

He wasn't alone. Two other Hellions also howled in mindless rage and began torching everything in sight. The animal fury in their eyes was chilling. All the more so because Oksana recognized it. Amid the haze and screaming, she was back with the Scarlet Embers, watching them destroy Linn. Were these Hellions *Snapping* the same way?

As those Tuliis lunged forward, hurling fire in every direction, many villagers fled into the forest as flames licked at their heels.

But not everyone retreated. The remaining villagers charged forward, shouting loud enough to rival the broken Hellions. Anu's aunt threw makeshift weapons to anyone in reach. The old man who'd strummed a kannel now darted forward with a pitchfork in hand.

"Death!" they yelled. "Death to demons. Death to our oppressors. Long live Vesimaa!"

"Hellions, *attack*," Haamer shouted, while raising the first flame. Lepik and Kraanvelt followed suit. Within seconds the square thundered with starters clicking, sparks crackling, fire roaring to life.

"No, stop!" Oksana stumbled, ash crunching between her teeth. But her voice was lost beneath the crash of windows bursting, glass shards pouring down like vicious rain. Everywhere she turned, flames ripped through houses and lives.

Anu's home. Oksana's knees went weak to see every cottage on fire. Even Anu's family, with rebellion stamped on their hearts, couldn't have wanted this. Meanwhile, everything she'd worked for, planned for, hoped for was destroyed the moment those Hellions broke like the Embers had. In all this mess, the only thing she understood was that she couldn't help any of them. That uselessness gnawed at her, darker than the smoke vomiting into the sky.

No, there was one she still might save. Pran, where was he? Oksana whirled around.

"Nayar's over there." The girl with the pale double buns gestured. He lay on the ground a few cart-lengths away, trying to stand. His bad leg gave out and he collapsed again, while a woman brandishing a pair of rusty shears sprinted toward him.

"STOP!" Oksana shoved aside villagers and Hellions alike, chasing away the woman with an enormous fireball.

"Look out!" Again, the girl from her barrack, screaming across the chaos. A force like a boulder slammed into Oksana. She was knocked clear off her feet and thrown to the ground, all the air battered from her lungs.

A heavyset Vesimaan man tugged Oksana upright and shoved her against a burning cottage. It was the knife-man from Anu's house. Her cousin.

"Peeter, don't!" Oksana shrieked, as he pressed that knife beneath her jaw.

The man froze. Stared, peering through the smoke and haze. "You?"

"None of this had to happen! Anu and I, we wanted to keep you safe."

"You swore they'd only light our fountain. I knew we couldn't trust you." He dug the knife against her skin until blood oozed beneath the blade.

"*Stop!*" She reached for her flint starter, but her hand came up empty. The starter lay on the ground, three steps behind Peeter.

"I wanted to believe my cousin," he said, voice breaking. "But only death comes from that fort."

Peeter shifted his hold on the knife to thrust it deeper, but toppled with a guttural groan as a flint starter cracked across his skull.

Pran hunched behind the fallen man, reaching for Oksana. "Are you all right?"

"Enough!" Kraanvelt bellowed across the square. The villagers' battle cries gave way to wails of panic and pain. Those still standing fled as the last homes erupted in flames. With shouts and sobs the rest of the villagers darted into the forest, where trees and shadows swallowed them up.

"Hellions, return to the fort," Lepik shouted. "You and you, help us bind these three."

Oksana yanked Pran's arm around her shoulder and led him from the village. Only the rasping sounds of his breath pushed her to take each step.

CHAPTER ELEVEN

OKSANA

The moment they passed through the gates, Pran was torn from her side. "He needs medicine!" Oksana cried.

Please, let her take care of one person tonight.

But the Nightmare dumped him beside the wall like a sack of stale bread. As he fell, Pran's swollen eyes blinked open. He reached for Oksana, and she elbowed another Nightmare in the ribs while lunging for him.

Before their fingers touched, a heavy hand grabbed Oksana by the shoulders, yanking her away. Kraanvelt's frosty eyes glinted down.

"Well, Artemivna. Tonight didn't go as planned."

The man marched Oksana across the fort grounds—half steering, half dragging as she struggled to keep up with his furious stride. He did not lead her to Commander Tower, as she'd hoped. Prayed.

He brought her to the prisons.

Oksana swallowed the scream ringing through her bones. She'd made the attack plan for Kivi, and it had ended in rebellion. There was no other place this night could have ended for her.

Still, as they passed through the prison's doors, her knees buckled. All she'd wanted was to protect one village. When so much seemed painfully out of reach—a hundred woolly lambs, mushroom hunting, fresh bread, music and dancing, her parents' smiles, her siblings' laughter—protecting one village hadn't seemed too much to ask.

But she'd greatly overestimated what lay in her grasp, all while she'd scolded Pran, *This is too much!* and *You have to think this through.* If she couldn't keep one village safe, what were the odds of them overcoming the Commanders, escaping Juhan, fleeing this fort?

She didn't want to risk more lives to find out.

When Oksana stumbled again, Kraanvelt thrust her forward, the heel of his hand slapping across her spine. The prison was colder inside than out. Its corridors narrowed as though the walls were closing in on her. Kraanvelt steered her upward, away from the cells, to the rooms where Commanders questioned troublemakers.

Where they tortured them.

He shoved her into a narrow chamber lit by a single chemical lamp and furnished with a metal table and two chairs. Kraanvelt pointed Oksana to one. When she dropped into it, he bound her hands to the back with iron manacles, then took the seat across from her.

"I'm sure you know why you're here, so let's get to the point: What rebellion did you organize with those Hellions?"

All the blood rushed from her head. If they thought she was involved with whatever those Hellions had done, if they tried to blame her . . . she'd be roasting on a pyre before the sun rose.

"S-s-sir!" She choked on her fear. *Slow down. Breathe. Desperation only makes you look guilty.* "The . . . the way those Hellions broke . . . they behaved like the Scarlet Embers. I saw the Imps when they ran through Mennick. They raged and rampaged exactly the same. That's not rebellion, that's madness. I don't know what's going on, but something's . . . wrong with them."

"Something is very wrong, indeed. Your plan depended on the people of Kivi being caught by surprise. But they were waiting for us."

She'd never dreamed warning the people of Kivi would end this catastrophically. *I'm sorry!* she pleaded, an apology no one might ever hear. "My plan, sir, depended on us performing a trick they neither expected nor could explain."

"You assured us they'd be distracted by the market."

"I underestimated their daring. These people assaulted councilors. If a scout spotted our approach, of course they'd resist our troop."

"Of course." Kraanvelt rose to his feet. "Of course they'd resist an advanced troop of Tuliikobrets, with minimal time to prepare their counterattack." The man circled, towering over her. Bound in this chair, her brow was barely level with his ribs.

"There was no scout. The people of Kivi were warned."

His shadow blocked most of the gray-green lamplight, casting Oksana into darkness. "Kivi is the home of Anu Tarvas."

Her stomach lurched like a living creature, but lying wouldn't help. "I . . . believe so."

He yanked the chair onto its back legs. Oksana stifled a yelp as her head slammed against the iron frame. "You know it. Seven years you've worked alongside her."

"We were brought to the fort at the same time. We were Novices together, along with dozens of other Tuliis."

He jerked the chair so it teetered on its left legs. Oksana scrambled, one foot brushing the floor, her manacles alone keeping her in the seat.

"Yet it was you who designed an assault that would leave minimal damage to that village. An assault those renegades were prepared to face."

He dropped the chair back in place. The impact as all four legs hit the ground jolted through Oksana's bones. Her whirling vision had barely settled when Kraanvelt slapped her so hard he almost tipped over the chair.

"Every Hellion in this fort knew of the plan. But there is not one Hellion with more motive than you for protecting Kivi." Kraanvelt grabbed her tunic collar. Oksana's joints screamed as her bound wrists strained against the manacles. "Unless you know otherwise, and wish to clear your name."

"No Tulii would dare raise trouble after watching the Scarlet Embers and their trainers be burned alive." She hated how small her voice had become, but she could barely draw in enough air to speak at all.

"And yet tonight those Hellions did just that." He dropped her. Pain flared through her spine as she hit the metal chair back. "You say they behaved like the Scarlet Embers. Well, someone encouraged those Embers to rebel. Do you know who that was, Artemivna?"

"I wasn't their trainer! I didn't work with the Embers."

Kraanvelt hit the striker on his flint. Sparks needled Oksana's cheeks. Their blazing orange lights brought back images of the Embers and their Hellion trainers screaming in agony. Then, as now, the Commanders needed someone to blame more than they needed actual answers. She didn't care about failing them, but Anu . . .

Hot tears stung Oksana's eyes. She should be the one to give her friend the news about Kivi. And Pran, she'd left him in agony. Would she even get to say goodbye? She prayed he wouldn't be in the courtyard to see . . .

Kraanvelt jammed his flint starter beneath her chin, tilted Oksana's face to his. "Did you tell Tarvas? Did she arrange this unfortunate plan to save her home?"

No no no, they couldn't think this was Anu! If she did one thing right tonight, let her steer them away from her friend.

"Tarvas is incompetent," Oksana said with all the venom she could muster. "She can't throw a fireball straight. She misses her own training. You think *she* arranged revolution?"

"I can bring Tarvas in here. Maybe that will jog your memory." He turned for the door.

It swung open before he touched the handle. "Kraanvelt! We've been looking for you."

The scent of rotten eggs and scorched metal wafted into the room. All the bile churning in Oksana's belly surged upward, and she gagged.

"What do you want, Rootare?" Kraanvelt moved between the door and Oksana.

"Emperor Juhan is on his way to the fort."

Kraanvelt deflated like his spine had been ripped out. "He's heard about Kivi?"

"He's not coming for tea and honey cakes." Rootare scowled from Kraanvelt to Oksana. "What are you doing to my Hellion?"

"*Your* Hellion?"

"Seems the message wasn't delivered before your . . . attack tonight. She's been given to my lab. I need her. In one piece, if you please."

As she gaped, Rootare met Oksana's gaze and lifted an eyebrow, daring her to argue.

If she did, Kraanvelt would keep at her, and the only way out would be either betrayal or burning. But the lab . . . This was not a kindness. This was Rootare forcing her hand. She thought back to when he'd first urged her to join him. *I'm developing another serum. Always stronger Tuliis for Vesimaa.*

He was up to something, and knowing him, it meant more suffering for Tuliis. She wanted no part in it.

But agreeing with Rootare meant leaving this room alive. And in his lab, she could make Pran's medicine. She thought of Pran, his face tight, barely able to breathe through his pain.

"Yes," she said, and that word sealed her fate.

"Go on," Rootare said, and Kraanvelt stormed from the room. The alchemist unlocked the manacles binding Oksana to the chair. His fingers lingered over the bruises on her wrists, but she jerked her hands away and staggered beyond his reach.

"Go on, Oksana." Rootare grinned. "Tonight, go to your boy. Tomorrow, I'll be waiting."

CHAPTER TWELVE

PRAN

Waking felt like clawing from a pit of viscous mud. Pran cracked his eyes open and struggled onto his elbows, but sitting made his head spin, and the cot beneath him seemed feather-soft, the most comfortable bed he could ever sleep on.

Most comfortable bed . . . Pran snorted and burrowed deeper into the blanket someone had tossed over him. The whole night was a fog; he barely remembered the long, awful walk alone to the hospital wing or the prick of the needle as he'd finally received his medicine. Its haze remained thick and sleep lingered a few breaths away, as it did when his mother used to sing him the golden parrot lullaby. Those notes chimed through his memories like tiny bells, celebrating the glimmering birds as they huddled together each night, their brilliant feathers safeguarding them till dawn. Pran's breath slowed as some unseen singer hummed the melody now, each measure carrying away a little more of his consciousness. But it wasn't his mother's voice echoing through his dreams.

It was Oksana's.

Pran jerked upright, heart beating so fast his pulse throbbed in his fingertips. Oksana . . . Kivi . . . the whole village ablaze . . . Kraanvelt at the fort gates, dragging her away . . .

And he'd been lying here, sleeping.

Every day, Pran hated what the Commanders had done to them, what this empire had done to their lives—not just being torn from their families and homes, not just that their bodies were changed, but that some like him were rendered dependent on Vesimaan medicines to function. He hated how often the pains overtook him, that they always came at the worst times, that they made Oksana worry, that both their lives were so much harder for these relentless bouts of agony.

But most of all, he hated that it kept him from being able to help her when she needed it. She'd been taken while he'd hardly been able to see straight. He'd despise himself for that . . . except it would only give the Commanders more power over him. They allowed his pain because they thought it trapped him in their control.

He couldn't change what they'd done to his body, but he would never hand them his will.

None of the physicians in the hospital wing stopped Pran as he clambered to his feet and staggered from the room. Outside Healing Hall, night still hung thick over the fort. He paused, unsure where Kraanvelt would have taken her, but a sour taste flooded Pran's mouth as he considered the possibilities. The Kivi attack had been Oksana's plan, and it had gone to chaos. Kraanvelt wouldn't ask gentle questions.

Pran hobbled toward the prison, his breath heaving as sweat trickled down his face despite the icy air. With each step, his bad leg wrenched, but Pran cursed it and refused to slow.

"Nayar!" a voice cried through the night. He knew it wasn't Oksana but turned anyway, heart in his throat, only to see Devak scurrying toward him. "Can you . . . please—"

"Not now, Devak!"

Flinching, the boy withdrew into shadows.

"Oksana," Pran whispered as he ran, as though his voice might reach her wherever she was trapped. He whispered again, because it drove him faster. "*Oksana!*"

He was nearing the prisons when another figure charged him. It was too tiny to be any Vesimaan, and when it passed beneath another lamp, the hair gleamed vivid red.

"OKSANA!" He lunged, pressing on when his leg threatened to give out.

She threw herself at Pran, winding her arms around his neck as they crashed into one another. At the impact, Pran's leg screamed, but he kept his mouth shut and clutched Oksana closer. On her face something shone, too dark to be tears. Pran turned her into the lamplight and sucked in a breath as the gray-green glow illuminated burns scattered across her nose and cheeks.

"Gods above. Are you all right? Do you need a physician?"

She waved away his words. "I'm fine. He mostly just

shouted. Thought I knew something about tonight's rampage. Or that Anu arranged it."

The night was cold, but inside Pran was hotter than the fire that had decimated Kivi. Because never mind the words Oksana gave him, she was so very far from fine, as evident from her trembling stance and haunted, hollow stare. Fury ripped through Pran like a lightning strike, and picturing the nearest lamppost as Kraanvelt's face, he slammed his fist into it until his knuckles bled.

"I'll kill him," he growled. "I'll kill him with a flame from his own flint!"

"Pran!"

He halted midway to another punch.

"We can't stay here." Oksana glanced toward the prison looming behind.

Of course they couldn't. Pran reached for her with the hand not covered in blood. "Let's move."

She clasped his fingers and hobbled after.

He led Oksana to the storage sheds, sat down among their shadowed, crooked frames, and for a moment believed he'd done well, as she curled against his chest and her trembling limbs fell still. But then she grasped his ring, strung onto her saint's necklace, and Pran's heart sank like a stone in the sea. Why bother with his worthless promises when he couldn't even keep her safe from Kraanvelt?

He didn't ask what had happened, didn't want to make her relive it so soon after she'd gotten away, but . . . *how?* The Commanders had burned the Hellion trainers who'd worked with the Scarlet Embers. For a plan that had gone to pieces, Pran had thought for certain . . .

No, he wouldn't poke at this turn of events, lest it shatter like glass. He'd be grateful, relieved. He held Oksana so tight her breaths echoed through his own lungs.

But then she sobbed, great shuddering cries that broke from the inside out.

"Shhh." Pran clutched her tighter. "You're away from him. You're safe."

"I'm bound to Rootare!" Oksana cried. "S-sold myself to him."

The medicine must still be affecting his brain, because what Oksana said made no sense. "*What?*"

She breathed, long and deep, until her sobs quieted. "He's been after me to work with him. That's why there's no medicine for you. He threatened to stop making it if I refused him."

"No," Pran breathed. He saw again Rootare eyeing her during their first session with the Novices, like he could take her apart fiber by fiber and discover how she worked. "Don't go near him."

"You'll keep hurting if I don't do something."

"I don't care, not if it means—"

"*I* care! How much of tonight do you remember?"

Pran didn't want to admit that so much of this evening—gods, so much of this *day*—was reduced to fragments. Snippets of conversations, blurs of scenes . . . He couldn't recall the walk to Kivi or the journey back. If it weren't for

Oksana's shoulder to lean on, her steering the way, the Commanders would have left him in the woods, having no use for a Tulii who couldn't stand on his own.

"I won't leave you suffering." She clawed at the hair tangling around her face. "I've failed everyone tonight. I thought warning Anu's family would help someone. But they fought back even worse, and Anu . . ." Oksana's face crumpled.

"It's not your fault Vesimaans threw away their village and their lives." But though there was truth amid these words, they still felt wrong against Pran's teeth. He understood those villagers' motives, at least. Sitting back wasn't safety, wasn't living. It wasn't protecting anyone but the people who already possessed too much power. "It's not your fault those Hellions lost their minds."

But he knew that wasn't so simple, either. Even if they'd gotten fed up and, independent of his own group, decided to rebel, Hellions could do better than set fire to everything like Novices who'd lost control of their flames. The parallels between their rampage and the Scarlet Embers' made Pran's throat go tight. To have two separate troops lash out so similarly . . . well, he'd never believed in coincidences.

Oksana's expression went sharp. "Something's happening. Rootare's involved. I'm going to find out what."

"When is he *not* up to something? Don't get distracted. Rootare, or freedom. Home. Which do you want?"

"I want home. I need you to be all right. One of those things I can actually make happen!" She glared toward his leg.

Pran could have screamed. *Frail, sickly, young.* No, he

would not hold them back. He'd prove to everyone—Oksana included—that he didn't need to be saved.

"Stop worrying about me and focus on the bigger picture. When you put home last, when you act like it's impossible, that's what keeps it out of your reach."

"Anu's family led a rebellion to kill us. How will we survive outside these walls if people only want us dead?"

Though the night was hazy to his mind, he was haunted by the clang of makeshift weapons, farmers charging fire warriors. *Death to demons! Death to our oppressors!*

But where Vesimaans saw soldiers no longer doing their jobs . . . surely the people of their home countries remembered the transformed Tuliis differently? Each one was stolen from their family to serve another nation's army, and giving up on them would be letting their oppressive emperor win. Pran had to believe their own people were better than that.

There was so little else to hold on to.

"Don't give up on your people because of what someone else's did. They deserve their own chance." He cupped his hands around Oksana's face. "Don't give up on home. I promised I'd get you there. Don't you trust me to do it?"

She pulled away from his touch. "How will you, if you can't even stand because you don't have medicine? I'm going into the lab. Someone needs to make it. And someone needs to find out what Rootare's doing, what it means for us. He can hurt us as badly as the Commanders."

"I still don't like—"

"I'm not asking for permission. If Rootare lights a fire beneath us all, you don't want to be caught unaware. When's your next meeting? I'll come, with whatever I've found out."

"No!" Pran shouted, and Oksana jumped, a wounded look stealing across her face. Gods, he hated startling her after all she'd been through tonight, but after Lepik's words outside the old armory, *Come talk with me after this mess with Kivi is over* . . . the thought of her among his Tuliis when Lepik had already come too close made every drop of blood in his body stop cold.

"What happened?" Her voice was soft, but there was nothing gentle about her gaze.

Pran swallowed a groan. Lying would do no good, she'd piece it together eventually, and he wouldn't insult her that way after everything she'd been through tonight. If he gave her the truth . . . she might not agree with him, but at least she might understand.

"Lepik caught me coming out of the armory last night. He knew something was going on, saw other Tuliis leaving the area." Why hadn't they been more careful? But they were Imps and Goblins, heady with the promise of freedom. *He* should have made sure the way was clear. "Asked me what was going on. I . . . couldn't say I didn't know. We're Hellions, we're *supposed* to know. I had to buy us time. So I told Lepik I'd be his spy, sniffing out trouble in the fort."

Oksana stared. "You did *what?*"

Gods, the look on her face, like he'd taken his flint starter and stabbed it through her heart. "I won't turn anyone over to him! That should go without saying."

"And how do you plan to do that? Pran, you have to know how this will turn out. You really think you can deceive the Commanders, while you plan to tear the army from their hands?"

"When Lepik thinks I'm on his side, he won't be watching so closely. This gives me time and space to create our freedom."

He reached for Oksana, but she scooted away until she was pressed against the next rotten shed. "I said you had to be careful. I said you had to think this through."

There was nothing sharp in her tone, but each of those words—the doubt and judgment in them—bit into Pran like thorns. "Did you think we could fight against people like the Commanders and keep our hands clean? That our choices would be easy and light? I said if we were going to do this, there'd be hard choices. This is one of those. Anyway, it's over. Done. Tomorrow morning, Lepik is expecting me to come."

She shook her head, eyes brimming with tears. "You're in over your head."

"Can't you trust me?" he hissed. "I'm doing this for *you*!"

"No. Do not put this on me." She rose to her feet. "I'm getting your medicine, that's my promise. Don't make me watch you fall into a trap along the way."

CHAPTER THIRTEEN

OKSANA

At dawn, all Tuliis were marched to the south courtyard. There, Anu caught Oksana in a suffocating hug. "No one would say what happened to you. They wouldn't say if you were condemned to be . . ."

On the platform, Commanders wrestled the three broken Hellions against metal stakes.

"I'm still here." Oksana cradled her friend against her side. "You are, too."

Bruises marred Anu's face and bandages peeked out from beneath her tunic. When Oksana's hands touched her back, Anu hissed in pain and flinched away. But she was *alive,* and in that, Oksana found the strength to keep standing.

"I warned you!" Juhan, flanked by two of his own Nightmares and joined by the twenty-one remaining Commanders, raged atop the platform at the gathered ranks of soldiers. "If you don't perform as expected, you *will* be replaced."

The man was uncharacteristically unkempt, his jacket wrinkled and hair hanging around his ears instead of slicked back. Dark circles ringed his eyes, and the Commanders' were similarly shadowed. It would seem none of them had slept that night.

With a signal from Juhan, Kraanvelt set fire to the Hellions who'd rampaged. The reek of scorching meat billowed through the yard while agonized screams split the air.

"Do as you are told," Juhan called. "*Only* as you are told." The man snapped his fingers, and his Nightmares raised an inferno that swallowed Commander Haamer whole.

"I do not tolerate failure from anyone." Juhan glared toward every Commander on the platform, each of them scrambling away as Haamer collapsed into the blaze consuming the Hellions. For a moment, the only sounds in the courtyard were the fire's roar and the shrieks of the dying.

Anu withered like a leaf in the blaze. "What happened in Kivi?"

The villagers' shouts echoed through Oksana's mind. "They took a stand. Recruited others to their cause."

"It was a massacre?"

"Those Hellions . . . it was just like the Scarlet Embers. They Snapped. Set fire to everything."

"My family?"

Oksana hadn't seen what became of Peeter, the aunt, or the old kannel player. "Many people escaped into the woods, even at the end."

Anu scrubbed her hands across her face. "Tadte taught me to sing. After my parents died, she sang every night until I fell asleep. We sang while cooking, tending animals, gathering herbs. We sang to work faster. We sang for good fortune. We sang for thanks. When I missed my parents, I sang to remember. It was like your prayers." Her voice caught. "What song do I sing now?"

Oksana had no words of comfort and certainly no songs to offer. All she could do was hold Anu until the flames on the platform huffed out and only ashes remained.

After, when the Tuliis were sent to training or patrols, Oksana turned to Healing Hall. Inside, a monster waited for her.

She would crush him.

Rootare's lab spanned almost the whole second floor of Healing Hall. When she entered, the first thing Oksana noticed was the reek of sulfur, strong as a fist to the face.

After she could breathe again, she studied the rows upon rows of wooden tables filling the room. All were cluttered with long-necked distillation bottles, brass scales, metal canisters, and round beakers with jewel-colored liquids bubbling over blue flames. Cabinets lined the walls, filled with raw ingredients or finished serums that would transmute a child into a Tulii.

Shuddering, Oksana turned toward a workstation surrounded by chalkboards. The station itself was nearly bare, housing a single beaker filled with a clear, syrupy liquid. But the chalkboards were covered with equations, alchemical symbols, and diagrams of minerals.

She waved away the beaker's sickly sweet smoke and

studied those diagrams. Focusing on them, she could pretend she was in old Professor Melnyk's lab back in her village, Novosel. After retiring from Horádim's university, the man found he couldn't live without chemistry. So he'd hired Oksana's father to furnish a new lab, ordering tables, benches, cabinets. The requests never ended. For each delivery, she and her older brother Borys tagged along, pretending to help but mostly gaping at the steaming beakers. Soon, the man paid Oksana's father in chemistry lessons for Oksana and Borys, and he didn't mind when the two invited themselves over to tinker.

Borys would wet himself to stand in this lab, larger than Melnyk's whole house and packed with the latest equipment. Or he would if there were a way to separate this place from its end goals.

Oksana hefted a glass jar, filled with a powder as red as spurting blood, from one of the tables.

"Careful," a voice said. "Bring that jar too close to a flame and it will explode."

Rootare stepped out from a closet in the lab's farthest corner, an open logbook in his hands and a grin on his face. "Powdered verikivi. The most dangerous element in this lab. Eons ago, those stones were left by the ancient fire demons for which you Tuliikobrets are named. Now they're the key ingredient for Demon's Tongue and my serums. Ingest too much and that verikivi will combust the mind. But in the right amount, they will—" He tipped his head toward her, and his grin morphed into a smirk.

Steady, Oksana urged herself. She'd chosen to come here, for Pran and the others.

Rootare shut the closet door and hobbled forward, lurching across the lab toward her. His movements were painfully slow, as if he were ancient. But when Oksana looked again, really looked, at his face free of lines and wrinkles—he couldn't be much older than her brother.

Oksana glanced at the chemicals bubbling in beakers all around the room, and shuffled closer to the doors.

Rootare had almost reached her when he burst into a hacking cough, each bark rattling thick and wet in his throat. He swiped at his mouth, and a dark stain smeared across his knuckles. From one of his lab coat pockets, he pulled out a flask and gulped from it until his cough eased.

A part of Oksana—one she didn't like—wasn't sorry to see him suffer. Part of her wondered if she could take advantage of his weakness.

But then he stuffed that flask back in his pocket and rounded on Oksana, leering as though she were a prize he'd won. Nothing weak about him at all.

"I know you don't want to be here, Oksana, so let's get to the point. Today, cleansing elixir." He gestured to a row of beakers boiling a silver-white blend. "This is what strips Novices of human limitations so they can be remade as Tuliis."

When Rootare had injected Oksana with this elixir seven years ago, it had felt like her soul was being eaten away. She was torn apart breath for breath, thought for thought, until she'd begged to die. That was the one time she hadn't risen quickly.

But some of the Novices never rose at all, and for three days Pran hadn't woken. Rootare had leaned over his cot, prying open Pran's eyelids, shaking his head at whatever he'd seen. He'd waved for a physician to drag the cot away when Pran jerked upright with a howl.

"We'll make a monster of you yet." Rootare had patted Pran's cheek, then walked away, ignoring Pran as he begged for water.

Choking, heart clenching, Oksana nearly bolted from the room. *Steady,* she urged herself again. *Remember why you're here.*

Through the steam wafting from beakers, she peered at Rootare. "You said if I helped, there'd be medicine for Pran."

"I'll grant that. After the serums." He handed Oksana a coat of her own, along with gloves, goggles, and a mask. "Put these on. Don't ever stand in this lab again without them."

While she slipped her arms through the sleeves, Rootare made a few more notes in that logbook. Leaning forward, Oksana tried to glimpse what he wrote.

Rootare slammed the book shut, then lifted an eyebrow while tucking it into his lab coat pocket. "Curious, are you?" His voice burred with sickening amusement. "Then follow me."

CHAPTER FOURTEEN

PRAN

Lepik's office was nearly as sterile as Tamm's, housing the same steel desk and wrought iron chairs, although on the far wall behind that desk hung a painting of a thatch-roofed Vesimaan farmhouse surrounded by cornflower fields. Pran tilted his head at it—he'd never seen anything like it in a Commander's office.

"Sit." Lepik pointed to a chair, and Pran obeyed gladly. The three flights of stairs up to this room had been murder on his leg.

The Commander, however, kept to his feet, pacing behind his desk. "I've had my eye on you for some time, Nayar. Tamm recommended your promotion, but I requested you for my troop. You were one of the weakest Novices we've had the misfortune to train, yet in barely three years you've advanced from Imp to Hellion rank. Even most of our able-bodied Tuliikobrets can't boast that, and in your condition . . . that takes shrewdness. You're resourceful, Nayar. A planner. You don't miss much. I need help like that on my side. Someone must keep these troops from being run into the ground."

A shadow passed across the Commander's face. "Mälk and I, we'd been friends since . . ."

Since their parents had handed them over to the emperor, most likely.

"My troops will be safe and well," Lepik continued, his voice rising. "I will sit on the emperor's council. So tell me, Nayar, of your plans to spy out trouble in this fort."

Despite Oksana's warning ringing through his mind, Pran barely hid his grin. Here was a Commander begging for help. For all seven years he'd been in the fort, there hadn't been a chance like this.

He had to make it count.

"The courtyard burnings, sir, are all very well for instilling fear." The words left a sour taste on Pran's tongue, but there was no time for squeamishness when a Commander dangled in his grasp. "But Tuliikobrets must understand their place in serving the empire. A sense of unique contribution ensures they don't just know that place, but *live* for it."

Lepik frowned. "That could stir up entitlement. Make them feel too important."

"Sir, consider the Nightmares. They guard this fort and are rewarded with prestige among Tuliikobrets. Consequently, the Nightmares immerse themselves in the work—they glory in it. They understand how each assignment contributes to the strength of the empire. It isn't their troops destroying Vesimaan villages, after all. You recall how the emperor had me remind everyone of our origin and roles? That could be useful on a personal scale. Might I be permitted to meet with small groups of Tuliis? In close conversations, I could boost their morale, inspire them to remember why we burn, and of course, what's at stake when the emperor is displeased."

He glanced pointedly toward the courtyard, and Lepik's mouth tightened in a grimace.

"I'll help you get the Tuliikobrets in shape," Pran promised, "in time for the jubilee."

When Lepik still looked doubtful, Pran leaned forward. "It is, of course, when I have Tuliis in my confidence that they'll open up and, intentionally or not, reveal the secret rebellions in their hearts. This is how I'll spy out trouble before it strikes again."

Lepik leaned against the wall, beside that strange cornflower painting, peering at Pran with his wintry stare. "Why are you doing this for me, Nayar?"

Because it was the only way Lepik would leave him alone. Because Pran was now a leader in this fort, in ways the Commanders must never discover, and he couldn't set up his Tuliis for another near trap like they'd walked past last meeting. If getting free of this fort meant talking and moving like a Commander—or at least, pretending to—Pran would do it.

There were hard choices, and he was making them. It didn't matter how dirty his hands got along the way; there'd be plenty of time for washing later.

But to Lepik, he said, "I was told Nightmare rank could be mine within a year if I served well. If this plan, however, proves to your benefit and helps you get that council seat . . . maybe we can make that less than a year?" He grinned conspiratorially.

If all turned out according to his plan, after Jubilee Night Lepik wouldn't have the power to give Pran so much as a cup of water. That was the dream he kept at the forefront of his mind as Lepik nodded. "All right, Nayar. Show me what you can do. But take care not to fail me. I do not like to be disappointed."

"I won't disappoint, sir."

Without Oksana, Novice training wasn't the same. Until she was gone, Pran hadn't realized how much of a presence she'd become in that yard: how the Novices had looked to her first for instruction, how when she'd shown a new technique with fire, they'd crowded around her closer than necessary. How after Sibul chewed them out for some small mistake, a smile or a nod from Oksana had instantly set the young Tuliis at ease.

Now, none of them smiled at all. "She's not here again," said the young Pakastran girl. The first days without Oksana, her shoulders had drooped, but today, she stood rigid with fury.

"You're supposed to trace squares with fire," Pran reminded her. Concentrating on specific, simple shapes helped beginners learn to control the flames.

After fiddling with her flint starter, the girl raised a few sparks. "They say she's working for the alchemist," she muttered, dragging one spark into flame. When she nudged that fire to the side, the whole thing sputtered out, but the girl hardly seemed to notice, glaring instead toward Pran. "I thought she was on our side!"

"She is." His words came out too loud and earnest, and Sibul scowled toward them from across the yard. He gestured back to the girl's flint starter.

"Then why is she helping that man?" The girl raised another flurry of sparks, creating a fireball so large she singed her eyebrows and the wisps of hair straying from her braid.

Of course the Novices despised Rootare, who was always tormenting them with new injections; of course they'd despise anyone who appeared to assist him. As Pran considered the seething girl, his own resentment smoldering toward Oksana huffed out. For all that he hated her being in the lab, he had only to look at what she'd accomplished after a mere few days: suddenly the medicine cabinets in the hospital wing were filled again, and Pran hadn't walked this easy in a long time.

And how could he have expected her to react any differently when he'd told her of his arrangement with Lepik? That plan *was* madness, but he still stood by the decision. These weren't reasonable people they dealt with; there weren't going to be comfortable solutions. Yet he didn't have to lash back so abruptly at her doubt. It meant she cared—about him, and what he meant to her, same as he didn't like her being near the devil who dealt in serums.

The real question was, how was Oksana faring alongside

Rootare? Surely that man must be letting her out to eat and sleep at some point, but Pran never saw her. And the not seeing, the not knowing, sent pain through his heart that rivaled anything he'd felt in his leg.

He had to speak with her again.

To the little Novice, hurling fire through the air as though she tried to burn flies, he said, "Sometimes you have to take a second look to find out what someone's really up to."

The girl did look—at his leg. And though her brow remained creased, she nodded, and the next flame she threw did not fly so crookedly.

CHAPTER FIFTEEN

OKSANA

Oksana stumbled from the lab positively reeking of sulfur, stomach cringing at the stench. She was desperate for a bath, but she had missed lunch and last night's supper, too, while searching through Rootare's notes, all scribbled in some alchemical code.

Although more than two weeks had passed since she'd started in the lab, Oksana had only just begun deciphering the symbols. The ones for elements were easier; she remembered some from her time in Melnyk's lab. With those, she pieced together others. Or tried to. There was far more guesswork than she'd like.

Truth was, she was no closer to finding out what Rootare was up to than finding a way to cut the moon from the sky. If only she could get ahold of his logbook. When he wasn't scribbling it in, he always kept it maddeningly out of reach in his coat pocket.

There had to be something important inside.

But for now, her head spun from hunger. Food always seemed trivial when it came to uncovering what Rootare was scheming. Yet after she'd staggered, dizzy, and nearly dropped a tray of serums, Rootare snarled at her to take a break. With Meal Hall moments from closing for the night, Oksana hurried down the path toward its doors, crunching through ice caked on the paths, batting away snowflakes tumbling onto her face from the low-hanging clouds.

But in the building's shadow, where the air was heavy with odors of burnt stew and stale bread, a hand grasped her shoulder. She nearly jumped out of her stinking skin. Kraanvelt, again—?

"It's all right!" Pran squeezed her arm.

For a moment, she wished it were Kraanvelt, because at least she knew how to respond to him. But Pran, emerging from nowhere and when she'd least expected . . . all the words from their argument crashed through her mind: *I told him I would be his spy . . . You have to know how this will turn out . . . Did you think we could keep our hands clean . . . Can't you trust me?*

Here he was now, eyes round and pleading, and she didn't have the strength for another fight. Oksana opened her mouth to tell him she needed rest, *food* . . . yet she couldn't dismiss him. He stood upright, not stooped with pain. So he was getting his medicine, at least. But it looked like he'd hardly slept since she'd last seen him, and he'd gotten so thin his wrist bones cast shadows across his skin.

Oksana couldn't keep from cupping a hand around his cheek. "Why aren't you taking care of yourself?" she asked, each word fogging the air between them.

"Can we talk? Now?"

Her stomach rumbled, so loudly she would have been embarrassed if she weren't utterly ravenous. As she glanced toward Meal Hall, its doors swung closed. She cursed out loud.

"No, look what I have for you." Pran stuffed a napkin into her hands, filled with black bread and a piece of sour cheese. "That's the best of what they served tonight, trust me. Now, can we talk?"

Staring from that bundle to him, Oksana was at a loss for what to say. She still had half a mind to make him wait until she'd scrubbed the stink of sulfur off her skin. But his shadowed eyes were so earnest that she couldn't refuse him.

Oksana nodded.

He tilted his head to the left and strolled away. Stepping in the opposite direction, Oksana circled back to the storage sheds, where he waited for her. When he stared at the bundle in her hand, it was clear he'd say nothing until she'd eaten. Oksana unwrapped the napkin and bit into the bread. Surprisingly, it wasn't stale . . . how had he managed that? She took three big bites, savoring each as though it were a feast. Never had plain bread tasted so heavenly.

Never had she spent two weeks in alchemical hell.

While she chewed, Pran seemed to shiver. At first she thought it was because of the snow glazing the air. But when she finally swallowed, he burst out, "I hate fighting with you! I hate not talking. I know you're worried, and you're right to be, because if we don't defeat these Commanders, we'll certainly die trying. But I hate it coming between us. I'm not sorry for my deal with Lepik, or any of the choices I make to set us free. But I'm sorry for how I spoke to you."

A classic Pran apology. Oksana rolled her eyes so hard they ached. He knew his convictions and refused to back down. Once he set his sights on something, he went for it, come hell or high water.

They were fire demons. It was always, *always*, come hell.

Setting aside the cheese, Oksana faced Pran. "If you make deals with Commanders, the things they'll expect . . . You can't make up stories and leave them chasing smoke forever. If you promise troublemakers, they'll want names. They'll want someone to *burn*."

Pran huffed a sigh that fogged in the icy air, blurring his face. "Someone would have burned that night, if I hadn't given Lepik a reason to trust me. There was no other way."

"And what will you do when he figures out you're playing him?"

"I could ask the same about you and Rootare." Pran grimaced. "Can we agree we're both doing desperate and probably reckless things?"

"*Probably* reckless?" She groaned, scrubbing at her brow and the headache forming there.

Pran caught her fingers and squeezed. "Yes, and every day I'm grateful you took a reckless chance on me. You never had to help me, and yet you take risk after risk to keep me alive. You taught me I could fight back, and gave me a reason to do it." He brushed his hand along her jaw. "Do you remember what you said on the tundra?"

That was a week she never wanted to remember, and one she could never forget. Only by focusing on Pran had she been able to keep going.

The tundra journey was the final test for Novices. In the middle of the night they were yanked from their barracks, crammed onto the train, and carted to Nyíta. Nightmares gave each of them a fur-lined coat, a flint starter, and orders to travel south to a camp on the Vesimaan border. Those who finished the trip in one week, and survived, were made Tuliikobrets.

Sometimes while wandering, they'd spot Nyítans in the distance. The clans sat bundled on sleds, guiding hundreds of reindeer along ancient migration routes toward their feeding grounds. At any sign of Tuliis, even young ones, Nyítans steered clear. They certainly wouldn't help Novices become cruel soldiers who'd come back to steal their children. Oksana didn't blame them, much. When it came to ordinary people and Tuliis, there was no taking chances. Kindness wasn't rewarded.

But that still left half-grown children, most who knew nothing about this tundra, to survive without assistance. It had been hard enough to scrounge up food, maintain direction in a land where every patch of ice and lichen looked the same, and keep from freezing when the wind screamed.

Pran had to do it without medicine. Four days he'd hobbled along, while the Novices melted ice for water, choked down arctic rodents, and huddled together to stay warm enough to breathe. On the fifth day, Pran had collapsed.

Oksana had dropped to her knees beside him and thumped his back. "Get up."

"I can't walk anymore," he'd groaned.

"If you stay here, you're letting the Commanders win. None of them expect you to reach camp. They took bets on how many days you'd last. How can you stand for that?"

"I can't stand. At all." He buried his face in the snow. "Leave me!"

Other Tuliis had done just that, trudging past Pran with only a glance, if they spared him attention at all. But she'd thrown herself on the ground beside him.

"Listen." She pressed her face against his hood. "I'm not giving up on you. Every day that you keep fighting, you show the Commanders how wrong they are. One day, you'll scorch that lesson into their hearts."

He'd tried to rise onto his elbows but tumbled down. "I can't walk anymore. I *can't*."

"Then we'll help you." With Anu, she'd lifted him. When he'd become too weak to even stagger along, Yalku had carried Pran on his back.

When they'd finally crossed into the camp, Anu and Yalku had sprinted ahead to call for a physician. Oksana had stayed with Pran, spreading her coat over him and cradling his head on her lap. "Be strong," she whispered, and hummed his golden parrot lullaby.

With a gasp, he'd pushed onto his elbows and pressed his lips against hers. "I love you. I want you to know." Then he'd slumped down, eyes fluttering shut, limp in the breathtaking cold.

She'd leaned over him, shielding his face from the stinging ice dropping from the clouds. "You won't die. I forbid it." And she'd held him until a couple of physicians came and loaded him onto a stretcher.

Now, among the crooked sheds, Pran stroked her lips with his thumb. His touch was as soft as the snowflakes tumbling down around them, painting the world white. "Don't you see why I'd do anything to set you free?"

She did, she really did. Yet now she worked alongside Rootare, the man who'd made them into monsters. *Sometimes you're a real hypocrite,* Anu accused, and saints, she was right.

The sooner they finished this fight, the sooner they would no longer have to burn their souls to stay alive.

"What's your plan for Jubilee Night?" she asked, clutching Pran's hand.

He settled against the shed, back in his element. "Eleven more nights until the emperor's celebration. We know he'll invite some Commanders to be honored at his party. The ones left behind, we'll need to separate, draw them out from wherever they're lurking and get them to scatter. If we set fires in key areas around the fort: the armory—"

Oksana's eyes widened. "You better get the barrels of Demon's Tongue out of there, or it will be the last thing any of us ever do."

"The stables—"

"Yalku will *kill* you."

"We'll get the horses out, too! Gods. Anyway, the Commanders' barracks and their tower."

An idea took root in Oksana's mind. For the first time in two weeks, her smile was genuine. "The lab. With Rootare's chemicals, I can rig a fine show. The Commanders will want to save his serums and notes; they'll run to the room in droves. I can even brew a little chloroform to send them to sleep when they come."

The rising light in Pran's face banished the shadows beneath his eyes. He pulled her in for a kiss. "You're amazing."

Oksana smiled again. "Don't you forget it."

CHAPTER SIXTEEN

OKSANA

Four days later, Oksana entered the lab to find one of the emperor's Nightmares inside. "I suggest you get your things together," he said to Rootare, voice gravelly. "Emperor Juhan wants a meeting. He does not want to be kept waiting."

Rootare spotted Oksana in the doorway and gestured for her to enter. Had the Nightmare's presence warped her mind, or was Rootare *relieved* to see her? "I must go to the palace." He packed diagrams into a leather bag. "The serums need tending while I'm away. Do not let them scorch, or I'll inject them into *you*."

Hefting the bag in his arms, he turned toward the Nightmare still waiting by the door.

Oksana realized her best chance was leaving with him. "Should you appear before His Majesty in a dirty coat?" She gestured toward the stains splattered across it: Black from antimony. Brown from celandine. And red, red, red like death, from the verikivi.

"His Majesty is waiting," the Nightmare growled. Though his flint starter remained clipped to his belt, Oksana swore the room grew warmer. Beads of sweat formed on her brow.

Heaving a sigh, Rootare shucked off his lab coat, leaving it on the ground where it fell. With the bag in his arms and the Nightmare at his heels, he disappeared into the hallway, slamming the door behind him.

The moment their footsteps faded, Oksana plucked the logbook from the coat's pocket. Ignoring the simmering serums, she got to work.

First, her chloroform for the Commanders on Jubilee Night: batches of chlorinated lime blended with alcohol. Once those were stuffed at the back of cabinets, in dark glass bottles labeled TINCTURE OF MAGNESIUM, she sat down with the logbook.

Oksana wasn't sure how long she bent over it. It was written in the usual alchemical code, of course. On scrap paper, she scribed her keys and translations, or attempts. There was still too much guesswork. And this book proved disappointingly similar to the stacks of notes: more recipes for failed attempts at the serum. All she learned was the astounding number of ways Rootare had gone astray.

One of the neglected beakers screeched until Oksana's mind splintered. Add to that, her lab mask had grown stifling, making it difficult to breathe, and her goggles were fogging up. Oksana yanked off both, shoving them in her coat pocket, then stood, ready to hurl the useless logbook into one of the burner fires. But as she hefted the thing up, pages fluttering like wings begging to take flight . . . something was written on the very back ones, after the blanks.

Though the beaker still screamed, its cries faded in Oksana's mind as she decoded their words:

Serum R remains too combustible to fully brew . . .

Increased ratio of antimony to verikivi. Serum boiled without igniting . . .

Injected Embers with Serum R. Subjects weathered it poorly but survived. Effects to be seen. Progressing to next stage, Serum R+, with additional verikivi for advanced Tuliis . . .

Embers rampaged with unprecedented strength and speed but lack necessary focus and control for proper coup. Injected several wounded Hellions with advanced serum.

Then, the night of the Kivi attack: *Hellions rampaged. Increased strength exceptional, but at the expense of strategy. Prognosis poor, without Tuliis strong enough to endure this serum.*

Saints alive. Oksana's shaking hands nearly tore the page. She swallowed hard, bile stinging her throat. What was it Rootare had said the day he'd cornered her? *I'm developing another serum. Always stronger Tuliis for Vesimaa.*

Vesimaa. Not Juhan. The new serum was his own scheme.

The shrieking beaker fell silent.

Rootare loomed behind her, hand on the knob beneath that steaming beaker. "I told you not to let these scorch."

Her pulse ratcheted so high it throbbed in her teeth. When had he returned? *How?* She hadn't heard footsteps.

The man snatched his logbook from her hands. Oksana leaped back, putting a row of tables between them. "You injected the Embers. With your new serum. You *wanted* them to Snap."

"I wanted them to end the Commanders. To have shown Juhan what it is to lose everything."

Oksana's legs nearly gave out beneath her. "You . . . you want to—?"

He laughed, a horrible bark like his lungs were coming apart. "Why the look of surprise? You think I want to be here? Because I'm Vesimaan? My parents gave me over to Juhan when I was fourteen years old. Let me assure you, not even the most patriotic Vesimaan child wants this. But I took what control of my life I could still claim, and I earned this position."

"And you want to tear the Commanders down—to what, replace them with yourself?"

"Sometimes you are such a simple creature. Maybe I once had such ambitions. I was supposed to go to university in Vaino and study chemistry. But instead my parents abandoned me here, and I was appointed a messenger." He tugged down the high collar on his shirt, uncovering the demon tattoo across his neck.

"I didn't give up then, oh no. I made my own studies, breaking into this lab and experimenting. They needed a competent replacement anyway; the former alchemist wasn't long for this world. Nobody in this position is. The mercury and verikivi are the worst, but prolonged exposure to any of these chemicals isn't conducive to long life. Just ten years I've been master of this lab, and already my time runs short." Rootare coughed thickly, then scrubbed a hand across his lips. His fist came away streaked with blood.

"Why do this to yourself?" Oksana whispered. "Is revenge worth your life?"

Rootare rolled his eyes. "It's more effective to rebel as imperial alchemist than as a messenger. With the right concentration of verikivi, I can make Tuliikobrets fiercer, stronger, more aggressive. Enough to take down the Commanders and emperor. Juhan stole my life. I'll steal his, and burn down his facade of an empire, too. Under Juhan's reign, this army cannibalizes Vesimaa. So I'll ruin these troops, and I'll end that coward's misrule."

"And along the way, how many people will you kill?" Oksana's skin went cold as she thought of the Scarlet Embers and those Hellions, burned for the crime of being poisoned by Rootare. "You imagine yourself some kind of hero, but you're no better than the Commanders."

"Foolish girl. This isn't about being *better* than the Commanders. This is about *stopping* them, and Juhan. Did you believe we could overturn their ilk without sacrifice?"

Pran had argued the same. Maybe there was truth to it. Maybe being good and moral wasn't enough to bring down a system so deeply entrenched in wrong. But saints alive, she couldn't give in to this plot. Not now, not ever.

"This is your plan? Cause as much chaos as possible, and hope that somehow, someday, the Commanders are slaughtered during a rampage?"

"Hardly." Rootare slumped against a table, looking impossibly old and young at once. "Strategy was always key. Neither the emperor nor Commanders will be taken down without a shrewd fight. Juhan is too ruthless, and as for the Commanders, there are simply too many. Yet every Tulii I've injected Snaps at the wrong time and rampages without reason. I don't want them wreaking havoc, I need them waging war. But without a soldier equal to its effects, my serum won't do its job."

The man's eyes went round. He jerked upright and gaped as though seeing her for the first time. "*You* endured your serum well."

Oksana's saliva turned to sand.

She spun on her heel. Leaped for the door.

Rootare grabbed her by the neck, fingers crushing her windpipe. She punched his jaw, kicked his knees, bit his fingers . . .

"*Enough!*" He slammed her skull against a table. Her vision dulled as she went limp, though her mind still screamed.

Countless times she'd been trapped in this man's presence, bound to a table, pricked, prodded, made to withstand whatever he'd injected beneath her skin. There was no undoing the transformation he'd forced on her, but she'd sworn to never again lie helpless at his hands.

As her vision cleared, Rootare crouched above her,

clutching a syringe filled with ruby-bright serum. "This will make you strong. Unstoppable. *You* will weather it well."

He was going to kill her. He'd already made her a monster. Now he'd make her break, ruining her like the Embers and those Hellions in Kivi.

With a swift kick, Oksana walloped Rootare in his stomach and lunged to her feet. She'd only made it a few steps forward when she slammed jaw-first to the ground.

Rootare had caught the edge of her lab coat. Twisting it in his fist, he hauled her back while she fumbled for cabinet corners and table legs, anything to grasp onto and keep away. The beakers atop the tables rattled, wobbling precariously.

But it was Rootare who dropped beside her, pinning her to the floor with his knees. "You, too, want to be rid of the Commanders. I'm helping you."

He jammed the syringe into her neck.

The serum burrowed into her flesh like a worm. Her blood turned to acid, cooking her from the inside out. She tried to scream, but sulfur seared her tongue and burned away her breath. Tears leaked from her eyes, stinging like brimstone, and her vision warped, dimming and darkening.

All the while, the hissing fires in the room sang her name, begging her to make them grow.

For seven years, she'd been a Tuliikobret. Now she did not know what she was.

She wasn't sure she wanted to know.

She would have no choice but to find out.

Oksana found her voice. She screamed until her throat went numb, until all her breath was spent.

In her heart, she never stopped screaming.

When she fell quiet, Rootare hauled her upright. "You'll be woozy the next few hours. Go to your barrack, sleep it off. When you wake, you'll be strong again. Don't come back here. I don't need you in this lab anymore. Take down the Commanders. *That* is your new assignment."

Beneath Oksana, the floor bucked. Walls spun. She staggered like Pran in his worst pains, lurching between tables. No matter how she ran, the lab doors seemed an eternity away. At last her hand closed around a knob, and she heaved herself into the corridor.

In her barrack, Oksana shucked off her lab coat. Collapsed near her bunk. Heat surged through her blood and sulfur slithered up her throat. She rolled onto her side and retched.

A Tulii at a nearby bunk whirled around, partway through changing into a clean uniform. "What's going on?"

Oksana's vision bobbed and blurred. A thousand years later, she finally recognized who stood before her: Sepp, the girl with the pale double buns.

She didn't much care who it was. "Rootare . . . injected . . ."

With a hand . . . five hands? . . . she gestured to her neck.

"What?" Sepp's voice echoed a dozen times over. "You need the hospital! You need—"

A shrill buzz throbbed through the room. It fed the flames

inside Oksana like Demon's Tongue. The fire ate through her, searing every writhing fiber in her body. Every breath hitching in her lungs. Every thought scattering through her mind.

She couldn't think anymore. Couldn't feel. Couldn't breathe.

Darkness claimed her.

CHAPTER SEVENTEEN

PRAN

Sepp arrived when he was moving through Meal Hall at midday, whispering messages to Yalku and their recruits about the next meeting: *Tomorrow night. Stables. Eighth bell.* At the sight of her, Pran glared. He didn't know who she thought she was, again intruding where she wasn't invited.

"What is it?" he asked as she stopped beside him.

Even for a Vesimaan, Sepp had gone pale. "You need to come with me."

"Where are we going?" Pran asked, following Sepp across the fort grounds. His heart knocked against his ribs as they marched toward Healing Hall. "What's happened?"

"Be quiet! Just come." As Sepp opened the hall's doors, Devak stepped out.

"Nayar." The boy hunched over, shoulders slumped, arms wrapped around his sides.

Pran's mouth went dry. "Devak! H-here for the physicians?"

"They won't help me." The boy's face tightened in pain. "I don't have a medicine token."

He must have been punished, probably for poor performance in training. Guilt surged through Pran, so bitter and rank he cringed. Each time Devak had come to him for help, he'd cast the boy aside. He had failed this Tulii, and now Devak stumbled along, beaten and shamed and alone. "I'm so sorry. I was going to teach you. I—"

Devak scooted from Pran's extended hand. "You're busy. Many need you. I get it."

Pran clenched a fist, empty as his promise. "When I offered help, I meant it."

A frigid wind wailed, flinging ice into their faces. Devak shuddered. "And freedom? Have you given up on that as well?"

"Never. Tomorrow night. The stables, eighth bell."

Devak straightened his bowed back. "I'll be ready."

"You coming?" Sepp's voice had gone curt, as if there weren't enough air in her throat. Pran darted after her, though his legs nearly gave out when she turned for the hospital wing.

If he'd eaten anything, he would have been sick. "What's going on? *Tell me.*"

Sepp opened a door to a room filled with cots and gestured toward one along the far wall. Anu sat by that cot, hunched over the figure bundled there: one with a dark red braid draped across the pillow.

Pran staggered, his hand on the doorframe the only thing keeping him upright. At his side, Sepp whispered, but he registered none of the words. All he saw, knew, was

Oksana limp on that cot, her face drawn and skin ashen. *What happened?* he asked again, but if his lips actually said the words, he did not hear.

"Go to her!" Sepp's voice rang obscenely loud in his ears, though Pran also knew that she'd spoken in little more than a whisper.

At the words, Anu turned toward him, eyes red and wet, while Oksana stirred, peering toward the door.

Sepp had disappeared, and Pran was grateful she didn't stick around—though he still would have appreciated answers. He thundered into the room and grasped Oksana's hand. "Can you hear me?"

She writhed, chest heaving. Those gasps came faster as she peered around, taking in cots, trays, cabinets. "No!" Oksana thrashed in the bed, fighting to rise. "Can't be here. Not near him, not—"

Anu pinned her in place. "That Hellion brought you here. Said she found you in your barrack. Said Rootare . . . *injected* you?"

Pran's heart shot into his throat. "With *what?*"

"He wants me to break like the others," Oksana whispered, voice rough as sand in an open wound.

"*Break?* Wait, you mean he . . ." Pran's knees gave out, and he thumped onto Oksana's cot.

She curled into him, fingers fumbling for the chain beneath her tunic, winding around that pendant of her saint—and his ring, with its once again useless promise.

"The Embers, those Hellions," Oksana rasped, "were his

doing. He's made a new serum. The details, they're in that logbook he always carries. Rootare wants us strong enough to defeat Commanders. But instead he destroyed those Tuliis."

"No!" Anu pressed a hand to her mouth. "The Scarlet Embers . . . that was *him?*"

"And he injected you with the same serum?" Those words tore at the very fiber of Pran's being. He'd known it was a terrible idea for her to go near that man. He'd *known,* and he hadn't talked her out of it. And now . . . *this*. He'd never seen her so gutted, broken. The sight flooded him with a terror like he'd never known. If he lost Oksana . . .

"This is his last mistake." She struggled to her elbows, lit with a fury he'd never seen from her. "Rootare thinks he's sculpted me into the perfect warrior for his revenge. But on Jubilee Night, I will end him along with the Commanders."

No. The refusal reverberated through Pran's bones, so powerful that for a moment he knew nothing else. He wouldn't risk her Snapping, her mind unraveling like the others', if the night's battle pushed her over the edge. He would not allow that to happen—not for anyone, especially himself. Oksana had kept him alive; it was his duty to get her free.

Even if he took the fort on Jubilee Night, if he lost her, the victory would be hollow.

"Listen to me." Pran squeezed her shoulders. "On Jubilee Night, I don't want you anywhere near that lab."

"I said I would help—"

"Well, you're not anymore."

"Why? Because I'm *sickly?*" Oksana arched one eyebrow high. "You hated when Nanda did the same to you. Speaking for you, deciding your limits."

"I'm not making up lies and using those as excuses! Look, we don't know what will happen to you. And I don't want to find out. I won't risk you for my plan."

"You won't?"

"Never!" As if that were even an option.

In one swift movement, Oksana was halfway to sitting, her face less than a handsbreadth from Pran's. "*You* get to decide what *I* risk on Jubilee Night? What battles I take on? Whether I fight at all? Why do you think you get to do that? After what he"—she jabbed a finger upward toward the lab—"decided for me? 'You want to be rid of the Commanders. I'm helping you.' That's what he said as he jammed the needle in my neck."

Anu let out a sob, tears spilling down her cheeks. Pran stalked between cots, shaking with rage. He wanted to punch something. Fury welled behind his eyes, congealing into a brutal headache. Oksana wasn't *listening*. Just like she hadn't listened when he'd said working with Rootare was a terrible idea.

Every day since, he'd wondered what that man might do to Oksana. He'd never dreamed Rootare would transform her again. Now he wouldn't be able to keep her from Snapping, couldn't stop whatever followed that storm.

All he could do, the only way he might protect her, was

to keep it from happening on the most deadly, dangerous night ahead.

"We saw what the Scarlet Embers did in Linn," he said. "What those Hellions did in Kivi. If you Snap on Jubilee Night . . . you could blow our cover or get someone killed. Everything might be ruined. And I've made promises to so many Tuliis."

"You made promises to me, too." She clutched that Horádimian ring.

"I promised you freedom. I can't give you that if you're dead." His voice broke over the words as something deep within his ribs cracked.

He reached to take Oksana's hand, clutch it to his heart, but she slapped away his fingers. "You don't know who will live and die on Jubilee Night, no matter what we do. I want to take the lab. Don't send other Tuliis there, if it makes you feel better. But I *will* bring down that place. And if I do end up Snapping . . . at least I'll rampage against the one who deserves it."

Pran shook his head, blood pulsing so hard he could barely hear his own words. "If a Commander gets hold of you, they'll make an example, same as with all the others. Even if we do survive, we don't know if you'll come back to yourself after Snapping."

"The Embers seemed like themselves after Linn," Anu said.

Pran turned on her, happy for someone to unleash his fury onto. "They'd stopped rampaging. That doesn't mean they were back to themselves! And we'll never know, because they were killed."

Oksana's eyes went wide and glassy. Distant. "I *am* going to Snap. Let me make it worth something." Her focus cleared and she rounded on Pran. Color flooded back into her skin and she sat tall, as though she weren't wounded anymore.

As though the serum made her stronger.

"This isn't only your fight, Pran. Let me decide how much I give. You don't get to make all the calls." Her face softened, and she cupped a hand around his jaw. "You don't *have* to."

But wasn't that what he'd signed up for, from the first night he'd voiced this wild plan for freedom? *There will be hard choices. I can make them.* He couldn't promise freedom only to back out when the way became hard. That wasn't being a leader.

He couldn't bear the failure, the shame, of not coming through on his promises.

Which meant owning up to the gut-clenching truths: Oksana could not fight on Jubilee Night. Not for the sake of the other Tuliis. Not for her own safety and life. He had to keep her far away from the battle. He had to do, say, whatever it took to make that happen.

There will be hard choices. I can make them. If he could go back to that night in the pub, he would thump past-Pran over his arrogant head.

Still, he couldn't deny it: he'd rather have Oksana furious with him and alive, than come to some fragile truce that ended with her dead.

Swallowing hard, Pran pictured barbs, cold flint, and unyielding steel, making himself as all those things. "I have to honor the promise to many over a promise to one. And I've promised freedom to Goblins and Imps, children who barely remember life outside this fort, who've just begun to believe they might have a world beyond these walls. Surely you wouldn't have me compromise their hopes for *your* feelings. The Oksana I knew wouldn't stand for that." He scowled. "But maybe you're not that girl anymore. Maybe this fort has changed even you."

"How dare you!" Anu was on her feet, shoving him away. "After everything she's been through, all she's done? Apologize."

The tears welling in Oksana's eyes spilled over. At the sight of them, Pran hated himself. His only comfort was that his cruel words had hit their mark.

"Get away from me," she hissed.

He did. And he left the broken pieces of his heart on the cot beside her.

When Pran stormed into the lab and no one was there, perhaps he should have known trouble was afoot—when was the alchemist *not* in his lab? Rootare lived for that place the way most lived for air, water, and sunlight.

But he wasn't thinking with reason. He barely thought

at all. His steps were driven by pure fury, agony, disgust, and outrage—at himself, this army, the whole insufferable empire. All that mattered was Rootare paying for what he'd done to Oksana. So in the lab with no one to stop him, Pran snatched a vial of serum, then ran for Commander Tower.

"I have news for the Commanders," he said to the Nightmares standing watch outside. "Urgent news. Treachery in the fort."

"They're in the meeting room," one said, and Pran hauled himself up four flights of stairs, bursting into the room with a shout.

"I have news! Treachery in the lab. The serums—"

Halfway through that door, he froze.

Rootare sat at the head of the long table, and set before him was a brown glass bottle.

Lepik, a few chairs from Rootare, lifted his eyebrows at Pran. "What a coincidence. We were just speaking of the lab."

Behind Pran, a Nightmare guard slammed the door shut.

"Rootare says he's found evidence of an impending attack, including this chloroform planted in his lab." Lepik gestured to the brown glass bottle on the table. "Perhaps you, Nayar, could provide us more information?"

CHAPTER EIGHTEEN

OKSANA

"I told that Hellion to bring him here. I'm so sorry." Anu wiped Oksana's brow with a rag and exchanged her sweat-dampened pillow for a dry one. "I saw her hauling you to the hospital wing. Thought he should also know what had happened. I thought it would help you, having him near. I'd never dreamed he'd—" Anu let out a string of curses, flinging the wet rag into the bowl at Oksana's bedside. "I know you love him, but sometimes he's a real prick."

Oksana sank onto her pillow, clutching the icon of her saint and Pran's ring beside it. Her fingertips clung to the engraved flowers, but when they brushed the words *Ya abetschayu,* she dropped it like a glowing coal.

Pran, always thinking he could single-handedly save the world, just to prove how much he could do. She loved that about him.

And hated it.

She wanted to rage at him for dismissing her out of hand the way his brother had done to him, which irked Pran so badly he'd willingly left with Nightmares to prove a point.

She wanted to rage against him stifling her decisions when there was so little else left to anyone in this fort.

But every time she opened her mouth to scream, she couldn't find her voice.

After all, he wasn't wrong to fear what might happen if she rampaged on Jubilee Night.

Saints, just the thought of it made Oksana want to crawl beneath this rickety cot and never climb back out. When the serum claimed her senses, would she be able to tell friend from enemy? Even if she intended to stay in the lab, would she have enough presence of mind to follow through?

There was no one to ask. All the others had been burned.

Oksana clutched her neck where the needle had gone in. "I can never go home."

"What?" Anu turned around, holding up another blanket she'd snatched from a cot, this one with fewer holes. "No, no nonsense. If there's one person in this fort who deserves home, it's you. And if there's one person who can get you there . . ." Anu scowled like the words were vinegar. "I should find Pran, slap him silly, drag him back by his ear, and make him apologize. But . . . if anyone can get us free, it's him."

Maybe once those words had been true. But Oksana had gone into the lab to fight the man who made demons, and instead he'd forced her to become something worse.

"We don't know what sets off the rampage. If I go back, then break like those others . . . I could lay the village to waste in minutes. My family, all my neighbors, everyone I once knew . . ." Her words dissolved to gasps. "I'm a danger to them all. I can't risk it."

She heard the words as though spoken by another mouth. To her ears, they made sense. Exactly what she'd caution someone else in this situation. But beneath her ribs, her heart unspooled, all her hopes unraveling. A hundred woolly lambs, mushroom hunting, fresh bread, music and dancing, her parents' smiles, her siblings' laughter . . .

They were only going to be memories. A part of who she was, never again who she'd be.

Burying her face in her hands, Oksana slumped forward with a cry that scraped her throat raw.

"Hey, don't!" Anu thumped down on the cot and wound her arms over Oksana's trembling shoulders. "Breathe. Talk to me!"

Only ever memories, a part of her past. They had to stay that way, if she was going to keep her family safe.

Oksana lifted her damp face from sodden hands. "I have to stop him."

"Pran?"

"*Rootare*. He's injected his last Tulii. I'll destroy his serums so he can't hurt another."

"How? Dump them down a privy?"

Oksana snorted. That would serve Rootare right. It'd also be the worst mistake she ever made. "And risk them leaking into the soil, maybe turning everyone in this country into Tuliikobrets? No."

"How, then?"

"I need to experiment." Oksana pushed upright and shoved away the ratty blankets.

Anu caught her elbow. "Where are you going?"

"To get a bottle of serum. I need to figure out what will destroy it."

"You mean, go back to the lab?" The girl's fingers locked tighter over Oksana's arm. "Not on my watch."

Oksana hissed in frustration. Did Anu think such words were helping? Every second she sat on this cot burned through her nerves. If she didn't move soon, Oksana wouldn't have enough courage left to face the lab.

If she were being honest with herself, the last thing she wanted, ever, was to go back there. The memory of Rootare suddenly behind her, knocking her down and injecting her . . . No, she didn't want to go anywhere near that lab. She wished she could sprout wings, fly so far away she'd find a people who'd never heard of Tuliikobrets or alchemy.

Anu squeezed Oksana's hand. "I'll get the serums."

Relief warred with a sick feeling in Oksana's heart. "Rootare won't let you inside."

"If he's there, I'll lure him out. You saw my handiwork with the Nightmares at the gate."

"Rootare is more dangerous than any Nightmare."

"Look, he injected you to destroy the Commanders. If he catches you in his lab, he might make you Snap, force you to do what he wants *now*. But me? I'm nothing to him. Just one of the oldest and most pathetic Imps, too incompetent to be any trouble." She winked.

"And pardon my bluntness," Anu added, when Oksana protested again and lurched to her feet. "But I've seen drunks with more grace than you." She pulled Oksana back onto the cot.

"Rest," Anu declared. "If you're going to take on that man, you'll need all the strength you can get. Stay here, think of ways to destroy the serums. I'll be back with some you can play with."

She tucked another blanket around Oksana's shoulders. The back of her hands were decked with new ink: *Demons came forth* on the left, *Avenging all wrongs* on the right.

Oksana touched a finger to that ink, as if within it was all the strength she'd ever need. "Yeva be with you, my friend."

Anu grinned, then passed into the hallway, out of sight.

CHAPTER NINETEEN

PRAN

"You promised to uncover secret rebellions inside this fort," Lepik continued. "I trust you haven't failed me. Who put this chloroform in the lab? Who's behind this planned attack?"

Pran's ears filled with the buzz of a thousand angry hornets, his vision dimming to that small brown bottle. How had it come to this? The deal with Lepik was supposed to deflect suspicion, give him time to coordinate every interaction with the Commander. But the alchemist . . . Pran's insides curdled at Rootare's sickening grin, and it took all his restraint not to snatch his flint starter and arc flame into the man's face.

But he couldn't lose his head. All twenty Commanders sat before him, and they wanted answers. Names. Pran must not give them any. He'd made promises to his Tuliis, promises to Oksana. He would die before he saw any of them handed over.

Pran threw back his shoulders and stared Lepik down. "It's what's inside the lab, sir, that's the most trouble. Rootare is responsible for the Imps and Hellions who rampaged. He injected them with serums that broke their minds." He held up the serum vial. "Take this, examine it, before he can lie again and cover up what he's doing. And look inside his log-book! The truth is written on those pages."

"These new serums are for Juhan," Rootare drawled. "Ask the emperor himself, if you don't believe me. I've just returned from a meeting with him. Meanwhile, ask this one"—he rose to his feet and strode toward Pran—"what else he knows. Clearly he's been poking around my lab. I'll take that back, thank you very much."

Rootare snatched the vial away.

Empty-handed, Pran faced the Commanders, all of them scowling at him in varying degrees of disgust. Nerves shook through him so badly that his teeth chattered, but he kept his voice steady.

"Those *are* what broke the Scarlet Embers, and those Hellions in Kivi." He gestured again toward the vial, now tucked into Rootare's lab coat pocket—alongside the outline of his logbook. "Take them right here, while you can! Learn the truth. Rootare will tear down the troops and turn the whole empire against us if he isn't stopped."

"How will you prove any of that?" Rootare stepped so close that Pran could see flecks like blood in the man's eyes. "I know how," Rootare added in a whisper. "We both know. Do what must be done. Give her up. Let them break her. Let her break . . ." He tilted his head toward the Commanders and grinned.

Any warmth left in Pran's body evaporated into the

tower's stale air. "That logbook reveals Rootare's plans!" Pran shouted over the alchemist's shoulder, his voice pitching too high as every nerve in his body went white-hot with rage. "That's all the evidence you need."

Rootare turned back to the Commanders. "He's deflecting. Ask again who hid chloroform in my lab. *He knows.*"

Lepik marched around the table toward Pran. "Nayar, enough. I warned you not to disappoint me. What do you know about this chloroform? The attack?"

The whole world narrowed to the space between Pran's breaths. "If you want the source of trouble, search the lab."

Kraanvelt joined Lepik beside Pran. "I see we must beat the truth from him."

With Lepik on one side and Kraanvelt on the other, they marched Pran across the fort grounds, through the prison, and into Kraanvelt's workroom. A metal table was set in the corner; beside it stood a tray laden with gleaming instruments.

"We don't have to do this, Nayar." Lepik caught Pran by the elbow, and deep within his eyes there was a flash of emotion almost like sorrow. "You promised to give me information."

Pran licked his dry lips, forcing his swollen throat to shape words. "If you want to find the source of trouble, check the lab."

Lepik shook his head, then yanked him toward the metal table. Pran dug his heels into the floor, but a spasm tore through his leg and he slumped forward with a gasp.

Steady. He pictured Oksana leaning over him, her hair tumbling around them both like a shield of flame. *Steady*. He pictured his Tuliis in the armory, fists in the air, gazing at him with hope and perfect trust.

Lepik tore off Pran's jacket and tunic. When Pran tried to shove the man away, Kraanvelt kicked his bad leg and Pran crumpled, his breath dissolving into a scream. Terror pulsed so hot through his veins that Pran was back on his feet the next instant, scrambling to break away. But fighting against Commanders was like fighting bears, and Pran was already dizzy from pain. Together, the Commanders heaved him facedown onto the metal table and shackled his limbs in place.

Kraanvelt sparked a flame and spun it thin, then swung it until the fire whip cracked with a vicious snap. "Last chance, Nayar."

Anything else he might give, even a lie, would make someone else suffer in his place. "Check the labs. Check the serums."

Kraanvelt whipped Pran across his back. The fire bit into his skin, scourging deep. Pran bit his lip to keep from crying out, and blood oozed down his chin.

"Well, Nayar?"

"Check the labs. Check the serums."

It was the only answer he gave, even as Kraanvelt struck him again, and again, and again.

The table was slick with blood and sweat and tears and spit. The air was rank from scorched flesh.

"Check the labs. Check the serums," Pran whispered. Another lash seared his skin and his mind shattered.

"Kraanvelt, enough!"

To Pran, the words were muffled as though uttered behind thick walls. They faded entirely as the whip tore again into Pran. This time he couldn't hold back his cry.

"Kraanvelt, stop!" the voice shouted again. "We have it. Nayar was right."

The whip stopped cracking. "What are you talking about?"

"We caught the rebel picking through the lab. Toying with serums." Tamm's voice.

"Juhan's here," she continued. "Wants the rebel brought to the courtyard. He'll make an example of her."

Picking through the lab. Toying with serums. *Her?*

. . . Oksana!!

Pran's swollen eyes flew open.

Lepik stepped up to the table, shaking his head. "What the devil were you thinking, Nayar? Why didn't you just give us the name?"

"He did lead us to the rebel in the end," Tamm argued.

Lepik scowled. "We'll let you live. For now. But another stunt like this and you'll burn on your own pyre."

None of that mattered, Pran *did not care,* not when Lepik's other words echoed with all the fury of the whip's cracks.

Her. Caught. The lab.

Pran would have been sick if there were anything in his stomach.

He'd tried to make everything right. It hadn't been enough.

Oksana . . .

Lepik unlocked the shackles and tossed Pran his tunic and jacket, along with a medicine token. "Get your wounds tended, then join us in the courtyard."

CHAPTER TWENTY

OKSANA

Sunlight changed angles through the hospital windows, going from golden to amber to crimson. As the room dimmed, physicians lit a few chemical lamps that stained the stone walls with an eerie gray-green glow. Oksana lay on her cot, exhausted but fighting sleep every time it tried to steal over her.

Anu had never returned.

Whenever Oksana tried to sit up, her head spun so badly she was nearly sick. Her legs, meanwhile, would hardly move, much less support her weight. But as the last bit of sunlight faded and physicians trundled out of the room one by one, Oksana forced herself to her feet. She couldn't ignore any longer the dread knotting beneath her ribs.

If Anu couldn't get into the lab, or hadn't been able to snatch the serum, she would have told Oksana. Had the Commanders dragged her off to another training? But even that would have ended by now; supper must be half-way through. Anu wouldn't leave Oksana waiting while she stuffed her face with cabbage-and-mince stew.

If she could have come back, she would have.

Ice spread through Oksana's veins. She hobbled from the hospital wing. Outside Healing Hall, the fort grounds were empty. No Tuliis wandered the courtyard. And across it . . . Saints alive. Meal Hall stood dark. The pub, dark. Even Commander Tower, dark.

Everyone seemed to have simply vanished.

Oksana's steps were small, her legs stiff with fear as she crept across the courtyard. "Anu?" she whispered into the night.

"Oksana!"

Her heart climbed into her throat as a figure lumbered forward. Pran.

At the sight of him, she staggered, nearly dropping to her knees. He was hunched over, bad leg dragging. His face was crusty with dark stains and blood oozed down his chin.

"What have they done to you?" she whispered, her eyes stinging with tears.

"You're alive." His voice rasped, scraped utterly raw. "All the gods and their teeth, you're *alive*!"

He fell into her, clinging to her neck. Tears leaked down his face and mixed with the blood. She tucked one arm around his shoulders, but he yelped and squirmed away. His tunic stuck to his back in patches. Dark, wet patches.

"Pran." She cupped her hands around his jaw. "What happened to you?"

He sagged to the ground, his whole torso quaking. Oksana crouched, yearning to draw him close but not daring to touch him.

"Tamm . . . ," Pran gasped. "Said they'd caught some-one . . . in the lab."

He said more, but Oksana didn't hear.

She didn't realize she'd fallen until she was on her hands and knees, scrabbling across the cobblestones. "What do you mean, 'they caught someone in the lab'?" Oksana grabbed Pran's shoulders, ignoring when he cried out. "Where is she? Where is Anu?!"

"South courtyard. Oksana, what—"

She whirled around. Smoke billowed above the court-yard walls, silhouetted against the moon.

"No." She mouthed the word, all the breath punched from her lungs. "*NO!*"

Pran gaped from her to the smoke, horror stretching across his face. "Oksana, don't!"

She threw herself down the fort paths.

Not Anu! Not Anu. *NotAnuNotAnuNotAnuNotAnuNot AnuNotAnu.*

If the saints had to claim a life, let them take hers. But not Anu, do not let Anu be . . .

She hadn't yet reached the courtyard when she heard the song rising with the smoke:

"Out in the mountains
The fires were born
With crackle and flame
On the earth's first morn.

One by one they left their lair
And lit the forests with piercing glare."

Oksana slammed into the gates, but they were chained shut.

"How many times must I tell you?" Juhan's wretched voice boomed across the courtyard. "*I do not tolerate rebellion.*"

Anu was on the platform with him, bound to a metal stake, flames rising up her sides. Smoke undulated across the yard like a coiling snake, and the Tuliis trapped within coughed and gagged.

Through it all, Anu sang on:

"Out in the mountains
The monsters arose
All embers and fire
To fight the land's foes.
With stealth and unflinching ire
They struck, and all smoldered on pyres."

"ANU!" Oksana threw herself at the gates. She tried to scale them, but they were so tall, and she was still too weak to climb them.

"Anu!" She slammed her fists against the bars, but there was no breaking past them. She could not get into the courtyard, could not run to the platform and its pyre.

Could not save her friend.

"Out from the mountains
The demons came forth
Avenging all wrongs
Wrought from east to north.
Tuliikobrets, come, come along!
Guardians to keep Vesimaa strong."

Someone grabbed Oksana's wrist. She whirled around, fist raised to strike.

Sepp. The girl caught Oksana's hand. "You shouldn't watch this. Come with me."

Oksana thrashed free. "I have to help her!"

"It's too late." Sepp steered Oksana aside. "I'm so sorry. They caught her in the lab. Rootare was carrying on about some impending attack, and when they found her inside . . . that was enough for them."

"How? The Commanders never go into the lab. Did Rootare send them?"

Pran staggered from the shadows. "No. I did."

"*What?*" Oksana wanted to scream, but the words coughed out like she'd been punched in the gut. "How *could* you?!"

His eyes were wide and wild, the whites stark against his blood-stained face. "Rootare, he . . . found your chloroform. Told the Commanders someone planned to attack his lab. And Lepik . . . my deal with him. To report trouble in the fort. He demanded answers." Pran scrubbed a bloodstained fist across his eyes. "I kept trying to give them Rootare, tell them what he was doing with the serums. When they wouldn't listen, I told them to go to the lab and see for themselves. Oh gods, Oksana, if I'd known, I never would have . . . why was Anu in the lab?"

"I let her go in my place," she whispered.

Oksana shuddered, remembering the terror of Rootare suddenly there, a creature born of smoke and air. Like all along, *he'd* been the demon.

Tonight, that terror had become her excuse—and Anu's death sentence.

She was Anu's death. She'd made the chloroform, thinking herself so clever, thinking she would bite back with chemicals of her own. But from the moment those bottles were discovered, of course the Commanders wouldn't rest until someone burned.

"Oksana?" Pran loomed before her, cheeks blotchy and eyes swollen. "I'm so sorry."

She couldn't hear Anu's song anymore. Because Sepp had pulled her too far away?

Or because there was nothing more to hear?

Pran sank to the ground, his shaking arms barely holding him upright. "If I could do this night over—"

"You can't!" She lunged forward, fists swinging, but Sepp dragged her back.

Oksana's hand twitched toward her flint starter, breath so hot in her lungs she might raise a bonfire with one spark. She didn't know whether she'd cast that fire toward Pran, or herself.

She didn't know, in this moment, whom she hated more.

"*We* killed her." She slumped forward, legs weakening, all fight snuffed out of her.

"Please, you have to believe—" Pran lurched to his feet, reaching for her, but Sepp swooped between them.

"Do not touch her. Not now." She tucked Oksana beneath her arm. "Will you come with me? Please?"

Oksana let herself be led away, her body an empty shell, everything dear to her scorched to ash.

CHAPTER TWENTY-ONE

PRAN

Yalku led him to the hospital wing. He peeled Pran's tunic off his raw back, eased him facedown onto a cot, and waited at his side for a physician to come. Pran sensed, in the stiff set to Yalku's jaw, that he was desperate to ask what had happened. But if Pran had to speak aloud those moments, if he had to relive them . . . he'd wish all over again he were dead.

"Leave me," he rasped, as Yalku opened his mouth. "Let me sleep."

Yalku frowned, but he left.

Pran did not sleep. He lay rigid on the thin mattress, every shallow breath shooting pain through his flesh, although the most agonizing flares extended deeper than the wounds across his back. The sick horror of those moments when he'd thought he'd gotten Oksana killed, when he'd discovered Anu was being burned alive . . . It would have been far less awful had Kraanvelt taken the fire whip to him again.

He hadn't meant for any of this to happen.

In the end, he'd protected his plan and kept his Tuliis out of the Commanders' clutches. But he wasn't certain he was fit anymore to lead them to Meal Hall, much less to freedom.

You've seen how quickly sparks can become a bonfire. And bonfires show little discretion in what, or whom, they devour.

Damn Nanda, being so right.

"We're ready for you, Nayar." A physician rolled a tray alongside his cot, the wheels' metallic screech like a knife boring through Pran's ears. The man frowned at Pran's leg, going crooked as the muscles seized. "When did you last have an injection?"

"Don't remember," Pran grunted.

"Double dose, then." The physician filled a syringe and pricked a vein in Pran's arm.

Relief flooded through him, the medicine numbing his mind along with his body. He drifted to sleep and dreamed that he was nothing, that the world was nothing, that there was nothing but nothing, and he floated weightless, senseless, painless through the void.

CHAPTER TWENTY-TWO

OKSANA

Sepp brought her to their barrack and sat Oksana on her bunk. "Lie down. Try to sleep."

Oksana pressed her back against the wall and curled her knees against her chest.

Sepp brought water mixed with a splash of something sharp-smelling from a flask hidden beneath her own bunk.

Oksana pushed the drink away. She rocked on her bed, chest tightening with each movement.

She'd never see Anu again. Her friend had been burned like trash. Like . . . nothing.

All because she'd let Anu do a job that was her own battle.

Yeva, why didn't you save her? Oksana sagged forward, forehead against knees. *Why didn't you warn me?*

Was this to punish her for giving in to her fears? Or was it simply the price of freedom?

A piercing cry slipped through Oksana's teeth. She did not want the freedom that came at this cost.

Sepp sat beside her on the bunk. "You planned something, right? Something big. And Tarvas helped?"

"I should never have sent her into the lab." Out of the corner of her eye, Oksana thought she saw flames, but it was only lamplight glinting off a gauntlet. She thought she heard a crackle, but it was Sepp unbuckling her greaves.

She thought she'd given her friend a truth, but it was a lie: *Not everything that comes from fire is terrible and ugly.*

Oksana buried her face in her arms and slumped across the bed. Now, she had more breath than she could ever bear. She stretched her mouth wide, sucked in one more gasp.

Then she howled. The sound pierced through the silent barrack, splintering the still air.

She didn't know how long she cried. Sepp didn't talk again. A part of Oksana hoped the girl had left, that she sobbed without an audience. But when her tears quieted, when she lifted her aching head, Sepp was still there.

The girl scooted closer to Oksana. "Whatever it was you planned to do, don't give up. You were plotting against the alchemist? If you need my help, you only have to ask."

Oksana pushed upright. Scrubbed her face dry, swallowed down the knot in her throat. Anu had died for this fight.

This was not how their battle would end.

CHAPTER TWENTY-THREE

PRAN

When Pran awoke, he was groggy and faintly nauseous. Outside the hospital windows, the sky was scarlet. Morning? No, that light came from the wrong angle. Evening. He'd slept the whole night, and the entire day. The physicians must have given him a third dose to keep him quiet while they worked on his back. He wanted to curl up on this cot and never leave it, but when the physicians saw him awake, they changed his bandages and sent him away.

Just as well. He'd promised his Tuliis a meeting tonight. He had to come through for them at least, make some promises come true. That wouldn't set things right for Oksana, but he might keep from hurting his own Tuliis.

He would not be the cause of one more broken life. That would be worse than failure.

This time, his Tuliis clustered in the stables, among the straw and feed. Yalku set to work grooming horses, whispering to them while he brushed their coats shiny, until Pran shooed him toward his post keeping watch at the doors.

All the other Tuliis arriving brought with them, as requested, additional recruits. They'd outdone themselves, going far beyond Pran's hopes, until he couldn't believe the number of Tuliis crowding around. Then Sepp arrived, leading dozens of Hellions and five Nightmares.

"We're *all* on your side," one of the Nightmares told Pran, speaking in that horrible, gravelly voice, though this time Pran's blood didn't chill at its sound. "All Nightmares wish to join you, though everyone could not abandon their posts tonight, else we'd raise the Commanders' suspicion."

Even as Pran's blood sang with hope, a note of caution rang through him as well. "You mean it?" he asked, glancing to Sepp as though searching for the trick.

"I explained everything to them," she said. "And after Tarvas . . ." Her words failed, and she bit her lower lip.

"Tarvas spoke to us through her song," another Nightmare said. "With her courage, she rebuked us. We knew, back when the Scarlet Embers were murdered . . . we *knew* then. But we were cowards. Now we're done with this life. We must atone. We wish to help others be free." The Nightmares peered around the room, at the younger Tuliis watching them in terror or disdain. Yalku scowled fiercely enough to curdle milk, shaking his head.

But Pran nodded at the Nightmares, searching their eyes and finding only truth. A part of him recoiled at the thought of these Tuliis coming to him because of what had happened to Anu. If there were any way he could take back last night . . . he sucked in a breath, barely holding in tears.

"Tarvas is already gone." Sepp's voice was all sternness. "Nothing will bring her back. Don't let her last actions have been for nothing. Don't be a fool, Nayar."

She was right, as usual. The Nightmares stood in silence, patiently waiting for directions. Though it would be strange to work alongside the ones they'd most feared—for what lay ahead, they'd need all the blue-hot flames they could get.

Pran took his place atop stacked bales of straw, lifting himself head and shoulders above the crowd so he could be seen, and couldn't help smiling at everyone gathered, so many Tuliis . . . until Devak wandered in alone. A bruise marred the boy's face and he limped with every other step, avoiding anyone's gaze and slumping out of sight behind a troop of Imps. Pran's heart turned inside out to see him this way, after all the life a few simple words of encouragement had bestowed.

Tomorrow, Pran vowed. *Tomorrow I'll help him.*

He beckoned his Tuliis forward and unfurled a map. "The jubilee is in six nights. Everyone gather around, and I'll show you our course of action."

They all huddled closer, peeking over each other's shoulders as Pran gestured to his charcoal sketches of the fort grounds. "Our aim is to lure those Commanders left behind into our traps. I'll assign groups to ignite fires at key locations across the grounds: Commander Tower and their barracks, the armory, and the stables."

"What about the lab?" a Goblin asked.

Pran's throat grew tight as he looked over the lab's floor

plan. That would have been Oksana's scene, and she would have done it exquisite justice, but after everything that had happened . . .

"The lab is too dangerous," Pran said, and several Tuliis nodded. "It has too much Commander attention right now, and explosive chemicals we don't know our way around. On Jubilee Night, we stay far away from it. Let's concentrate on areas where we can ambush the Commanders and still maintain the upper hand. We'll ignite our key locations moments apart, which should stir the Commanders into panic and force them to separate as they deal with those fires. At each spot, with large enough groups of our own, we can capture them."

"Then burn them?" one Tulii asked.

Pran waved a cautious hand. "They're better as leverage when the others return from the jubilee. With their lives in our hands, this fort will be ours before the night is through."

Imps and Goblins pumped their fists in silent assent, smiles on their faces and shoulders no longer stooped. They were eager, effusive with hope, and Pran felt it alongside them.

"All of you will be assigned to groups with a Hellion or Nightmare as leader." Pran nodded to Sepp's recruits. When the younger Tuliis saw the trust in his gaze, they stopped squirming away from those Nightmares. "Each group will be assigned a location to burn. Lie in wait until the Commanders come running, but be prepared to spring the instant they arrive. Surprise is our only weapon against them. Everything they've taught you about wounding with fire, this is your chance to show them—"

The stable door slammed shut. "Pran!" Yalku hissed.

Every head whipped toward the boy.

"Kraanvelt." All color leached from Yalku's face. "He's coming. He's not alone."

Gods, *no*. Pran's stomach sank into his boots.

Panicked Tuliis stampeded for the door like animals fleeing a blaze. Pran cursed. If they made this much noise, every one of them would burn before the sun rose.

"Not that way," Pran hissed, then gestured to his right. "Everyone, out those windows. Climb through and scatter. *Quietly.*"

Some Nightmares heaved the windows open and the rest of the Tuliis poured through, dropping one by one to the ground and sprinting in every direction. Meanwhile, with Yalku's and Sepp's help, Pran shoved straw bales across the room to block the door, slow down Kraanvelt and anyone with him. After kicking the last in place, they followed the others through the window. Hugging the stable walls, they slipped into the shadows, their black uniforms blending with the dark. Kraanvelt's booming voice cut through the otherwise quiet night, but no footsteps pounded after the Tuliis. Still, no one dared to slow as they looped around the weathered building, running for the barracks.

As they ran, Pran listened for signs of recruits captured: scuffles, crackling flames, Commanders shouting in triumph, young voices crying out in terror or pain. But the only sounds were their pounding feet and a few curses from the stables.

Up ahead, a lone figure raced toward them through the shadows. Pran halted, thrusting out an arm to stop Yalku and Sepp before they could be seen, but the figure was too small and clumsy to be a Commander. It tripped, yelping as it struck the ground. Pran lunged forward and the Tulii—Devak—wailed, throwing his hands over his face.

"Be quiet. Come with me." Pran shoved the boy forward, after Yalku and Sepp. Only when they were deep within the rows of barracks did the four pause to catch their breath, huddling in the shadows cast by the low buildings.

Yalku paced like a caged animal. "How did Kraanvelt know?"

Pran sank to the ground, clutching his throbbing leg. "The bigger question is, how *much* does he know? Is he searching for *us*?"

Sepp staggered against a wall. "There'd be nowhere to hide."

"There's been a traitor," Yalku said. "Someone did this to us." He rounded on Sepp.

"It wasn't me!" she cried.

If Yalku should be threatening anyone, it was Pran; it had been his job to keep something like this from happening. He glanced to Devak, crouched low and rocking on his heels, worrying the seven knots across his braided wristband until one broke between his fingers.

A sick feeling bubbled up Pran's throat as their gazes locked. How many of his other Tuliis also hunkered in dread, afraid for their lives?

This was not the freedom Pran had promised. He would not fail this mission before it began.

He would not watch any of them burn.

"We have to figure out how much Kraanvelt knows." Pran heaved to his aching feet. "Whether the Commanders have our names, if they're searching for us specifically. Yalku, Sepp, sneak near the tower—get in, if you can—and listen to what the Commanders say. Devak, come with me. We'll return to the stables, and if Kraanvelt is there, we'll—"

"Don't go back there." Devak twisted his wristband so tightly another cord snapped.

"Would you rather wait here? I'll come for you after. Or you could hide in the pub." Pran fished a drink token from his pocket with difficulty—his hand had gone slick with sweat.

Devak ignored the token. "Don't go back there."

"Nayar!"

Pran and Sepp drew their flint starters. Yalku sprang ahead, lunging into the shadows. A yelp sounded, followed by a thud and a groan as Yalku tackled the newcomers. He dragged them forward—two Goblins from Pran's original recruits.

"We've been looking for you," one hissed, his hands in the air. He beckoned and several more Tuliis crept into the narrow alley. "Kraanvelt has an informant," the boy continued.

"We heard him talking. Someone gave him the time and location of tonight's meeting."

Pran's heart hammered against his ribs. "Is he searching for *us*?"

"I didn't hear him mention names," another Goblin said. "But we didn't stick around."

"Do you still want us to spy in the tower?" Sepp asked.

"Yes. If they aren't already talking about the stables, they will be soon. Yalku, you—"

"Where's he going?" Yalku barked.

Devak was scrambling down the alley, away from everyone. In a single leap, Yalku was on him, dragging the boy back by his collar.

"Why are you running?" Yalku shook him until Devak's teeth clattered. "It isn't safe until we figure out what Kraanvelt knows. So where are you going?"

"Release him." Pran could barely hear himself over his shrieking nerves. "Can't you see he's scared? This is more than he bargained for."

Yalku shoved the boy against a wall. Devak thrashed and flailed, reaching for Pran. "Kraanvelt doesn't know it's you. So don't go back to the armory, or he'll figure it out."

"How do you . . . ? *No*." Pran stumbled as the ground swayed beneath him, his brain finally acknowledging what his instincts had screamed since he'd fled the stables. "Devak, you *didn't* . . ."

"Traitor!" Yalku slammed Devak back against the wall.

"You said you'd help me!" The boy strained over Yalku's

shoulder, fists swinging toward Pran. "You said you'd help, but you didn't. So I helped myself. When the Commanders came for me again . . . I thought if I reported rebellion, they'd give me another chance."

Yalku wrapped a hand around Devak's quivering throat. "You sold us out. And expected mercy from the Commanders? You're twice a fool."

"They were going to kill me! But when I talked, they let me go."

It should never have come to this. Not for any of them. Pran staggered back, reaching for a wall to cling to, but they all seemed to have retreated. So had his Tuliis, gazing from him to Devak with widened eyes—except for Yalku, who seethed in a way that made even Pran's breath catch. That, and Devak glaring with a fervent hatred Pran wouldn't have believed the lonely Imp was capable of.

Pran stopped fumbling for a wall and rocked forward, all his weight on his own feet. This mess with Devak was his responsibility—his promises once again unraveling. He had to make it right. He turned to Devak, facing the boy's fury straight on.

"I meant to help you." Each word was molten in Pran's throat, all the more so as Devak swelled with outrage. "I made you promises, and I let you down."

With a steadying breath, he forced himself to stop shrinking, made himself be the leader he'd sworn to become. "But you could have gotten our recruits captured or killed. Maybe you still have." His Tuliis' panicked cries as they fled the stables echoed through Pran's mind, and he was sick again at the betrayal of their trust and dedication. "Your grief was with me. How could you condemn the others?"

The boy spread his empty hands wide. "When have they done a thing for me? When has *anyone* ever done a thing for me? You said you'd help me. But it was all a lie. You only said those things to get me on your side. To *use* me."

Pran's heart seized. "Devak, I meant them! I just . . ."

Bonfires show little discretion in what, or whom, they devour. I don't want you overtaken by the blaze.

He'd made more promises than he could keep, and the fallout would be far greater than a few hurt feelings. Pran wished there were a hole he could throw himself into. But though he might dig until his fingers were worn to the bone, it would never be deep enough to hide his shame.

Devak's lip curled as he looked Pran over. "You're no different from anyone else. In this place, there's only one truth: You take care of yourself because no one else will. Otherwise, you die. So that's what I did. If anyone got hurt, they weren't doing their own job."

Yalku lunged forward, his face inches from Devak's. "When you joined this group, you swore to protect our cause. You've betrayed us all."

A violent flush smoldered across Devak's cheeks. "All I told Kraanvelt was the time and place of the meeting. I didn't give names."

"You gave enough," Yalku said. "They know our group

exists. You betrayed us. Now, you pay." He jabbed a finger toward the flint starter in Pran's belt.

"No, you can't hurt him!" Sepp pushed between Yalku and Devak.

Pran's head spun. "Let's . . . not be hasty. Devak is young. He's frightened. We all know what it's like to be bullied by the Commanders."

"He gave us away and almost got us killed," Yalku raged. "If the others find out you let this little traitor walk away unpunished, they'll never trust you again."

"I hurt him," Pran rasped, no more air left inside him. "I let him down. It's my fault."

"Look. This isn't about making a point or taking revenge," Yalku said in low tones, so only Pran could hear. "Devak has spilled information to the Commanders. He's put a target on his own back. When they don't find us tonight, they'll come to him for more. They'll make him talk again, and they'll make him suffer while they do it, until either they've killed him or he's given away every one of us. *Or both.* Either he goes, or all your other Tuliis end up on pyres."

Pran's senses burned with the reek of smoke and sting of heat as he remembered the Scarlet Embers. The Hellions after Kivi. Anu, singing even as the flames swallowed her.

His Tuliis would not be next. He had to do anything to keep that from happening.

There will be hard choices. I can make them.

Gods, he hated himself.

A shout barked through the air. One of the Goblins scrambled to the end of the alley. "Commanders! They're coming this way. Lepik's leading them."

The last of the warmth in Pran's veins evaporated. Of course it would be Lepik.

"We can't keep him around." Yalku thrust Devak forward. "But we can make it quick. The Commanders won't."

The shouts grew louder, closer.

Sepp grabbed Pran's shoulder. "Don't do this! He's only an Imp. He's one of us."

Pran's knees threatened to buckle, but he forced himself to stand. "He might have cost everyone their freedom. He definitely will if we keep him around. And the Commanders will show him no mercy."

They never did. Everyone knew that. Pran swallowed hard but couldn't banish the taste of metal and bile coating his teeth.

Devak lurched toward him, straining against Yalku's hold. "Please! I . . . I didn't know what else to do."

Pran knew what he had to do, and wished to the marrow in his bones there was anything else. He turned to the Goblins crouched at the alley's end. "Get out of here. Run!" he said, then eyed Sepp. "You, too. Leave, if you don't want to see."

Devak tried to flee as well, but Yalku grabbed him back. "Please!" the Imp shrieked. "Please. I'm sorry!"

Pran wanted to tell the boy he understood, wanted to forgive him.

I have to honor the promise to many over a promise to one. The words were crueler now than when he'd first spoken them.

Didn't make them any less true.

He placed a hand against Devak's jaw, lifted the boy's tearstained face. "I'm so sorry I let you down." Pran met his terror-stricken eyes. His own stung, burned. "I've made terrible choices. But you did, too."

His next moves were a world apart, as if he watched someone else in a dream. As Yalku kept the boy pinned in place, Pran clicked his flint starter to raise sparks, and sent tiny flames into Devak's open, wailing mouth. As those flames tumbled down Devak's throat, Pran urged that fire to burn faster, stronger, fiercer, until the heat instantly torched Devak from the inside out.

"I'm so sorry," Pran whispered as the boy crumpled to the ground, never to rise again.

Yalku scrubbed his hands across his tunic sleeves. "It's done. He can't hurt us anymore."

"Go." Pran spoke to Yalku, though he did not lift his gaze from Devak's limp form, smoke still trailing from between the boy's lips. "Don't let Lepik see you."

Yalku vanished out of the alley one moment before Lepik rounded the opposite end. "Nayar?" The Commander staggered to a halt. "What the hell is going on?"

"Caught a traitor for you, sir," Pran declared.

Then he slumped against the wall and vomited.

CHAPTER TWENTY-FOUR

OKSANA

Sepp arranged the deal with one of her messenger friends. The next time a letter arrived for Rootare, this boy carried it to the lab himself. While Rootare grumbled over the document, that messenger left with serum vials smuggled beneath his jacket, along with a jar of verikivi.

For the next five days, in the dead of night, Oksana turned Meal Hall's kitchens into her laboratory. She and Sepp crept from their barrack while everyone slept. As Sepp kept watch outside, Oksana experimented with her own serum.

"You should kill him," Sepp said, ducking into the kitchen as dawn lit the horizon.

Oksana wiped her sweaty hair off her brow and stirred the mixture boiling over a cook fire. "There are fates worse than death."

"If you're trying to be less cruel, I don't know if this is worth it."

"I don't want to go easy on him." If anything, death was too good for the man.

And yet even after all he'd done, ending another's life

was more than Oksana could bear. It wouldn't honor Anu's memory, wouldn't bring her back. All it would do was force Oksana to live with another stain on her soul, for however many days she had left in this world.

Rootare had stolen more than enough. She'd give him nothing else.

"It'll be better for everyone when he's gone," Sepp pressed.

"Oh, he won't hurt anyone again. He won't have the mind to do so. It will have *combusted*." She nodded to the bubbling brew.

Sepp looked unconvinced. "How will you get this into him? Slip it in his tea?"

"There'd be no way to hide the taste. Besides, I was his apprentice for a time. I thought I'd take a leaf out of his book, this once." She held up a leather gauntlet.

Sepp's mouth opened in surprise, then stretched into a grin.

While her serum simmered, Oksana turned to Rootare's. She didn't dare bury it or dump it down a drain. Mixing it with water would only make more of a mess to dispose of. The best thought she'd had was to burn the serums with the same flames they'd spawned.

"It'll take forever to dispose of these if you have to burn them drop by drop," Sepp mused while Oksana tipped a tiny amount from a vial onto a tin plate.

"With all the verikivi in this serum, if I burn too much at once, it'll explode. And I told you to stay back. I don't have gear for you." At least she'd had her own still in the barrack, where she'd shed it after Rootare's injection. The goggles, left in her lab coat pocket, were cracked after the tussle with Rootare, but still better than nothing. Oksana adjusted them across her face, then raised one tiny flame with her flint starter and cast it onto the tin plate.

White-hot sparks crackled and roared, launching into the air and across the kitchen counters as smoke billowed up.

"Get down!" Oksana threw herself in front of Sepp, covering them both with her lab coat.

When the room was quiet, she pushed to her knees and poked her head above the table's edge. The tin plate was a scorched ruin, stained black and warped like wrinkled paper.

The serum, on the other hand, gleamed as red as if it'd still been in the vial.

Sepp's shoulders slumped. "It didn't work."

Oksana shook her head at the drops, shimmering arrogantly in the kitchen's dim light. "There has to be a way. At the right temperature, even rocks melt. I just need a fire hot enough to do the job."

Like a spark flaring to life, an idea lit up her mind. "I need Demon's Tongue."

CHAPTER TWENTY-FIVE

PRAN

All throughout the next day, Pran's Tuliis confronted him—at Meal Hall, outside the privies, among the barracks, or between training yards.

"You caught the traitor?" some demanded, their eyes blazing coals. "You brought him to justice?"

Others staggered toward him, slack-jawed and pale. "You killed him? One of our own?"

"He betrayed us," Pran said, over and over. "He would have destroyed us. I swore to defend all of you."

The words were practically engraved onto his tongue, but that didn't make them easier to say. He hadn't slept or eaten since, haunted by Devak's face everywhere he turned.

I'm sorry, I'm sorry that I promised more than I could give . . .

An apology the one who needed it would never hear.

Sepp cornered him outside Healing Hall at his worst—while he limped and hobbled, due both for medicine and a bandage change. "I trusted you," she seethed. "I thought you'd be a different kind of leader, not another brute like the Commanders."

"You know what the Commanders would have done when they caught him." It was all Pran could do to keep his chin lifted, to meet her searing glare and not stare at the mud staining his boots. "Devak wasn't going to survive the night either way. And at the Commanders' hands . . . he'd have wished for death a hundred times over, before they ended him."

Whatever she was going to say next, she caught between her teeth. "Don't pretend there isn't still blood on your hands. It will catch up to you."

And though he stood by what he'd said, she wasn't wrong.

"How many have I lost?" he whispered. "How many Tuliis will no longer join us on Jubilee Night?"

Sepp sucked in a noisy breath. "All will still fight. Because all are on the side of freedom."

Freedom's side. Not his.

That was fair. Until he came through on a promise, that was more than fair.

When the letter arrived three days later, the copper crown waiting on the roof of Pran's barrack, he almost lit a fire and tossed the paper in without reading. The last thing he needed was another guilt trip from his brother.

But as he reached for the flint starter on his belt, something made him stop. Pran held on to the letter and walked instead to the storage sheds, unfolding it amid their shadows.

This letter was bright with the illustrations he usually received from Nanda, sketches made vibrant with watercolors: The mountains surrounding their city, lush with mist and vegetation. Waterfalls like ribbons of white silk stretching down cliff sides. Impossibly thick trees dripping vines as if they were melting candle wax. The bright red hornbill who'd knock at their kitchen window every morning with his enormous beak until someone gave him a fig or slice of guava.

There were people, too: Nanda and his partner Jiyn, the two young men hand in hand, looking through books in a street-side market. Their father with a cup of masala chai, his head tipped up, watching the stars. Their mother frying parathas in a pan. Pran's mouth watered, remembering all the mornings he'd woken to the smell of those flaky flatbreads. Best was when his mother stuffed them with spiced eggs or cheese. Then he'd march off with the whole plate while his mother alternately laughed and scolded him to bring it back.

Only three sentences were written across this letter. Pran read them over and over until he could have recited them in his sleep:

Remember all you come from. Remember the people who love and stand by you. You will overcome and thrive when you lean on the shoulders of the strong people at your side.

Tumha Bha'uu

This letter, Pran did not burn. All of them he'd had to, eventually—it was too much of a risk keeping them around. Someone would find them no matter how he hid them. But this one he tucked within his tunic, holding the words at his side.

If his plan came through, if he took the fort, he would never have to let this one go.

The next day, Pran snuck a letter of his own onto Oksana's bunk. More than once he'd been tempted to crumple the paper and toss the whole thing aside. But he could not let her slip away, at least not without one more effort on his part. So he'd gritted his teeth and captured his words in ink before his heart failed him.

I am so sorry. I cannot say it enough. If there were any way I could change that night, any price I could pay . . .

Oksana, I hope you are not alone. I hope you are with those you can trust.

Maybe one day, he'd be among that group again.

CHAPTER TWENTY-SIX

PRAN

In his office before a full-length mirror, Lepik adjusted his new council livery—black broadcloth trimmed with braid spun in the Tuliikobrets' colors of red, orange, blue, and white. Earlier that day, he, Kraanvelt, and Tamm had received the livery along with invitations to be honored at the jubilee that night with appointments to the Imperial Council—a reward for catching the rebel who had planned to destroy the Tuliikobret lab.

Pran wanted to tear that uniform to pieces, then set each scrap on fire. Instead, he stood beside Lepik's desk, hands clasped behind his back, jaw so tight every tooth hurt.

"I nearly demoted you." Lepik glared at Pran through the mirror. "When we raised you to Hellion rank, there were strict expectations for your behavior, and you've failed every one."

"Yes, sir." Pran dipped his head in a semblance of contrition. The man expected him to cower, but Lepik's scorn tumbled off Pran like rain from an oiled coat. Come morning, Pran would either command this fort or lie smoldering in ashes. There was very little that man could do now to hurt him.

Lepik blathered on, as if any of his words still mattered. "Eventually you did lead us to those traitors, but you should have turned Tarvas in without games. And as for Devak, you should have brought him to us for punishment, not taken it into your own hands."

Pran met Lepik's glare without blinking. He'd never stop feeling sick over what he'd done to Devak, but he did not regret sparing him from the Commanders.

"While I'm away at the jubilee," Lepik continued, "you will patrol the fort walls alongside the Commanders staying behind. Any suspicious business and they'll have you bound for a pyre by sunrise."

Pran glanced to the south courtyard, its corner visible from the window in Lepik's office. His lips curled in a grin. One way or another, those walls would reflect flames tonight.

But when Pran spoke, he kept his voice meek, the picture of a reformed rebel. "As you wish, sir."

OKSANA

She waited until sunset, watching from the shadows beside the armory as the Commanders set out for the jubilee. Lepik, Kraanvelt, and Tamm strutted like proud foxes in their council livery toward the fort's gates. Juhan waited there, along with a handful of nobility he'd brought to view the fort. No doubt this was some privilege given to them in return for one favor or another. Those stuffed shirts peered about in various degrees of unease or terror, none of them venturing forward, as though at any moment, Tuliis might launch from the roofs and attack like feral animals.

Or maybe they simply didn't want to get their clothes dirty. The women paraded about in such enormous bell skirts it was a wonder they could move at all, while the men pranced in formal coats with tails so long they swept the ground. Oksana was disappointed that nobody tripped.

When Lepik, Kraanvelt, and Tamm reached the gates, they greeted the visitors, bowed to Juhan, then climbed into a crimson carriage. A cluster of other Commanders, those invited to attend the celebration, climbed inside a second carriage. Juhan and his entourage piled into a third, their own golden ride, and all the carriages rumbled onto the street, turning toward the festivities.

The moment the gates slammed shut, Oksana strode toward Healing Hall, where burner flames flickered in the second-floor laboratory windows. One of her coat pockets was heavy with her serum for Rootare. In her other pocket, she'd stuffed a bottle of Demon's Tongue.

Yeva, guide my hands. Help me put an end to the one who's stolen so much.

As she stepped through the lab doors, a voice called amid the beakers and steam. "There you are, Oksana. I'd hoped you'd join me tonight."

CHAPTER TWENTY-SEVEN

PRAN

He strode across the fort walls, decked in battle gear: scaled greaves, gnarled antlers, night-dark eyes, and a staff topped by a tiny chemical lamp. The sun had barely set, yet Mennick's streets were packed with those celebrating the emperor's jubilee, dressed in vibrant fire-colored clothes. Many carried chemical lamps on poles, swinging them while they chanted Vesimaa's anthem, praising the flames that had freed their country.

"No one challenges the flame!" one bold-voiced man proclaimed. "No one defies the flame! No one defeats the flame!"

On the horizon, the Imperial Palace gleamed. Atop its turrets burned bonfires of every color, the towering white walls reflecting their swirling glow. Opposite palace and fort, tucked in the farthest corner of the city, Ceremony Hall loomed against the Terhi River, which watered all of Vesimaa. Only the wealthiest and highest-ranking aristocrats would be permitted within that hall to attend the jubilee, but street vendors lined every path along the way, making merry for Mennick's ordinary folk. The scents of their food wafted through the air: roast lamb and pork, layered honey cakes, and fresh-baked cinnamon kringle. Other vendors offered glittering red scarves and sparklers, and children played with these as if they, too, could cast flames.

But many Vesimaans did not tread so joyfully. They walked in small, silent groups, waving no lights, twirling no scarves, ignoring the street vendors and their tempting wares. Like the scents of food, the tension rolling off these groups could be sensed from atop the fort walls. Pran's scalp tingled and he squeezed his staff until his knuckles popped.

Beside him, a Commander paused. "Anything of interest out there, Nayar?"

"Nothing that merits concern, sir." Pran scooted from the wall's edge, but the Commander was no longer paying him any mind, instead glaring sulkily toward Ceremony Hall and the celebration he hadn't been invited to join.

In Imperial Square, the bell tower tolled and a sea-green bonfire ignited atop it like a crown. Jubilee Night had officially begun.

Pran peered down into the fort grounds, where Yalku waited in the shadows below. As though swatting aside snowflakes, Pran flicked his hand from his chest. Yalku tapped his brow in acknowledgment, then crept off to settle the Tuliis into their starting positions. After Lepik's threats of pyres, Pran had picked a new place to kick off tonight's chain of fire, and the Tuliis had cheered when he'd shared the news.

May that fervor carry them far.

Pran's blood thundered as he resumed his fake patrol. For all the hundreds of lives depending on him this night, one kept sweeping to the front of his mind: a pale face framed with fire-bright hair. He was certain Oksana wouldn't sit idle tonight. Whatever she had planned, Pran pleaded to anyone who might listen—even that saint of hers—that she'd be safe.

"I'm thirsty." The sulking Commander eyed Pran. "Go to the pub and fetch me a mug of—"

A roar ripped through the night, followed by a blinding gleam and a wave of heat that scorched Pran's skin.

He spun around, putting everything he could into appearing alarmed. With his heart pounding as though it would erupt, that took surprisingly little effort. "Trouble in the south courtyard!" he called.

"What—?" The Commander shoved past him.

The courtyard blazed, all its stonework doused in Demon's Tongue. Some Nightmares had smuggled it out from the armory, and Pran poured it there himself before ascending this wall. The act was symbolic only, as the whole courtyard—with its execution platform—was designed to withstand fire, but nevertheless the sight of that hated space ablaze was the sweetest serum Pran had ever known.

Commanders raced across the walls. "Sibul, Leok, Teder!" one barked. "Get down there."

The three had hardly descended the stairs when the stables ignited. All the horses within had already been moved to safety, but of course the Commanders didn't know that, and four more rushed toward it, shouting.

A third roar. "There! And there, and there. The Commander barracks!" Pran shouted, as each row, tucked into the four corners of the fort, burst into flames.

"Don't just stand there, Nayar! Help put out those fires." A Commander slapped Pran across his back, but he scarcely felt the sting to his wounds. He ran down the stairs leading from the wall top to the fort grounds, counting silently. Before he'd reached the last step, the armory lit up.

"Forget the barracks," a Commander screeched. "Put out the armory before the Demon's Tongue ignites!"

Of course, Pran had removed those barrels. And of course, the panicked Commanders didn't know that, either.

"Get them," he whispered as he passed Sepp in the shadows.

She led her group of Imps out of their hiding spot with a whistle and a hiss. Their whole group ran silently forward to ambush those Commanders and bind them in chains Nightmares had stolen from the prison.

Pran grinned to see his Tuliis moving so seamlessly. Time to meet Yalku and guide their own group to ignite the last fires. Sparking flames, he turned for Commander Tower.

The fort's alarm erupted to life, bells clamoring as if the whole world were dying.

CHAPTER TWENTY-EIGHT

OKSANA

Rootare leaned smugly back in his chair, studying Oksana as if he'd sculpted her from clay.

"I knew you'd weather my serum well. Yet you disappoint me. Why haven't you taken down the Commanders? Well, I'll give you one more chance." He stepped to the nearest window and opened it wide. Outside, the fort's bells screamed as if they were roasting on a pyre.

"I'm not your rat to use as you please." Fury seared through Oksana, scorching away all fear. "Maybe your serum didn't work on me. Maybe I'm stronger than it. Stronger than *you*."

"Is that what you believe?" He smiled indulgently. "If that were true, why have you given yourself to my power?"

"*Given* myself?" Oksana spat. "You threatened Pran. Injected others with a serum that's broken them. I never came to help you. I came to *take*!"

Tipping his head to the side, the man watched her as though considering a fascinating chemical reaction. "Such a simple creature. Those little morals and virtues you cling to make you so easy to manipulate. Clearly, you envy me."

Oksana recoiled. "You have nothing I want. You *are* nothing I want."

"Don't misunderstand. You also hate me. And fear me, which is why Tarvas and not you was caught in my lab and cooked alive. But you absolutely envy me."

He rose to his feet and circled Oksana, his footfalls echoing across the lab. "I was only fourteen years old when I was dragged to this fort, remember. Like you, it wasn't by choice. Unlike you, I made myself into someone of consequence. Because unlike you, I didn't cower before my fears. Didn't hide behind a wall of so-called morality that kept me from what I wanted. No, I made ruthless choices, and through them I brought about *real* change."

Acid seared her throat, burning worse than any fire. "You make Tuliikobrets. Give Juhan reasons to steal more children from their homes."

"Look wider, my dear. The army is in disgrace, the troops in disarray. The Commanders divided. I got to kill one with my own poison, and they had to watch. *That* is power. I could torment anyone I wanted. Protect anyone I chose."

He brushed a hand over her cheek, lingering on the burn marks left from Kraanvelt's interrogation. "You cannot claim the same. Your boy is broken, your friend dead. And you didn't stop any of it."

Those words hit like a boot to the gut. They dragged her down, pulled her beneath waves of grief. In their depths, she saw Anu's face, hair drifting like seaweed in a current. The girl smiled, but her eyes were hollow, lifeless.

And Pran . . . she saw him as she last had, bowed by pains she couldn't begin to understand. He'd thought he could save the world with bold words and clever plans. Instead, they'd pushed each other so far apart, she had no idea how to bridge the gap.

Rootare lifted an eyebrow high, then leaned out that open window. "Up here!" he yelled, waving his arms. The white sleeves of his lab coat were stark against the deep night. "*Up here!* In the lab."

"What are you doing?" Oksana ran forward, one hand raised to shut the window. With the other, she reached for the bottles hidden in her coat.

But Rootare caught her arms and pinned them still. "Make the most of the hand you've been dealt," he whispered between the bell's clangs. "I've shared my power. All that remains is to Snap. Help me destroy the Commanders and this army that eats Vesimaa from the inside out. Snap, and ruin them with the flames they forced you to wield. And if that still doesn't work . . ."

He shifted his hold on her, and from his pocket, pulled a syringe with a serum dark as the void. "Stick the Commanders with a poison strong enough to end their kind in abject misery. So help me, they will not last this night."

CHAPTER TWENTY-NINE

PRAN

The fort's alarm clanged with such fury that each knell echoed through Pran's bones. Staggering to a halt, he gaped toward the tower. Had one of the Commanders slipped inside, set off the alarm?

It would bring back, too early, those who'd gone to the jubilee.

Someone had to watch for them, warn the others when they arrived. Pran looked around, but all his Tuliis were occupied taking down Commanders at their assigned posts. He turned on his heel, to sprint to the wall and watch himself, when shouts barked out from Commander Tower, followed by young voices screaming in terror and pain.

Yalku was in there, along with a pack of Imps assigned to him for the night.

Pran clenched his jaw, then ran for the tower.

Inside, the lower floors blazed. The Tuliis had done as he'd asked, breaking windows, stacking documents and furniture beside them, and lighting it all up so the flames would be visible and draw Commanders inside.

Pran sprinted up the spiraling stairs, cursing his leg each

time it threatened to give out. He clung to the walls, the steps, shoving himself forward whenever another frightened cry cut through the air.

Halfway up, he found them, in the flaming ruins of an office. Yalku lay on the floor, barely stirring, a goose egg swelling on his brow. The Imps were backed against the wall, uniforms smoldering, faces burned and soot-stained, but still trying to stand tall and face down the two Commanders stalking toward them.

Only surprise was on Pran's side. Summoning the deepest, hottest breath he could muster, Pran lunged into the room, screaming and sparking a flame that licked the ceiling.

OKSANA

She stared from the syringe to Rootare, his face twisted in a mockery of kindness. His glasses caught the glare from a nearby burner. That took her back to every time she'd been trapped in this lab, when all she knew was the flash of light against those lenses. Waking nightmares, always followed by the sting of serum in her blood, until the day she was declared no longer human, but a true Tuliikobret.

Oksana spat at Rootare. "Without you, there are no Tuliikobrets. Your time is over."

When he released her to wipe his face, she snatched the serum and Demon's Tongue from her pocket.

Rootare glanced at the bottles, unconcerned. "Put those away," he said, as footsteps pounded down the hallway toward the room. "For what's next, you'll want your hands free."

The lab doors screeched open. Kraanvelt, Lepik, and Tamm rushed in, still in their council livery, though it was disheveled now from their haste.

"Put your hands in the air," Kraanvelt barked at Oksana.

Like hell. She yanked her flint from her belt, but before she could spark, Kraanvelt caught her by the neck and pinched a nerve that dropped her to her knees, breathless with pain.

Rootare cackled. "You three back already? My alarm worked better than I'd dreamed. So glad to have each of you leap when I call."

Lepik stalked forward. "What's going on, Rootare? Is this Tulii threatening you?"

"By all means, keep roughing her up," Rootare said, as Kraanvelt kicked aside Oksana's flint starter and twisted her arms behind her back. "You might finally get her to Snap. She's been especially challenging, my little gem."

The Commanders stared.

"You *were* behind those attacks," Tamm said.

Kraanvelt dropped Oksana and turned his flint starter toward Rootare. "You're under arrest."

"Going to torture me?" The alchemist sneered. "You're just an overgrown Tulii. I create your kind. Without me, you are nothing."

"You're a traitor," Tamm said. "We'll finally prove it to the emperor." She sprang toward the alchemist, Lepik hot on her heels.

Oksana snatched up her flint starter and scrambled back, but her body was slow and clumsy after Kraanvelt's abuse. The man rounded on her, clicking his flint starter and raising sparks.

"I should have killed you after Kivi, girl." He lobbed a fireball, one that swelled as it swooped toward her.

Oksana's pulse stuttered. Her fire wasn't enough to fend off a Commander's. Her fingers closed around the bottle of Demon's Tongue in her pocket.

She tugged it free.

Pried off the cap.

Threw it toward Kraanvelt's flame.

Dove beneath a thick table piled with leather-bound notebooks.

The explosion rocked the whole room. It didn't drown out Kraanvelt's scream.

When Oksana peeked from beneath the table, half the lab was on fire and Kraanvelt was on the floor, hands over his face, thrashing into tables. Beakers toppled, raining serum down on him and the floor.

Rootare's laugh barked over Kraanvelt's cries. "I knew you'd come through for me, Oksana."

PRAN

As the Commanders whirled toward him, Pran ducked before they could turn his own fire against him, half running, half rolling to the far side of the room. A few of the Imps tensed as if to sprint away. But Pran motioned for them to hold their ground, and not a moment too soon: the Commanders sent flames roaring through the doorway that would have consumed any escapees. Then one stalked toward Pran, the other to the Imps, both Commanders summoning new rounds of flame.

Pran's mouth went dry. There'd be no outburning these men, but there was nothing else he could do against them. So he drew in a breath, sparked his flint starter, feinted to the left while searching for an opening on the Commander's right.

Yalku sprang up, bludgeoning both Commanders across their skulls with his flint starter. He moved like wildfire, so unearthly fast that Pran gaped, nearly getting his head burned by the Commanders' half-formed blaze.

"They should have made you Hellion," he said once both Commanders slumped, unconscious, across the floor.

Yalku thrust his flint starter beneath Pran's jaw. His eyes were unfocused, his hand wobbled, yet his stance was nothing but fierce. For a moment, Pran was truly afraid of his friend. "Say that again," Yalku growled, "and I'll drop you like these monsters."

Pran lifted his hands in surrender. "All I mean is, I'm glad you're on my side."

He reached to steady Yalku, but the boy peered behind Pran and lunged forward, flint starter swinging again. With a cry and a thud, one of the Commanders toppled back to the floor.

"I always have your back," Yalku said. "Aren't you lucky I'm an excellent friend?"

Pran was leaning down to bind their newest prisoners when shouts wafted through the broken windows.

"Fire! The lab is burning!"

Pran nearly tumbled onto one of the fallen Commanders. He hadn't assigned troops to the lab . . .

Yalku jerked his head toward the door. "I'll finish here. Go see what's happening. Don't let anyone tear this night from us."

"Never." Pran sucked in a breath, steeling himself as he began the long run down the spiraling tower steps and across the grounds to Healing Hall.

CHAPTER THIRTY

OKSANA

"Watch out!" a familiar, dreaded voice screamed from behind.

Oksana froze, something inside her turning to stone. She couldn't look at Pran, not even from the corner of her eye.

Another shout. Lepik lunged at her, a fireball the size of her head spinning in his hands. And there was no more Demon's Tongue in her pocket to meet it.

For the first time, she yearned to Snap. If ever she had to attack with the mindless ferocity of those Hellions in Kivi, it was now. But she didn't know how to awaken the monster inside.

She wanted to scream until the stars shook from the sky. If she'd had to endure the serum, had to wonder helplessly how it might destroy her, why couldn't it rear its head when she needed it?

An enormous ball of flame roared from the doorway, bowling Lepik over. When Tamm rounded toward her next, Oksana raised a white-hot flash of fire. As Tamm staggered back, arms thrown up over her face, Oksana sprang for

Rootare, the man dodging fires and broken glass, lurching across the lab toward its open doors.

PRAN

Lepik dodged the second flame Pran hurled, then swung his flint starter. Pran barely ducked the blow to his skull.

"I granted you power," the Commander growled. "But you played me for a fool."

Pran feinted low, then spiraled a flame high and dropped it onto the Commander. "I played you as you are."

Inside his gloves, his palms were slick with sweat, and more slipped down his brow, dripping into his eyes. Pran swiped at his face with the hand that wasn't holding flint. *Of course* the Commanders had returned while he'd been distracted in the tower. He couldn't let any more of this night unravel. Pran tried dodging around Lepik, all the while searching for where Oksana had gone, but Tamm limped forward, blocking his way. Even Kraanvelt hauled to his feet, a ruin of blistering burns, his hair and uniform still smoldering. Pran couldn't help being impressed—and horrified—at Oksana's handiwork.

Let no one ever underestimate her again.

"Think you can take us on your own?" Lepik clicked his massive flint starter, raising sparks as long as his fingers. "You're dead, Nayar."

"But I'm not alone." Footsteps thundered up the hallway and burst into the lab: Sepp, along with Yalku, carrying a dented, soot-stained Commander's helmet.

OKSANA

She barreled into Rootare before he made it halfway across the lab. They hit the floor in a tangled heap beside the wreckage of a workstation.

"You want me to destroy the Commanders," Oksana hissed, crouching over him, "but won't stay to watch it done?"

Thick, choking gasps heaved from the man's throat. Blood stained his teeth and pooled in the corners of his lips.

He laughed. "I knew you'd fight them for me. Knew you'd do what was needed."

"I never came to help you. I came to destroy!"

"I admire your ambition, thinking you can be rid of me so easily. But I didn't become imperial alchemist by creating work that could be undone by a half-trained child. I've left my mark on you forever." He touched a finger to the spot where he'd injected her.

"SHUT UP!" Oksana slapped away his cold hand.

He shook his head. "You'd be so much *more* if you weren't afraid to reach out and grab what you want. Quit hiding behind excuses and grow a spine. If you refuse . . . well, maybe another Tulii has the grit to make lasting change."

Everything inside Oksana went sour. She could not let him torment one more Tulii.

She had to make that impossible.

Beside her lay Rootare's syringe of poison.

Did you think we could keep our hands clean? Our choices easy and light?

The words, everything within them that she'd resisted for so long, blared through her with all the fury of the fort's alarm until her mind was a ruin of tiny broken pieces. Screaming, she struck Rootare across the brow with her flint starter, knocking him back down. Before he could move again, she scooped up his syringe of poison and stabbed the needle into his neck.

As the serum oozed into his flesh, Rootare squirmed, hissing and groaning.

"Not so nice, is it?" she said. "Think of every Tulii who's suffered under your hands."

Saliva and blood bubbled in Rootare's mouth. He tried to spit, but his throat and tongue strained . . . into another laugh. "Felled by my own venom. The most beautiful way I could have gone out. Thank you, my dear, for this last gift. This final mercy."

His eyes lost focus, his breath faded. When Oksana touched his neck, there was no pulse.

She dropped the empty syringe and lurched to her feet. Staggered to the open window and vomited over its ledge, heaving until her ribs ached.

Rootare was a monster. He'd used her. Would have kept

using her, hurting her, hurting others through her. The man had to go.

Still, the stain of murdering him bled through her heart. Not because she'd killed a terrible man, but because she hadn't been able to *escape* that. All these years in the fort, there was an evil she'd been desperate to keep apart from.

But in the end, that evil had overpowered her.

CHAPTER THIRTY-ONE

PRAN

As Tamm and Lepik hurled fire, Sepp and Yalku lunged alongside Pran, the three of them meeting the onslaught with their own flames. The Commanders were relentless, their blazing pillars nudging Pran and the others against the wall. Pran's face grew tight from the heat and sweat poured into his eyes, but he kept throwing flame after flame.

Until he was only bones and ash, he would not stop.

As their backs touched the wall, as the Commanders summoned one last incandescent round to scorch them through, more feet pounded into the lab: Nightmares, Hellions, and Goblins. All of them pit their fire against the Commanders until the room was noon-bright and the Commanders were trapped in one corner of the lab.

Pran barely felt the ground beneath him as he stared down their former masters, now bedraggled and smoke-stained. It was all he could do not to laugh, that he'd taken down the people who for seven years had made his life hell. That he, who nearly hadn't survived transformation, now led Hellions and Nightmares in revolution.

Though his head spun in nauseating circles, when he

spoke, Pran's voice was strong. "Drop your flints," he ordered those Commanders.

"You do not give orders," Kraanvelt rasped. "*You* obey *us*." His words would have had more impact if he weren't clinging to the wall to keep standing.

"The Tuliikobrets have sworn allegiance to a new authority."

Across the fort, cries reverberated, drifting through the open lab window: *"Freedom to the flames! Freedom to Tuliikobrets!"*

"We have your fellows." Yalku kicked forward the battered Commander's helmet he'd brought. "We can treat them as you've treated us. Except I see we already have." He glanced toward Kraanvelt, who was making a valiant effort to remain on his feet, though anyone could see from his gritted teeth and shaking limbs how much agony he was in.

"When the emperor hears what you've done," Tamm said, "he'll destroy you."

"Worry about yourself," Pran said. "You think he'll come to your rescue? Perhaps we should drop you outside the gates and see how you fare under his mercy. Or we can end you here."

Every Tulii in front of the Commanders clicked their flint starters and raised sparks.

Lepik's eyes went round with terror. "Nayar, let us live and we'll hear your terms."

"Drop your flint starters. You'll join your fellow

Commanders in prison. Any resistance, any attempts to fight back, and we'll roast you."

As the Tuliis, led by Sepp, clapped the Commanders in chains and steered them away, Yalku stepped forward. "There's an envoy from the emperor at the gates."

Pran heaved a sigh through his teeth. Even with the Commanders locked away, this fight was far from over. "Let them in, but make them wait. Please. I just need . . ." He nodded to Oksana clinging to the windowsill.

Yalku pursed his lips. "Don't be long."

His footsteps had hardly disappeared down the hallway when Oksana screamed.

OKSANA

She was barely aware of the raw sound tearing through her throat. Beneath the weight of this fort and its evil stain on her, Oksana collapsed, slumping forward until she sank to her knees.

Deep within her, something unraveled.

"Oksana?"

Pran, calling to her from across the lab. Striding toward her. "It's over! The fort is ours. We're safe."

His words rang with confidence. But when she focused on him, she saw the cracks within. He'd played the Commanders' game, while she'd refused.

Both had lost, and they'd done it to themselves.

Oksana leaned out the window, tears dripping off her jaw, and screamed again into the night. Her heart beat so violently that pain throbbed through her ribs, up her spine, and into her skull. Each beat tore through her, mangling her cries, thoughts, senses, until only a single emotion remained.

Rage.

As consuming as the need to breathe.

Oksana clung to the windowsill, scrambling to hold on to her mind.

She was Snapping.

She couldn't, not now! Rootare was dead, he had no more power over her, she'd *killed* him to make that so. She couldn't let him win again, after everything she'd lost.

Oksana pinched herself, slapped herself. Leaned farther out the window until the cool night air numbed her face. None of it diminished the heat surging through her veins, vowing to purge the world of everything that would hurt or betray again.

With a feral scream, Oksana snatched up her flint starter and lunged for Pran.

CHAPTER THIRTY-TWO

PRAN

Her pupils dilated until her eyes were nearly black and sparks exploded around her as Oksana leaped forward, face contorting into a snarl. She wasn't decked in battle gear: no antlers, no scaled greaves.

She didn't need them to be terrifying.

Pran's instinct was to flee the demon charging forward with death in her eyes. But he could not accept—could not believe—that after all she'd done to separate herself from the Commanders' and Rootare's demands, she could be lost in an instant because of a serum in her blood. She was stronger than that.

So he threw off his antlers and met her charge, shouting her name. For one moment, recognition flickered across her face. For one moment, her steps faltered, her sparks dimmed.

One moment was all Pran needed to know she was still in there.

"Oksana!" He lurched forward, reaching for her.

She crashed into him with the force of a charging bull. He was thrown onto his back, screaming as pain lanced through his torn-up flesh.

"It's me!" he cried. "Come back, Oksana. *Remember.*"

She shrieked again and swung her boot toward his face.

Pran scrambled away, scarcely dodging her blow. While he floundered, she raised a flame that lit the lab like hell itself, sending sparks skittering across the ceiling beams and igniting shelves stacked with charts and diagrams.

"Come out of it!" Pran begged.

With a gasp, she faltered, the fire fading in her hands. She gritted her teeth as she wrestled back her howl. But then she blinked, and fresh rage swept across her face. She hurled another fireball, and kept throwing as Pran staggered around the room, barely avoiding each flame by a mere handsbreadth as his bad leg slowed his steps.

"Dammit, stop!" he cried. "This isn't you."

Oksana arced another flame toward him. Pran ducked beneath it, too slow. His cry of pain was muffled by the fire's roar as the blaze singed the back of his tunic.

But the moment those flames were gone, he was clambering to his feet. "I know you're in there," he shouted. "*Wake up!*" He feinted to her right, then tossed a handful of fire to her left.

She vaulted over a workstation and sprang toward him, kicking his right thigh where the muscles hurt worst. With a howl, Pran collapsed to the ground. "Oksana . . . s-stop . . ."

When she kicked again, pain darkened every corner of his mind. He doubled over, retching. "Please . . . come back to me . . ."

She slammed her flint starter against his brow, pushed

him onto his back, and threw herself on top of him, reaching for his throat.

"I'm so sorry!" He wrenched her shoulder nearly out of its socket until, crying out, she tumbled off him. But he was only halfway to sitting when she smashed her fist into his face. Hot blood gushed from Pran's nose into his opened mouth, and he gagged and spat.

Oksana knelt over him, hands on his throat. Her eyes—pupils still enormous, swallowing all color—were unfocused and didn't meet his, as though she didn't see.

Didn't *want* to see.

"Oksana," he whispered, "I'm sorry. So sorry."

She squeezed his neck until his breath hitched.

"I wanted you . . . free," he choked. "But the more I tried . . . the more I hurt you."

"You took away Anu." Her voice had gone gravelly like a Nightmare's. But she spoke, unlike the others who'd stormed through Kivi and Linn, their voices lost to feral screams. "When I became too much trouble, you pushed me away."

"I wanted . . . you . . . safe. Wanted . . . future . . ." He fumbled for the ring dangling from her neck, flashing in his face like a taunt. "Ya . . . abetschayu."

Around his neck, her fingers shook.

"Ya . . . abetschayu," he said with his last breath.

She released him—Pran gasped as air burned back through his lungs—but snatched up her flint starter and held it over his face, thumb on the striker, one click from flinging sparks.

"Maybe you can't give me freedom. Maybe it's not yours to give. Or maybe . . ." Her hand went limp. The flint starter clattered to the floor. "Maybe I haven't earned it. People were hurt because of me. *Anu died.* And I still became Rootare's monster."

Slipping off Pran, Oksana gaped at the ruins of the lab surrounding them. One tear, then another, fell from her night-dark eyes.

"Please," Pran croaked, scrabbling to his knees. "We were only trying to do what seemed right in the worst circumstances."

He reached a hand toward her face, cupping his fingers around her cheek. Beneath his touch, she flinched and hissed. But she didn't strike him, nor pull away. Something flickered deep in her eyes, and when he peered close, Pran saw a little color cut through the black.

"You still have more to do," he whispered. "Maybe everything you've done hasn't been perfect. But you still have more to give. There's so much left to you in this world. Don't keep yourself from it."

A shudder ripped through Oksana. She stumbled back, gasping and blinking. Her pupils were still large, but they were shrinking. Her eyes brimmed with tears and then spilled over.

Wrapping her arms around her ribs like a shield, Oksana staggered to the window. The alarm bells had fallen silent and the fort's beacons had been lit, their flames blazing across the sky.

"Will these people ever see us as anything but monsters?" Oksana pressed her hands to the sill, staring across the city. "I don't know how to help them. Or us. I don't know what's right anymore. How to make a difference. Whether it's even possible."

Pran pushed himself to standing, gasping as pain surged through him. "It'll take time. Time and a lot of Tuliis working together to defend our people and lands. We're far from done, but together—" He clasped Oksana's hands, her scent of cloves and woodsmoke more soothing than any medicine.

But she pulled away, curling in on herself as she shivered. "That was always your goal. Not mine."

"You want to go home!" Each word was stone-heavy on his tongue. He couldn't go with her yet, not with the emperor still to deal with. But he'd made a promise to her. "I'll get you to Horádim, even if we have to sneak you in."

Oksana shook her head. "I don't know if I belong there anymore."

The hopelessness in those words was more frightening than when she'd Snapped. "You've thought of your homeland every day," he told her. "You wear that saint's charm around your neck. At night, your dreams of Horádim get you through to the next morning. Why wouldn't you belong?"

She rounded on him, eyes bright with tears. "I attacked you. Like a monster. Because that's what I *am* now. Not the girl they took from Horádim. I don't deserve to be there."

"None of that's true!" He reached for her, but she didn't accept his outstretched hand.

The space between them felt as wide as the whole Vesimaan Empire. He didn't know how to breach that distance, and it left him feeling as helpless as a child being snatched by Nightmares. "Look," he pleaded, "I don't care that you attacked me. It wasn't you."

"*I* care. What if I turn on someone who can't fight back?"

Fire still crackled in parts of the room, embers smoldering everywhere he stepped, but Pran had never felt colder. "Oksana, don't give up on yourself. Please."

She turned from the window, refusing to look at him. "I have serums to destroy."

"They'll still be here in the morning. Come out of this place."

Again, she ignored his outstretched hand. "I'm not going with you."

He opened his mouth to argue—if he could persuade frightened Tuliis to rise against their Commanders, why couldn't he convince this girl he loved more than life to give herself the world she deserved?

But Yalku was back in the doorway, tapping impatiently against the frame. "Pran, the envoy—she's demanding to speak with you."

"Go," Oksana pressed, when Pran moved toward her instead of Yalku. "Finish what you set out to do."

"But—"

"Just . . . go."

It was not what he wanted. Deep down, he didn't believe it was what she did, either. But arguing more would only drive Oksana further away.

So he turned to Yalku. And he left.

PART TWO

THE DEMONS CAME FORTH

CHAPTER THIRTY-THREE

PRAN

As Pran turned from Healing Hall to the fort's gates, Yalku stopped him and held out a Commander's helmet, the vicious horns on it stretching nearly as long as Pran was tall. He wasn't sure he'd be able to walk beneath its weight, especially with his leg already throbbing. And even if it wasn't, the Commanders' gear wasn't something he wished to embrace.

"Get that thing away from me." Pran shoved it aside and tried to slip past Yalku to the gates.

But Yalku thrust the helmet onto Pran's head. "It's a sign of power that the envoy will understand. With the emperor and his crew, you need all the help you can get. That's not criticism," he added, as Pran opened his mouth to protest, "it's the truth. You have to send a clear message now about who runs this fort and the army, or all of this was for nothing."

The helmet turned out to be far lighter than it looked, though it still wasn't comfortable, too large and slipping down his brow. But with Yalku's words ringing in his ears, Pran gestured to another horn, broken off a Commander's helmet, lying in the dirt across the yard. "Bring that to me."

Yalku furrowed his brow in confusion, but did as he was asked. Grasping that horn, leaning on it as a staff, Pran shifted all the weight off his aching leg and exhaled in relief. With this, he'd be able to keep standing. And the horn served as a stark reminder of what he'd just done, who he'd taken down. Marching across the courtyard with his horn staff, Pran approached the opened copper gates and the envoy standing inside them, flanked by two of the emperor's own Nightmares.

In a moment like this, when so much rested on the next exchange, Oksana would pray to her saint. Pran could hear her as if she walked beside him: *Yeva, guide our steps, our words . . .*

But *he* had made the promise to his Tuliis. *He* had to see it through himself, not pin his hopes on the assistance of some unseen, supposedly benevolent spirit.

The envoy waiting for him was a towering Vesimaan woman in a uniform like the fort messengers', though hers shone amber instead of gold and the fire-demon tattoo stretched like a mask across her face. The blowing snow and ice didn't faze her, and Pran forced himself likewise to stop shivering.

"Yes?" he asked the woman. "Why have you come?"

"I bring a message," the envoy called, "for the one in command of this fort."

"I am he," Pran said, glad the pompous helmet Yalku had forced onto him gave the appearance of much-needed height.

The envoy started with such absurd surprise Pran barely held off his scowl. "On your head be it"—the envoy lifted one shoulder in a shrug—"if you're lying and your real leader is too careless to prevent that from happening."

"I thought you had a message to deliver," Pran said, with all the haughty confidence he did not feel.

The envoy grinned. "You've supplanted the Commanders. Emperor Juhan doesn't wish for you to relinquish the fort and army back to their control. By losing, they've betrayed him. Instead, he offers a trade: reaffirm the troops' commitment to him, and he'll appoint you their leader."

Pran snorted, leaning forward and flicking his hornstaff with a finger. "A weak agreement, offering what I've already taken. And reaffirm our commitment? You mean burn whatever he wants, when he wants it. My troops didn't defeat the Commanders to bow before your emperor once more."

"Then face his wrath, Hellion. Emperor Juhan does not view insubordination kindly."

"We are the Tuliikobret army. What can he do against us?"

"He killed a Commander with a handshake."

"And we've killed the one responsible for that poisoned glove. He'll have to try a new approach."

"Do not tempt fate, Hellion." The envoy stalked back through the gates, with the Nightmares close behind.

Pran turned to the Tuliis gathered around him. "Time to send a real message. I need emissaries to our homelands, Tuliis from each nation to visit their countries. We must spread word that we've claimed the fort, that we mean to return home and defend them with our fire. See if they'll help us along the way."

When the Tuliis cheered, many hurrying forward to volunteer as emissaries, a few of the splintered pieces of Pran's heart slid back into place.

The next days he spent planning routes and writing the emissaries' missives from Lepik's old office—one of the few tower rooms that hadn't been burned on Jubilee Night. Though the stairs were still murder on Pran's leg, it felt fitting to have claimed his former Commander's quarters. Perhaps he'd even replace that painting of the cornflower field with sketches from Nanda's last letter.

He'd sent the final emissary on her way with a sealed message to her home village in Pakastra when there was a tap at the window, like a pebble hitting glass. Pran rose from his chair, heart thundering against his ribs, as his gaze locked on that window . . . and the copper crown fluttering outside it.

How had the bird known to find him here? He'd never understood this creature, how Nanda trained it to always know where Pran was. Throwing open the window, Pran drew the bird inside.

Once again, Nanda's letter contained no sketches, only three lines.

What have you done, bha'ee?

Are you planning to come home?

What help do you need?

Pran's hands clenched over the letter. It was at once disconcerting and strangely relieving that Nanda already knew, but he did tap telegraph lines. The better question might be what he *didn't* know.

At least this time, Pran didn't have to immediately send the bird away for fear of being caught with something he shouldn't have. So he let the copper crown hop around the desk, poking at the assortment of nib pens and ink bottles, while Pran wrote his response.

You know full well what I've done. The fort and army are in my hands, and I will lead every one of us to freedom. We come to defend our homes with the fire in our veins. Look for me. I'll show you exactly who I've become.

Pran sent the copper crown on its way, watching as the bird shrank to a dark silhouette against the sunset. *Frail, sickly, so young.*

Never again.

CHAPTER THIRTY-FOUR

OKSANA

She wasn't sure how much time had passed, but Oksana hadn't left the lab since she'd killed Rootare. At least his body wasn't still there, thank the saints. Two Nightmares had taken it away, arriving with a stretcher—and without their burning-soul masks.

At the sight of their bare faces, Oksana had frozen where she'd stood. Never had she seen Nightmares unmasked, and it turned her world inside out to see they were ordinary people. One was even Horádimian. She recognized the soft vowels in the woman's accent as the two Nightmares spoke to each other, figuring out the best way to heave the alchemist's body onto the stretcher.

None of this should have been shocking. It was, after all, the argument Anu's family had failed to grasp. The one people must understand if Tuliis would ever live outside this fort: they were people, many still *children*, who only wanted to go home.

Yet for as much of the future as Oksana could foresee, this lab would be her home. With every breath, the sulfur turned her stomach. She'd never grow comfortable with its stench. Most Tuliis had enough sense to stay away from the place.

Here, she could avoid hurting others.

She didn't remember much of Snapping. One moment, she'd mourned everything she'd hoped for, strived for, gone up in smoke. The next moments . . . rage coursed through her, as though her blood itself had gone molten. At the mere sight of Pran, the sound of his would-be soothing words, she'd launched into him. This boy who'd been half her heart and all her reason! Every single one of his pleas while she'd attacked, she'd heard and *not cared*. All that had mattered, in those moments, was her fury.

Never had there been a more sickening scene in her life, and that included all seven years of living in this fort. She didn't know how she'd look herself in the mirror or meet another person in the eye. And if she crossed paths with Pran again . . . would she rampage once more? If snippets of a folksong or words inked across a hand reminded her of Anu, would she lash back with flames no one could counter?

Her tunic might still bear the Hellion's orange demon, but she was well and truly a Nightmare.

Oksana grabbed hold of the thin chain and yanked it—pendant, ring, and all—over her head.

Yeva, I can't give back lives. Can't erase the harm I've caused. But please, help me make amends. Help me be rid of the monster lurking inside me.

Help me be, like you, a defender of life.

She tucked the necklace into her pocket, unworthy to

carry the saint's image over her heart. And Pran's ring, his promise . . . the sight of it hurt so much she could barely breathe.

So she set her sights on a different mission: purging the last of Rootare's vile alchemy from this world.

Once again, Oksana donned a lab coat, goggles, and gloves. Then she mixed the serums with Demon's Tongue and burned them, drop by drop, until the sunrise lit the windows with amber.

"How long have you been up?"

Yelping, Oksana whirled around, a vial of serum nearly tumbling from her hand. Sepp stood in the doorway, cradling a basket in her arms.

Now that the Tuliis had taken the fort, Sepp could be doing anything she pleased. And yet she'd chosen to find Oksana. It was a ray of light in the gloom of burner smoke and steam, to see a friend standing near.

If only she deserved such a friend.

"Do you need something?" Oksana asked, burning more serum until only ash remained.

Sepp squinted. Oksana imagined the sight she must be, hair spilling from the knot pinned high on her head, face streaked with soot except where her goggles rested.

"Let me rephrase," the girl said. "Have you slept at all?"

A ridiculous question. "Who can sleep?"

Sepp huffed. "If you won't rest, at least eat something." She placed her basket on a table.

"I'm not hungry." The burning was all Oksana needed to keep going. She stood a world apart from her body. And that was a relief. When she felt separate from it, she didn't have to worry what it might do next.

When she might Snap next.

But when Sepp pulled the cloth off the basket, releasing aromas of cinnamon, butter, and almonds, Oksana's stomach rumbled like a living creature.

Sepp nodded, unbearably smug. "I thought this would get your attention."

"Babka?" Oksana edged toward the basket. Its scent spoke of long winter nights by the fire, bread in one hand, a mug of caramelly baked milk in the other, while the air thrummed with her family's laughter. The bread smelled so much like her mother's baking that Oksana nearly burst into tears.

Sepp's smile faltered before a wicked grin stole across her face. "Cinnamon kringle. Horádimians aren't the only ones who can bake. Let me show you what we Vesimaans can do."

From the basket, she lifted a ring of braided bread, layered with thick cinnamon paste and sparkling with chunks of sugar. She broke off a wide wedge and held it out.

Disappointment drenched Oksana like a cloudburst, to have a piece of home seemingly in reach only to be wrong.

She almost went back to burning the serums. But her stomach erupted in a growl that all but echoed off the stone walls. Sighing, she stripped off her gloves, washed her hands, and accepted the bread. Sepp stared, one eyebrow lifted high, while Oksana took a bite.

Saints alive, it tasted even better than it smelled. In three bites, Oksana wolfed down the rest. "Where did you get this?" she asked, tearing another piece from the loaf.

Sepp tipped her chin high. "I made it."

Oksana stopped mid-chew. "You—"

"So much surprise. Should I be offended?" Sepp ripped a fat wedge from the ring and perched on a windowsill, nibbling at the thickest patches of cinnamon.

"My parents ran a bakery in our village," she said between bites. "Most kids grow up with lullabies or folk stories. I was raised to the tune of bread rising. At night I fell asleep listening to my parents kneading dough. Mornings, I woke to the smell of bread in our ovens. I started helping as soon as I could hold a mixing spoon. It's been years, obviously, but seems I remember a thing or two about baking. And when none of the kitchen staff came back . . . well, there's no one here to stop me from working a different kind of magic. Anyway, I need to practice, if I'm going to help my parents once more."

The bread in Oksana's belly went rock hard. "You think you can just go home and bake bread like none of this happened?"

"I . . . thought you wanted home, too." Sepp frowned, setting aside the bread. "I know Nayar dreams of leading this army to victory and vengeance, but I thought your dreams were more personal. Taking back what's yours."

"Taking back." The words were so bitter on Oksana's tongue she nearly choked. "A hundred woolly lambs, mushroom hunting, fresh bread, music and dancing, my parents' smiles, my siblings' laughter. It's everything I miss about Horádim. Everything I loved. But even if I get all of that . . . it won't be the same."

"What do you think will have changed?"

"I'm not the girl who was taken. Even if we free ourselves from the emperor . . . how can I belong in my village again?" She grabbed a fistful of the bright red hair spilling from her bun. "I love the story of my grandparents. Yes, it made me different from everyone else in the village, but at least my family and I were different *together*. And having a Scamall grandfather didn't make me a monster." Oksana touched the spot on her neck where Rootare had injected her and cringed.

Sepp turned a piece of bread over in her hands, as though an answer were scrawled in the cinnamon. "Sometimes life's about making new homes. Look what you and Nayar did for each other all these years. Sorry," she added, when Oksana flinched. "I know things aren't great between you and him."

"I don't *want* a new home!" Oksana protested, heart shattering against her ribs. "All I want is Horádim. I was happy there."

"I'm not saying you can't have Horádim," Sepp said. "But

if you still want it in your life, you'll have to connect in a new way. Create another home there, one that suits who you are *now*. Then it can still be yours, even if it's shaped a little differently."

Oksana felt the truth in Sepp's words. But it wasn't just a matter of changing her thoughts; with the new serum inside her, she was a danger to everyone around. Until she changed that, she wouldn't belong anywhere.

Yeva, help me find a way, Oksana prayed, touching the icon hidden in her pocket. But the silver frame around that image was icy against her fingertips.

Was that her answer?

Scrubbing at her eyes before Sepp could see the tears, Oksana turned again to the serums and got back to burning.

CHAPTER THIRTY-FIVE

PRAN

"Your bandages needed changing yesterday, Nayar," the physician groused when Pran stopped by the hospital wing as dawn broke the next morning.

Although there were no more wretched rules about earning medicine tokens before treatments, it was harder than ever for Pran to get help. Only one physician remained. After Jubilee Night the messengers had fled in terror—and Pran hadn't stopped them, certainly wouldn't force anyone to stay and risk them rebelling—and most of the kitchen workers and physicians never reported back for duty. They'd been, after all, political prisoners, or working off a family debt . . . no one *chose* this fort.

Pran was grateful that at least this man, Mikkel, had stayed. Still, with many Tuliis hurt on Jubilee Night, or struggling with old injuries, Pran was left with only odd hours to claim his own medicine. Added to that, their supplies were limited. The emperor had ceased all deliveries to the fort; they had to make do with what remained on the shelves, and already their stock was dwindling.

Physician Mikkel, however, had different worries. "If

these wounds become infected, I'll tie you down until you're healed."

"Is that how you speak to one who wields fire?" Pran clicked his flint starter, raising a warning spark. Mikkel rolled his eyes and scrubbed none too gently at the worst of Pran's whip wounds.

Pran hissed in pain and cursed the man under his breath. All the same, there was some comfort in hearing the physician fuss, proof that someone not a Tulii could care, at least a little. "Thank you," Pran muttered, as the man cut new bandages, "for staying with us."

Mikkel gave an undignified snort. "If I hadn't, Juhan would have captured me, too."

"Captured?" Pran peered over his shoulder as the man mixed salve.

"He wouldn't risk anyone spreading the news of what's happened in this fort. Trust me, the ones who deserted have been dealt with. I stayed out of self-preservation."

Pran opened his mouth to ask about these people *dealt with* by the emperor, but the words dissolved into another hiss as the physician spread salve across Pran's back.

"Stop squirming," Mikkel said. "This would hurt less if you'd come on time."

Pran very much doubted that was true, and was about to tell the man not to talk nonsense when the hospital door creaked open. "Could someone bring more Demon's Tongue to the lab?" a voice called. "I'm running low again."

Oksana. Suddenly, Pran didn't feel anything except his heart thunking against his ribs.

She stood in the doorway, swallowed by a too-large lab coat splotched with smoke stains. Her eyes were sunken, shadowed. It looked like she hadn't slept since Jubilee Night.

All he wanted was to take her in his arms. Only five days had passed since the jubilee, but it felt like fifty years. For all he'd had to do since taking the fort—including inventorying the food cellars and assigning rations—he still wondered with every other breath how she was doing.

Mikkel frowned at Oksana. "Fresh air would do you a world of good. You should fetch that Demon's Tongue yourself."

But she didn't seem to hear. Oksana stared at Pran, her face a hollow mask. He couldn't tell if she was angry to have stumbled across him. It was so strange, *so wrong*, not to know at a glance what she was thinking. When he tried to stand, the physician clapped a hand onto his shoulder, holding him to the cot.

"I'll send Sepp." Oksana was gone before Pran drew his next breath.

He exhaled, his insides a ruin worse than what Kraanvelt had wrought across his back.

Mikkel finished his work in silence, but again held Pran in place when he tried to stand. "It's been too long since you've had a dose for your leg."

He was filling a syringe when Yalku appeared in the

doorway. "Pran, there's . . . something going on with the Commanders. You should come."

Seven gods and all their *piss,* he couldn't even have a moment to wallow in his own misery. Pran shook his head when the physician held up the syringe.

"I'll come back for it," he said, lifting his eyebrows as though to add, *See why I'm not here every day?*

Flanked by half a dozen Nightmares and a few chemical lamps, Pran descended the prison steps to the cell block—chambers dug deep into the earth and fronted with copper bars thick as men's arms, each with one Commander inside.

When the Nightmares had locked them up, they'd confiscated the Commanders' flint starters. When the Commanders were fed, it was with wooden bowls and spoons. They were given ample food, and water for drinking and washing. Though Pran would have loved to see them rot, he wouldn't starve them, even if that was what they would have done to a Tulii.

"Miss us, Nayar?" a voice croaked. "Is leading more difficult than you dreamed?"

Slumped on the wooden bench in his cell, Kraanvelt looked positively feral, bandages stuck to the burns across his face. Tangled hair hung before his eyes and his fingernails were torn to the quick, probably from attempting to dig through the packed-earth walls. There were no prisoner uniforms sized to fit Commanders, so they were all in whatever clothes they'd worn on Jubilee Night. For Kraanvelt, along with Lepik and Tamm, that meant their council livery, now in a sorry state, wrinkled and filthy.

Pran couldn't deny the thrill of standing outside a cell with Kraanvelt in it, knowing *he'd* put that man inside. But Kraanvelt's guffaw was cut short by a hacking cough. He slumped against the dirt wall, chest heaving. A chill shot through Pran as drops of blood flew from the man's mouth, spattering across the floor. And his face was skeletal, skin stretched across bone.

Turning from Kraanvelt, Pran gaped across the cells, his pulse spiking. Every Commander shook like a withered leaf in an autumn storm, gaunt and strangely gray.

"What's happening to you?" Pran asked. "You're being fed. Your wounds are tended. Why do you all look like you're halfway to the grave?"

Every Commander glared at Pran, jaws clamped shut. But pain loosens lips, as the Commanders themselves well knew.

Tamm leaned against her cell bars. "We had a serum. Took it daily. Kept us strong."

Some Commanders glowered, hissing for Tamm to be silent, though it was no great shock to Pran that their transformations were different. They weren't so much stronger because they were that much better than every Tulii. Still, Pran hadn't expected they'd continued to receive a serum, or that without it they'd decline this rapidly. Were their bodies dependent on the poison to function?

And he'd thought his fate as a Tulii had been horrible.

"Please." Tamm clung to the bars with trembling fingers, face damp with sweat, eyes bloodshot. "Let us have the serum. Even a little. Without it, we're . . ." She hunched forward, keening in pain.

This could have been an extraordinary moment, knowing he had the power to ease or extend their suffering. So why wasn't seeing them in pain more thrilling? As he looked them over, every one slouching with shoulders hunched, breath strained . . . they'd only ever been overgrown Tuliis, all the more vulnerable because their transformations never ended. None of them had chosen this role. Ultimately, they'd all been at the mercy of whatever the emperor and his alchemist chose to inflict.

Still, the Commanders had participated in every abuse against the Tuliis, heightening their suffering.

Pran crouched before Tamm until their eyes were level. "Tuliikobrets must earn their treatments. You need a medicine token before receiving anything for your pain. We can permit you a half dose now, but if you wait until after patrol, you'll receive a full one. Oh, and there's your favorite line: true Tuliikobrets are strong enough to stand on their own."

Tamm set her jaw. "Cruelty doesn't suit you, Nayar."

"I've done nothing to harm you. But I don't have to help, especially when it means handing over power you'd only use to hurt us."

"Just make the pain stop! We can't go on like this."

"We can't." Pran stood. "That's why you're coming with me."

"What?" The woman scrambled back, the whites of her eyes stark against her ashen face.

"That's right." Pran turned to the Nightmares behind him. "Take our council members. Make sure they're bound well. I don't want anyone escaping while we pay the emperor a visit."

Outside the fort, the streets were silent and empty—no surprise there, with another storm dumping snow across the city. It was the time of year in Vesimaa when smart people stayed indoors, huddling around their fireplaces and sipping hot drinks. Pran wished he could do the same; these icy winds only made his leg ache worse. But he had even bigger problems within this carriage lumbering down the snowy roads.

Six Nightmares rode inside that carriage, keeping tabs on the Commanders there. This carriage was not intended to hold so many; they were smashed onto the benches shoulder to shoulder, but Pran wouldn't risk any Commanders breaking out.

He rode in the driver's seat along with Yalku, who drove the carriage and *whistled* while he did it, actually enjoying the snow. Pran barely held back his eye roll.

"Exactly what do you hope to accomplish?" Yalku asked,

guiding them around the fort's wall and onto the street that led toward the palace.

Pran was still trying to figure that out. "We have to convince the emperor to let us go," he said, as the horses pulled them beneath stone archways and past guttering chemical lamps on the verge of burning out. "We can't kill him, or rise in open rebellion and risk bringing down Scamall on us. We have to persuade Juhan that he's better served relinquishing all claim on the troops rather than forcing us back into his power. I have an arrangement that I hope gets him listening."

Yalku scowled. "Because your 'arrangement' with Lepik turned out so well."

Shame gnawed through Pran. "People like these won't give anything unless they believe they'll receive more in return. I just have to make that happen without putting us in greater danger. Last time I made too many promises. I will do better."

As they approached the palace, the emperor's own Nightmares emerged from the shadows and followed the carriage. They were all Vesimaans—Juhan would trust no one else with his personal safety—and maybe their boots made them taller, but some of their heads were level with Pran's, and he was perched on the driver's bench high above the ground. He swallowed hard, glancing to the nearest Nightmare, and as their eyes met, her lips curled into a vicious grin. She darted forward, ushering the carriage to the palace gates.

"Representatives from the Tuliikobrets, here to speak

with Emperor Juhan," Pran told the Nightmare guards there, his voice so much steadier than the blood screaming through his veins.

"Surrender your flint starters," one rasped. "All of you."

After handing them over, then being frisked none too gently, the emperor's Nightmares beckoned the group through the gates. Yalku steered the carriage inside, and the palace's towering bronze doors groaned open. Emperor Juhan, garish in an unearthly red cloak and bronze livery, promenaded down the amber steps into the courtyard.

As the man's stare, and every other set of eyes, fastened expectantly onto Pran . . . the chill weighing on him deepened until he could scarcely breathe, much less string together two thoughts. Pran licked his dry lips, flexed his fingers, sucked in air until his lungs ached—anything to remind his body and brain to work. *You are running out of chances,* he scolded himself. *Do not disappoint the Tuliis again.*

When he clambered down from the carriage to meet the emperor, that man frowned. "I know you. How?"

It was the annoyance in Juhan's gaze, the dismissal, that snapped Pran out of his funk. After all, *he* held the troops and fort, their fire power and strength. Yes, the emperor knew him. And Pran would make sure that man never forgot.

He dipped into a mocking bow. "'Refresh your comrades on the Tuliikobrets' history,' you told me."

Emperor Juhan scowled. "Was I too generous that day, letting you live?"

"But I come with gifts." From the carriage, the fort's

Nightmares dragged out Kraanvelt, Lepik, and Tamm, all of them cringing at the sunlight. "Your newest council members."

The emperor recoiled as though Pran was offering plates of maggoty meat. "They failed me. Never even made it to the jubilee, because the troops fell apart as soon as they left. I don't want . . . I *do not* treat with rebels!"

"Oh, you will. If you're going to keep your throne, you'll have to win back the Vesimaans' loyalty and trust. I come with a solution."

Pran gestured again to the Commanders, and the fort's Nightmares shoved them to kneel at the emperor's feet. "You wanted Commanders on your council to aid with Vesimaa's needs. Show your people this was the right choice. Tell them of a new plan for Vesimaa's security, thanks to advice from these Commanders."

The emperor lifted an eyebrow. "*New plan?*"

"The Tuliikobret army as you know it is ending. We've killed your alchemist. Your Commanders are weakening. You have no way to force the troops to do your bidding."

"Is that so? How will you survive without fresh food and supplies?"

Pran smirked. "Your Commanders trained us to get by on very little. And you, Your Majesty . . . you won't have winter on your side forever. Once the snow melts, your people will be back on the streets, watching the fort and asking too many questions. You cannot risk them—or Scamall—finding out you've lost control of Vesimaa's military. And the fort is too well made; you can't breach its walls without an assault that would draw the wrong attention. So yes, if you wish to keep your crown, you'd better figure out a new plan."

Emperor Juhan paced. The way he kept his gaze on the ground let Pran hope the man felt the gravity of his situation, a nation slipping out of his reach.

But when the man faced Pran, his gaze was anything but worried. "With this army, my grandfather freed Vesimaa from decades of invasion and war. Under my father's direction, the Tuliikobrets made Vesimaa into an empire of matchless power. I will not fail my family's legacy. Nor will I let this army be taken by a Pakastran child who thinks he knows better than I how to govern *my* empire. No way to force you to do my bidding, you say?"

With a flick of his finger, the emperor gestured to one of his Nightmares, who disappeared inside the palace. Far too quickly, that Nightmare returned, leading two prisoners in tarnished chains. Their clothes were torn and dirty, faces bruised and swollen. Pran recognized them anyway: two of the emissaries he'd sent out from the fort only days before, one Horádimian, the other Nyítan. Of all the Tuliis who'd volunteered, these two had been among the most eager and determined. Now their eyes were so empty Pran felt he was peering at ghosts.

"What have you done to them?" he whispered.

Another of the emperor's Nightmares caught Pran, pinning him in place. Meanwhile, Emperor Juhan pointed to the Horádimian Tulii. "You. Hold out your hand."

The Tulii did it as if moving in his sleep.

"You." The emperor pointed to the Nyítan. "Bend back his finger until it breaks."

"What? No!" Pran thrashed against the Nightmare's hold, but it was like flailing against marble. Panic surged through his veins as the Nyítan girl reached for the boy's hand.

"Don't do this," Pran shouted. "Don't listen to him. I'll get every one of us free."

Both Tuliis ignored him. Did they hear only the emperor, or were they so broken by whatever the man had done to them that Pran's words meant nothing? The girl grabbed the boy's littlest finger and yanked it back until a crack sounded through the courtyard. The boy lurched and grimaced. The girl gave no reaction, as if she'd done nothing more than snap an old twig.

"Good." The emperor circled around the chained Tuliis. "Again. Another."

"Please, don't," Pran begged, when the girl reached for the boy's ring finger. Pran's heart turned inside out, then crumbled to dust, as the boy didn't even try to protect himself. "Look at me. *Look at me!* You don't have to obey him."

Crack.

On and on it went, until the girl broke the boy's thumb and he let out an animal howl. Still, he didn't move away or lower his hand. The girl waited, impassive, for her next command.

Emperor Juhan shoved them aside. "Do you see? I don't

need alchemists or Commanders. I can get any Tuliikobret to do as I wish. Either those troops reswear allegiance to me, or I will wear you down until none remember why they dared rebel. No, I won't give up the army. In fact, at this month's end, my people will once again light the flames of Fire Night. They'll recall how the Tuliikobrets brought Vesimaa out of darkness and will go on to make us unstoppable."

Fire Night was an ancient Vesimaan tradition that Emperor Juhan's grandfather had repurposed for celebrating the Tuliikobrets. On the longest night of the year, Vesimaans lit bonfires until sunrise, dancing around and leaping over them, paying homage to the flames—never the people—that had liberated them. It was a truly sickening display.

The emperor stepped so close, Pran had to crane his head all the way back to meet the man's stare. "Any little spies you send out, boy? Anyone who sneaks out for food, or who tries to run? My Nightmares will find them. They will end them. All."

Emperor Juhan snapped his fingers, and his Nightmares released both broken emissaries from the chains and shoved them forward. Pran caught them, staggering beneath their weight. Neither Tulii met his gaze; they just stared at the ground like empty-eyed dolls.

Pran gingerly handed off the broken Tuliis to his own Nightmares. But when he faced the emperor, the man who'd caused every bit of pain in this yard and beyond . . . all Pran knew was fury—for himself, his Tuliis, every nation caught under this man's tyranny. "Do not underestimate how far any of us will go for freedom."

The fort's Nightmares surrounded Pran, crowding him, the broken Tuliis, and the Commanders into the carriage. One took Pran's place on the driver's seat with Yalku, keeping watch as the carriage sped back to the fort.

Inside the carriage, Kraanvelt croaked, "We know the emperor. His weaknesses, his flaws. We can help you break from him . . . if you make it worth our while. *The serum.*"

Sitting taller, reclaiming some dignity, Pran shook his head. "You're not getting any."

"You can't defeat that man alone! Don't be proud and obtuse, Nayar."

Once, he would have taken those words as a challenge, desperate to prove himself smart enough to outwit the Commanders. But if he was going to keep fighting for his Tuliis, he could not stumble into the same trap. "I've been both those things. Not anymore. I will never give in to the emperor, *or* to you."

He only wished his mind would more quickly concoct another plan.

CHAPTER THIRTY-SIX

OKSANA

The past days, Sepp had come to the lab time and again, trying to get Oksana to leave for food, fresh air . . . a never-ending list of nuisances there was no time for when there was still alchemy to wipe out. Here she was again, nagging about eating, and Oksana was losing all patience for it.

"Save the food for Tuliis who are actually hungry." Oksana hunched over the lab burners.

Sepp elbowed between her and the workstation. "You've been in here for five days. You will have a proper meal today, or so help me . . ."

With a hiss, Oksana snatched the bread the girl held out—stale rye, no more decadent kringle. They'd run out of milk, butter, and sugar.

"If you want me out of here so badly," she said while gnawing the slice, "help me finish this job."

"Fine. One hour. But then you *will* take a break from this place." Grimacing, Sepp picked up one of Rootare's notebooks like it had fangs.

When she wasn't burning serums, Oksana destroyed Rootare's records. This proved the more maddening task, as their leather covers turned out to be flame-resistant—a wise choice, in this lab. But the man was gone, and Oksana would have his work vanish with him. Leather bindings would not defeat her.

Snatching another book off the pile, Oksana yanked it open and ripped out pages, dropping them by handfuls onto burner flames. Soon the air was a chorus of tearing paper and crackling fire.

Oksana paid little attention to what was written across those pages. Rootare didn't deserve the energy, and anyway, most were covered with his bizarre alchemical code. But one book did catch her eye: a leather cover warped like it had been dropped in water and speckled with spots that looked like dried blood. The handwriting inside was harried, more scrawl than script . . . and in Vesimaan, not code.

She could practically feel the despair bleeding through the ink as she read: *My last additions to the serums failed. The Novices appear to have weakened in power.*

Oksana's heart thumped so loudly she was sure the whole fort could hear.

"What's wrong?" Sepp stared over the edge of another book, half-torn pages twisted in her fingers.

Silently, Oksana handed over the journal. Sepp's jaw went slack. "How?"

Oksana pointed to a corner of the page, where a date was scrawled. This entry was more than thirteen years old. Rootare had only been imperial alchemist for ten.

I made my own studies, breaking into this lab and experimenting.

"This would have been from his first attempts," she said. "Before he was alchemist. And he'd *weakened* the Tuliikobrets' power."

"You're not thinking you might also . . ."

Oksana's heartbeat pitched to a fevered note. "If it was possible once, why not again? Look, here are notes on how he made that batch of serum!"

Sepp frowned. "By now, he's surely accounted for those weaknesses, made his new serums strong enough that they couldn't be erased by any other. The man left nothing half-done."

"I should still try. If we can weaken our fire, maybe even destroy it completely . . . we'd have a whole new life outside these walls. People would have no reason to fear us. They might trust us again. At the least, we wouldn't be stuck with these powers the emperor forced onto us."

She couldn't erase anyone's time in this fort, but maybe she could neutralize the serum in their veins. This could be how she fit back in at home.

This could be her redemption.

"Redemption?" Sepp pressed her lips together so hard they went white, as Oksana realized she'd spoken those last words out loud. She backed away as Sepp set aside the notebook, then prowled between Oksana and the mound of burning pages.

"If you're ever going to leave this lab—and you must—you have to get control over your Snapping," Sepp said. "If we spar together, try different techniques—"

"There's no getting control of it." Oksana felt as hot as the flames waiting to break out of her. "I don't know what will set me off. The best thing is to weaken it. End it, if I can."

"But you did get control," Sepp pressed. "You came back on your own. No one had to attack you with Demon's Tongue or wrap you in chains."

Maybe Oksana had broken out of the Snap, eventually, but she hadn't kept it from happening. "You didn't see how I tore into Pran," she whispered, each word scratching her parched tongue. "I don't want to hurt you, too."

"If you don't get control over it, you *will* hurt someone," Sepp said. "You must get it in check. Come on, spar with me."

They took the east training yard, chaining the gates shut at Oksana's insistence. "If I escape this yard, nobody wants to see what I'd do to the fort."

Sepp bound on her greaves and turned to three other Hellions she'd recruited. "Step in only if I need help, understand? The goal is to get the Snapping under control, not antagonize her."

The Hellions, two Vesimaans and one Horádimian, all looked less than thrilled to be closed into this yard alongside Oksana. "You say she rampages like those others?" one of the Vesimaans asked.

"The Commanders barely got them under control," the second Vesimaan muttered.

"Stop talking about me like I'm not here!" Oksana said.

None of the others looked sorry. "This is a fool's errand, if you ask me," the Horádimian said, hand wrapped tight around the flint starter in his belt.

"Good thing I didn't." Sepp glowered until they fell back a step.

Oksana faced the doubters. "I've pulled myself together before. It can be done."

Defending herself felt strange. She still didn't quite believe these words, but speaking them aloud softened her heart to the idea. If others had no faith in her, who else did she have on her side but herself?

"We're learning to manage it," Sepp told the others. "Go stand against the wall. You're backup only if I need you. Which I won't, because she'll do fine. We're just being careful."

Before Oksana could slip on her own gauntlets, Sepp caught her hand. "Would you do something for me?"

Instantly, Oksana tensed at the unknown. "All right . . ."

"I just want you to call me Kati. My given name. Like my friends back home."

Oksana let out a shaking breath. Tuliis hadn't often called each other by their first names. It was against protocol. Doing so, in private, had been an act of defiance against the Commanders. A risk, too, getting so close to someone.

None of those same threats remained, yet it still felt

strange, taking a new friend inside this fort. Oksana wanted to say no, but she did need someone on her side. "All right. Kati."

"How do we begin?" Kati peered between her flint starter and Oksana's. "The Hellions in Kivi broke after they'd been attacked. Do I . . . need to punch you in the face or something?"

Oksana turned the flint starter over in her hands. The time she'd Snapped . . . yes, she had been punched—straight through the heart. Gutted from Anu's murder. Gutted by Rootare's twisted manipulation. Her hands were so steeped in death that if she closed her eyes she could still feel its stain, sticky like blood.

Gutted, too, because Pran had stood in front of her, asking her to come back to him. As if she *deserved* love and comfort, promises and hope. After all she'd done, who was she to . . . how could she *ever* . . .

A cry split the air, like someone's heart had been torn from their ribs. She opened her eyes, turning to see who was hurt. But Kati's other Hellions were pressed flat against the far wall, bodies tensed, flint starters lifted high.

The grating cry had come from Oksana's own throat. Her sight narrowed to the Hellion prancing before her, clutching flint starters in both hands, already throwing sparks. "Come and get me!" the Tulii taunted.

With one click of flint and steel, Oksana raised a pillar of fire that roared above the yard walls.

She'd show them what a monster could do.

CHAPTER THIRTY-SEVEN

PRAN

"They stopped our emissaries? How many have they caught?"

Pran stood surrounded by Tuliis in Meal Hall, mostly Nightmares and Hellions, all glowering after he'd disclosed what had passed during his visit to the emperor. As soon as they'd returned, Yalku had ushered the captured emissaries straight to the hospital wing, but enough Tuliis had spotted them along the way and seen the emperor's handiwork. Now they crowded around Pran, demanding answers.

"He only showed those two," Pran told the group. "If more had been caught, Emperor Juhan would have flaunted it."

"But we don't know for sure," a Hellion protested. The rest glared in degrees of disgust, dismay, and outrage.

Pran slumped against a table's edge. His whole body ached. All he wanted was a few moments to soak in one of the Commanders' copper tubs. He needed time to pull himself together. He needed . . .

Red hair, tumbling down like a veil . . . eyes dark as earth, gazing back at him . . . strong hands holding him while his breaths evened out, slowed . . . soft lips caressing his brow, cheek, mouth until he was steady enough to kiss back . . .

No. Pran shook himself, scrubbed his hands over his face. He couldn't have her now; she wouldn't have him. Above all, he must not become distracted.

Waving away the memories like smoke, Pran faced his Tuliis. "Juhan can't let word of what we've done get out. He can't let his people discover that he's lost control of the fort. They'd burn him themselves."

"So we tell them!" a Hellion shouted. "Let them know exactly who's in charge here."

Other Tuliis rumbled their assent, but Pran shook his head. "If Scamall finds out the emperor no longer has an army at his command, they'll march on Vesimaa. We don't want to bring Scamall on our heads, not while we're still—"

Shouts erupted outside Meal Hall.

Pran opened the hall doors to a flurry of Tuliis running by, mostly Imps and Goblins. He snagged the first one in reach. "What's going on?"

"Hellion fight in the east training yard!"

Gods above, couldn't they hold themselves together for one day?

Pran chased the crowd to where they pooled around the east training yard. Behind its walls, shouts echoed, sparks sizzled, and flames roared.

"Let me through!" Pran barked, and Tuliis parted so he could reach the gates—which were *chained shut*?

"Enough!" he bellowed through those gates. "Stop this immediately."

But none of the Tuliis in the yard paid attention. They were too busy scattering, yelping, retreating. The moment they broke apart, Pran realized what was happening.

Oksana. She'd Snapped, raging against four other Hellions, and all of them together could not get her in check. Around the training yard, stones were scorched in wide patches and the air was rank with burnt leather and hair. The Hellions stumbled and scrambled, their flames missing Oksana entirely. All the while, she moved—it was almost graceful, a true battle dance, vaulting and spinning through the air, bending away from everything the Hellions threw against her while raising another fireball of her own, splitting it in four, and hitting her attackers square across their chests, instantly knocking them to the ground.

"Artemivna. *Artemivna!*" one of those Hellions shouted, launching back to her feet. Sepp. "Get ahold of yourself. Remember why we're doing this."

In response, Oksana screamed, so loud half the Tuliis around the gate covered their ears. "She's gone round the bend," an Imp declared, grotesquely delighted.

"It's like Kivi." A Hellion turned to Pran. "How will we calm her? *Can we?*"

Pran turned to a Nightmare. "Can you break these chains on the gate? I need to talk her down."

The Nightmare gaped. "You want to go *in* there?"

"*Can you break the chains?*"

It took only a moment for the young woman to raise a blue-hot fire in her hands and heat one of the links until another Nightmare pulled it apart. The second the links were torn from the gate's iron frame, Pran threw himself inside. "Everyone stay out," he shouted, slamming the metal bars behind him, then sprinted for the battle, his ears ringing with its shrieks and snarls.

Those cries were all too familiar, dredging up memories of transformation when the serums devoured him from the inside out. In those darkest hours, Oksana would crawl to his cot, curl up alongside him, and breathe until his own gasps slowed to match her rhythm. That had cleared his mind, given him something to focus on beside the pain.

He didn't know, now, if he could help her. But as the other Hellions fled a round of ravenous flames, Pran threw himself between her and the singed, frantic Tuliis. "Please! Come back to yourself. You don't want to hurt them."

Oksana's eyes, pupils so wide they were almost solid black, smoldered with hatred. But her steps faltered, and her hold over her flint starter loosened.

"Please." He swooped forward, catching her in his arms. With one hand, he knocked her flint starter away. With the other, he cradled her head. "*Remember.*"

And as she'd done for him, Pran breathed slow and deep, whispering the words of the golden parrot lullaby she'd sung until he slept. He closed his eyes, shutting out the world, and focused only on Oksana.

He didn't know how much time passed, but her breath

mirrored his pace until their ribs moved in unison. When Pran opened his eyes again, Oksana's had returned to their earth-brown tones, shining bright with tears. Cupping his hands around her face, pale as starlight, Pran wove his fingers through the hair slipping from her braid. When he tipped his face down to hers, he breathed in that scent of woodsmoke and cloves, and for the first time since Jubilee Night he felt warm.

"I miss you," he whispered, the confession slipping out before he could stop it.

She turned away. Pran's stomach sank, but then she rested her head against his shoulder. They swayed together as the wind gusted, Pran shivering as its ice lashed at his exposed neck while Oksana burrowed into his open coat.

"Stay away from me," she murmured.

Pran's heart crumpled as she yanked from his touch. "I'm sorry! I didn't mean—" Gods, he wanted to break as she stepped back, his arms aching for her warmth.

Oksana peered at him over her shoulder, eyes red-rimmed. She gestured to his battered nose. "I did that to you."

"And I've hurt you, *worse*. Just because those wounds don't show—"

"That doesn't make it okay!" She retreated, her arms wrapped around herself like a shield. "*I hurt you*. And until I do something about my Snapping, no one should come near me."

"You should go straight to the emperor," a Goblin yelled

through the gates. "Nayar, why are we ignoring the obvious? *Kill the emperor*. Send *her* to do it."

"I'm not killing anyone! Anyone *else*," Oksana whispered, her voice breaking.

"Murdering Emperor Juhan isn't an option." Pran stepped between Oksana and the crowd. "The man has no heir. The power struggle that would ensue as distant relations grappled for the throne would leave this nation vulnerable to Scamall."

"Who cares?" another Goblin shouted. "To hell with Vesimaa!"

A part of Pran agreed with that sentiment. Let this whole nation burn if it meant escape. But that wasn't the answer, not least because the Vesimaan Tuliis watched him with growing consternation in their shadowed eyes.

"If Scamall advances on these lands," Pran said, "each one of us would be caught in the cross fire as we tried to run."

"What's your plan then, other than to keep getting Tuliis killed?"

A hush fell over the yard, and an icy chill shot down Pran's spine. He looked toward the boy pressed up against the gates. Marten, his name was.

"Do you have something to say to me?" Pran stepped toward the gates, fighting to hold his voice steady.

Marten—a Vesimaan, towering over Pran even from this distance—tilted his head down, mouth curling into a sneer. "We know you got Tarvas burned alive."

A sick feeling swept over Pran, and his shivers had nothing to do with the ice in the air. "That was an accident," he whispered.

"And when you *accidentally* ruin more of us? Like those emissaries?"

"Devak was no accident," a Goblin spoke up.

All the Seven Gods and their crooked teeth. Pran would have been sick right where he stood if he weren't so utterly numb. "Devak betrayed us. I did what I must, to keep everyone safe."

"Is that how you absolve yourself?" Marten demanded.

It was simply the truth, not absolution. "I did what I had to."

"Meanwhile, we're trapped behind these walls, eating rations like prisoners." Marten whirled toward the other Tuliis. "How can we trust Nayar? All he leads us toward is death."

CHAPTER THIRTY-EIGHT

OKSANA

The acid tang of mutiny soured the air. Tuliis of all ranks crowded around that cast-iron gate. Imps and Goblins rattled the metal bars. Hellions and Nightmares murmured together while casting Pran dark looks. If any got hold of him, Oksana had no doubt Pran would be torn down in this yard.

After all, he'd shown them how it was done.

Part of her wanted to let it happen. He'd *destroyed* Anu. Not on purpose, she understood that. Didn't change that her friend was gone, burned alive. That Pran had promised freedom but delivered death.

And what was this about Devak? Oksana thought she knew the name, an Imp who often lurked alone. She didn't know what had passed there, though she knew by the pain twisting across Pran's face that whatever it was cut him to the bone.

Pran might not believe in gods or souls, but whatever he'd endured had shredded his spirit.

And she hadn't been there to help him, through any of it. Oksana swallowed hard but couldn't banish the bitter film coating her throat and tongue. She wasn't sure how Pran was even standing, much less leading these troops and running the fort. But here he was on his feet. Crookedly, all the weight off his bad leg, probably because he wasn't getting his medicine, because he was too busy taking care of everyone else instead of himself.

How much did he have to suffer to be forgiven?

"He warned us the price would be steep." Oksana barely heard her words over the shouts at the gate. She turned to face those Tuliis, raising her voice above their cries. "Warned us that challenging the Commanders and emperor wouldn't be easy. So why are you upset when the fight gets tough, when the emperor doesn't lie down and hand over his power? As if it would ever have been that simple, no matter who led the fight?"

Everyone at the gate fell silent. Marten sneered at Oksana through the bars. "Tarvas was your friend. Taking Nayar's side means betraying her."

"Tarvas was brave enough to go where I wouldn't. She risked everything to help me. And that's what Nayar's been doing, for all of us. Don't talk like you would have done better, when none of you acted *at all*." She glared especially at the Hellions and Nightmares, all of them in the fort years longer than Pran.

At her words, many of them had the decency to look ashamed, or at least uncomfortable.

"Everyone here wished for freedom," Oksana said, "but Nayar was the only one who reached for it. He wants to protect us, but that's messy when we're pitted against those who will do *anything* to keep their power. Think about that before you turn against him. He's doing what no one else here dared try."

Though defending Pran stung, she knew each word was true. And she couldn't watch these Tuliis tear down the one who'd done so much more than simply wish for freedom.

The one who'd first given her a reason to fight behind these walls.

Across the yard, Sepp—Kati—met her gaze. Nodded once.

Finally, Oksana saw what Kati did. Though it would have been more comfortable to have never left the lab, to stay there burning, taking quiet vengeance on the man who'd warped them all, there was even more she could do. In this fort with so many Tuliis hurting, wanting more out of their lives but not knowing how to get it . . . for seven years, that was all she'd fought for.

She could help them.

"Nayar has a vision for our future," Oksana continued. "Keep listening to him, following his orders, if you want a life outside these walls."

At her side, Pran moved closer, trying to take her hand. She tucked her fingers under her arms and kept her attention on the gates. All these words weren't for him, not really.

At least not in a way that left her yearning to hold him close.

She missed him. The purpose he gave her, outside herself. The team they'd made, forever helping each other along. The reason for rising above whatever this fort threw at them.

The promise, the vision, the shape of a future.

No. She couldn't think like this. Couldn't have the distraction, not when there was so much work ahead. Not when she still wasn't sure they'd earned back the right to that future. Maybe Pran deserved forgiveness, maybe they both did.

But that didn't mean they deserved each other.

"Listen to Nayar, or what?" Marten countered. "You'll rampage on us, too?"

His attitude was so petty in the face of all their suffering. Oksana was sick of it. She stared him down through the gates, meeting his challenging smirk without flinching. "Far from it. I may have a way out of fire, completely."

All the Tuliis surrounding the training yard grew so quiet, Oksana could hear the ash crumbling beneath her boots.

"I'm already destroying the serums. There will be no new soldiers." She paused, sucked a shaking breath through her teeth, then forced herself to confess this wild dream. "And in Rootare's records, there are notes about weakening Tulii fire. If I can diminish our power over flame, maybe destroy it completely . . . there will be no Tuliis at all. We'll be human again, can go home as we were. No one will have any reason to fear us or hate us, or *use us*. One way or another, we'll force Juhan's hand, make him let us go. We'll truly be free."

Kati shook her head, lips curling in a frown. Well, Oksana already knew she doubted. Maybe it simply didn't matter to her, with her dreams of going home and baking bread like nothing had changed.

But a shadow loomed over Pran's face as well. "I know why you want this. But, Oksana . . . we need our fire to escape the emperor. He's more relentless than we dreamed. We'll need every ounce of strength we possess to break from him."

Oksana couldn't meet his eyes. She looked past him, staring at a speck of ash drifting above his shoulder, though avoiding his gaze felt like another betrayal.

"Let me give us the option," she choked out. "For after. All of us in this fort have had too few choices for too long."

Across the yard, a Tulii rattled the gates. An Imp, so young she could not have been a Tuliikobret for long. "If I don't have to carry this power forever, I don't want it. I want to be free, completely. I'll fight for that."

"And us!" a trio of Goblins called.

"Get it out of me," another said, scratching at his hands as though the fire were something that could be scraped away. "Make me human again."

"Let me try," Oksana said, making herself face Pran. "For those who want it. I won't force it onto anyone. But no one should have to keep these powers we never chose to have."

Pran looked like he wanted to argue further, but only nodded. "Just be careful."

His lips parted as though to say more, but his mouth hung empty.

"And?" Oksana prompted, the word almost inaudible on her ghost of a voice.

"I'm sorry." Pran's shoulders bowed as though something deep inside him was breaking.

Oksana could feel herself falling. If she didn't move, she might never rise again. So she left without speaking, Pran's words echoing like bells in her ears.

CHAPTER THIRTY-NINE

PRAN

He couldn't sleep. Again. Each night, he'd doze off for an hour or two slumped at the desk in Lepik's—*his*—office, then startle awake. He'd sit up, looking for whoever had woken him. Another Tulii, reporting bad news? The copper crown, with a message from Nanda?

But no one was ever there.

For nearly three weeks, Oksana had barely emerged from the lab, working on that concoction she swore could end their power over flame. He wasn't about to surrender his own; the Vesimaans had pushed it on him, and now they could watch him claim it. All the same, he hoped she did succeed, if only so it might bring back the brightness she'd once carried.

Until that returned, neither of them would truly be free.

Pran heaved a frosty breath toward the ceiling. If he was going to lie awake, he might as well take a turn at night watch, let someone else rest. Leaving the tower, he ascended the fort wall and found Yalku staring over the city.

"I didn't know you were assigned to watch tonight," Pran said, joining him.

"What do we do next?" Yalku asked.

Just once, Pran would like to have an answer. At least they still held the fort against the emperor and his Nightmares. Its outer walls were thicker than the Nightmares were tall, and the copper cladding was alchemically treated against fire and blunt force. Didn't stop the emperor from watching the place night and day. Even in the worst weather, Pran often spotted the man's Nightmares lurking in the shadows or slinking through the streets, making sure no one came out of the fort, and that nothing went in.

"How much food is left in the cellars?" Pran asked. He'd never dreamed there'd be a day he'd miss cabbage-and-mince stew—and he *didn't*, that slop was disgusting—but at least it had kept their stomachs filled.

Yalku grimaced. "We're down to the last barrels of flour, and sacks of potatoes with eyes longer than my fingers. We might be better off distilling those and drinking them."

Adding liquor would only worsen tempers. The Tuliis tired of waiting for the emissaries to return with news from their homelands. "Our people will help us," Pran assured them daily.

But he hadn't even heard from Nanda in weeks.

As Pran surveyed the starlit sky, still no copper crown in view, his throat went tight. He didn't know how much longer he could keep his Tuliis going on nothing.

Beside him, Yalku went rigid. "Someone's coming!"

Sinking down, Pran peered over the wall's edge through

the snowflakes tumbling onto the street. A handful of shadowy figures scurried toward the fort. They were too far away and the snow was too thick; he couldn't tell who they were or even how many marched among their group, only that they ran like fire licked at their heels.

Other Tuliis on watch darted along the wall. "Should we attack?" a Hellion asked—Marten again. Gods above, would the boy never give him a break? "A little bit closer and the Nightmares can launch fire at them."

Something deep inside Pran warned against acting hastily. "We do nothing until we know who they are."

"If it's the emperor's Nightmares," Marten countered, "we should strike before they know we've spotted them. This is our chance."

"If we don't act soon," Yalku said, "whoever it is will be close enough to see us and know they're being watched."

"*Quiet.*" Pran leaned over the wall's edge. "Those aren't the emperor's Nightmares."

The figures had drawn close enough to be seen through the moonlight. There were five, all running together. One limped, clinging to another. Of the other three, one sent up a flurry of sparks, then a flame that swelled into the shape of a copper crown, wings spread in flight.

"The emissaries!" Pran yelped. "Open the gates!"

Their Nightmares on guard reached for the wheeled winch that hefted the copper gates.

"Wait!" Yalku shouted, as another set of shadows sprang from side streets. These didn't move like people trying to escape fire; these moved *as* fire, a blaze tearing through straw. One of the five runners threw flames at those newcomers, who raised their own blaze quick as drawing breath—blue-white fire that stood out like lightning against the night.

Yalku blanched. "*Those* are the emperor's Nightmares."

"Open the gates!" Pran screamed down to the guards. "Let our emissaries in."

"You'll let in the Nightmares!" Marten protested.

"Not if ours get them first." Pran jabbed a finger at the guards. "*Save them!*"

With three mighty cranks of the winch, the gates lifted enough for the fort's Nightmares to slip out. The emissaries, reacting instinctively to any Nightmares charging toward them, faltered in their run. Some turned around, others tried to fend off those Nightmares with their own much smaller flames. Unperturbed, the fort's Nightmares snatched up those Tuliis, threw them over their shoulders, and sprinted back toward the fort.

It all happened before Pran and the others made it down the wall to the gates. "Come on!" Pran shouted, and they set to work turning the winch, closing the gates. Their Nightmares, with the rescued emissaries, slipped through moments before the fort closed. The emperor's Nightmares blasted torrents of blue-white fire against the gates, but though the walls quaked and rumbled, that alchemically treated copper held strong.

"We're safe," Pran declared, as the emperor's Nightmares slunk back toward the palace. He uncurled his stiff hands from the winch and faced the emissaries as they untangled themselves from their Nightmare rescuers. "You're all right. You're safe now."

The injured emissary burst into a hacking laugh. "We are so far from safe."

The boy couldn't stand on his own—stained bandages peeked through his torn pants—so Pran crouched down to his level. "We were worried the emperor's Nightmares had caught you on your way out."

He shifted his gaze to the other four emissaries, still catching their breath, hair plastered against their brows with sweat and melted snow.

"They almost did," the wounded boy replied. "Chased us to the city's edge. We dove into the Terhi River to escape them."

Pran ached thinking of the ice chunks that collected along the banks this time of year.

"It was the only way," the boy continued. "They would have tracked us through the trees. We'd have sent word back to warn you, but with those Nightmares on our tails, we had to keep moving."

Pran's heart beat so hard he could feel it in his teeth. "You did the right thing. And . . . you delivered your messages?"

Almost as one, the emissaries looked away.

"The messages?" Pran pressed.

"We spoke to every village on our route," the wounded boy said. "They want nothing to do with us. 'You've been too long in Vesimaa. We can't trust you. None of you belong here anymore.' Their words."

Pran sank to the ground, heedless of the snow soaking through his pants.

Maybe he should have known better. Some of the Tuliis had spent more time living in this fort than among their own people. And when Tuliikobrets marched through villages, stamping down every rebellion, when Nightmares came time and again to steal children . . . why would anyone believe Tuliis should be welcomed back?

"Even free, we can't go home," an emissary whispered. "What do we have to fight for?"

CHAPTER FORTY

OKSANA

Days slipped past like stray snowflakes dropping from the sky. At last, she'd destroyed the final bottles of Rootare's seemingly endless serum hoard. When she hadn't been burning those, she'd pored over the notes in his journals and experimented with different formulas. She ate only when Kati bodily dragged her from workstations and sat her down before food. As for sleep, more often than not it came in hour-or-two bursts, slumping across a workstation when her eyes refused to stay open any longer. Sometimes, she worried the reek of sulfur was permanently steeped into her hair.

But finally, one dark morning when the sun had yet to rise, she turned triumphantly to Kati as the girl shoved through the lab doors.

"Up already?" Kati grumbled. "Or no, let me guess—you never actually slept? Again. Oksana, you can't go on like this."

She wouldn't. Because she didn't have to.

"It's done! I have it." Oksana doused the burner fire, then held up a syringe filled with a silver, shining liquid.

Kati froze where she stood. "That will weaken your fire?"

"Snuff it out completely, I hope. Along with my Snapping." Oksana cradled that syringe the way she used to hold her icon of Yeva. She hadn't been this proud of something she'd created since she'd made her first smoke bomb in Professor Melnyk's lab. That day, she and Borys had made their little sister Iryna shriek with laughter while they set off bomb after bomb in a nearby field, until their neighbor chased them away with a broom.

But instead of looking elated, Kati eyed that syringe like a plague. "You sure about this?"

If Oksana was being honest . . . no, she wasn't. There were so many ways this serum might be wrong. And the only way to know if it would work was to inject it.

She wished Kati hadn't come in time to watch.

As the girl leaned closer, hands outstretched as though to snatch the syringe away, Oksana scooted beyond reach. Putting her back to Kati and her panicked expression, Oksana focused on the syringe. *Stop doubting,* she scolded herself. She had to be strong, had to believe.

She'd do this for the other Tuliis, that they might have a chance to be free. And for her home, because she couldn't risk ruining them if—*when*—she lost control. It would only take one time, one Snap, for her to lay the whole village to waste.

She'd do it for Pran, because his Tuliis needed all the motivation they could get to keep fighting. And he deserved a break, someone on his side.

Oksana shoved her goggles onto her forehead. "I've

studied these notes so many times I dream about them. Gone through other journals to review how Rootare created his formulas. Compared the effects of different blends together. This is the best I can do."

It was the truth. She could take comfort in that, at least.

But Kati shook her head. "Are you sure you want to take this?"

Oksana blinked in confusion. "You . . . think I should wait until after we've escaped the emperor?"

"No, I mean, should you take it *at all?* Is this really your answer?"

"I want to be myself again! Other Tuliis do, too. Now I've created a way that might make it happen. All that's left is to test it."

Before Kati could protest again, and before she could lose her own nerve, Oksana stuck the syringe into her arm and injected the serum.

Kati cursed. "Saints' teeth, *how could you?*"

Oksana set the empty syringe on the table, her hand barely holding steady. She lifted her head, gone heavy as a boulder. Squinted toward the girl gaping at her.

Then she collapsed.

A cry echoed through the lab as Oksana hit the floor. She convulsed, her jaw clenched so tight her teeth nearly cracked. Fire shot through her heart and lined the inside of her skull.

A thousand bells thundered through her mind. Her guts were being pulled apart, turned inside out. Someone, somewhere, shouted her name, then shook her so hard her head snapped back. Or maybe that was the earth breaking. Oksana stretched a hand through the fog suffocating her.

Regret coated Oksana's heart and lungs in a thick, sticky film. She should have talked with Pran first. Should have said goodbye. Should have told him she was sorry, for abandoning him to bear the weight of an army alone.

The only mercy was that Pran wasn't here to see her die.

Fog closed in, smothering her brain, flooding her throat and lungs, chasing away her breath. She was about to give in, let it crush her, but a frantic voice snatched her attention, catching her every time she began to drift. "Oksana? OKSANA! Can you hear me?!"

She opened her eyes. When had they closed?

Kati leaned over her, arms around Oksana's shoulders and cradling her head.

"Can you hear me?" Kati's voice was thick with tears. "Can you move?"

Oksana dragged herself up through the fog. Stretched her jaw, reminded her tongue how to speak. "I'm . . . all right."

"There is *no way* you're all ri—"

"I'm all right." Oksana heaved herself to sitting, breaking from Kati's hold. She hefted her arms up, turned her hands over. The fingers still shook, but they curled into fists when she willed them to.

"I'm taking you to the physician." Kati clenched her shoulder. "All the saints, Oksana, how could you—"

Oksana turned to meet her friend's red-rimmed eyes.

Her heart beat so hard she could feel it in her fingertips. "My fire . . . the heat in my lungs . . . I don't feel it anymore."

Kati snorted. "I doubt you feel much of anything. I'm still taking you to the—stop that, don't try to stand, what if you—"

Using the table for support, Oksana hauled herself to her feet. Her vision blurred for a moment, a wave of dizziness crashing over her. Kati grabbed her by the waist, swinging one of Oksana's arms across her shoulders.

Oksana leaned against the girl until her legs stopped shaking. "I mean it. I can't feel my fire. At all!"

Those words almost lifted her into the sky.

Kati's brow furrowed. "You really believe that means . . . ? And your Snapping?"

Oksana grounded herself with a breath. "The only way to know that is to test it."

CHAPTER FORTY-ONE

PRAN

Though the sun wasn't yet risen, Pran called all Tuliis to gather for a meeting. Yet the emissaries' news still spread before Pran could round up anyone to present it himself. At once, it seemed everyone knew how the emissaries had been received—or rather, how they *hadn't*.

Some Tuliis shut themselves back in their barracks, but most flocked to the pub, until the little wooden building couldn't hold them all. They smashed the cellar locks and hauled up the last barrels of ale and bottles of liquor.

There'd be no pulling this crowd to order now, making them listen to reason no matter how Pran gilded his words. He retreated to the tower, his office there, staring through the window toward the pub, lit green from all the chemical lamps inside.

"It's not your fault, Pran." Yalku sat at the iron desk, clutching his own enormous mug of ale—now nearly empty.

"Not my fault, maybe, but it's my job to get us past this, if we're not going to waste away behind these walls." Pran couldn't shake the feeling that there was more he should have done: stronger words sent with the emissaries, a compelling fight during the jubilee—something so grand their homelands could never have doubted their intentions.

Had everyone forgotten that the nation who'd taken them in the first place was their real enemy? Pran leaned against the window, gazing past its frosty panes, watching the lamps dim one by one as their chemicals burned out.

If he hadn't been looking so closely, he would have missed them. But as he peered out, seven shadowy figures staggered from the pub, across the courtyard, and through the gates.

Any little spies you send out, boy? My Nightmares will find them.

"No!" Pran was on his feet, lumbering down the tower stairs after the departing Tuliis.

Behind him, Yalku panted, clinging to the walls to stay upright. "What's going on?"

Outside in the courtyard, Pran gestured toward the gates. The Tuliis were already disappearing from sight, turning around a street corner. Their flint starters were in hand, orange sparks crackling high.

"They *can't*," Pran said. It was one thing to drink away their sorrows. But leaving the fort while the emperor's Nightmares lay in wait, and not even sober . . . "Where are the Nightmare guards?"

"I . . ." Yalku clutched his head, slumped against the tower wall. "Saw a lot of Nightmares in the pub, when I got my mug."

Pran shoved the boy toward that pub. "Get them. Tell them there are Tuliis on the loose. Send them after us."

"*Us?* What are you—"

Pran lurched across the courtyard and through the gates, his own flint starter in hand.

CHAPTER FORTY-TWO

OKSANA

She found three Nightmares in the pub, chins in their hands, surrounded by too many empty mugs. Drinking before dawn . . . what was wrong with everyone?

"What's gotten into you? Pull yourselves together." She shoved away their mugs and poured them cups of water. At least it was so much easier to talk to them now that they'd quit wearing those gut-wrenching masks.

They stared at her with hollow eyes. "You haven't heard."

"What, that everyone's decided to see how fast they can burn out their livers?" She scowled at the enormous amounts of alcohol being consumed throughout the pub.

"Some emissaries returned," one Nightmare said.

"So they did get out of the city!" But her stomach sank, as she looked again around the pub. This was not celebratory drinking. Throughout the room, there wasn't one smile.

"They don't want us back," she whispered. Her worst fears, in five words.

The Nightmares stared into their cups of water.

Oksana swallowed until the pain in her throat eased. Then she glared at each Nightmare. This was, after all, exactly what they'd heard from Anu's family and the people of Kivi. The real question was why anyone thought they could put their Commanders in chains, march out of this fort, and be welcomed back by the world with open arms.

"We always knew this might happen," Oksana told the Nightmares. "I have a solution that might make the difference."

If they were no longer fire demons, there was no reason to fear them.

"It's time to test it," she pressed. "I need Tuliis who can challenge me. I need to make sure I can't Snap anymore. Then I'll know this serum has worked."

One lifted an eyebrow. "You're the broken one. We're supposed to fight *you*?"

"I'm not broken." The words always seemed wrong, until she had to defend herself. Then, somehow, they tumbled from her lips with little prompting. "If my new serum has countered Rootare's, I can fix all of us. No more life with these powers, no more fire on our breath. If I've succeeded, you can be the first I free from the flames. Will you help, or not?"

She didn't want to chain the training yard gates, didn't want to believe it was still necessary. But she knew better than to tempt fate.

After they were secured, Kati stood against the wall. Oksana hadn't wanted her to come into the yard and risk getting hurt, but Kati had refused to remain outside. "When Nightmares are in a fight, they get intense," she said, as Oksana geared up with greaves and gauntlets. "I want someone on your side nearby, in case they forget they're not the Commanders' pet monsters anymore."

"And how would you step in against three Nightmares?"

Kati smiled. "I won't have to, right? I'm here as a precaution."

Oksana would have felt better if that gesture reached the girl's eyes. Alone, she marched to the center of the training yard, where the trio of Nightmares waited.

"How do we start this thing?" one asked.

"Try coming for me." None of the Nightmares moved. "Don't be afraid of hurting me," Oksana pressed. "If there's any chance at all that I might still Snap, it won't happen unless I'm about to break. I must know if it's really gone."

The wary looks the Nightmares shot each other betrayed their true concern: *she* wasn't the one they were worried about getting hurt.

Maybe she should have felt powerful, that even Nightmares were afraid to fight her. For years she and the other Tuliis trembled whenever they'd stalked past. After all, these brutes tore children from homes. Terrorized Novices. Kept so-called order in the fort by rounding up Tuliis to be burned. Were so far under the Commanders' thumbs that yes, she was surprised to find that beneath their masks they still looked human, that their bodies weren't as warped as their souls must have been . . .

These Nightmares *dared* to fear her? As if she were the one who hurt without conscience, who followed orders blindly, never seeing the faces of those condemned . . .

A feral screech erupted with all the fury of Demon's Tongue. Oksana lunged forward, sight narrowed to the three cowards before her.

They would pay for their crimes.

This time, the fight wasn't reduced to scraps of sound and flashes of flame. This time, Oksana was aware of everything that happened. She saw one Nightmare leap back, raise a flame, and throw, all while she charged. Saw his face slip into the concentration of battle.

But he was slow, so pathetically slow. How had the Commanders ever trusted the Nightmares to do their work? Why had Tuliis ever feared them?

She had no reason to fear a Nightmare anymore.

The other two held back at first. But when she vaulted onto the shoulders of the first Nightmare, spiraled fire around him, then clenched her hands into fists to close those flames over him, they finally moved. One hurled a flame at Oksana, so she had to leap off the Nightmare's shoulders, losing hold of the flame she'd spun around him. The third launched fire at Oksana before her feet touched the ground.

She tried to turn in midair but didn't quite make it. The blue flame slammed into her torso, biting through the leather battle tunic and scorching her flesh beneath. Ignoring the pain, Oksana fired back, three flames at once, knocking each Nightmare to the ground.

On and on it went. They were good. She was better.

When they thought they knew her next move, she'd change it, their flames falling on empty air. Meanwhile, they scrambled to avoid her fire, yelping as heat bit through their uniforms. Their faces shone with sweat, their counterattacks growing erratic. Sloppy. One by one they fell to the ground, nursing raw, blistered burns.

Oksana tipped back her head and laughed, while dawn lit its own fire in the sky. These creatures of terror . . . she'd shown them what it really meant to fear.

Sparking flames, Oksana raised a piercing blue blaze that hurt her own eyes, so tall it towered above the training yard walls. She was gearing up for another round when she spotted Kati pressed against that wall, her face taut with shock.

Saints alive. Oksana snuffed out the flames and dropped her flint starter, the ivory handle searing hot. What had she been doing? She kicked the starter away and collapsed to her knees.

Kati was at her side in an instant. "Are you hurt?"

No. And that made it so much worse. "I'm stronger. I've made my fire *stronger*!"

Around the yard, the Nightmares limped and hobbled like Novices after a dismal training session. *She'd* done that. It shouldn't have been possible.

"I warned you," Kati's voice echoed as though she spoke

from the opposite side of the training yard. "Rootare would have accounted for those old weaknesses, safeguarded against them in his new serums."

And Rootare's own words whispered through Oksana's mind like a taunt: *I didn't become imperial alchemist by creating work that could be undone by a half-trained child. I've left my mark on you forever.*

"I thought . . . ," Oksana gasped, each word piercing her throat. "I thought this was how I could save us all."

Kati crouched down, her face hard lines of fury. "Did you really believe being weaker was the answer? With all we still have to face?"

"Not weaker," Oksana protested. "Human. So we could be accepted."

"What did I tell you about connecting in a different way? You have a much bigger issue than being accepted by Vesimaans or even Horádimians. You don't accept *yourself.* You keep searching for other ways to fix our situation, rather than face it straight on and make use of what you've been given."

The words were so heartless, Oksana could feel herself Snapping again. Only through sheer force of will did she hold herself together.

"Why should I have to make use of a power I never wanted?" she snarled. "Why should I have to accept that?"

Kati snorted. "Nayar wasn't off base when he talked about using our fire to protect. Look, no one had to talk you down this time. You did it on your own. Fought when you had to, then stopped. You're strong enough now to control your flames. Isn't that what counts?"

Oksana grimaced, but Kati had a point. As usual.

There was still work to do, the Snap to get completely under control. But this time Oksana had fought only to defend. She'd fought against the ones who could destroy, who'd already done so. And when they'd stopped, she had too, because she'd seen that the fight was over and didn't want to cause more pain.

If she could do that much, she could do more. Rootare hadn't broken her, even now.

"Think about this." Kati scooted closer, until Oksana met her gaze. "You can fight off Nightmares. What are you going to do with that?"

CHAPTER FORTY-THREE

PRAN

When his leg buckled, he clung to walls, carts, barrels, or hitching posts for horses. There was no time to coddle his pain, so Pran gritted his teeth and flung himself through the snowy streets, following the slurred voices and boisterous shouts of his escaped Tuliis.

Those shouts dissolved into the shatter of breaking glass and the crackle of flame.

No.

No no no no no no no no no!

Pran rounded a corner and found the broken window, glass shards splayed across the street like tears. The slurred voices barked from behind those jagged panes: a spirit shop, the paint on its walls flaked away. Inside, Tuliis stuffed bottles into their jackets and hurled others to the floor, cackling as glass smashed and liquor bled across the wooden slats.

"They wanted us to burn," one shouted. "So we burn!"

The group lifted their flint starters. Sparked.

"No!" Pran lunged forward, glass crunching beneath his boots. He threw himself at the window, cutting his hands on the jagged glass. *"Don't."*

But sparks became fire, and fire ignited the spilled liquor.

Pran clambered through the window, slicing his legs on the broken glass. He stomped on the flames, but there were too many. The fire spread beyond his reach, racing toward the walls, lined with bottles and barrels.

"GET OUT," he yelled at the Tuliis, who protested even though they barely seemed able to stand. "Get back to the fort!"

While they lumbered outside, Pran searched for anything he could use to douse the flames, but the room held nothing of the sort. This building, stacked floor to ceiling with shelves of liquor, was done for.

Pran shoved the last tottering Tulii through the window and tumbled out himself, hot blood from his sliced-up legs dripping onto the snow. But there'd be no true escape from this; everyone in this city would know who'd set the fire—and worse, these flames screamed their exact location. He had to get them all back to the safety of the fort.

But it was too late.

A trio of the emperor's Nightmares stood in the street, watching through the blood-red sunrise as the drunk Tuliis whooped at the growing flames. When the oafs finally spotted those Nightmares, they fumbled for their flint starters.

"Think you can hunt us like animals?" one yelled, sparking an embarrassing excuse for fire. "We will end you!"

"SHUT UP!" Pran barked. "Go back this instant, or I'll lock you away with the Commanders."

Pushing ahead of the louts, he stared down the

Nightmares. Two more had joined the group, and another ambled up the street. None of them displayed the least concern about these Tuliis escaping.

Because this wasn't going to be a battle.

"You were warned, little Hellion." One of the Nightmares stepped forward, shaking her head. "This time, we won't spare you."

Pran clutched his starter, raising warning sparks, even as his stomach dipped. His thoughts flashed to Oksana, safe—*safe?*—in the fort lab. *I love you,* he thought, and maybe her saint would carry those words back for him.

Sparking his starter again, Pran reached for every scrap of heat within his lungs and blew a fire that grew steadily brighter. Behind its cover, he muttered to his Tuliis, "When I throw, you run back to the fort. That's an order. Run, and tell the guards to shut the gates."

"We're staying to fight!" one yelled. The others bellowed, "Freedom to the flames!"

Pran almost turned his fire onto them. "Run, you unbelievable fools, or you'll be ashes under their boots!"

He launched a blaze toward the Nightmares, then raised six fireballs in quick succession until he gasped for breath and his lips were scorched.

It wasn't enough.

All that fire was swallowed up by a torrent of blue-white flames surging forward. He dived beneath them, shielding his face as the searing heat threatened to cook him.

At least that heat finally sent the other Tuliis running.

A leader gave himself up for his people, if the situation required it. That didn't mean, if there did turn out to be an afterlife, that Pran wouldn't come back as a ghost and make those blockheads sorry.

Lurching to his feet, slipping on the blood still weeping down his legs, Pran arced two pillars of fire forward, one after the other.

Both were swallowed by another torrent of blue flames.

Beneath the blistering wave of heat that sent sweat dripping into his eyes, Pran cursed. Only four Nightmares stood before him. Where had the other two gone? Slipped off after the Tuliis? He wanted to look but didn't dare take his eyes off the group before him. With fire alone, he'd never fight them off, but if he could distract them . . .

Down the street, the steam train thundered into the station.

Pran clicked a spark, breathed it into fire, but before he could throw it toward that train, smoldering blue flames billowed toward him, so wide there was no way around. He launched his fire anyway and watched the blue swallow it whole.

He staggered back, but flesh couldn't outpace flame, and he was growing dizzy from the blood spilling down his shins. Clicking his starter, he raised another flame—if he was going down, he'd go burning—when a wave of blue roared from behind him and met the blaze.

Hands snatched him by the shoulders and threw him to the side of the street.

A dozen Nightmares from the fort gathered around Pran where he'd fallen. They all charged the emperor's crew, except for two who remained at Pran's side. "We have to get you to the fort, Nayar," one rasped.

"Wait! There were seven Tuliis, all drunk," Pran said as a Nightmare hauled him to his feet. "I told them to go back to the fort, but I think Nightmares went after them."

"Get him back," one said to the other, then turned to join the battle of blue, the street incandescent with the fire of Nightmares versus Nightmares.

"Did you see them?" Pran pressed the one still at his side. "If any Nightmares went after them, they don't have a chance—"

"Neither do you, unless we leave now." Ignoring Pran's protests, the Nightmare heaved Pran over his shoulders and ran. Slung backward, Pran had an unbroken view of what they left behind. The fort's Nightmares were petrifying, slinging fire so tall and bright it would have dropped any other Tuliis where they stood.

Yet for everything they threw, the emperor's Nightmares met it more fiercely. The street was as warm as a summer's day, ice and frost steaming into the night. Nightmares leaped around each other so smoothly that if he tuned out the screams, it might have been a beautiful dance.

But this was no dance. It was death, only death.

Slung over the Nightmare's shoulder, Pran saw the emperor's crew raise a swath of flame that devoured the fort's Nightmares.

❦

The fort's gates slammed down the second Pran was inside.

"Let me go!" he bellowed, kicking loose from the Nightmare's hold so that he tumbled down in a heap.

A crowd of Tuliis gathered around the gates. Pran didn't care that they saw him scrabbling on the ground, smearing his blood in the snow. The next moment, he was back on his feet, faster than he knew he could move. Near those gates, sobbing Tuliis hunched, two of the seven fools. They were soot-stained, reeking of smoke, their clothes and hair smoldering.

"Where are the others?" Pran demanded. They only wailed harder.

Two Nightmare guards stared from the gates to Pran and the lone Nightmare at his side. "Where are *our* others?"

A few weeks ago Pran wouldn't have believed it—Nightmares, defeated by flames. Now, the image of those Nightmares swallowed up in one burst of blue fire would be forever etched into his mind. He rounded on the two crying Tuliis.

"*What the hell were you thinking?!*" Gods, it felt good to scream. "Why would you do that when you *know* what's out there?!"

"Why wouldn't we?" one of the Tuliis shouted back. "We're trapped behind these walls."

"We're going to starve in here," the other yelled. "This

fort is our tomb. You lied to us, Nayar. We are never going to be free."

Every eye in the courtyard turned to Pran. Many were bright with either tears or too much booze, or perhaps both.

He fought to still his own racing breaths. "Our fight isn't over—"

"It *is*," an Imp cut in. "That one who Snapped . . . Artemivna . . . her serum didn't work. She promised to get rid of our fire. Instead, she made hers *worse*. We have nothing to fight for anymore!"

Oksana.

His instinct was to run to her, find her. But when he turned too fast, he stumbled, another bout of dizziness sweeping over him. His shredded pants were soaked with his blood, and more kept spilling.

And his injuries aside, there were too many Tuliis surrounding him, expecting answers. Without homes to welcome them back, no one trusting them to use their fire, and no way to get rid of it . . . If even their Nightmares couldn't fight against the emperor's, what chance did *any* of them have?

But he'd declared himself their leader, planting in their heads the escape these Tuliis had never let themselves dream of. He didn't get to despair.

He faced the others, looking them over even when they didn't meet his gaze. "There's a place in this world for us, if we make it ourselves. *We* are what's left. If we look out for each other, we'll never be alone. That's as much as anyone can ask for."

"But how do we get there?" a Tulii asked.

If he stepped past these Tuliis, if he climbed the stairs and stood on the wall, if he turned south, he'd see the white marble palace with its jagged spires. Inside lurked the man who stood in their way. "The emperor must let us go."

CHAPTER FORTY-FOUR

OKSANA

Hours later, the fort had finally gone silent, everyone retreated to the pub or their barracks, out of the cold. Oksana figured it was safe, at last, to enter the hospital wing and get her burn tended from the Nightmare fight. She needed the place to be empty, needed to be alone. She did not want to endure the inevitable stares and questions, the shame of her failure.

But she'd guessed wrong. Even when she hadn't seen another Tulii walk the fort grounds since the sun had risen high above the walls, someone was already there. First thing she saw, when she passed through its door, was Pran slumped across a cot.

Oksana's knees locked. She wasn't ready to face him. To confess how she'd completely failed, that her serum couldn't end anyone's fire. She'd run from the room if she could get her leaden legs to move. But as she staggered back, her elbow knocked against the doorframe.

At the sound, Pran jerked upright. Spotted her. Pushed himself to sitting.

Their silence wrapped around Oksana's throat like a

cord. For what seemed an eternity, they simply stared at each other.

"We've got to find another place to cross paths," Pran said at last. His face was a mask of lightness, yet his haunted eyes betrayed his nerves.

"I just need . . . the physician . . ." Oksana glanced around, relieved for an excuse to look away, but the man was nowhere in sight.

"He ran out of bandages. Went to find some clean rags." Pran gestured to his legs. His pants were torn off at the upper thighs, the remains of the dark fabric in a heap on the floor. Rags were wound up and down both legs from mid-calf to mid-thigh.

"Falling apart worse than usual?"

She didn't know why she said it. Some lousy attempt at a joke? Nothing was funny here. She'd heard the stories whispered before everyone disappeared into their barracks: The Tuliis despaired. Pran had tried to save them. He'd nearly died with them.

Saints alive. All she wanted was to hold him until they both stopped shaking.

Pran grimaced. "Everything I do falls to pieces. Why not me, too?"

"I'm . . . sorry for the emissaries' news," she choked out, then could say no more, fury and despair waging war in her throat.

"Am I such a fool?" Pran's own voice cracked. "I thought

I could succeed. But no matter what I do, everyone suffers." He swept a hand across his face, hiding his eyes.

Pran was no perfect leader. He was a *boy*. In Horádim, no one was considered grown until they were twenty years old, and until that time, they remained children, with a child's freedom from burden and worry. Yet Pran had taken up a mantle of unimaginable responsibility.

It was what she admired about him. *Missed,* until the ache throbbed through her bones.

"What would succeeding look like?" she asked. "Everyone alive and unharmed? You always said there would be a stiff price. Hard choices."

His jaw tightened. "Maybe I wasn't the right one to make them."

"But you *did*. When no one else would. That counts, Pran. It counts for everything."

"It wasn't all me," Pran whispered. "The rest of the Tuliis, all those Nightmares . . . they joined after what happened to Anu. Her burning. Her song."

For a long moment, Oksana couldn't breathe. All those Tuliis on Pran's side—why did it happen only after such enormous cost? Yet warmth also trickled through Oksana's veins, to know that others had risen up. It was the best way to honor her friend.

"Anu was braver than anyone gave her credit for," Oksana said, when she found her voice again. "And Pran . . . so are you."

She stepped to his cot. Sank to her knees. Gently cupped her hands around his face, brushing a thumb across the shining scar on his cheek.

"Ever since the Nightmares dragged me from Horádim," she said, "all I've wanted was to go home. But I've always been scared of getting there. For the longest time, I barely let myself dream of it, because it seemed impossible. So I threw myself into looking out for others. That started as my rebellion. But it became my excuse. In the end, it wasn't enough to protect anyone. Not Anu. Not you. Not even myself."

A chill bit through her until Oksana could barely feel her fingers against Pran's face. She dropped her hands before the frost could pass onto him and turned away.

"Can you . . ." The words tangled in her throat. She didn't know if she deserved to speak them. But she felt Pran's gaze, like the sun on her shoulders. It loosened her jaw, unlocked her tongue. "Can you . . . ever forgive me?"

Pran caught her chin, tilting her face up. "Can we agree we've both done really reckless and probably desperate things?"

When he held out his arms, Oksana couldn't help but sink into them.

After the physician returned and finished tending to both of them, Oksana thought she ought to leave. Pran lay on his cot in a clean uniform, drowsy from medicine. His gaze was unfocused—she wasn't sure he even knew his surroundings.

But when she tucked a blanket around him and stepped away, he called after her. "Stay?"

Barely understanding what came over her, and definitely not questioning it, Oksana climbed beneath the blanket with him and curled against his back. Pressing her face to the curve of his neck, she breathed. Once, twice, three times. As she'd done when they were Novices. As he'd done for her, in the training yard when she'd gone wild on the Hellions. Each breath came long and slow, filling her whole chest, her ribs expanding against his spine. He copied the rhythm until their breathing matched.

Tucking an arm around him, Oksana held Pran tight. She couldn't stop whatever this world threw at them next, but she could make sure he didn't confront any more of it alone.

Just when she was wondering if he'd fallen asleep, Pran turned over on the cot, facing her. The room was dim, but his eyes shone brighter than she'd seen in weeks. Maybe not since the night he'd given her his promise and ring.

His ring, still stuffed in her pocket. Suddenly Oksana felt unguarded without it hanging over her heart.

Pran pressed his lips to her forehead. "I've never stopped needing you. I'm sorry I pushed you away and called that protecting you."

"I know why you did it. It was wrong—don't do it again. But I get it." She scooted closer until her breath blended with his, until their heartbeats knocked together, a quiet duet in the dark.

Pran shifted uneasily against her. "You're so warm. Are you . . . do you feel . . . ?" He rose onto an elbow, squinting at her. "They said your new serum, it didn't . . ."

No more hiding. Still, Oksana's throat knotted over the words. "I . . . can't get the fire out of our blood. I can't keep my promise to the Tuliis. I'm so sorry."

"You could try again . . ."

"I tried everything. I don't know what else to do." Before she could stop it, a scalding tear slipped from her eye and cut down her cheek.

Pran sank back onto the cot, his whole face hollow. "That makes two of us. Between the emperor and his Nightmares—when our own are no match for them, I don't know how we'll ever escape them."

Beneath the blankets, Oksana caught his hand. "You'll do it with help. Don't you see, Pran? It's never been up to you, alone, to figure out all these answers."

Saints alive. She had an answer. She wished it were any other. But she couldn't look him in the eyes and hold this back.

Leaning close, she whispered, "I know someone who can defeat Nightmares."

CHAPTER FORTY-FIVE

PRAN

He hobbled from the hospital wing with Oksana at his side. Though his head was still fuzzy from medicine and he would probably do better to sleep, Pran couldn't wait another moment to tell the Tuliis they had their way out.

Before they reached Healing Hall's doors, above the sounds of the howling, stormy wind, voices thundered in the courtyard. "Freedom to the flames! Freedom from traitors! Freedom from liars!"

Beside him, Oksana's steps faltered. "Are they . . . trying to take the fort . . . from *you?*"

She looked thunderstruck, but it wasn't so impossible to believe. *Bonfires show little discretion in what, or whom, they devour—even the hands that made them.*

"Stay behind me," Pran whispered.

She caught his arm. "Want to rethink those words?"

Right. He had to get hold of himself, if he wanted to face those Tuliis without losing everything he'd worked for. "Keep watch, please? Let me know if you see real trouble."

With her on alert, flint starter in hand, he pushed open the hall doors.

A roar greeted them, wind flinging jagged ice into his face. Furious Tuliis stood shoulder to shoulder before the building.

"We're through with you, Nayar," Marten bellowed. "We're through with waiting and dying."

"We fought for you," a Goblin shouted. "Did everything you asked. But you've only given us a cage. Anytime someone steps outside it, they die. And we'll starve if we stay in here."

An ugly part of Pran, all barbs and thorns, wanted to demand what they'd have done differently. The stronger part of him stamped down those words. He had much to atone for. "I know things have been bleak—"

"You promised freedom," another Hellion interrupted. "And *you*"—she jabbed a finger toward Oksana—"promised to end our fire. If neither of you can keep those promises, we'll replace you like we replaced the Commanders."

"You'll do no such thing." Oksana shouldered in front of Pran, staring down the Tuliis, her red hair whipping in the wind. "I can't end our fire. And I'm sorry for it."

Her voice broke, and Pran's heart ached. Catching her hand, he squeezed her fingers until she clutched back.

"But I *can* get us out of this fort," she shouted over the Tuliis' cries.

"How?" Marten scoffed. "Rampage on everyone?"

"Only on the emperor's Nightmares."

"No one can fight them," an Imp called out. "If our Nightmares can't defeat them, no one has a chance."

"I can defeat the Nightmares."

"It's true," one spoke up, fresh bandages peeking from beneath her tunic.

"You have to understand all we're up against," Pran called out, his heart pounding in time with the angry murmurs reverberating through the yard. "The Commanders were only the beginning. The emperor is desperate to uphold his family legacy; he has much more to lose than the Commanders. His reign is in trouble. That makes him too stubborn to reason with. All the man has going for him is that Scamall hasn't invaded yet."

"So, we take that away," Oksana said. "Give them the power to invade."

Every single Tulii in the courtyard gaped.

"You wouldn't," Marten snarled.

Pran huffed. "Of course we won't. The emperor only has to *think* that's what we're doing."

The Tuliis quieted, though most of them—especially the Vesimaans—still shot Pran and Oksana dark looks. Pran met their stares, keeping his own gaze soft but his chin tipped high.

This was the last chance for everyone inside the fort. He would see it through.

Marten stalked forward, sneering. "What exactly will the emperor *think* we're doing?"

Pran stepped aside, nodding toward Oksana.

"My new serum made my fire stronger," she said. "Maybe it will do the same for another: Demon's Tongue."

CHAPTER FORTY-SIX

OKSANA

Hellions carted a barrel of Demon's Tongue from the armory to the south courtyard. There, Oksana mixed a beaker of the new serum into the barrel.

Another Hellion brought over a small battle tank, one they'd carried on their backs while attacking Kivi. Oksana filled it with the serum-Demon's Tongue mixture. Once it was full, that Hellion pointed the tank's nozzle toward the wood stacked on the execution platform.

"Only a little," Oksana cautioned. "Until we know for sure what it will do . . ."

The Hellion pumped the claw-shaped handle once, sending a single splash onto the wood.

"Everyone stand back," Oksana called to the Tuliis gathered around watching. "Outside the gates."

Only Pran remained with her, along with a trio of Hellions who stood with more tanks, these filled with water. Pran had insisted on them. Though if this new Demon's Tongue went awry, would those even be enough?

Oksana's mouth went dry. What was she getting them into, this girl who played with fire? Staggering back, she nearly told the others to forget it, that they shouldn't trust her. After what her dangerous ideas had done to Kivi, who was she to try anything else?

But . . . who was she *not* to? She glanced at the Tuliis pressed against the gates, waiting. Kati stood at the front of that crowd, nodding when their gazes locked.

Oksana glanced at Pran, standing taller than she'd seen in weeks, his face tranquil as he watched her in perfect trust. She couldn't end their fire, but she wasn't useless.

Out in the mountains the monsters arose, all embers and fire, to fight the land's foes.

Help me be, like you, a defender of life.

Oksana sparked a flame the size of her thumbnail and hurled it across the courtyard onto the wood wet with Demon's Tongue.

White-hot flames exploded toward the sky like a million stars combusting.

"Saints alive." She winced at the heat scalding her skin from all the way across the yard.

The Hellions with the water tanks whooped and punched the air. "The emperor will piss himself when he sees this!" one yelled with glee.

Oksana retreated from the bonfire's relentless heat, yet as the air filled with Tuliis' cheers, she couldn't help smiling. *Not everything that comes from fire is terrible and ugly.*

Maybe those words still held some truth.

Pran rubbed his hands together and faced the Tuliis

behind the gates. "Tomorrow is Fire Night. The emperor will host another party in Ceremony Hall. Shall we give him a show?"

"Another deal?" Yalku called through the gates.

Pran shook his head. "No more deals. An ultimatum."

CHAPTER FORTY-SEVEN

PRAN

"Where will we go after?" Marten called.

Gods above, Pran would be glad to be through with this jackass. "There's a whole world beyond this empire. We can explore it, find places where we belong. Create them ourselves, if we have to. With our fire, we can protect ourselves. With freedom, we'll build lives worth living."

He stepped closer to the gates, sweeping the gazes of every Tulii leaning against the bars. "I'm sorry for the response from our homelands. I expected better."

"We can't control anyone else's reactions," Oksana said to the group. "Only our own."

"Will you waste away in mourning," Pran called to the Tuliis, "or will you prove your worth to the world? Will you fight with me . . . one more time?"

When he gestured to Sepp, and she unlocked the gates, the Tuliis milled inside the courtyard, surrounding Pran.

"One more time," Marten said, and the troops around him nodded.

"I'll do everything in my power to set us free," Pran said.

When they looked unimpressed, Oksana stepped forward, raising a blue-white fire from the tiniest of sparks. "Remember how much is in our power now," she said, and to Pran's amazement, Marten stalked away without complaint.

Glancing at the Goblins and Imps watching her and that fire, Oksana tossed the flame onto another pile of wood beside the platform, raising a bonfire that stained the courtyard eerie shades of blue.

The Tuliis held their own Fire Night a day early, staying up until dawn building bonfires around the courtyard and leaping over them while bellowing the festival's anthem:

Jump the flames with me, my love
Jump the flames so high
Jump the flames with me, my dear
Together we will fly

On the edge of the platform, Pran sat with Oksana, watching her study the dancing light. Snow and ice had finally stopped falling, but patches here and there glistened on Oksana's coat, glittering like crushed gems. Her vibrant hair lifted in the breeze, curling around her jaw. Her eyes seemed darker than he'd remembered; there were definitely new shadows beneath them. Yet they possessed strength as well, a depth like the expanse of night sky.

She was beautiful. She'd always been beautiful. She was

the light that kept him going when all else seemed hopelessly bleak.

He took her hand, squeezed it so she looked at him. "Will you jump with me?" He nodded toward the nearest bonfire, Oksana's blue-white blaze.

Her lips parted. The Vesimaans had a fable about jumping the flames on Fire Night: a couple who held hands while leaping over fire, and kept that handhold through landing, would never be torn apart. Pran had little interest in Vesimaan traditions, but the act of rising together, as one—that they knew forward and back.

"Please," Pran said, his blood buzzing with how much he wanted, *needed*, this jump before the fight ahead.

Oksana stood, tugging him along. Tuliis parted, making way for them, their singing louder as Pran and Oksana paused beside the flames. The others' voices faded as Pran's senses narrowed to the soft touch of Oksana's palm against his.

"Ready?" Her earth-dark eyes shimmered in the firelight.

He could only nod, all speech stolen from his throat.

When Oksana moved, he followed automatically. As one they leaped, sailing over the blue flames. For a moment, that fire beneath them seemed as wide as the sea, yet they kept flying across it, fingers entwined, rising higher and higher like they might join the stars.

But what rises must always fall, and eventually the ground loomed toward them. Oksana clung to his hand. "Don't let go."

"Never," Pran said.

When their boots hit rock, they stumbled, but their palms didn't part. The Tuliis cheered before turning back to their songs, and Pran drew Oksana closer until his lips were a breath away.

"Whatever our future holds," he whispered, "I still want to share it with you."

She pulled something from her pocket—the necklace with her Yeva pendant and his ring—and slipped it around her neck. "That is a future worth fighting for."

Oksana leaned in and kissed him until all that mattered to Pran was the feel of her lips against his.

The copper crown came with the dawn, bearing a message between its wings.

Bha'ee,

I'm sorry I didn't write sooner. The past weeks, there's much I've fought toward. That's no excuse; I know you can say the same a hundred times over. But when we heard rumors of how your emissaries were—or weren't—being received, Jiyn, Mother, Father, and I met with people across our city and beyond, pleading your case. I can now promise that there are some here prepared to offer sanctuary to any Tuliis who need somewhere to go. We do mean all Tuliis, not only those who are Pakastran. Let us know if we can help bring any here, and where we can meet you along the way.

Come swiftly home to us, bha'ee. It's been too long since your laughter and stories brightened our home.

Tumha Bha'uu

Hand shaking so hard he nearly dropped the letter, Pran climbed the platform in the south courtyard and shouted, his voice echoing until every Tulii turned from the dwindling fires toward him.

"We have a place to go!" he yelled, and the Tuliis cheered as he told them of Nanda's offer. They sparked their flint starters, casting fireballs toward the sky—and Pran was grateful they were too busy to notice him barely holding back tears, that after all these years Nanda had never stopped reaching out to him.

And that for once, Pran accepted that hand.

CHAPTER FORTY-EIGHT

OKSANA

In Meal Hall, Oksana helped Pran spread a city map across a table.

"Tonight," Pran told the Tuliis gathered around, "Oksana and I will go to the emperor in the midst of his Fire Night celebration. We'll tell him of the new Demon's Tongue and exactly what will happen with it if he doesn't set us free."

"But how will you get into that hall?" Kati pressed. "His Nightmares will be keeping watch. They'll see you coming, put the emperor under lockdown, and you'll never reach him."

"I'll sneak in under their noses," Oksana said, "then get Pran in through a servants' door."

Kati lifted an eyebrow. "*You* will sneak into an imperial ball?"

"I can make myself look Vesimaan. Anu showed me how."

In the Commanders' barracks, she and Kati rooted through the trunks of every female Commander, searching for an outfit befitting Juhan's celebration.

"None of this livery." Kati shoved aside another armful. "That'll draw the wrong attention. You need to blend in, look elegant enough to be ordinary."

Oksana rolled her eyes. "Because that makes lots of sense."

But Kati crowed when she found her prize: an off-the-shoulder gown with a full bell skirt, made of fabric that changed from red to orange to gold depending on how the light hit it.

"Saints," Oksana gasped. "When would Tamm have worn this?"

Kati grinned wickedly. "Maybe she wanted to be pretty for a special someone."

Commanders in love, romancing each other. Oksana gagged at the thought.

The dress was hopelessly too big, but Kati leaned over the fabric, her mouth a determined line. "If we take it in here and here, then shorten the hem . . ."

"Can you do all that? It's so much work."

The girl waved a hand. "Well enough to last one night. You only need to get through the doors, not win a marriage proposal."

While Kati enlisted other Tuliis to help alter the dress, Oksana went to Anu's barrack. She stood so long outside the door her feet cramped, but still she couldn't bring herself to reach for the handle.

"Where are you now, Anu?" Oksana whispered. "With your parents? Are you happy?"

Anu should have been happy *here*. She should have been looking forward to freedom and all she'd do with it.

"This should have been your victory," Oksana said. "It *is*. If I'd gone into the lab that night, it would have been me burned. I'm alive because you looked out for me."

She couldn't waste Anu's sacrifice crying when there was still so much to be done. Swiping the tears from her cheeks and sucking in a long breath, she pushed through the door. When she knelt beside Anu's bunk and lifted three of the floorboards beneath, Oksana uncovered the box that held Anu's makeup powders and inks.

"Still looking out for me." Oksana took up the box in her arms, then paused and rested a hand on the pillow. "May the saints keep you, my friend."

CHAPTER FORTY-NINE

PRAN

"For the first step of our plan," he told the Tuliis that afternoon, everyone gathered again in Meal Hall, "we need the train."

Each night between the first and fourth bells, the steam train sat silent in its station. While it cooled from daily travels, the crews refilled the coal cars and mended any parts needing attention. That would be their best chance.

"Fire Night will work to our benefit," Pran told the Goblins, Hellions, and Nightmares, all who'd help seize the train. "Less crew around, while everyone celebrates. Any crew present will be easy enough to capture or frighten away. It's the emperor's Nightmares we must watch for. We won't be able to avoid them; our job is to be ready when they find us."

"That's where the new Demon's Tongue comes in," Oksana spoke up beside him. "Well, one part."

Onto the handcarts once used to transport stolen children, they loaded the barrel of strengthened Demon's Tongue, along with every other barrel of ordinary Demon's Tongue left in the armory plus a few empty barrels as well, to fill the rest of the carts.

"It must *look* like we have a lot," Oksana said. "We want the emperor's Nightmares noticing that." She turned to the fort's six remaining Nightmares, along with Hellions and older Goblins carrying tanks filled with the new Demon's Tongue. "Stay back from the emperor's Nightmares, understand? Do not challenge them directly. They'll be no match for this Demon's Tongue, but those flames won't make *you* move faster. Don't let them reach you."

Sepp would stay at the fort with the Imps and Novices. "Stuff Commander Tower with straw," Pran told them, "then burn it. The flames will draw the Nightmares' attention, keep them from spotting us quickly. But the fort gates—keep them shut, understand? Don't open them for any reason. If one of those Nightmares gets in . . ."

The young faces paled.

"Watch for our signal," Pran said. "When you see it, you know what to do."

They pumped their fists in assent.

"What about the Commanders?" Sepp asked.

One of the Hellions tasked with prison duty stepped forward. "They're fading. Begging at all hours for their serum. Most refuse to eat or drink anymore. I doubt they'll last the night."

Pran grimaced, though his heart ached more for the Tuliis standing guard over them. "The Commanders didn't ask for this life. None of them chose to be where they are. But they did choose to be cruel. Tonight, we leave them to their fate. When it's time to flee the fort, unlock their cells. I won't leave them caged like animals. But if they want out of this place, they're on their own to get there."

Oksana nodded. "It's time to show the emperor what we've done with the fire he's forced into our hands."

CHAPTER FIFTY

OKSANA

When the cloud cover was thickest, the moon tucked away as if beneath a woolly blanket, they set out from the fort. One by one the carts lumbered through the gates and into the snow-covered streets, each one pulled by Goblins, Hellions, or Nightmares swathed in cloaks like peddlers out to earn extra coins on Fire Night.

Outside, they turned in different directions, all heading to the train station. Lone carts would draw less attention than a procession. Each one was flanked by two more Tuliis carrying tanks of Demon's Tongue beneath their cloaks. Yalku, armed with a tank, nodded to Pran before departing with his cart.

Oksana and Pran followed the last cart, clutching their flint starters. On her back, Oksana also carried a leather bag stuffed with the dress Kati had fixed for her. She didn't know what sorcery Kati had invoked to have folded that massive dress hardly larger than a bread loaf.

"Tonight, you'll set us free," Kati had said as she'd presented the bag. Her hands had lingered against Oksana's. "I'm proud of you, everything you've done. I know it's been hard. I know you were hurt. But you are strong."

Oksana had snorted. If it hadn't been for Kati, she might still be in the lab hiding behind smoke and serums. "Thank you, for everything," she'd said, then could say no more past the knot in her throat.

"That's enough. No tears!" Though Kati's own voice had gone suspiciously thick. "Get out there and show those Nightmares how to *really* fight with fire."

But so far, the streets nearest the fort were empty. Anyone still awake, still braving the cold and snow, would be hunkered around the fire fountains at Imperial Square or at Ceremony Hall with the emperor himself.

All the better for sneaking around. The carts left unfortunate tracks in the snow, but everyone's biggest concern was getting to the train station quickly.

Oksana and Pran, with their cart, had barely crossed a few streets when Commander Tower went up in flames. There'd be no missing that from anywhere in this city. Surely it would draw the Nightmares' attention, keep them preoccupied at least a little while.

Still, only a few streets from the train station, the emperor's Nightmares closed in. Through the snow's haze, Oksana spotted the dark figures slinking toward them.

"Get the barrels onto the train," she whispered to the Tuliis pulling their cart. "I'll hold them off."

Beside her, Pran hesitated, staring at the blurry forms. "I don't want to leave you alone with them."

She understood his worry. If the situation had been reversed . . . it took one type of courage to make plans, another altogether to bring them about. But if there were ever a time for both kinds of courage, it was now.

"Go. You know the plan. I *will* find you again," she added, when Pran's face creased with fear. "If I don't meet you at the station . . . look for me at Ceremony Hall."

Pran clasped her gauntleted hand, kissed it, then disappeared into the veil of snow with the other Tuliis.

Oksana planted her heels against the cobblestones. Though she stood alone on this street, she felt anything but defenseless as three Nightmares drew near.

"Stand down, Tulii," one said. "This will not end well."

Of course they'd dismiss her. To them, she'd appear nothing but a spark—flaring fast, quickly spent.

But they had never seen her fight. "You're right. It won't end well."

Her nerves screamed. She'd never burned to kill. She still didn't want to. But so close to the station, where Tuliis would load barrels brimming with freedom onto that train . . . she could not trip up. Every Tulii in the fort depended on her. She had to be strong for them, or Anu would not be the only person who died because of her fear.

Oksana lifted her starter, clicked until a spark burst into life, and faced her Nightmares.

This would be for Anu. Pran. Kati. Her own family still in Horádim. Any Tulii ever torn from their homes.

For home.

Home.

Home.

All of it—fury, despair, passion, hope—Oksana poured into a flame so bright it looked like the sun had returned in the dead of night.

PRAN

"To the train!" Pran called to the Tuliis pulling the cart. They lunged forward, barrels knocking together as wooden wheels crunched through snow and ice, crossing the last streets to the station. Several other carts arrived at the same time. Pran was relieved to see Yalku among them, breathless from running but unharmed, still grasping the nozzle on his tank of Demon's Tongue.

The train loomed on the tracks ahead, brass sides glinting as if radiating their own light, its smokestack sculpted like a bonfire erupting toward the stars. "Watch for any train crew," Pran said to the Tuliis. "I doubt they'll try attacking, but we don't want them raising an alarm, either."

"Look out!" Yalku pointed back the way they'd come.

A trio of Nightmares approached.

Pran's stomach turned inside out. These weren't the same . . . they hadn't . . . No, Oksana said she was strong enough to fight them, and he trusted her. He had to.

"You know what to do," Pran said. "Don't let them get closer."

"Ready!" Yalku called, signaling to the others carrying

tanks. As one, they pumped furiously, unleashing the liquid. The Nightmares ducked and dodged the spray, moving with inhuman speed. But they were outnumbered and couldn't avoid the Demon's Tongue from every angle. The deep red liquid splashed onto them, and when they whipped out their flint starters to throw flames at Pran and his Tuliis . . . they ignited themselves instead, transformed into living torches, blinding white-hot flames blazing through the snow.

The heat was stifling, and more than one Tulii dropped to their knees, arms shielding their faces. Pran's skin felt like it was withering across his cheeks. When those flames finally expired, there was nothing left but char that Pran didn't want to look at too closely. He couldn't help being a little horrified at what Oksana's work had wrought.

She was two sides of the same coin—the gentlest soul he knew, yet also the fiercest. Maybe one didn't truly exist without the other.

He was never prouder to have her on his side.

OKSANA

Her flames overpowered every pillar of fire the Nightmares hurled, swallowing them like one snake devouring another. Still, the Nightmares came at her. Oksana whirled past their fireballs. Blasted through walls of flame. When a storm of sparks bit at her, she formed a blazing shield above her head with her own blue fire.

Then she launched into the Nightmares, arcing flame toward them left and right, above and below. Looped it around until it seared them from behind. They pushed back, struggled, but she kept the fire coming. Sweat poured down her face and her palms grew so slick her gauntlets nearly slid off. Her skin screamed for relief. Something deep inside her felt it was being cooked through.

After so much fire, would there be anything left of her? Even Nightmares weren't immune to flame, made clear by their howling as they cowered beneath her onslaught.

Still, they kept coming.

If she did one thing tonight, she had to hold off these Nightmares until the others got the train moving.

When one lifted his hands, summoning a fireball, Oksana raised another faster, until her blue flames burst toward the sky and roared down both ends of the street. It caught every one of those Nightmares, swallowing them like flies.

They shrieked. At least, she *saw* their mouths stretching wide. Their cries were drowned beneath her own screams, the heat threatening to scorch everything inside her. It was too much.

But she didn't let go. She kept the fire coming to keep those Nightmares away from the station. In the grip of that endless blue flame, they toppled, bodies turning to charcoal, then crumbling to ashes while she burned the life right out of them.

As the flames roared before her, Oksana blinked tears from her eyes. No matter what the Commanders had thrown her way, through all seven years in that fort, she'd never once wanted to kill.

Yet she'd always yearned to protect. *Help me be, like you, a defender of life.*

PRAN

As he'd suspected, at the sight of the warring Tuliis, the station crew didn't stick around, absolutely no match for the fire. He let every one of them escape without pursuing them, except for one—an engineer to drive the steam train.

"We're not here to hurt you," Pran said to the man, while Tuliis loaded barrels onto the cars. "Do as we say, and you'll leave this train uninjured. You'll tell your family how you helped free Vesimaan children from the Tuliikobrets."

That got the man listening.

Moments later, Yalku was at Pran's shoulder. "The barrels are on board. We're ready."

An odd itch rose in Pran's throat. "Straight off to Nyíta for you, after this?"

"My people don't turn their backs on each other. It's not our way. I'll help them remember and understand."

"Make sure all the others get off the train safely, when it's time. Always have someone watching for the signal. And . . . take care in Nyíta, all right? Don't go falling through ice or letting some reindeer stomp on you."

Yalku rolled his eyes. "I was born there, remember? I'm made for the place."

The itch in Pran's throat got stronger, pricking at his eyes, too. "Goodbye, Yalku. Come visit, all right? We don't have reindeer in Pakastra, but there are other animals you might like."

Yalku smiled. "What is it your brother calls you? Bha'ee? Goodbye, bha'ee."

They thumped each other on the back, and then Yalku boarded the train with all the other Tuliis. A few crouched in each car beside barrels of Demon's Tongue. Marten was among them. His gaze met Pran's, and for a moment the two stared at each other, Marten's cheeks reddening.

"Off to my freedom," the infuriating boy declared, throwing his shoulders back as though he'd been crowned king.

He could be Divine Emperor of his own world as long as Pran never had to see him again. "You don't have to thank me. Just use your freedom wisely, all right? Maybe with a little more compassion for those around you."

Marten snorted and slammed the door.

Though he wasn't sorry to see this one go, Pran wished him—all his Tuliis—the best this world had to offer. He waved to the ones still leaning out their cars, that annoying prickle in his eyes about to make them spill over. Before he became a mess, he signaled to the engineer, and with a piercing screech and an almighty belch of steam, the train lumbered from the station.

The Tuliis cheered until one shrieked, pointing behind Pran. "Oh gods, look out! That one's not dead."

A Nightmare rose to her feet. She'd been farthest back of the three who had charged the station, and while she was so badly burned she could barely stand, the look she cast Pran was anything but broken. "The emperor will hear what you've done."

He grinned. "We're counting on it," he said, as that Nightmare crawled into the shadows.

"Pran!" Oksana darted through the gloom, flint starter in one hand, a blue fireball crackling in another. He almost sank to his knees, dropped by utter relief at seeing Oksana uninjured and racing toward him.

She opened her mouth again, but the words were drowned by an earsplitting clamor. Bells.

The fort's alarm.

CHAPTER FIFTY-ONE

PRAN

Pran gaped toward the fort. "This wasn't part of the plan."

The fire in Oksana's hand fizzled. "We left Sepp with all the Imps and Novices. Are they in danger? Did a Nightmare breach the fort?"

"It could be a trap." He staggered back. "A Nightmare could want to draw us there."

"Pran!" Oksana caught his arm. "We can't ignore that alarm."

Every nerve inside him screeched as the world tore in two. She wasn't wrong—gods, if something happened to those Imps and Novices, he'd never be able to live with himself. But to turn from the plan now . . . if they didn't get inside Ceremony Hall fast, they'd miss their chance. The train charging from the city, loaded with its treacherous contents, was the best leverage they'd ever get against the emperor.

"We can't let this go," he whispered, sick to his stomach. "If we don't talk to the emperor tonight, no Tulii will ever be free."

Oksana's eyes shone glassy with tears, but she didn't let

them fall. "You go to the fort. I'll get into Ceremony Hall, find the emperor. I'll tell him about the train."

All the blood drained from Pran's face. "I can't leave you to face that man and his Nightmares alone!"

"You have to. I can sneak into the hall, blend in among Vesimaans." She gestured to the bag on her back with the ball gown. "But the others . . . if they need help, you can't leave them alone. Get to Sepp. Save them."

Leaving her to do by herself the work that was supposed to be shared—him keeping close watch at her back—felt like another sort of betrayal. He'd promised her safety, freedom.

To bring about both, he had to abandon her.

"Pran." Oksana touched a hand to his cheek. "I'll find you again on the road to Horádim. Ya abetschayu."

He yanked her close, crushed his lips against hers. The kiss was salty, tears streaming down both their faces. "May your saint watch over you."

He clasped her hands, squeezing tight, then charged toward the fort. Whatever was happening in there, whatever had torn him from Oksana's side, he'd destroy it.

OKSANA

The windows of the spired Ceremony Hall glowed like lanterns—proper ones lit by fire and not chemicals. From where Oksana stood, tucked between a darkened milliner's shop and a restaurant, she could see Vesimaa's aristocrats and top-tier politicians inside the hall, bedecked in fire-colored finery, sweeping past the windows in elaborate dances.

But within the plaza in front of that hall a crowd had gathered, farmers and craftsmen with dirty faces and worn-out clothes. They thronged before the half-dozen Nightmares standing guard at the hall doors, voices raised in a clamor.

"What's happening in the fort?"

"The tower is burning!"

"Is the city under attack?"

"Are the Tuliikobrets rebelling?"

In her dark, narrow alley, Oksana shivered. The alarm had stopped clanging almost as soon as she and Pran had parted ways. Had it all been some ruse to separate them?

Yeva, do not let Pran walk into a trap. A part of her ached to turn back and find out what was going on. But Pran was right. Their freedom depended on reaching Juhan, speaking to him, while that train still roared along the tracks.

She had to get inside the hall.

In the alley's shadows, she changed into her dress. Kati and the others had done an outstanding job fitting it to Oksana, the bodice now snug around her narrow torso. The skirt was still too long, but that was to hide the ridiculous high-heeled boots they'd cobbled together. Wine corks were stacked and nailed to their soles, giving Oksana some desperately needed height. Even in these, she'd be short for a Vesimaan, but not so much that she'd instantly stand out as an imposter. Oksana prayed she could walk in them without wobbling.

In this getup, she felt beyond absurd, pale shoulders bared to the world while the skirt had enough fabric to wrap her from head to toe half a dozen times. Using a window's reflection as a mirror, she did her makeup as Anu had, blending the powders and pastes to pale her skin even more and make her cheekbones rounder and eyes wider. With a shimmering scarf Kati had found in another trunk, she covered her very un-Vesimaan hair, twisting the fabric into an elaborate headdress.

As she worked, she sensed Anu beside her. That stilled her racing heart and made her feel less alone. With the last of the mudroot paste, she inked across her wrists the words Anu had worn the final night of her life: *Demons came forth* on the left, *Avenging all wrongs* on the right. And into her bodice, she slipped her necklace with Yeva's icon and Pran's ring. *Ya abetschayu.*

When she looked again at her reflection, a stranger peered back, an elegant Vesimaan aristocrat with an imperious stare.

Oksana swallowed hard. She wished it hadn't come down to *her* to face Juhan, to have the weight of everyone's freedom on her bare shoulders. Pran was the one good with words! Fortunately, she had something else to rely on: through slits that Kati had slashed into the bell skirt, she bound a pouch of Demon's Tongue vials to her left thigh, and her flint starter to her right.

Words might fail, but chemicals, properly mixed, always came through.

Drawing a long breath, Oksana emerged from the alley and strode toward the hall. Looping around to make it appear that she came from the line of carriages still delivering guests, she fell into step with the emerging aristocrats. The new arrivals ascended the stairs to the hall, and when Oksana did wobble in her heels, she lifted her chin high, daring anyone to criticize her.

"And you are?" a Nightmare guard asked, collecting names to announce each guest.

"Katariina of Hämarik." Oksana rolled over the syllables she'd practiced with Kati, making sure she flattened all traces of her Horádimian accent.

The Nightmare stared. "I don't recall that name on the list."

Oksana's heart knocked staccato beats against her ribs, but she funneled that anxiety into rage. "I don't recall needing a Tuliikobret's permission to accept the emperor's invitation. It was extended as a great honor to my father, to repay certain contributions he's made in our nation's service. Neither he nor His Imperial Majesty would be pleased to hear that you kept me waiting in the cold." She glared at the snowflakes dusting her gown.

A few guests frowned at the Nightmare. "Let the girl pass," another woman called.

Scowling, the Nightmare waved Oksana inside.

CHAPTER FIFTY-TWO

PRAN

As he ran through the snow-covered streets, Pran watched the fort go up in flames. It was Jubilee Night all over again but turned on its head, with him on the wrong side of the walls. He'd told the Imps and Novices to burn the tower, and the tower only. Had they gotten carried away, or . . . ?

On and on he ran, pleading to anyone, *anything*, that the youngest Tuliis were all right. His bad leg throbbed and buckled, throwing him to the ground, where he skinned his cheek on a rough patch of stone. He should have had another injection today, but it would have left him too sleepy and slow. Now, the pain spurred him onward. *Pain keeps Tuliikobrets alert.*

"Open the gates!" he screamed as the fort loomed into view. "It's Nayar! Let me in."

But those mighty barriers remained shut, no creaking chains or groaning hinges even hinting that they would move.

"Let me in!" Pran hunched forward, choking on the smoke billowing over the walls. "Is anyone there?"

A tiny, shadowy figure—an Imp, or maybe just a Novice—peeked over the wall. "They broke the chains! We can't open the gates."

Who broke the chains?

"Throw down one of them," Pran yelled back. "Get some bigger Tuliis to help you. Heft it up the stairs, toss it down the wall toward me. I'll climb it to you."

The Tulii disappeared. So much time passed—each minute dragging by—Pran wondered if the boy had even heard his instructions.

He pounded his fists against the gates. Glaring at the walls, Pran searched for some way to climb them—these unbreachable barriers even the emperor's Nightmares hadn't overcome.

"Look out!" a young voice cried from above. A clink, then a crash of metal. Pran barely leaped out of the way in time as one of the enormous chains once tethered to the gates dropped in front of him.

"I'm coming up!" Bracing his feet against the wall, he climbed that chain so fast his palms were raw by the time he reached the top.

"Nayar!" Sepp lunged up the stairs, face bloodless beneath soot stains and burn marks. "They got out of their cells, I don't know how, they weren't supposed to be unlocked yet."

Pran's heart stuttered against his ribs. "The Commanders?"

"They attacked the Tuliis keeping watch, stole their flint starters, and set fire to everything. When I ran for the gates, they broke the chains before I could get anything opened, then took the physician captive, demanding their serum."

Flames flashed through Healing Hall's second story windows. They'd gone into the lab.

OKSANA

The celebration was in the largest room she'd ever seen, bigger than the south courtyard many times over. From its entrance, the back wall was barely visible, the ceiling lost in shadow. The floor gleamed with polished marble tiles in every shade of red. Amber-curtained glass doors opened onto narrow balconies lit with chemical lamps. Gold-plated pillars, sculpted as bonfires, stood sentinel down the room's length in even rows. A small orchestra played in the corner, in between suits of armor with pikes and swords—relics from the days when Vesimaa had battled like an ordinary nation.

Keeping to the walls, Oksana sidestepped women in bell-shaped dresses and men in long-tailed jackets. All the guests sipped wine or nibbled food from bronze trays. The drinks flamed and desserts sparked, tiny cakes topped with sugared nuts set ablaze.

And there, on a dais at the far side of the room, stood Juhan himself, nauseating in his fire-colored celebratory robes and shimmering gold crown. Like a proud father, he gazed at the people dancing and laughing around him.

Somehow, he missed Oksana glaring all too vehemently back. But she did not miss when a servant looped from behind the dais to whisper in Juhan's ear, or when Juhan turned to follow that man from the room. As he went, Juhan smiled and waved to people in the crowd, but some of the brightness vanished from his face, replaced with a stiffly set jaw.

A young man appeared at Oksana's side, hand extended, asking if she'd dance. Ignoring him, Oksana strode across the room after Juhan. She scooped up her enormous skirt so she could move faster. By the time she got behind the dais and squeezed out the door hidden there, Juhan and the servant had disappeared.

Biting back a curse, Oksana peered around. She was in a dark corridor so narrow that if she extended her arms she could touch both walls with her palms. Clearly, this was not meant for guests. Where had Juhan gone? Shutting her eyes, holding her breath, she listened for voices or any trace of footsteps.

There, to her left.

Train . . . gone . . . fort . . . fire.

Oksana yanked off her boots, tossing them aside. They'd done their job; the precarious cork heels were now only a tripping hazard. She followed the voices down the corridor. Her stockinged feet moved softly over the stone floor, the silk of her skirt swishing against the walls. Somehow, she kept her breath silent even as her heart pounded hard enough to hurt.

Reaching through the left slit in her skirt, she touched the vials bound to her thigh. A few words from her, a spark to a single drop of their contents, and Juhan would have to agree to her offer or risk the ruin of his empire.

These chemicals would never let her down. They'd bring her, everyone, home. Steeling herself with that truth, she hurried onward.

"Katariina of Hämarik?" The voice rang out behind her, echoing down the narrow corridor. A flint starter clicked, and sparks crackled on the cold, damp air.

Oksana lifted her hands, as if in surrender, then glared over her shoulder. "You don't want to light me up, with what I have on me."

CHAPTER FIFTY-THREE

PRAN

"Get the Novices out of here," he said to Sepp. "And the Imps. Those broken chains, throw them down the walls, climb them into the streets. Lead everyone to Horádim. Go to Novosel, Oksana's village. My brother is meeting us there."

"But, the signal?" Sepp glanced toward Ceremony Hall. "It hasn't gone up. Oksana hasn't convinced the emperor to—"

"She won't fail us. Get everyone out so Oksana has someone to save. I'm counting on you."

As Pran darted down the stairs into the fort, Sepp leaned after. "What are you doing?"

"Rescuing Physician Mikkel." That man was the only one who'd stayed. He didn't deserve to endure whatever the Commanders would inflict on him.

"Don't go down there!" she yelled. "If the Commanders don't kill you, the flames will."

"I won't leave anyone to suffer. There's too much of that on my conscience already." Pran leaped down the final steps.

Sepp yelled something else, but he didn't hear it over the flames' roar. Commander Tower came down, its red-shingled roof collapsing on itself. Around him, Tuliis screamed and fled up the wall, shouting at him to follow, but Pran barreled deeper into the fort. Any stray Tulii he came across, he sent toward the gates. When he found no others, Pran turned for Healing Hall, charging through its vacant corridors and hobbling up the stairs toward the lab.

From that room, glass shattered and something heavy hit the ground.

"The serums!" a voice screamed, echoing down the hallway. "Make them!"

OKSANA

"I mean it," she said to the Nightmares. There were two, and even more footsteps echoed down the dark corridor. "What I have on me . . . if you throw a fireball, you'll blow this whole hall to the moon. You don't want to kill every political leader and aristocrat here in one burst. So put out that flame and let me speak."

The Nightmares leaned together, whispering so softly she couldn't catch a word. In the end, neither of them put their flint starters away, but the flames on their palms shrank a little. Warning fires, a reminder of what they could do.

"Speak, then," one said, in the Nightmares' gravelly tones.

Step by step Oksana turned, empty hands still raised by her head. It took every ounce of mettle she possessed to keep those hands from shaking. "My words are for the emperor. It's a matter of national security. I can tell him what's happening in the fort."

"Give us that information and we'll deliver it."

Oksana's throat grew tight. What would Pran say to get someone hopping exactly where he wanted?

She turned up her lips in the sparest of smiles. "For now, that crowd outside only complains, but soon they'll riot unless the emperor gives real answers. I have something Juhan must *see*."

The Nightmares scowled so fiercely Oksana's whole mouth went dry. But finally the soldiers beckoned her down the narrow corridor. "Keep your hands up, where we can watch them."

One Nightmare in front of Oksana, the other behind, they marched through the corridor and back into a larger hallway where music and laughter drifted from the grand room. With every step, Oksana's heart pulsed in her throat. This was it. Either she'd leave this meeting with Juhan free, or she'd leave as a bag of ashes.

Her saint's icon—tucked into her bodice—pressed against one of her ribs. Beside that icon, Pran's ring dug into her skin. She wished she'd slipped it onto a finger so she could see it with every glimpse of her hand. *Ya abetschayu.*

Never had she felt more insignificant, stocking-footed in this gaudy dress cut for a woman twice her size. But Pran had promised. So would she. They'd all be free.

She'd make it happen.

The Nightmares pushed open a door at the end of the hallway. Oksana winced as vibrant light poured from the room. It seemed to be some kind of reception hall, with a polished banquet table in the center set for an elaborate meal. The creamy walls were painted with ivy and cornflowers. On the far side of the room, opposite the door, towering sixteen-paned windows looked down on the plaza, where the crowd's voices rose to a fevered pitch. Juhan stood beside those windows arguing with two Nightmares, their voices low and ominous.

As Oksana passed through the doorway, hands still lifted in the air, the emperor turned to stare. "Who are you?"

All words vanished as she stood before this man. Here was the one who'd grasped their lives like threads he could, and did, snap any time they no longer suited him. With one word, Juhan could have her murdered where she stood. He could have the fort razed, the Tuliis inside killed in retribution for what she said. He could send Nightmares after any who escaped.

Here was the man who'd ordered Pran onto a platform, forced him to tell tales, then had him struck across the face with fire. He could have killed Pran while making her watch. He *had* killed Anu, sneered as flames consumed her. Out of the corner of her eye, Oksana saw Anu's words stained across her wrists: *Demons came forth. Avenging all wrongs.*

Her tongue unlocked. She would never stand silent before a man like him again.

"It's Fire Night, Your Majesty. I've come to give you a show."

CHAPTER FIFTY-FOUR

PRAN

"I don't know the formula." Physician Mikkel's voice frayed along the edges. "I can't brew it."

Pran lunged through the lab doors. How the Commanders expected Mikkel to make anything, he'd never understand, with the way they'd wrecked the place. Whole tables and workstations were overturned, a sea of broken glass winked from the floor, while red and white powders were strewn across the wreckage.

A Commander hurled another jar toward the physician, pinned to a chair beneath a collapsed workstation. The glass smashed on the wall behind him, spraying Mikkel with sickly gray powder. "Make it!" the Commander screamed.

Pran expected Kraanvelt, for all the mania, but when the man turned it was Lepik, blue eyes bloodshot and gray hair missing from his head in patches.

"Nayar!" The Commander lurched forward, jabbing a finger so unsteadily it made Pran queasy. "Our serums! We want them."

"They're gone." He almost felt bad, if only because he

knew the awfulness of a body needing something it couldn't have. "Everything's destroyed."

Oksana had burned all the serums and elixirs, though many of the ingredients remained. There'd been simply too much, and most too dangerous to burn in their raw forms. Those were what the Commanders pawed through on the shelves, overturning jars, bags, and boxes, everything that wasn't their fix.

"I mean it," Pran called over the racket. "There's nothing left."

"Damn you, Nayar!" Lepik hurled a jar. Pran almost didn't duck in time as his leg seized so badly he could scarcely breathe, much less move.

"You don't have to be like this," Pran said, as Kraanvelt overturned a cabinet, as Tamm threw bottle after bottle off a shelf, as every other Commander screamed and raged. "It's gone. But you can find a way to go on without it."

"We can't!" Lepik screeched, and the others howled in agreement.

Any sympathy Pran possessed for them steamed away. "You made *me* go on. Every day, for seven years. I was a child, I was sick, but you forced me to endure. The rest of my life, I'll have to bear what you've done to me."

Lepik stared so long his eyes went glassy. "We're not like you, Nayar."

"I've noticed."

"No." Lepik's voice quieted, almost calm. "We're not like you. We never will be. But you know that. You've known it since you snatched the fort from our hands." Deep in the man's gaze, there was something almost resembling respect—or would have, if it weren't stained through with resentment.

"Serum!" From the back of a cabinet, a Commander dragged a tray of bottles filled with bright red liquid.

For a moment, Pran's heart clenched. But the liquid sloshing inside was too runny, its acidic red too lurid. Some sort of verikivi? Oksana would know at a glance.

"Don't drink that!" Pran said. "It's not serum—it could kill you."

The Commanders ignored him. Like starved dogs they charged forward, shoving, kicking, elbowing, snatching bottles off the tray or from another's hands. They howled while yanking at the corks stoppering the bottles, then downed the red liquid in throaty gulps. Smacked their lips and tossed the emptied bottles aside in a chorus of shattering glass.

Kraanvelt lurched toward Pran, red liquid dripping off his chin, eyes bright with triumph. "Now you'll pay, Nayar."

But the words had hardly left his tongue when screams erupted throughout the room.

Hands clutched throats, tore hair, clawed faces. Scratched tables, chairs, each other. One by one, the Commanders sank to their hands and knees, writhing, convulsing. Some retched while others curled onto their sides, screeching until Pran thought his ears would bleed.

Almost as one, they stopped, the lab falling silent so fast

Pran nearly went dizzy. In the whole room, only the physician's eyes moved, looking across the fallen bodies.

"I warned them that might happen," Mikkel whispered.

OKSANA

Juhan glared at the Nightmares standing on either side of Oksana. "Take her away."

Oksana dodged the Nightmares' hands. "You don't want to do that."

"Who *are* you?" Juhan demanded again.

"Katariina of Hämarik," said a Nightmare, though his voice was laced with doubt.

"Oksana Artemivna," she corrected, dropping the phony Vesimaan accent. "A Hellion from the Bronze Bonfire troop."

Juhan's brow furrowed. "A Tuliikobret?"

The Nightmares lunged, but Juhan stilled them with a raised hand. "What's happening in the fort?" he asked Oksana.

"A whole new kind of fire. If I may give a demonstration?"

When Juhan nodded once, Oksana reached through the left slit in her skirt, retrieved one of the vials from the pouch at her thigh, then stepped to a narrow table standing against the wall near the doorway. This one was set with a silver tray filled with goblets and a decanter of wine.

"I'm sure Rootare told you all about Demon's Tongue.

That's what we used to create the burning water fountain in Kivi." Oksana gestured toward the wine. "If I may?" When Juhan nodded, she poured a little ruby liquid into one glass.

When she moved to add Demon's Tongue to the glass, every Nightmare lunged toward her, shouting in protest.

"One drop," Oksana said, far more calmly than she felt. "I promise. You can watch, take it away if I pour more."

"You said with what you had on you, you could blow this place up," a Nightmare growled.

"You're no stranger to Demon's Tongue. One drop will barely warm the air, and you know it."

Holding her breath, her whole body rigid, she poured a single drop into the glass. Then she pulled her flint starter from her right hip, raised a thumbnail-size flame, and tossed it into the glass.

Fire roared in a brilliant blue-orange sheen, licking the air for a full three seconds before sputtering out.

Juhan stared from the glass to Oksana in silent question.

"I've made some additions to this weapon you'll want to know about." Pulling another vial from her thigh pouch, she poured a second drop into the wineglass, then set that glass on the banquet table in the room's center. After returning to the doorway, she clicked the starter to raise a spark and hurled it toward the goblet.

Glass shattered. Flames roared so violently the room shook. The banquet table cracked, sending porcelain dishware crashing to the stone floor. A wave of heat rocked through the room, forcing everyone to cover their faces.

When they could see again, smoke billowed and scorch marks stained the ruined table and ceiling. Every Nightmare stood tensed to fight, sparks crackling, flint starters pointed toward Oksana.

"That's what one drop of the new Demon's Tongue can do." Oksana held the vial between her fingers, swirling its gleaming contents. As she took in the room's wreckage, pride surged through her like she'd never felt. *She'd* made this. And these Vesimaans wouldn't forget it anytime soon.

Juhan's expression, as he gazed at Oksana, was a blend of exasperation and admiration. "I suppose you intend to trade this weapon for your freedom?"

A smile, semi-delirious, tugged at Oksana's lips. This was where the real work began.

"We're making a trade, yes. But not with you. Not with Vesimaa. The barrels of this new Demon's Tongue are on board the train, headed straight for Scamall."

The only sound in the room was an ember crackling on the ruins of the table.

"You lie," Juhan whispered.

The horror on his face made it easier to keep speaking. "You know I'm not. Tuliikobrets stole the train. It's headed north. We loaded barrels onto it. You know all these things. Yes, we're making a trade. When that train reaches the end of the tracks, the Tuliikobrets on board will carry those barrels over the border into Scamall. We'll offer this Demon's Tongue to them, unless you set every Tuliikobret free and leave us in peace for the rest of our lives."

Even the Nightmares were too stunned to move.

"A weapon like that . . ." Juhan wobbled as though Oksana had torn that golden crown from his head and broken it across his skull. "If Scamall gets hold of it . . . that would be the end of Vesimaa . . . Y-you wouldn't—"

"Of course I would." Heart thundering, Oksana pulled away her headscarf, letting her bright red hair tumble across her shoulders. "I am a Scamall. Why wouldn't I help my people?"

Her people were Horádimian. Scamall to Oksana was only that story about her grandparents. But for this moment, Juhan must believe she had real ties with the place.

Juhan opened his mouth as though to protest, but there was no arguing with that hair, the symbol of everything Vesimaans hated, and feared, about the land to the north.

"Your empire is crumbling," Oksana said. "All that keeps you on the throne is that Scamall hasn't invaded. Lose that, and you lose everything."

She paused so the voices of the protesters outside could leak through the windowpanes.

"If you fail one more time"—Oksana nodded toward their shouts—"your own people will tear you apart."

Juhan sank onto a chair beside the ruined table. "You Tuliikobrets have been a thorn in my side since you ravaged Linn."

Oksana approached the table, leaned over it until her eyes were level with Juhan's. "You placed that thorn in your own flesh, Your Majesty, when you forced us into this army.

Did you really believe abusing children would make your nation strong?"

"I am still your emperor." Juhan straightened in his chair so fast, Oksana swore she heard his spine creak. "Vesimaa reigns over the lands we've taken. It's right that you serve the greater nation."

Oksana pointed to her flaming-red hair. "You do not rule Scamall. And unless you want Vesimaa to fall once and for all into their hands . . . Well, I've shown you what I can do. Now, I need your decision. Will you release the Tuliikobrets? Or will you allow your enemies to obtain a weapon unlike any this world has seen?"

Juhan stared for so long that it seemed he was trying to intimidate her into giving up. She held her ground.

When the man finally spoke, his words were so soft she had to lean in to hear them. "If I let you go, how do I know you won't hand over the Demon's Tongue to Scamall anyway?"

She grinned. "Oh, you'll know when I call off the train. There'll be no question whether it reached its destination."

"Go," Juhan whispered, his eyes burning coals. "All you Tuliikobrets, leave this country. I'll find another way to keep my people strong."

Oksana could sink to her knees whispering prayers of gratitude to Yeva the rest of the night and all the next day. But she held her legs steady, kept her eyes dry. Her work wasn't through.

"One more thing, Your Majesty: Do not come after us.

Ever. You see, what we have on that train isn't *all* the Demon's Tongue. There's a reserve hidden of my new batch, along with instructions for how to make more. If you send your Nightmares or anyone else after *any* Tuliikobret, that Demon's Tongue will be given to Scamall. But leave us in peace forever, and we will keep it safely out of their hands. Understood?"

Juhan staggered from the table. "Get out of my sight."

"Not yet." Oksana raised a spark, nudged it into blue fire. "Juhan Edvin Visnapuu, if you ever again hurt anyone I love, I will return. And I'll make you regret the day your family gave us power over flame."

With a flick of her finger, she sent that fire rushing forward to lash against the emperor's cheek, leaving a burn twice the size of the one he'd put on Pran.

"Something to help you remember," Oksana said, then saw herself out of the hall.

PRAN

He ducked through the wreckage to Mikkel's side. Together they lifted the collapsed table until the physician slipped around it, climbing to his feet.

"Go on," Pran told him. "Go free. You showed us mercy when you didn't have to."

Mikkel blinked as though he didn't understand. "I told you, that was self-preservation. You don't owe me anything."

"I do. Because you were here for us, helped when we needed it. Go in peace."

Without another word, Mikkel ran. When he was gone, Pran faced the lab, jaw tight as he took in the remains of this place he despised more than any other in the world.

"Good riddance."

He raised a fireball and cast it to the middle of the room, where it caught on the wreckage of a table. Pran backed away as the fire spread greedily from one workstation to the next. When it reached the cabinets with the leftover raw ingredients—all that verikivi—those would make short work of this whole fort.

Never again would this hellhole plague another Tulii.

OKSANA

In the streets, she shot a blue flame toward the sky. As it roared upward, it stretched taller, wider, until far above Mennick it unfurled into the shape of a copper crown.

She was on the city's outskirts when an explosion rocked the northwestern mountains. At her signal, the Tuliis on the train had lit long fuses, then evacuated, detonating every barrel of Demon's Tongue.

Rootare's creations were truly no more. Well, most of them.

From the pouch at her thigh, she drew out a dozen vials

of new Demon's Tongue. These she'd hide deep in the forest, along with those instructions for making more, just as she'd threatened. Only she would know their location. But she would come for them, if Juhan or Vesimaa ever gave her a reason.

After all, she was a girl of her word.

But for today, they were free. Out in the mountains the Tuliis set out, choosing whatever paths pleased them.

And Oksana at last did the same, following the road from the city, never once looking back.

EPILOGUE

Hand in hand, they walked through the trees. Night had fallen hours ago, and the clouds were thick, making it hard to avoid tripping over gnarled roots or fallen branches. But neither Oksana nor Pran could wait until dawn. Leaving Sepp at their camp to watch over those Tuliis seeking refuge in Pakastra, Pran and Oksana had continued ahead, finishing the trek to Novosel.

As the trees thinned and they could glimpse cottages between them, Oksana's hand shook. Pran squeezed her fingers, then lifted her hand to kiss her knuckles. "Remember the message the copper crown brought. They know we're coming tonight. They're happy to see us."

"It's just . . . it's been so long, and they haven't seen what we've become, and . . ."

Her words died when through the trees a man came into view, chopping a huge pile of wood behind a thatched-roof cottage. He had hair as red as Oksana's, though his was peppered with gray. That man lifted the ax again but paused when his gaze met hers.

"Papa?" she whispered.

He dropped the ax and sprang forward, lifting her into his arms. "My little lamb! You're home."

Oksana pressed her brow against his, laughing and sobbing. "I'm here! I'm *home*."

The back door to the cottage flew open and three people rushed out. In an instant, Oksana was surrounded, arms thrown about her, heads knocking together. A woman in a long dress with a scarf around her head caught Oksana's face in her hands, kissing her cheeks over and over while sobbing, "My girl, my girl, my girl!" A young man with untidy brown hair and overlarge ears thumped Oksana's shoulder, while a girl of about fourteen hopped on the balls of her feet, hands pressed against her mouth.

Pran stood back, giving the family space, rubbing his arms against the chilly air nipping at him once Oksana had stepped away. Her mother caught sight of him and grinned, beckoning Pran over. He started to approach, until a new voice stopped him in his tracks.

"Bha'ee?"

Another group stepped out of the cottage: a man and woman, brown faces lined and black hair streaked with silver. They were followed by two young men, one stepping slightly behind the other, hand clasping his shoulder.

"Bha'ee?" the first one said again, his eyes bright with tears.

Pran was moving, *running*, before Nanda even reached out his arms, and yanked his brother into a hug. His forehead bumped Nanda's chin—Nanda would forever remain the bigger brother. Another day, Pran would be annoyed about it, but this day, he clung to Nanda.

“You are so brave,” Nanda whispered. “You didn’t need me to save you.”

“They didn’t break me.” Pran leaned back, looked his brother full in the face, his own eyes prickling. “Because I had help from the best people I know.”

Another hand closed around Pran’s, squeezing tight. Oksana was back at his side, leaning so close he could feel her heart pounding.

She smiled at him, then turned to their families. “We were strong because we remembered where we came from. We know who we are. And we know where we belong.”

ACKNOWLEDGMENTS

This book lit a fire in me the moment the first idea sparked in my mind. It's a project I did not want to give up on, yet despite all my efforts, there was a time I genuinely feared it would only ever be a lonely file hidden away on my iCloud. Then one day I received an email from Emily Settle saying Swoon Reads wanted to talk to me about this book. That offer brought light and hope in a time when I needed both in my writing journey, and I'll be forever grateful to Swoon Reads for making *this* story into a book. Thank you, Jean Feiwel, for creating this imprint, and thanks to everyone on the team who picked my story to be a part of it.

Tremendous thanks to my awesome editor, Emily Settle, for loving this story and its characters, for asking all the right questions, for making sure every word counts . . . and for coming up with much better titles than I ever could. Great books don't happen without excellent editors, and I'm so grateful you're on my side.

Thanks also to my cover designer, Mike Burroughs, my stunningly talented cover artist, Bastien LeCouffe-Deharme, copyeditor Valerie Shea, and production editor Mandy Veloso. Big, big thanks as well to every Swoon Reader who took time to look at this story and leave ratings and comments. I wouldn't be here without you either!

Shout-out to my agent, Alli Hellegers. Though we didn't cross paths until after this book was picked up by Swoon Reads, you deserve thanks for being such a fierce and loyal advocate. Your guidance, expertise, and encouragement have brought peace and clarity to my publishing journey. I'm beyond lucky to have you in my corner.

So much gratitude to the Swoon Squad for all the laughs, advice, insight, and support. There's no better group to share this publishing journey. Squad Goals forever!!

This book went through many revisions over several years, and I was fortunate to have a lot of different readers along the way. Thanks to everyone who offered feedback on all or part of the manuscript: Alyse Allred, J. A. Andrews, Christine Arnold, Ian Barnes, Danielle Carriere, E. M. Castellan, Nita Collins, Kimberly Gabriel, Sara Hagmann, Andrea Jakeman, Alisha Klapheke, Rajani LaRocca, Kara McDowell, Brook McKelvey, Leenna Naidoo, Dana Nuens, Alexandria Rogers, Erin Sullivan, Rosiee Thor, Erin Tidwell, ReLynn Vaughn, and Kip Wilson. Special shout-out to E. M. Castellan, who checked in with me numerous times throughout my writing and querying journey, somehow always knowing when I most needed a kind word of encouragement. You are truly awesome.

I have been abundantly blessed with amazing writer friends. Shout-out to my Glastonbury writers' group for welcoming me when I was new to Connecticut and giving me a place to share my stories, learn more about publishing, and celebrate/commiserate the ups and downs of this journey. You ladies really helped me find my place.

Lindsay Hess, your kind words (and excellent feedback) kept me going in a time when I wasn't sure my stories had a future in publishing. Thanks for teaching me how to write kissing scenes! And another of your suggestions led me to write "The Demons' Ballad," which has become such an important part of this book. For that, you deserve a whole platter of tacos.

Kim Smejkal, I'm so glad we crossed paths. Your enthusiasm for this story meant so much in a journey that was often filled with self-doubt and uncertainty. (Kim also designed the fiery cover this book got to wear while it was up on the Swoon Reads site! Acts of kindness like that really stick with a person. May we all have such friends.)

Huge, huge shout-out to Kim Mach and Lyla Lawless. Your feedback and support during the wild revision ride of this story were invaluable and a true gift. This book is much better (and was finished so much faster!) thanks to your stellar insights. A writer could not ask for better critique partners.

To Wendy Burk, my college creative writing adviser: Your encouragement during college and every year after gave me strength as I honed my writing voice and discovered the stories I *needed* to tell. I'm so glad to have your friendship and gentle guidance.

Thanks to my family for celebrating this book along

with me. Special thanks to my mom and sister Savanna for visiting while I was on deadline and watching my toddler so I could slip away to the library for hours each day to tackle revisions. Thanks most of all to my husband, Steve, for believing in me when I was losing faith in myself, for listening to my story ramblings, for supporting my hours spent writing, and making sure I had time and space to do so. Love you!

And to North. Whenever I wanted to give up, I'd think of how I wanted you to see that we can stick with our dreams, even if the path is long and hard and we don't reach our goal on the first try (or even the second). Can't wait to see what you reach for and where you go, little star.

Baby Oak, you were with me as I finished this book (and probably heard it read aloud more times than any person should). You arrived during a pandemic and the increasingly chaotic 2020, and also had health challenges to face when you were only weeks old. But like the characters of this book, you handle whatever life throws your way. Little red king, you are mighty like the flame, and you will grow stronger still.